MADE IN L.A.

MADE IN L.A.

VOL. 1
STORIES ROOTED IN THE CITY OF ANGELS

MILA WRITERS

RESONANT EARTH PUBLISHING

MADE IN L.A.
Stories Rooted in the City of Angels

FIRST ANNUAL ANTHOLOGY

Cover design by Allison Rose

Visit Made in L.A. Writers online at
www.madeinlawriters.com

ISBN: 978-0-9987607-1-1
Library of Congress Control Number: 2018936365

Published by Resonant Earth Publishing
on behalf of
MADE IN L.A. WRITERS
P.O. Box 50785
Los Angeles, CA 90050

TABLE OF CONTENTS

Introduction

INTRODUCTION

In 2017 four indie authors first came together under the Made in L.A. banner to support each other and share a booth at the Los Angeles Festival of Books. We passed out bookmarks, watched as kids made away with our candy, chatted with a few questionable characters, and found many new fans. We expected all of that.

What surprised us was how many people approached our booth with a version of the Question: Are these books all set in L.A.? Our reluctant though truthful response, "Not really," didn't satisfy them and it didn't satisfy the four of us, who saw a missed opportunity to "give them what they want," a line and theme that echoes throughout the first tale in this anthology, a novella, by Allison Rose titled "Between Broken Pieces." By presenting an assortment of stories set in L.A. by local authors, we hope we're giving you what you want.

Dissatisfaction and unrequited passions are neither unfamiliar nor unique to Angelenos, but they are, perhaps, all the more notable in a place that has for so long been associated with "living the dream." Gabi Lorino's stories, "Going With the Flow" and "Wild Irish Rose," tease out the frustrations and hopes that so often collide with hard truths like paying the rent and looking for ways to reach your goals, while in the meantime having to tell yourself, again and again, maybe next year.

What emerged as we assembled the stories for this anthology was a rough sketch of the past, present, and future. The past came to life in brutal and haunting ways in Bonnie Randall's story, "No Vacancy," which asks us to consider the cost of following our dreams. In Dario Ciriello's "Dry Bones," the question becomes about what remains when a relationship sunders, and just how much of L.A.'s haunted past of cults and occultism we've left behind.

The stories I contributed to the anthology—"Little Woman," "Salt in the Hell Mouth," and "Unquiet Baggage," a triptych of fantasy shorts from the perspectives of marginalized, queer, and dismembered characters—explore the present-day struggles that emerge when violence erupts in our relationships. The protagonist in Andre Hardy's "Negro in a Hot Tub" grapples with what it means to resist as a black man and as a writer when sharing a tub with his worst nightmare.

Genre fiction has long flourished in L.A. From detective noir to science fiction and fantasy, the tableau lends itself to the odd, the novel, and the unconventional. Amy Sterling Casil's traveling freakshow in "Chromosome Circus" and Jude-Marie Green's music-loving stellar refugee story in "Endless Summer" both explore a blend of quintessentially Angeleno subjects, adding futuristic layers of the quirky and cosmic.

These stories will change how you look at Los Angeles. We all carry a map in our heads. The local geography is literally too widespread for any individual to know comprehensively; the scenes are too niche and diverse to go deep into all of them. Each map varies: home, workplace, local haunts, and favorite destinations are all idiosyncratic; as are the hazy, circumstantial, and rumored zones nearby that we've only heard about or looked up online. We are all discoverers, explorers, and creators of experiences in this great city; we've each only peeled the onion a layer or two deeper than the skin.

– Cody Sisco

BETWEEN BROKEN PIECES

Allison Rose

The City of Angels

A HAUNTING STILLNESS creeps over the hill, soaking fallen leaves in a suffocating density, until the trees open up and she appears, sweating, heaving and racing through the woods. The thumping of her footsteps matches her labored breaths, high-pitched, feminine gasps. She runs. And runs. And runs from whomever is chasing her.

Dare she look back? Of course she does. The wind sweeps her hair in a wave, exposing her terrified yet beautiful face. She's slender, but strong enough to outrun and outlast her chaser, and when she stumbles she finds her feet beneath her.

There is another voice. A man's, deep and jagged and forced. The voice sounds out of place, not from whoever is chasing her. It belongs to someone else.

Up ahead shines a porch light, a beacon on a dilapidated house that serves as her only solitude. In two steps she scales the stairs, thumps across the porch, caring not about how much noise she makes. She wants to be heard.

So does the outsider's breath. It gets louder. If she hears it, she makes no move to find the source.

She goes for the door handle, a rusted knob that won't turn despite how many times she twists on it. With both hands, she pounds on the door. "Help! Somebody help! He's going to kill me!"

Sure as her warning, a shadow falls on her, a ghostly hooded figure. Gloved fingers curl into the collar of her button-up and pull, ripping the threads that secure the buttons to expose her breasts.

The outsider breathes again. It does not belong here, there's no doubting that now. Someone else is watching. Someone not here in the woods, but from some other vantage point. Perhaps from some other time.

Unable—or unwilling—to cover up her nakedness, she pleads with her captor. "Please. Please don't kill me."

The predator grabs a handful of her breast, and squeezes. She cries out in pain. Maybe also pleasure.

The outsider's breath hitches. Goes silent.

A knife catches the glint of the porch light an instant before it rips through her trachea. Blood sprays everywhere, flows down her bare breasts. Her hands find the gaping hole in her neck. She gags. Cries. Slumps to the floor.

The outsider's voice returns with a gurgling, orgasmic moan.

Glass suddenly encases the horror on the porch, separating her and her captor safely from the outsider. This is not real life, this morbid and oddly seductive scene; this is make-believe. This is a movie, playing on a living room television.

The film goes silent, muting the noises of the beautiful victim's final gasps for life. All that is left is the conclusive sound of a fastening pants zipper.

ONE
Alice

By THE TIME he zipped his pants, we were well into the danger zone. That the kids hadn't caught me bent over the kitchen counter with their father up my ass was impressive enough. That Matt actually climaxed was the real miracle.

Time had ticked by on the wall clock, the lurch of the second hand marking each agonizing moment, until the TV caught my eye. There she was. I had expected her to make media circuits to promote her latest film, but I didn't expect she would be intoxicated at 6:30 in the morning for a network spot, hunched over the desk, cleavage barely hidden by the lower-third graphic: "MALLORY BRAUN, STAR OF *BETWEEN BROKEN PIECES.*"

There was something about her, something about the way she leaned into the camera, like she was falling through the screen onto the counter next to me. Those beautiful eyes filled with dread and boredom. It was invigorating. It was sickening. I couldn't look away.

Bowed over the desk, Mallory lamely grasped for her composure, a magician about to accidentally spill the secret of the trick while knowing full well the audience was not fooled. "I have done enough sex scenes to know how to make it look good," Mallory said, each word dripping with a persistent midwestern inflection.

The reporter's eyes flickered down her shirt. "There's a lot of Oscar talk surrounding this film. Are you excited to be part of such a noteworthy project?"

Deep in her own story, Mallory ignored the question. "The scene takes place in a cemetery, which is a weird place to do it, but there's this part where he has me bent over a headstone, and he's pounding into me—"

That was when Matt climaxed, gurgling and gasping. As he cleaned himself with the dishtowel, it occurred to me that he had also been watching the interview, bathing in the same experience. Was that was the reason he actually came, and in a reasonable amount of time?

Matt went for the remote and I turned to look at him, on level ground from my heels. It was odd to see his face after feeling only his body. I noted the disconnect.

"Leave it on," I said.

"Alice, the kids will be down soon, and this is getting a little risqué."

"You'll fuck me in the kitchen while the bagels toast, but you're worried about the kids watching *Rise and Shine, Los Angeles*?" I said.

"We can control ourselves. There's no controlling that."

His fingers hovered over the off button, but his eyes lingered on the TV. I followed his gaze to see Mallory's shirt open up, milky breasts heaving with every breath. Her eyebrows rose as she looked at the reporter, having not heard his question. If only Matt knew what was brewing inside that girl. Were he aware of the fermenting filth beyond that arousing exterior, would he still fantasize about emptying himself inside her?

The TV went dark just as the kids burst in, and I stared at the blank screen, wishing to see her again.

As a reporter, Mallory Braun was my wet dream, the vessel of a tragic story she didn't know she possessed, my ticket out of the sludge of *The Hollywood Express* and into the big leagues of legitimate journalism.

4

As a wife, and a mother, and a woman, I wanted her to go away.

There was an accident on the 101. Some schmuck's bad luck never failed to add annoyance to my day, but that accident was something else. It was the sort of wreckage that once you witnessed the gloriously gruesome sight, you were grateful for the delay. I was grateful for the fuel.

As I wove through the white cubicles of *The Hollywood Express* bullpen, my heart raced. I was amped. Trevor stepped into my path, dark muscles shining through his white dress shirt, struggling underneath tightly woven fabric, a presentation decidedly meant for misconception. Who was he fooling?

Trevor's downturned frown attempted to threaten my enthusiasm. "You're late."

"There was an accident," I said, swerving around him. "Tell me you saw the *Rise and Shine* shitshow this morning."

"I don't watch A.M. spots. It puts me in a bad mood for real life."

It wasn't his inability to recognize the carnage that made him weak; it was his unwillingness to even look in that direction. "Mallory Braun described the sex scene from her new movie," I said, and watched as light filled his dark eyes.

"You're joking."

"I need my exclusive, Trevor. Put pressure on the studio."

"Everyone wants that exclusive. She's a hard girl to catch. You should have tried back when she was just *that chick who dies in horror movies.*"

"There's a story there," I said, "and I need it."

"There's no story, Alice. She's just another cute girl with daddy issues. If you want that promotion, sell me a real story. There's a space waiting for you at the top."

"I've been told that before," I said, "and then they hired you."

Trevor stopped in his tracks, and I made my way to my office. I knew he'd follow. He spent more time in my office than his own, and his had a view.

"Don't close the door," I said as he did just that, then sat across my desk.

"Pitch it to me, Alice."

"I've emailed you three proposals."

"Paint the picture. Make me see why it's so important to you."

Just like that accident on the freeway, my argument needed to sell not the droning familiarity of a traffic crawler, but the seductive charm of destruction in mind-blowing slow motion.

"I saw the wreck on the 101," I said, setting the scene. "Drove right past it. Mercedes pancaked into the k-rail, it was a mess."

Skin pulled around his nose in a frown. "You want to compare Mallory Braun to a car wreck?"

"Not just any wreck, but a luxury vehicle wreck," I said. "See, were it a minivan, you'd get a little teary-eyed and worry about how many kids they had in the back seat. If it were a semi, you'd cringe, because who hasn't been next to one of those at seventy miles an hour. A Prius? Well, who gives a fuck about Prius drivers. But a Mercedes? That's different. Makes you think, oh of course he crashed. He was probably speeding, cutting people off, driving like an asshole, and now he's got to figure out how to pay off the lease for his under-insured car, and probably also bail since you know he was on something, and now I'm late to work because some douchebag in a C-Class couldn't keep his hand off his dick long enough to make it to the off-ramp."

Trevor blinked at me. "Alice, I drive a Mercedes."

6

I nodded. "It's a sexy car. One that people who drive decade-old Hondas aspire to own one day. But when they see one totaled on the freeway, not only do they blame it on the driver, but they want evidence to prove they saw it coming. That they knew it was all a matter of time before every self-important jerk in a fancy car ends up in a crumpled heap on the freeway. People don't just want after photos. They want the lead-in. The set-up. Time to place bets. It's all part of the experience."

"I still don't know what this has to do with Mallory Braun, but if you want to capture a play-by-play, join the junket."

"The junket is for amateurs," I said. He still wasn't grasping my pitch. "I need an exclusive."

"You'll have to go through Juliette Fairchild, and we both know she won't give you shit."

"Juliette pretends the press is her enemy, but even she knows in order to sell her new star to Academy voters, she has to do better than *Rise and Shine, Los Angeles*."

"I just can't see what you find so special about this girl."

"This is about more than Mallory Braun," I said. "It's about what she represents."

"Which is what?"

"The fall of the Hollywood playgirl," I said, gaze drifting to the window, visualizing that line as the title of my op-ed.

Trevor stood, towering over me. "Just don't push too hard, Alice. Not everyone is made of brick like you are."

The seduction had been lost on him. How could he not see what was so glaringly obvious? I knew him as a man of instant gratification, someone used to showing up right at the spark of ignition. I, however, was familiar with being held on the edge in eager anticipation of the climax.

There was power in that. Trevor, like most of them, didn't know what he was missing. He needed me to show him. They all did. They needed me to bathe them in the experience.

TWO
Juliette

THREE TIMES was too many for the phone to beep. I had told her before; if I don't answer after two, leave me the fuck alone. On the fourth beep, I'd about lost my shit.

Lifting my hand from the keyboard, I jabbed the blinking button on my office phone. "What."

Hope's voice whispered through the speaker. "Alice Welsh is on line one."

"I'll take it." I jabbed another button, and went back to typing. "I'm going to tell you the same thing I've told everyone else. If you want to talk to Mallory Braun, join the junket."

"Mallory has the potential for Oscar buzz. A solid interview could push that." Alice's voice sounded higher than usual. No doubt she'd seen the *Rise and Shine* spot and thought she was on to something.

"Not that you'd care, but I'm up to my tits in legal paperwork."

"I can't give you divorce advice, Juliette."

"I'm giving you some. For the inevitable future."

"My marriage is fine."

"I know what you're after, Alice. You're not an advocate for truth, you want to watch the world burn."

"The world is already burning. I'm just here to report on it."

"And I'm here to make movies about it. I don't see the difference."

Her silence ate up too much precious time. I was about to hang up when she finally said, "You need my help to sell her, Juliette. You don't need some social media schmuck whose main job is writing online quizzes."

"This film will get me an Oscar nom. There's your story. Quit trying to find the failed human behind the art. That's what HBO specials are for."

I jabbed the End Call button, but Alice's voice echoed in my ears. She had a way of doing that. Which is precisely why I'd kept her the fuck away from my people.

I went back to typing. No time to waste on thirsty journalists. The screening was a day away and every hour I was back on damage control, pushing that steaming shit-pile uphill. It wasn't my first rodeo. My wall of film posters read like a lapel of war medals. One open shelf sat waiting for the ultimate prize. That was why I'd stuck it out for those twenty years; for a shiny gold dildo-shaped statue of a man.

The door opened, and Mallory entered like it was her own office she'd stepped into. No knock. She never knocked. Once Oscar made it onto my shelf, I would have to invest in a security system.

"You busy?" she said.

"I'm always busy," I said, barely looking away from my computer.

Mallory plunked herself on the couch and stared at the newest poster on my wall. *Between Broken Pieces*, featuring the smug photograph of the very girl who stared at it as though that was the first she'd seen of it. I had to look at it every goddamn day.

I got tired of waiting. "If you're here to beg me to push back the junket, don't bother."

She tilted her head. "And what if I am?"

"This is the biggest film of your career. The screening is tomorrow, the premiere on Friday. Academy voters are sniffing around and I have the H.F.P.A. drinking from my cunt as we speak, so no, we can't push back the junket."

Mallory toyed with a loose thread escaping from a seam in the couch. "You saw the interview this morning, didn't you?"

"I don't watch the news."

"The words just, kind of, flew out of my mouth before I could stop them. What do they call it? Word vomit?" She tugged on the thread, pulled it out an inch.

My nerves flared. "Have you even seen that therapist?"

"I had an appointment this morning. And I'm not here to ask you to push back the junket."

"How was the session? Are you going back?" Years spent in network meetings full of men made me a pro at keeping a conversation on track. I wasn't about to be diverted, despite the destruction of my couch.

"I like the junkets," she said. "Out of all the movie bullshit, the junket is the best part. A whole line of wannabe reporters waiting for one perfect sound bite. The anticipation, the hope I'll give them something juicy and memorable—ooh," she squirmed, "it's so exciting."

"The whole point of me paying for your therapist is for you to babble on someone else's couch."

"Sorry." She pulled the thread out from the seam. It was six inches long. "I'm just… tired."

"You've been in the business all of three years. You can't be tired."

"You have no idea what it's like for me."

"You're right. I don't. My career isn't based on how many social media followers I have."

"That was literally what got me my first gig."

"It's my job to sell you, but you need to present a version of yourself people actually want to buy. Buck up, get out there, and sell your fucking movie."

She smirked. "Give the people what they want, right?"

The door pushed open as though to offer me an easier way to throw her out. Luke Connelly strutted in wearing that smile that made women cream themselves. At least, that's what he said.

"Ladies! How are ya? Mallory, good to see you." He gave her a wink, and Mallory leaned against the couch arm, shoulders rolling back, pushing other things out. "You were amazing on *Rise and Shine*. I want to see more of that. Can you give me more of that? Juliette, let's book more of that. I want to see this face everywhere I look."

"You can look at it all you want," Mallory said with that languid midwestern drawl that came out around men. Her smug grin matched the one in her poster. Luke's eyes drifted down her body.

I decided then that Oscar would live on my desk. So I could use it as a mallet.

"Mallory, give us the room," I started, but Luke waved me off.

"She should be here for this," he said. "Besides, I don't want to be left alone with you."

Mallory tossed back her head and laughed. Luke made that annoying guttural chuckle he made when he couldn't decide if he was embarrassed or aroused.

How cute. So fucking cute. I still couldn't see what he found so damn appealing. Her eyes were red and foggy, yet her face was camera ready. There was an indestructible quality to girls like her; no matter how dissolved they were on the inside, they remained perky and tight on the outside. It made me want to inject her with battery acid to give her a sense of mortality.

"Why not just parade her down Hollywood Boulevard?" I said. "She could join Spiderman and that millionaire who pretends he's homeless."

"That's not what I mean." Luke's voice hardened. "No one will give a shit about this movie unless we make them. We're already fucked by a bad release date—"

"Which you didn't fight to change," I said.

"And the marketing campaign is as thin and dry as a decade-old wallet condom—"

"Because you didn't leave enough budget for a push."

"No one will vote for her if they don't see her."

"Don't talk to me like I'm green, Luke. I know how to do this."

"Then do it. Get her out there. I want to be sick of Mallory Braun. I want to see so much of her that I wish she would disappear."

When she spoke again, the drawl crawled out her mouth like a venomous snake. "I'll give you what you want."

The two of them locked eyes, as thought they'd come up with the most brilliant idea ever, as though no one in the entire entertainment industry had ever faced the uphill battle of film promotion, as though I hadn't formulated a plan while Luke was busy working his morning wood to *Rise and Shine, Los Angeles.*

Struggling to do my job was a color I didn't like wearing. Most actors were eager to do the legwork. But the only work Mallory's legs did was gliding her in like a goddamn Disney On Ice princess.

Mallory fucking Braun. A child in a queen's body. A girl who didn't seem to care at all if her movie flopped, if it became the laughing stock of the year, if the only good thing that came out of it was that a few million creeps watched her have sex on the big screen.

I Googled the effects of battery acid. That Oscar would be mine, for fuck's sake.

THREE
Riley

DRAIN WATER. Mid-ocean sinkholes. Fresh beer tapped into a glass.

Things that swirl.
Like my brain.

In my skull sloshed an alphabet soup of incoherent thoughts, whirlpooled around by that insane fairy some would call my conscience.

I called her my evil seductress.

Yes, I needed the money, but only the wicked elf of my frontal lobe would have suggested this way to get it.

My phone buzzed in my hand. I shook my head, tried to align figurative noodle letters in my brain as I squinted at the screen. Four missed calls from Juliette. Not one. Not two. Four.

Call her back, nefarious nymph whimpered in my ear.
Fucking fairies.

"These are… nice."

I silenced my phone and looked up. The girl behind the shiny desk was easily fifteen years younger than me. She had the perky tits to prove it, framed by a teal blouse that perfectly contrasted her skin. I loathed her from the start, and those tits were just one reason.

"I have more," I said. "I've shot some pretty important people. I used to do film posters."

She thumbed my iPad, acrylic nails tapping on the screen. "Are those pictures in here?"

"No. I keep the best ones on my computer. You know what they say."

"Sure. Yeah, totally," she said, nodding. She didn't know. No one under twenty-five knew anything about anything. A few more years and she'd know what it felt like to watch the world crumble around her like a dried-out sand castle.

She'd paused on a photograph of a model passed out on the floor. He had been high. I didn't know then that he was in the process of overdosing. He traded his pain for artistic expression.

It was a brilliant fucking photo.

"I know my style can be jarring," I said. "See, most people just want to look hot. Instagram fuckable. But it's unrealistic. I want to capture people in their most raw, unfiltered moments. That's reality. That's what people connect with."

The girl's eyes went cloudy.

"You don't like it, just say that."

"I'm just not sure it's appropriate for our publication. We focus on body positivity here, and a lot of your work is—" she scrolled to the next photo and lit up. "Wait. Is this Mallory Braun?"

She had found a portrait of Mallory. A washed-up hooker in front of a smoke shop on Hollywood Boulevard. One of my favorite pieces.

"That wasn't supposed to be in there."

"Do you know her?"

"Sort of."

My phone buzzed. It was Juliette. Again.

"We spent months trying to get Mallory Braun featured on our website," she said.

Oh, here we go.

"It's not going to happen."

"What's not going happen?" the girl asked, her face scrunched like a child told it was time to stop playing.

"You're not going to convince me to sell you those photos."

"Oh, I don't want these photos." She looked down at the iPad, then swiftly handed it over. "No, that doesn't fit our publication at all."

"You just said you've been trying for months to get her in your magazine."

"We only publish photos shot in-house," she motioned toward me, "and that is not the Mallory Braun we want associated with us."

What a firm-boobed, contoured-faced, annoyingly successful floozy piece of work. How dare she assume anything about Mallory. She didn't know her. Nobody did. Not like I did. What they saw was what juvenile fashion editors put in their magazines. Pretty patterns. Colorful backgrounds. Clean and airbrushed and proper enough to bring home to Mommy.

No one could capture the real Mallory. Not like I could.

"You'll never get any good photos of her. Only I know how to shoot her. And anyway, Juliette Fairchild will never let her anywhere near a place like this."

"Oh, you don't know, do you?" The girl smiled as a ray of sunlight twinkled across her bright white teeth. "She's, like, in the middle of a shoot right now."

Son of a bitch.

Two steps out of the office, I returned Juliette's phone call.

"Jesus mother fucking Christ," I said as soon as she answered. Everyone in the bullpen stared wide-eyed as I passed through. It had been a while since I had been out in public. "You would rather sell Mallory to a pre-pubescent fashion magazine than let me shoot her?"

"For fuck's sake, calm down." Juliette's voice was harsh over the phone. Not that it was ever any different. "That magazine has gotten a lot of notoriety for its political ballsiness. They have a progressive vision for their online edition."

"I am the only one who knows how to shoot Mallory Braun."

"So you keep saying."

The woman had ground my nerves so many times they should have been as smooth as stones in a river.

"That poster is an atrocity. You made her look like a nun getting head under her habit."

"Don't make me regret calling you, Riley. I only did it as a courtesy."

Juliette called for me when she was in a bind, and not just of the photographic sort.

"You're losing her, aren't you? Juliette, I keep telling you, the more you try to direct her into a particular shape, the quicker she's going to break the whole mold apart."

"Jesus with the analogies."

"You were supposed to keep her safe."

"I'm keeping her career safe, which is why I'm keeping her away from you."

As I prepared to scream into the phone about what a stupid fucking idea it was to sell the girl to a half-baked fashion magazine, the door I blindly shoved my way through opened into the dark and cold cavern of a photography studio.

There she was. Backed against a stark white cyclorama. One light shone down from the rig, as though she were being beamed up by aliens. Her detached expression was alluring in the same way that one might find a wilting flower attractive.

"Yes, that's it." *Shuk-cha*. "Make me believe you don't care." *Shuk-cha*. "Let me feel how much you loathe everyone around you." *Shuk-cha*. "I'm beneath you, Mallory." *Shuk-cha*. "I'm so far below you're going to step on my balls on your way to the top." *Shuk-cha*.

The douchebag shooting her flailed and shimmied. Mallory sat atop a stool, and that was all she did. She might as well have been a department store mannequin for the amount of enthusiasm she put into it. She had on too much makeup—or not enough, it was hard to tell under those lights. Despite how her dark clothes contrasted with the cyclorama, she sunk into the background, drawn into her own black hole.

That was not the Mallory Braun I knew.

How dare he even try.

"No, like this." Mr. Douchebag nudged at her shoulder. Stiffly, she bounced back. A bottom-weighted punching bag. Without the creepy painted-on smile. "Oh for the love of Kanye, it's like trying to shoot a tree branch."

Shielding my eyes from the spot lamp, I walked over. It wasn't my cyc being covered in boot prints, what did I care.

Mr. Douchebag sure cared. "Who the fuck are you and why are you in my shot?"

"I'm trying to help."

Mallory looked up at me. Squinting. Like she didn't recognize me. I brushed the hair out of her eyes. There was a hollowness in them. I pulled the hair back forward.

"Have you ever shot anyone before? Because it feels like you're new at this."

He crowded me. Shouted and spit in my ear. "Seriously, lady, get out of my studio or I'm calling security."

The way Mallory ran her fingers through her hair made me shiver. I wasn't sure why. I also wasn't sure it was

17

a shiver. "I'm going to be featured on their website," she said, smiling.

"So I heard. Gonna be a real shake-up, I'm sure."

"They didn't go for my nude suggestion, though." She smirked, her voice drenched in that midwestern drawl that came out when she was intoxicated. Fake eyelashes weighed down her eyelids. The plain ensemble made her look fifteen, not twenty-five.

I hated myself for thinking she was beautiful.

"Juliette told you about the shoot, didn't she?" Mallory said.

"I found out about it barely three minutes ago."

"I preferred it when you did it," she said. "You're the best photographer I know."

Nope. Not a shiver. That was definitely a throb.

"That's the last time I'll say it, lady."

Her eyes warned me he was coming. Hand on my shoulder. A swivel around. Arm whipping out, into his camera. Crashing and skidding into the cyc.

The room went silent, all eyes on the camera. The lens was broken, cracked through the middle like ice on a lake. Rage built in Douchebag's face. Bellowing heat singed my neck.

Time to ditch and run.

Mallory's hand in mine, we ran. Me with my iPad of second-rate photos and her in expensive wardrobe that was likely meant to be returned after the shoot.

We burst onto the street like a couple of bank robbers. Mallory scanned the block for the getaway car. I wondered when the paps would spot her.

"You don't have to put up with whatever Juliette tells you," I said. "You can make your own decisions."

"I'm thinking about reinventing myself," she said, waving to the street. I stepped back. Those long arms were dangerous when flailing. "That's what people want, right? To watch me change before their eyes, like phases of the moon?" Her arms dropped to her sides. "Dr. Shea thinks I'm full of shit."

"Wait, you're seeing Fiona Shea?"

"It was Juliette's idea." Mallory tugged a fake eyelash, pulling it from her lid. "I don't want to see her again. She's depressing. Actually, that's probably on purpose. You know, job security."

She peeled the eyelash off. Threw it into the street, like it were a skin she was shedding, the new one fresh and shiny underneath. Her phases were already changing. It was fascinating to watch.

It would be even more fascinating to capture. And I would. Because I could do it best.

FOUR
Fiona

THE ROOM NEEDED WINDOWS. Every patient I had reminded me so. Medical journals heralded the power of Vitamin D, but no amount of vitamins ever kept a suicidal patient alive. If it did, I'd have chained my fiancé to the fence post and let him sweat it out in the sun. But he wasn't suicidal. He was a liar.

The door buzzed. I hated the noise. It should have been something soothing, like a bird chirp, or a church bell, not the teeth-grinding hum of electric shock.

Alice Welsh was at the door, stiff and unsmiling. "Sorry I'm late. It's been a crazy day."

I hadn't noticed she was late. "It's fine. Just keep in mind I can't go beyond the hour."

Alice moved to the couch with urgency. "It's my husband's birthday today, which normally doesn't bother me, but this year he's brought out all the stops. What forty-two-year-old insists on anal sex as a birthday present? A nice evening out, sure. I'd even be down for a random threesome. I mean, stuff your dick in some twenty-year-old's asshole, why force it into mine?"

Speed talker. Self-absorbed. Possibly narcissistic, pending further evaluation. "Do you not like anal sex?"

"I love anal sex. Who doesn't love anal sex?"

"A lot of women, actually."

"Doesn't mean you get to fuck it just because it's your birthday. Are you married, Fiona?"

Eyes on my left hand. I had been rubbing my naked ring finger. Abrupt subject change. Classic deflection.

"Here's the thing," Alice said, crossing her legs. "I got where I am by writing a shit-ton of material for my journalism portfolio. It makes me wonder how much of life psychiatrists are required to live before they're allowed to analyze people."

No other patient spent a hundred and fifty dollars an hour to talk shit to my face. "I'm sensing some resentment."

"Not resentment. Just… bemusement."

"About the extent of my life experience?"

"Who's fault was it? The end of your relationship, I mean."

The door buzzed. I wasn't expecting my next patient until later. Alice frowned, upset she'd lost my focus. I was grateful for the interruption.

"Excuse me," I said.

Upon opening the door, I found Mallory Braun hunched around the doorframe, hiding from view. She spoke in breathy, rapid bursts. "Hi, I'm so sorry I missed our meeting. I didn't mean anything by it. I'm sure you're great at your job. I'm just a fuckup."

A practiced apology. Glancing back to see if Alice was watching—which she was—I snuck into the waiting area. "Your appointment was three hours ago."

"I said I'm sorry." Mallory slumped against the wall. "I thought I was strong enough to get through this alone. I guess I'm not. So here I am, asking for help."

For two hour-long sessions I had subjected myself to her near silence while I waited for her to say something of note. And there she was, on her own accord, needing something from me. It was my chance to get what I needed from her.

It needed to be her idea.

"Would you like to come in and talk?"

A glance to the outside door. "Yeah. Okay."

"Wait here."

I returned to my office to find Alice pitched forward on the couch, ear turned to the door. "Something wrong?"

"I'll have to cut our session short. I have a bit of an emergency."

A frown, exaggerated. "Does this mean you'll add minutes to the next session?"

The thought of spending additional time with the woman—and the unfortunate discussion of anal sex—made my stomach churn. "Anything you'd like. Now, please."

Alice neared the door, and her body stiffened. "Who is this patient? I can't help but feel I recognized her voice."

Instantly I'd realized my error—I knew the nature of Alice's profession—but her hand was on the doorknob and she pushed into the waiting area. Mallory sat huddled in a chair in the corner. A fashion magazine hid her face. Alice passed through. Mallory moved the magazine as I shut the outside door. Just before the lock clicked, I heard Alice gasp.

"At least you're good at getting people to leave," Mallory said. She ushered past me into the office and fell onto the couch.

Her outfit seemed extravagant for a Wednesday afternoon. One fake eyelash hung half detached from her eyelid. Some young women could be in the worst of ways and still look more beautiful than a woman who'd spent hours trying. I hated that about her—how she could be so effortlessly memorable, how she was undoubtedly pulling the wool over my eyes in order to get from me what she wanted. My fiancé was the same way. They were all like that.

I held up my cell phone. "Do you mind if I record this session?"

Eyes narrowed. Head tilted. Easily suspicious. "Isn't that against some kind of regulation?"

"Not if it's agreed upon by the patient."

In the space of her silence, I caught the red light of my office answering machine. On the seventh blink I pleaded with myself to stop counting. By the twelfth blink, Mallory finally shrugged and leaned back.

"Whatever you're into, Dr. Shea." Pushback. A diversion of unease.

Pressing *Record* on my cell phone, I settled myself. "You mentioned you're going through a stressful time. Why don't you tell me about that?"

After a deep sigh, she said, "I hate movie releases. There's so much going on. I fly to New York in three days, London after that, it's nuts. I do a million interviews in what feels like minutes. I'm on magazines, in commercials, at bus stops. I can't even explain the surreal moment when you see your face on a fucking billboard along the

Strip." Her body was open and relaxed as she described her anxiety. Casual. Comfortable.

"It must be a lot of pressure to be the center of so much attention."

She nodded. "I get anxious just thinking about walking down that carpet, you know? Cameras flashing, people yelling, and all I'm thinking about is how afraid I am that one of my tits is going to slip out of my dress."

"And thinking about that makes you anxious?"

"Yeah. I'm stressed all the time. And tired. Like, I can barely keep my eyes open." She paused, then said, "They make stuff for that, right?"

"You mean, medication?"

"Yeah. You know, something to take the edge off."

Quick to the punch. I had expected more of a set-up, more of a sob story. "Let me ask, Mallory, are you hoping to make acting a life-long career?"

She stiffened, shoulders pulled inward. "I guess. Why?"

"As your therapist, I have concern for your ability to deal with this level of stress long term. I certainly wouldn't want you to become dependent on medication."

The façade cracked. Body started to recoil. First her arms, which she folded across her belly. "It's not my fault I'm a celebrity. I just want to act."

"What makes you so stressed about being a public figure?"

"People just need to see me, that's what I've been told." Her gaze danced around the room. Unable to settle. "Did you realize this room didn't have windows when you signed the lease?"

"What do these people want to see when they look at you?"

She tucked a leg beneath her. "People expect a lot of me. All kinds of things. I want to give them those things,

I do. I just need help finding the way to do it." Her gaze landed on me. "That's what you have to understand, Dr. Shea. I have to give the people what they want."

I could see right through it, that perfectly practiced prompt—the one spoken by a girl who didn't care how her actions affected others, a girl who had been modified and hatched into a Hollywood siren. So many innocent people would perish at the edge of a cliff because of her.

It wasn't my job to bring her back to the real world. What I needed to do was prove I was right.

"I'm sorry," I said. "I don't prescribe medication anymore."

Limbs sprung out like a released spring and she jolted forward. "What do you mean 'anymore'? Did you just decide that right this second?"

Aggressive outburst. Unnecessarily so. "I have a professional reason for not prescribing medication."

"You're fucking kidding me. I heard you were good for it."

"I don't know who gave you the idea that I doled out prescription drugs like candy, but—"

"That's exactly what she said," Mallory interrupted. "She said I could get what I needed from you."

That caught me. "Who told you?"

"Whatever, it doesn't matter," she said, getting to her feet. "Thanks for wasting my time."

I stood to stop her, but she was easily five inches taller and I withdrew. "Mallory, who told you about getting pills from me?"

Her breath was heavy and forced. "Why does anyone bother coming to see you if you can't even help them? What the fuck is your purpose?"

It was a damn good question, one my fiancé failed to answer. Mallory forced guilt on me, tried to make me feel bad for the fact that I was refusing her ability to abuse my position and think she could get away with it, but she had no idea the reason why. It wasn't about her. Not everything was about Mallory Braun.

I wasn't going to let it happen again.

Five
Juliette

"WE'RE HERE," he said, as though I couldn't see the giant red *W* looming in the car window. I had my hand on the door when he said, "Is this some kind of movie event? Or TV? I love TV."

Rideshare drivers had a habit of being nosy. "It's just a party," I said, getting out of the car.

"Yeah, but a movie party, right? Holy shit, is that Mallory Braun?"

No way had she beaten me there, wandering in public unattended. Her late entrance was planned on purpose. Of course she hadn't paid attention.

Whipping around, I prepared to scold the insubordinate twat when I saw her picture. What the rideshare driver had spotted was that goddamn poster plastered all over the front entrance of the hotel.

"She's here, isn't she? Oh my God, I want to marry her."

"It's a private event," I said, then slammed the car door shut.

The driver rolled down the passenger window. "Think she'll take a selfie with me?"

"Go away."

"I picked you up from your house!" he called. "I know where you live!"

The posters lined the walk inside. Yes, fine, Riley Westcott would have done a better job with the portrait, but I sure as hell was not about to admit that to her. I had a reputation, for fuck's sake.

Claustrophobia was named for events like these. Nothing about screening parties gave me the least bit of joy. I would have preferred to spend the evening at the DMV, but I was there to sell my movie, even if my star refused to. Making the rounds early, I needed a feel for the intellectual opinions in the room before Mallory arrived and everyone would be distracted by their reproductive organs.

Two minutes in, I found myself in the crosshairs of Alice Welsh. She beelined for me, weaving around stiff-necked critics and catering trays. Alice had a way of being simultaneously intrusive and apathetic. Terrible traits for a reporter.

"Verdict is coming in," she said.

"You were at the screening," I said, eyes on the cell phone held out in front of her.

"You knew I would be."

"Does that mean you signed up for the junket?"

"Junkets are for newbies."

"Last I checked you didn't have the credentials to push for much more."

Turning her credentials lanyard to face her stomach, she held her phone closer to me. "Do you think the response for the film will outweigh the salacious events of today? I also have reason to believe she's seeing a therapist."

"For fuck's sake, the film will speak for itself."

"Do you really believe that, though?" Alice leaned in, focusing her beady eyes on my lips. "Do you really believe you can keep Mallory Braun under control?"

"You sound like you want her to fail."

A smile tugged at the edges of her mouth. "Don't tell me you've gone easy on the girl. I know how you work, Juliette. She's your biggest asset to date. Maybe a little too big for you to handle these days."

"I've had plenty of practice keeping talent under control," I said. "My success is my own doing, and not easily undone by someone like Mallory Braun."

"I don't doubt it." A full smile broke across Alice's face, and she backed away. "I'll be watching, Juliette. You'll wish you'd given me that interview."

I knew how Alice Welsh worked. She would be picking away at the critics, forcing me to defend my talent when I needed those people focused on their appreciation for the film. I had an aptitude for swaying opinions. Minds were feeble shortly after watching a movie, like a tired child throwing a tantrum instead of doing the reasonable thing and going to sleep. I warned Luke, *don't load a gun and put me in a room with those people*. He laughed. He didn't think I was serious. Which was precisely why I was at that party when even I knew I shouldn't have been.

"She added such a nuance to her character," said one man. He'd worn that same suit to every screening for the last seven years. It had gotten increasingly tight around the middle.

"She and the director did a fabulous job exploring the character together," I said.

"Yes," he said, nodding thoughtfully. "Miss Braun really draws you in."

"The message was loud and clear: women are taking over the world," said a flamboyant young man. He and his partner had matching handlebar mustaches. "But the execution was confusing. Why did she lack so much screen time? I hardly saw her face."

"It was an artistic decision to force the viewer through her perspective," I said.

"I get that, but you've left us wanting so much more," he said.

The partner fondled his mustache. "People will go anywhere to get what they want."

When I made my way to the most hard-nosed woman in the critic's circle, I knew I was in trouble. She went on about the Bechdel Test, about the misleading implications of the sexuality of young women in film, about all the things that I agreed with but had no desire to discuss at a screening party. Telling a woman in Hollywood that there needs to be more women in Hollywood is like telling a single mother of five that parenting is hard. No shit, sweetheart.

"Maybe it's the feminist in me talking," she said, "but when women are forced to believe that intelligence is only sexy when matched with attractiveness, it defeats the purpose of intellectualism altogether."

"That's the message of the film," I said while trying desperately not to throw my drink at her. "It shows us the process women go through when determining their place in the world."

"You can leave men out of that process," she said. "They're not even necessary to the story."

My arm had moved to raise my glass when someone spoke up beside me. "What this film does so brilliantly is demonstrate how both sexes are part of the equation. If you're going to pretend women aren't also part of the problem, then we're simply asking the wrong questions about how to fix it."

The critic's eyes went soft as she stared at the person beside me. The tall, obscenely confident young woman named Mallory Braun. Her presence caught attention, and suddenly every sucker in the room crowded around her.

"You can't possibly believe there's any advantage to showcasing the negative role of women in this, when it was men who spawned it," said the critic.

"*Between Broken Pieces* shows us both the negative and the positive. It shows us how women have the potential to do consequential things together. We'll only truly know our collective power when we accept the potential of our own self-destruction."

The crowd clapped and cheered and took her picture, and Mallory smiled and waved back at them as if she were the goddamn princess of Wales. Every pair of eyes, every lust-drunk smile, every awkward laugh made my stomach knot. She had enchanted the whole room, except for Alice, whose enthusiasm had waned.

I escaped the carnal feeding and went to Alice, brimming with the pride of my win.

"Still want that interview?"

Alice frowned at me. "What did you do to her?"

"I didn't do anything. I told you, there's no story. It's just me and her and an Oscar-contending movie." Patting her on the arm, I said, "I'll pen you in for thirty minutes after the junket tomorrow. Congratulations, Alice. You got your interview."

Relief washed over me as I walked away, looking back as Mallory hunched over in a fit of laughter, everyone laughing along with her. Mallory had finally learned to sell herself, and people were buying in bulk.

SIX
Riley

SOME PEOPLE WERE NOT hard to find. Wednesday evening. West Hollywood Whole Foods. Herbal remedies aisle.

Or the wine aisle, depending on the mood she was in.

I found Fiona near the diet detox pills. She whispered into her phone. "How is he not available all week? Have you told him it's an emergency?"

"Quite the emergency," I said.

Fiona swiveled around, covered the mouthpiece with one hand while balancing a handcart full of clanking wine bottles. Dressed in yoga pants and a jean jacket, she fit right in with the single Hollywood wannabees fifteen years her junior. She mouthed *I'm on the phone* and moved down the aisle.

I followed.

"Please tell him I called," she said into the phone. "It's important that I speak with him. In person." She ended the call and glared at me. "Why are you here?"

"I'm shopping," I said. She looked, but I wasn't carrying a basket. "It's a specific kind of shopping."

"I tried to get you to stop being so cryptic." Fiona walked away, pretending to browse. "Vagueness is not an effective communication technique. It won't get you what you want."

"I want drugs."

She halted. Glanced around, twitching like a strung-out tweaker. "Don't say shit like that around here."

I threw my arms out. "Dude, this is WeHo. Nobody cares."

"You were doing fine without them. You haven't need-ed to see me in months. Why are you suddenly cornering me in a grocery store?"

"You're my therapist. You tell me."

"I don't do that anymore," she said. "We're in the mid-dle of a prescription drug crisis, that stuff is everywhere. There's a retired woman in my building who practically has a pharmacy in her closet. Why bother me for it?"

"What can I say, I believe in customer loyalty."

Her eyes darted around the aisle. "I won't get caught up in that again."

The woman needed a lesson in deadpan. She was too easy to read. Less guilt, more *muh muh muh muh p-p-p-p-poker face.*

A man came into the aisle. Even in his baseball cap and sunglasses, he was recognizable enough for me to do a double-take like a transplant on the Star Tours bus.

I called out past him to Fiona. "You won't? Or you can't?"

Her jaw clenched so tight her teeth clattered. "Riley. Enough."

"I just need something to take the edge off."

"You won't get them from me."

Famous actor dude stopped and looked around, as though startled to find himself in that particular aisle, but not surprised by the conversation.

"Dealer?" he asked me.

"Therapist," I said. "A bit ineffective, if you ask me."

He nodded, reached into his jeans and pulled out a baggie with two round blue pills. 10mg. Child's play, but better than nothing. "Mine gives me extra when I cry."

"You're really not helping," I said.

"You want them or not?"

I nodded sideways, and he handed me the pills.

"Might want to look into a new shrink," he said.

Famous actor dude moved on down the aisle, and I was about to declare the outing a moderate success when the detox aisle suddenly filled with a horde of women jabbering on about the celebrity in the parking lot.

"I'm pretty sure it was her," one said.

"She's got a movie coming out, she's too busy to be hanging out at Whole Foods," said another.

"I'm so excited for that movie, though," said a third. "I'm, like, really intrigued by that sex scene."

"You're gross," said the first.

"What?" shrugged the third. "I can admit when a woman is hot. And Mallory Braun is hot."

The girls laughed as they passed. It didn't take much for Mallory to be noticed. She was like a strip club magnet on a fridge covered in children's drawings.

Once the gaggle was out of earshot, Fiona approached me.

"You can't be serious," she said.

"We're all struggling, Fiona. Some of us more than others."

"She's not struggling. She's playing you. Just like she tried to play me." She shifted, tilted her head back. "You're the one who told her to ask me for pills, aren't you?"

"Did they blame you for what happened to your fiancé? Is that what this is about?" She flinched. I'd hit a raw nerve.

She crowded me, wine cart swaying dangerously close to my knees. "There's not a single authentic thing about that girl. You'll see. Just like I did. And then it'll be too late."

With that, she stormed off, knocking two women out of her way like a couple of bowling pins.

When I walked out of the store, my rideshare driver was in the middle of an argument with the parking lot security guard. Something about double-parking and why can't immigrants get more respect, the normal sort of L.A. shit. I slid into the backseat and hoped I wouldn't get stuck paying extra charges.

Mallory was slumped against the opposite door. Hem of her dress hitched up to her hip, showing off those impressively long legs.

"I got it," I said, presenting the baggie of blue pills. I waited for a show of appreciation, or maybe even joy. Something. Anything.

"I feel like I'm living behind a two-way mirror," she said. "They're watching me, but they can't tell I'm watching them."

Beyond her window, several people with oversized cameras hovered near the car. They knew someone notable was inside, in spite of the darkness.

"Better than living in a fishbowl," I said.

"What do you think they want?" she said.

"I honestly don't know anymore." I studied the photographers as they danced, jostling for prime position. Our driver swore at the security guy in a foreign language. Someone threw a lit cigarette at the tire.

The side door opened and Mallory slid off the seat and into the parking lot. Flashes showered her. The photographers shouted her name. Random shoppers in the parking lot turned and gawked and recorded it on their phones. Mallory stood there, swaying. Intoxicated with attention. Blinking into the strobing lights.

My rental house off La Cienega and Melrose was set up for moments like those. The lights were in place. Windows covered with thrift store drapes. Pre-arranged props. Each room with different theme. Reclaimed mid-century modern. Steampunk industrial. 1980s dive bar. Joan Crawford-era noir.

That's where I put her.

Music pulsed in my ears as I set up the tripod, focused on the subject lying on the red velvet couch in a silky trumpet gown. Tipping martini glass. Veronica Lake peek-a-boo bangs. Eyes blank and staring into the distance.

I wasn't sure if she was conscious until the shutter went off.

Shuk-cha.

Mallory blinked. "Am I doing this right?"

"You're doing great. Just relax. Find that empty spot in your head, and live in it."

She took a sip of the martini. Red lipstick smeared the rim. I wasn't sure if it worked for or against the shot.

"I don't know how long I can pull it off," she said. "They expect me to be a particular thing, and they don't want anything else."

"Just relax."

I told her the effects were stronger and faster when she snorted the blue powder. It helped her get there. Helped her forget, for just one fucking second, who she was.

Mallory became someone else in my house. Someone new. Someone real.

She sat on the desk. Leaned back. Opened her legs and herself. Vents unsealed and all that built-up, condensed steam came whistling out. Heat like that would scare most people away.

Not me. I wanted her to foam me up like a frothy cappuccino.

Her fingers knotted into my hair as I bent down to put my head between her legs.

"Everyone just wants to fuck me," she said, voice muffled by her thighs against my ears.

"Sex sells. Everyone knows that. It's not something you can change. You can fight it, or you can sell it."

Let me buy it. Let me buy all of it.

"You think I have a choice. But I don't. Do you think they'll accept me if I decide I don't want to be that person anymore? I don't even know if I can be anything else, if I know how to be anything else. If they'll still want me if I'm something else. They just want me to give them what they—*oooh.*"

I wished she could see what I saw then. Hair strewn back, catching the illumination of the spotlight. Eyes squeezed closed, casting long eyelash shadows on her cheeks. Jaw slacked, letting her plump and red bottom lip hang out in the open. Strong collarbones forced out, pushing against the straps of her dress.

If only she understood. If only she could see. It wasn't what she did that made it work. All she needed to do was be there, caught in the moment.

SEVEN
Alice

THE GIRL that sat across from me was barely recognizable. Unnervingly still, dressed in an oversized hoodie, red eyes staring into the distance. The previous night, I feared I'd gotten a raw deal, that Juliette Fairchild had brainwashed her new starlet into a prim and proper debutante, but Juliette wasn't there. Cleared of all signs of the morning's junket, in that hotel room it was just Mallory and me.

The concept of celebrity had always been a fascination of mine. Some were the epitome of their projected self, a caricature worn as a daily outfit. Others blended and formed into their environments, social chameleons for self-preservation. Then there were the few steadfast in flimsy armor, declared masters of ego in complete denial, a mere step away from full consumption by the instinctual id.

They were all fragile, desperate, and severely insecure, and while I thought I had met every variation of Hollywood deplorable, how could it be that the girl sitting across from me appeared so deliberately alien?

Pressing *Record* on my phone, I leaned back, cleared my throat, and found my first question. "Can we talk about what happened at Whole Foods last night?"

Rubbing one eye like a child just woken up, she grumbled her response. "The cops said the fight started because I got out of the car."

"You did make a scene."

"By existing."

"The photos are… revealing."

A smile crept across her lips. "Everybody likes to see a little skin."

What she lacked in vulnerability she made up for in talent of misdirection. "Are you saying you did it on purpose?"

Her smile dropped. "They said I flashed my vagina to the cameras."

"That was discredited," I said.

"They're still talking about it on the internet."

"It takes longer for real news to override clickbait bits."

"It was a better story anyway," she said, then turned to look out the window.

I had seen the censored version of those photos on the news. Then, like everyone else, Matt and I found the originals online. There was enough exposure to remind the viewer that yes, half an inch to the right was a hot young woman's pantiless pussy.

I had to wonder if Mallory could smell Matt's sex on me, if she'd be pleased to learn she was the catalyst for it, if she knew my purpose for bringing up the Whole Foods incident in the first place.

"*Between Broken Pieces* is getting a lot of critical attention," I said, trying to clear my head of the photos, trying not to match them with the girl sitting across from me. "There's even talk of Oscar nominations."

"Is that a question?"

"I'd like to know your thoughts about it."

She shrugged. "It's cool."

"Cool?"

"What do you want me to say? That the movie is awful and the critics are idiots?"

Doing my best to soften my voice, I said, "I want you to say whatever you feel like saying."

"You're a terrible journalist if this is how you do press gigs. You sound more like a shrink."

"I only want the truth, Mallory," I said.

Her eyes drifted to my phone as it sat between us on the coffee table. "I decided to do things a little differently this time around," she said finally. "For example, I actually read the script."

"You don't normally read your scripts?"

"I read my lines. The rest is pointless bullshit. You saw that horror movie I did last year, right? I didn't even know I had a topless scene until I showed up on set that day. Might have turned the gig down if I knew, but by then everyone was so stoked to see my tits, I figured I had to go along with it. I never saw that actor's face. I had no idea who was feeling me up, but I could tell he was into it."

There it was, uncensored word vomit, just like *Rise and Shine, Los Angeles*. "But you read the script for *Between Broken Pieces*?"

"It was read to me. The director invited me over to his house and acted out every single scene while I watched. The original script was practically soft core porn, so there I was, in the fucker's living room, watching him act out a hundred and twenty pages of sex scenes."

"Was it your idea to tone down the sexual nature of the film?" I said.

"Of course not. I mean, some of the things he acted out were a little weird, but it was the studio's idea to combine it all into one massive sex scene. I spent three days naked on set. When you spend that much time pretending to fuck for a crowd, it messes with you psychologically."

I had been prepared for her to be candid. I did not expect she would lead me by the hand into the depths of her reality. Mallory had somehow peeked at my cards, and she was using them against me. It had turned into a completely different game. Moby Dick had beached herself on shore.

"Messes with you how?" I said, though I pretty confidently knew the answer.

"You get used to it, I guess. You go from being insecure to full-on exhibitionist. By day three I wasn't acting for the camera anymore. I was fueled by the room."

My ears rung with the sound of her gasping voice, replayed in my head from the screening the night before. How many times did she attempt that one whimper before it was declared good enough to print? Or did she take her time with it, make the director beg for that perfect sound, the one that would make everyone believe—without a doubt—that what she had pretended to feel was real?

"If you've never had sex in front of a camera, you don't understand how it works," she said suddenly.

I almost laughed. "Who says I haven't?"

"I'm not talking 'homemade sex tape'. I'm talking choreographed fucking. Cued orgasms. C.G.I. lust."

"That's the science of filmmaking," I said.

"And now everyone's going to assume that's exactly how I fuck. Just like everything. They only know what they watch on screen, what they see in photos, what they read in interviews …"

Her fingers fidgeted with the zipper of her hoodie, pulling it up, then down, an inch further each time. Was she aware of the act, or was she creating exposure through muscle memory?

"This film could gain you some real clout in the industry," I said. "People are starting to recognize your talent."

She huffed, shaking her head. "No, they're not. They'll give me decent lines and assign their favorite director, but at the end of the day, all they want is to watch me run around naked. Right? Isn't that what everybody wants?" Swiftly, she pulled the zipper to the hem of her sweatshirt, revealing unquestionably naked skin. She looked down at her chest, grabbed an exposed breast and squeezed, just like the predator from that horror movie. "I mean, you can't really blame them."

What little empathy I felt washed away like footprints in the sand.

"Is that how you want people to see you?" I said.

"It doesn't matter, as long as they do see me. At least, that's what I've been told." She'd left her sweatshirt open, baiting me to look.

"And you're okay with it?"

"It's not up to me to be okay with it," she said, voice hardening by the syllable. "I'm a placeholder. There are a thousand other girls like me wandering L.A., waiting to be captured and put in the right slots. And when the mold shifts and the slots take a different shape, those girls go back into the slush pile. We're all closer to losing our place in the mold than we realize. That's why you have to solidify yourself, before it's too late."

Mallory's eyes bored into me, and I no longer cared to stare at her exposed skin. If she was so aware of her fate, why did she go along with it? Why endure the fallout if it was so easily prevented?

I could have stretched out a rescuing hand, I could have made her believe she would be better off getting out before it got worse. But I didn't. Hers was a story I had spent a lifetime searching for, and here was the subject, handing it to me. No analogies needed. No interpreted passages, no reading between the lines, no piecing together broken bits.

It made me question if had my microphone pointed in the right direction.

EIGHT
Fiona

"JUST LISTEN TO HER TONE." I pressed *Play* on my phone. Mallory's voice came through. That cocky midwestern twang.

"*I'm stressed all the time. And tired. Exhausted. Like, I can barely keep my eyes open. They make stuff for that, right?*"

My voice followed. "*You mean, medication?*"

"*Yeah. You know, something to take the edge off.*"

"You can hear the exaggeration in her voice," I said, pausing the playback. "Not a word she says makes me believe she's at all stressed by her career."

"Fiona, tell me you're not driving." I tried to focus on the subtle notes of Dr. Lam's intonation, but I couldn't hear anything over the ticking of my turn signal. Annoyance, predominantly. Irritation over my call to him at home. Ten at night was considered an off-hours consultation.

"Listen to what she says next."

"*People expect a lot of me. All kinds of things. I want to give them those things, I do. I just need help finding the way to do it. That's what you have to understand, Dr. Shea. I have to give the people what they want.*"

The silence lasted for eight ticks of my blinker. Too long for Dr. Lam to have had a planned response. Unusual. "You said she became aggressive during your session," he said finally. "How did you react to what she was telling you?"

He was leading me. Baiting me to present evidence that made sense to his pre-established conclusion.

"I asked if she was prepared for the life-long stress of her career."

"What was her response to that?"

I hesitated. Pressed *Play*. I would not tell him I had skipped a part of the clip. "*Why does anyone bother coming to see you if you can't even help them? What the fuck is your purpose?*"

"There's a lot of anger in her voice," Dr. Lam said. "A lot of resentment."

"Yes. At me. Because I didn't buy into her bullshit."

"Her bullshit?"

"She's not coming to see me because she's mentally ill. She wants to use me."

"For what, Fiona?" His voice was cool and calm.

My lungs vibrated. I needed to maintain control. I had driven the route I was on enough times to know it by heart, yet none of the landmarks seemed familiar. I must have taken a wrong turn.

"There is no other reason for her to come see me if she weren't after prescription medication. And not because she needs it. Because she wants to abuse it, just like she does everything else."

"You still aren't cleared to prescribe."

There had been no prompt for him to bring that up. Across the street, bright red lights of a liquor store sign caught my attention. I would have to merge over, make a U-turn on a street with no center lane. The light ahead had just turned green—it would be several minutes before the oncoming traffic allowed enough of a gap to squeeze through.

Dr. Lam's voice was unexpectedly sharp. "Maybe you should call me when you get home."

I wasn't going home. I wouldn't be home for at least another two hours, but he would have no reason—or need—to know that.

Focusing on each breath, I spoke slowly. Kept my tone in a lower register. "Mallory Braun manipulates everyone around her with little concern for consequences. She'll prey on weaknesses, force sympathy, all while taking advantage of whatever avenue there is. My fiancé was the same way." A tremble filled my voice. "He took advantage of me."

"Your fiancé committed suicide by swallowing a bottle of pills," said Dr. Lam. Sharp precision of word choice. "Which you prescribed him."

My tongue swelled in my throat. Traffic rolled forward and the liquor store disappeared from view. "He tricked me, Dr. Lam. He tricked me and he used me."

"And now he's dead."

"They're actors. Professional liars. He knew what he was doing, and so does she."

Another several second pause, until finally he said, "What did Mallory mean when she said, 'I have to give the people what they want'? Did she elaborate on that?"

"No."

He wasn't listening. He still didn't believe me.

"And you didn't give her any medication?"

"Of course not. I can't."

"Good," he said, his tone brighter. He'd made a conclusion. Or perhaps a decision. "The next time you see her, Fiona, just listen to what she has to say."

The call ended before I could tell him that I would not be seeing her again because there was no point. She was wasting my time. She was wasting everybody's time.

When I arrived at the duplex, the familiarity came back—the cracked and weedy sidewalk, the telephone pole with corner pieces of paper held on by thousands of rusted nails and staples, the wrought iron fence detached from the cement post.

I ascended the narrow carpeted stairs of the building to the second floor. Five knocks. The door opened.

"You're late," said the tall, lanky man in a Laker's jersey.

"I missed the turn."

"It's the construction, trips people up," he said. "Putting in a Trader Joe's, or some shit. Like folks around here wanna shop at Trader Joe's. Fucking white people. No offense. You want vikes or oxy?" Chatty. Excitable. A user of his own dealings.

"Both." I handed him my envelope of cash.

"Hey mama, how you doin'?" He wasn't talking to me. He was looking past me. At her.

Mallory Braun stood at the top of the stairs. Hair wet. Nipples visible through her thin T-shirt. It had been a chilly night, a fact she seemed to ignore.

"What are you doing here?" I said, my voice high enough to raise awareness of my surprise. "Did you follow me?"

"You're an easy person to track. You drive fifteen miles below the speed limit." She stepped closer. Small spaces like that hallway gave her height an added illusion.

"Hey, wait." The dealer looked her over. "You're that actress chick, aren't you? Don't you have a movie coming out?"

Mallory straightened. Shoulders rolled back. "The premiere was tonight. Just finished, actually."

The dealer pulled his cell phone out. "That's coo'. Say hi, beautiful. You're live on video!"

A smile flickered on Mallory's lips. Her chest pushed further out. "I feel bad about how I yelled at you. That wasn't fair."

"Mallory, you're allowed to call me if you need to talk, but following me out here?"

"I didn't expect such a trip. You know you don't have to go below the 10 to do this, right?"

"Never buy drugs in your own neighborhood," said the dealer. "You never know who you're gonna run into."

Mallory looked directly into the cell phone camera. Then turned to me. Her stance shifted. Arms folded across her chest, closing herself off. "Dr. Shea, I really need to talk to you."

She'd said my name. The video was streaming live, and Mallory said my name. "Turn that off, please." I reached for the dealer's phone, but he swatted me away. "I'm asking you nicely to turn that off."

"And I'm nicely saying to fuck off," he said. "This is good stuff right here. Gonna get me lots of hits. Come on, girl, give the people what they want."

Mallory came in closer. "Dr. Shea, this is important."

"Don't say my name."

"I'm having a crisis, Dr. Shea, and I really need to talk to you. Please, Dr. Shea. I need your help."

Desperately, I tugged on the dealer's arm. "I'll buy whatever you want if you shut that thing off."

He looked into the plastic grocery bag of pills, then pulled out a Ziploc. A colorful cocktail. "This'll cost you two hundred."

I held out the cash, and he accepted, dropping the phone to his side. Once the bag was in my hand, I tossed it to Mallory.

"I know why you're really here. Now leave me the hell alone." Breezing down the hallway, I pushed past her to the stairs. My forehead connected with her shoulder. She jerked, and I feared she might shove me into the wall. Mallory had cornered me on purpose. She was stalking me. Baiting me. I gave her what she wanted so that she would leave me alone.

I reached the weedy sidewalk empty-handed. I needed to find a liquor store.

NINE
Juliette

"Fuuuck," Luke Connelly said from my passenger seat, drawing out the word. "This is intense. Getting a lot of reblogs. Have you read it?"

He knew better than to bait me to take my eyes off Coldwater Canyon and glance at his iPad. "I haven't had time. Instead of reading internet comments, I have been running defense."

"The premiere went fine," he said. "It was probably a good thing she didn't show, considering how the junkets went. You probably should have been there for that."

"I'm an executive, not a publicist."

"I'm no babysitter, either, but when you let someone like Alice Welsh have a thirty minute interview with someone like Mallory Braun, there needs to be a chaperone."

I would have smacked Luke with his own iPad were I not traveling down the tightest zigzag of the drive. He was right, though. I'd fucked up. Mallory had me convinced she would present herself as someone who actually gave a shit about her career. She did the complete opposite. I was grateful she didn't show up to the premiere, despite how many times I had to repeat the mantra to every fucking internet blogger with a camera: "Mallory Braun is feeling ill tonight and will not be attending the premiere, but she wishes everyone a happy viewing."

At least I didn't have to watch the gaggle drool over her all night.

"You saw the photos, right?" Luke said. "Say what you will about Riley Westcott, but she's a damn good photographer. I wonder how much *The Hollywood Express* paid her."

The car accelerated through the turn. Luke reached for his *oh-shit* handle. I had seen the photos. They were everywhere. Mallory Braun as a noir actress, dead-eyed and soulless. They would be attractive were they of someone I hadn't spent the last several months trying to make look alive.

We pulled up to her house and Luke insisted on taking his iPad with him. "I want to see her face when she reads it."

"Wait in the car," I said. "She could be indisposed."

His eyes lit up.

"Stay," I said, and left him behind.

I rang the doorbell. "Answer the door, Mallory," I said into her security camera, then rang again. Nothing.

I dialed her number in my phone. It went straight to voicemail. "*Hey, it's Mallory. Leave a message, if you must.*"

I yelled into the phone. "Answer the fucking door, Mallory!"

A jolt of anxiety pulsed through me. I couldn't explain why. I was angry with her, pissed she had turned out to be exactly what I feared she would, despite my best efforts to shape her. Mallory was no professional; she was a hot chick with a lucky talent and a sexy body. She represented everything I had come to loathe about my job.

Behind me in my car, Luke was busy thumbing his iPad. I snuck around the side of the house. The patio furniture was in disarray around the pool, as though a party had happened and no one bothered to finish the cleanup. If Mallory had stood up the premiere to get lit with her friends, there would be no stopping my fury.

I found the back doors unlocked. Aside from the mess, the house was quiet, unnervingly still. "Mallory, where the hell are you?"

I found her in the master bedroom. On the bed. Tossed among the covers. Naked.

"Life imitates art?" Luke was beside me, iPad held out, comparing the published photograph to her current state.

He snapped a photo of his own and glanced around the room. "Better clean her up. She's got to get ready for New York."

I couldn't move. I didn't dare. When Luke stepped forward, I whipped my arm out to stop him. "Don't."

Luke halted.

I studied her, took in every detail of her surroundings. The expression on her face. The way the bed sheets covered her, but not in a way that hid her exposure. The way her eyes were partly open, staring blankly across the room. She wasn't breathing. And when I touched her leg, she was cold.

"For fuck's sake."

TEN
Alice

"You're not supposed to enjoy this," I said, lost for breath.

"Literally impossible not to."

I let my gaze drift down to the couch. In the morning sunlight, Trevor's dark mahogany skin contrasted against mine. It was startlingly obvious, beautiful and obscene, delicious to my senses, luring me to devour it, to savor the momentary sovereignty before Trevor returned to his throne as the admonisher of desires.

Pushing down, I forced him to fill me. His hands gripped my hips, tried to dictate the movement as though this had anything to do with him. I moved him where I needed him, deep inside, until I felt the surge. I couldn't hold my moan.

"I got that interview on my own."

"I know you did."

"How many people tried to get an exclusive with Mallory Braun?" I said.

"Thousands."

"You're so much sexier when you keep your mouth shut."

"Fine. Dozens."

"Juliette gave it to me."

"Damn straight. You played the white witch like the bitch she is."

I stopped moving and looked down through the hair stuck to my forehead. His eyes were glued to my breasts. What exactly did he see? Was he aroused by my inferiority, my inability to push past him up the ladder? Or was this a sign of a neglected cuckold, a man in power who secretly longed for impotence?

If I talked while I fucked, could I prevent him from enjoying it too much?

"She's really good at her job," I said.

"Oh, now you're defending her?"

"I'm just saying, Juliette fought hard to get where she is."

"She's also divorced and living alone in that huge house in the hills."

"Hollywood breaks people down," I said. "It's a tough, unforgiving world. A whole city bidding on the same pot, forcing unplayable hands, everyone a half-step from ending up alone and despe—*ughh* ..."

I tensed around him. Trevor held on, watching me twitch. Was he even listening?

"My job here is done." As usual, Trevor returned to his boorish nature as soon as he evacuated my vagina. He pushed me off as he stood and waddled to the bathroom, chiseled ass cheeks clenching the whole way.

"Where the hell are you going?" I asked.

"To beat off in the shower."

"You're joking."

"I'm starting to question your motives. You're one hot piece of MILF ass, but I'm not interested in fathering any mixed babies at this point in my life."

He disappeared into the bathroom, and I was left cooling off on the couch, my sweat-slicked body sticking to the leather, wondering whom Trevor thought of when it was his time for self-appreciation.

It was true, the interview was my holy grail and I got it on my own. Uploaded early that morning, the published piece was accompanied by a photo set from a photographer I had heard about in passing. There was a raw honesty to the subject in those photos. Matt gasped when he saw them, and then put me in charge of taking the kids to school, by excuse of bathroom troubles. No doubt he'd spent the morning masturbating.

Had every man I fucked done it to the thought of her?

Not that I cared. Not really. I had been close to Mallory, inches from her, practically inside her head, a fact that drew people in as though she'd implanted a magnet in me. I felt indestructible.

While I waited for the obligatory grunt to come from the shower, my cell beeped, and I pulled it from my purse. It was a text from someone in the office.

The thumping of my heart made it difficult to breathe. "Holy fuck," I gasped. "Trevor!"

"I'm a little busy!"

"Mallory Braun is dead."

Trevor appeared in the bathroom doorway, dick in hand, quickly going flaccid. "You're joking."

"No one had time to read my story first."

He let his dick swing free. "You're fucked up, Alice."

I went for my pants. "Get dressed. We can't be MIA when this goes down."

ELEVEN
Riley

CARS AND PEOPLE swarmed the street like flies around a shit pile. Cops. Paramedics. Reporters. Paparazzi. A whole crowd of onlookers. Pointing and shouting. Seizing with sobs. Howling at the sun.

The Hollywood spectacle.

"What do you think is going on?" My rideshare driver had pulled over, drawn to the scene. "Do you know who lives here?"

I looked at my phone. It was flooded with text messages and emails and app notifications, all congratulating me on the amazing photographs that were published by *The Hollywood Express* that morning. I didn't read the interview. I refused to.

There was a voicemail from Mallory, left at three in the morning. I had listened to it eleven times on the ride over. She had been upset and crying. A maniac's blubbering. In the background, I could hear the sounds of a movie. A very particular movie. That horror flick she was in the previous year. That one.

It didn't mean much until we pulled up across the street from her house. I watched a cop pull yellow caution tape across the front door.

"I hope everything's okay," said the rideshare driver.

Juliette drove past in her white Tesla. Relief washed over me. If Juliette was leaving the scene, then it couldn't have been that bad. She wouldn't dare leave her precious cargo unattended.

I got out of the car and waved to a cop who looked more like a TV detective than an actual policeman. "Hey! I need to go inside. That's my friend's house."

He shook his head. "Gimme a break. No one's going inside."

"I'm serious, I'm practically family. Look." I held out my phone. "She called me last night. Even left a voicemail. Want me to play it for you?"

The cop grabbed my hand and squinted at my phone. "Shit. 3:03. That matches the timeline."

"What timeline?"

He shouted past me. "O'Toole!"

The cop tried to move past but I got right in his face. "What happened to Mallory?"

The spectators on the lawn erupted. Shouting, and crying, and hollering, and making a horrible mass of noise.

Then I saw it. Three paramedics pushed a gurney through the front door. Black body bag on top of it.

No. No no no no no.

NO.

"Tell me that's not Mallory."

A bald man in a tight black shirt approached. Spoke to TV Cop as though I weren't even there. "Who's this?"

"Says she's a friend of the victim. Voicemail matches the timeline."

"What was the voicemail about?"

"That's what I'd like to find out."

"Must not be that good a friend if she didn't answer."

"It was three in the morning." I didn't like feeling blamed.

They both looked at me.

"Bring her in," TV Cop said. "I want to know more about that voicemail."

The bald one grabbed my arm and pulled me away. I was stuffed into a cruiser as the body bag was pushed into the back of an ambulance.

You always looked beautiful in black.

TWELVE
Alice

NEVER HAD *The Hollywood Express* bullpen buzzed with that much excitement. Everywhere I looked, people were reading on their computers, talking on their phones, whispering to each other. What were they saying? Did they debate the details? Who bet on the outcome? Was there a prize for guessing correctly?

"Rumor is she O.D.'d on pills. Found a bowl of them. Oh God, someone leaked a picture of her body." Trevor trailed behind me, thumbing his phone. "Alice, your article is the most viewed page on *The Hollywood Express* website. Ever."

I could see the excitement in his eyes, the thrill of being absorbed in the drama, and maybe that was enough for him. It was enough for some to drive past the destruction on the freeway, to see that beautiful, grossly expensive car crumpled over the side rail, steaming, whirring, freshly destroyed. I knew that deep down Trevor wanted more. They all did. They wanted the set-up, which I had delivered, just a tad too late. No one had time to absorb it, to immerse themselves in it, to make their predictions. She was gone. The story had ended.

As I turned the corner, an intern stepped in front of me. "Mrs. Welsh, you have visitors."

I found them in my office. Two men, thick and muscular like Trevor, but worn and aged like an old bookcase. Sturdy like one, too. The shorter one had a mustache. I wondered what his wife thought of it.

"Mrs. Welsh, I'm Detective Davila with the L.A.P.D. This is Detective O'Toole. We'd like to ask you some questions."

I shouldn't have been surprised the cops had come to see me. At least, I didn't want to be. I closed the door on

Trevor before he could ask to join, and motioned for the detectives to sit across the desk.

"We're trying to lay down a timeline leading to the victim's death," Davila said, thumbing a tablet.

"Why do you need a timeline?" I said. "I thought it was ruled a suicide."

"That's not official," said O'Toole, gaze boring into me.

Davila nodded. "It's my understanding you published an article this morning that was based on an interview you had with Miss Braun yesterday, is that correct?"

"Our standard morning post is 6:00 A.M.," I said.

"Three hours after the presumed time of death," said O'Toole. He barely moved when he spoke.

"Is that official?" I asked.

Davila looked up. "Did she suffer from emotional distress at the time of the interview?"

"No. Actually, she was pretty lucid."

"Any hint of intoxication?"

If the cops were interested in my observations of Mallory, why wouldn't they have simply referenced my interview? "I can't comment on that."

O'Toole took the tablet from Davila. "You stated in your published interview—and I quote—'Braun had the air of someone existing in a pocket of emptiness in their head. Purposefully, if not chemically directed.'"

So they had read it. And they were playing me. Two large men against one woman. Their story had to have holes to require that much muscling. "It was an observation. I've seen enough people under the influence to know if she's—"

O'Toole finished my sentence. "If she's on drugs?"

The crime scene was piecing together in my head. I tried to picture what the detectives found: a beautiful, young starlet, having drowned herself in pills on the biggest night of her career. Tragic, and profoundly believable.

If there were breadcrumbs, I wanted to find them. "Did she leave a note?"

Davila's mustache twitched. "A note?"

"A suicide letter."

O'Toole huffed. "This is the twenty-first century, ma'am, people don't write letters."

"These days, people are a lot more obscure with their public declarations," Davila added.

With a tap on the tablet, O'Toole went on, "Now it's Facebook likes and Twitter posts. Such as the tweet Miss Braun wrote at 2:34 A.M. to the handle @AliceWelshReports."

"That's me. That's my Twitter handle."

"We know," said O'Toole.

My spine shivered; I did what I could to hide it. "What did she say?"

Davila read from the tablet. "If anything happens to me, be grateful that @AliceWelshReports has the key to all my secrets."

O'Toole raised an eyebrow. "Care to comment?"

Was that their plan, to corner and blindside me in my own office, all because I had predicted it so perfectly? "I assume she's talking about the interview."

"Any idea what secrets she's referring to?" Davila asked.

"It's all in the article."

"Is it, though?" Davila said. "I'm asking because I understand you have audio recordings."

Trevor. He had to be the reason they knew that. They were going to take it away. They were going to let me bring everyone to the edge, and then refuse their right to finish. It wasn't my fault Mallory killed herself and ruined the surprise.

Mallory flashed through my mind, the way she used her body to completely halt the forward progression of a situation. I didn't have that talent. I needed a different diversion.

"Have you spoken with Juliette Fairchild?"

"Why do you ask?"

"She would have been the last to see Mallory," I said. "She watched over that girl like a hawk. I find it surprising that anything like this would have happened, knowing how Juliette is."

"And how exactly is Juliette Fairchild?"

"She's… obsessive."

Both men tilted their heads back. "Interesting," O'Toole said.

"So you've spoken with her?" I said.

"We can't discuss that," Davila said.

"But we'll note your concern," O'Toole said, and winked at me.

By the time the cops left, the entire staff of *The Hollywood Express* was outside my office door. Trevor managed to squeeze his way through the crowd.

"Now what?" he said.

Studying my colleagues, I recognized the hungry eagerness. I had been right. I had seen it coming and made myself a part of it. I was going to help them see it through the end. What was the harm? After all, the girl was already dead.

THIRTEEN
Fiona

THE CAT WOKE ME. He'd meowed, jumped onto the bedside table and knocked over a glass of water. I lurched up, instantly feeling the throb behind my eyes. I blinked, lay back down to level myself.

It was almost noon. The cat meowed again. I shoved him away.

I checked my phone. Dr. Lam had to have wised up to his mistake and called to apologize for second-guessing my observation.

I had eight missed calls from an unknown number. The first was at 2:27 A.M. The last, just after three. No voicemail. It wasn't unusual for patients to call my cell. The number hadn't been assigned a contact name. When I called back, it went straight to voicemail.

"Hey, it's Mallory. Leave a message, if you must."

My hand flinched. The phone dropped into the puddle of water. She was still doing it—trying manipulate me, expanding her charade of lies—but Mallory Braun would never fool me. No one would ever fool me again.

While making coffee in the kitchen, someone knocked on the front door. It had to be Mallory. The girl was obsessive, hyper-focused on the task she had not been able to achieve, unwilling to give up until someone put her down. The cocktail of prescription pills had only been enough to make her want more. I should have known better. Don't feed the animals, Dr. Lam used to say.

The second knock was a thud, an aggressive declaration. Not the nervous tapping of a strung-out junkie.

"Miss Shea, this is the police."

A man's voice. A strong, powerful man. A man eager to demonstrate his dominance.

It wasn't until I opened the door that I realized I was barely dressed, in sleeping shorts and a tank top. The man in the hallway was tall and bald, with muscles that bulged through his skin-tight black shirt. Muscles that could restrain me. Muscles that could suffocate me.

"Can I help you?"

The man looked me over. "Are you Miss Shea?"

"Doctor Shea."

He leaned forward at the waist. An excessively polite introduction. "I'm Detective O'Toole with the L.A.P.D.

Can I come in?"

"Of course." I stepped aside, flattened myself along the wall, let the large man pass into my living room. He brushed against me. I tried not to flinch.

His eyes caught three empty wine bottles in my trash-can. "Did you have company last night?"

"No, I was alone."

"Huh." He sat on my couch. The cat went scurrying.

"Can I help you with something?"

Detective O'Toole looked me over, from head to toe. Observing. Studying. Judging. "I take it you haven't heard the news."

"I don't watch the news. It's all fake anyway."

"Mallory Braun is your patient, right?" He tossed an arm on the back of the couch. A relaxed pose to put the interviewee at ease.

"For now."

His head tilted to one side. "For now? Why do you say that?"

"I'm going to get her transferred."

"Any particular reason why?"

"I believe she wants to abuse prescription drugs."

"What drugs? Pain killers?" Casual yet direct questions. A man of purpose, not sport.

"Amphetamines, mostly."

"Ah. I bet that's why most people go to see a shrink." He leaned forward, put his elbows on his knees. A more persuasive stance. I took a step back. "Mallory Braun was found dead this morning. Overdose. Amphetamines, mostly."

His voice was firm on that last word. It caught me before I could process the other thing he'd said, about Mallory. That thing about Mallory being dead.

"The medical examiner is still running the tox screens, but it was quite the cocktail. Found a whole mix of shit next to her bed, like a goddamn candy grab-bag."

"I'm not authorized to prescribe medication," I said a little too quickly. A little too sharply.

"I'm not accusing you of anything, Miss Shea—"

"Doctor."

"Dr. Shea." He nodded. "I just want to know why a young woman at the start of her career would toss a handful of prescription amphetamines down her throat. Somebody had to see it coming. Didn't they?"

No. No one saw it coming because there was nothing to see. If there were, my fiancé would have survived to our wedding day—but that was the point, my whole argument to Dr. Lam. There was nothing to see coming because every action and word spoken was drenched in a thick syrup of lies. Had Mallory been a normal person, I would have seen the signs.

"I would imagine it was hard for anyone to know what Mallory Braun was thinking. You have to remember, she is an actress." It was a good answer. A solid diversion. Put the focus back on her.

"Was," O'Toole said.

"Yes. Was. She was young, and pretty, and popular, and a little arrogant, if I'm perfectly honest."

"She hasn't been dead twelve hours."

"I'm not blaming her. I've had a lot of patients in the business. There's always a bit of exaggeration."

"You're saying this was all part of an act?"

"Maybe. It could have been something else. I could tell right off that she was pretty vulnerable. Maybe a little too sensitive for the business."

He squinted. Eyes found my ring finger, which I had absently rubbed raw. The pain shot up my hand, even after I forced my arms to my sides, revealing—once again—that I was superbly underdressed.

"Here's what I'm wondering, Dr. Shea," he said, "how did you have this insight into Mallory Braun's psychology, but no idea she might kill herself?"

"If she was suicidal, I would have done something."

He leaned further forward. Inching his way toward me. "Would you have?"

"Yes." My voice quivered. I cleared my throat. "Of course I would have."

O'Toole stared at me for thirteen ticks of my wall clock before rubbing the top of his bald head with the palm of his hand. "Well, I guess it's just a surprising tragedy for everyone, isn't it?" He was still asking questions, still searching for the elusive answer.

When he finally let himself out, I felt the wetness between my legs. I had pissed myself out of fear.

FOURTEEN
Riley

THEY HAD TO DO IT on purpose, the layout of the room. The space was too big; it dwarfed the table. The view from the windows was one I wouldn't mind having from a town house or an office. But a conference room in a police station felt wrong. They could probably see Mallory's house from there. They probably even knew it was happening. They probably knew all the terrible things that went on across that vast landscape and did nothing about it.

The flags didn't help. There were too many of them at one end of the room, throwing the balance. The American stripes of red and white always seemed to fly with aggression. A forced declaration of freedom.

I didn't feel free.

I was not under arrest, but I certainly did not feel free.

When TV Cop sat across from me, he avoided looking in my direction. His mustache twitched as he thumbed a tablet. An off-brand one. L.A. cops didn't get fancy toys.

"Sorry for the hold-up, Miss Westcott," he said. "It's been a busy morning."

He set the tablet on the table, and there it was. That fucking article. My photos seemed tainted against the text.

I wanted to read it now. If only to have something to hold onto.

"I'm Detective Davila. You said you're friends with the victim?"

"Yeah. We go way back. Can I read that?" I motioned to the tablet.

"It's evidence."

"The internet is evidence?"

"Why don't we start with why you were at Miss Braun's house this morning."

I hadn't done anything wrong. But I couldn't explain why my stomach was a swirling cesspool of nausea and acid.

"Mallory is my friend. Was my friend."

Fuck.

Davila typed something into the tablet. "It will take some time to process the loss, but you'll recover." What a cop-out. Pun intended.

Something had to rattle this guy.

"I also fucked her on occasion."

His eyes never flickered. "You're stating you had a sexual relationship with the victim?"

"Yeah. Does that do something for you?"

"The victim is dead."

"So, no?"

He set the tablet down. "Is there something you want to say?"

"I'm not the one who wants to say it."

Finally, his mustache twitched.

I knew why I was forced to wait forty-five minutes alone in the conference room. They were checking up on me, doing a social media search, breaking down my background into compartmentalized pieces. Davila knew I had taken those photos of Mallory the night before she died. The way she was found made it impossible not to consider a correlation. Everyone was talking about it. I just wished he'd hurry up and spill already.

"The victim made a large number of phone calls and texts in the hour before her declared time of death," Davila said, reading from the tablet. "Several were made to you. According to the log, one call at 3:03 A.M. lasted five minutes and forty-eight seconds. Why don't you tell me what the call was about."

"It was a voicemail."

"Can I hear it?"

"I deleted it."

Don't flinch. He'll know the lie.

"Do you remember what she said?"

"She called to invite me over."

"Did you visit her?"

"No."

"How did she sound?"

"Tired. Maybe high."

"High on what?"

"That's a tricky thing to hear over the phone."

With a slow nod, Davila gazed through the window. I was right. These cops did nothing but stare out that fucking window all day. "Anything else?"

"Not really."

"The voicemail was nearly six minutes long. She had to say something you remember."

What I remembered most was the sound of her voice. The way it flowed with that drawl, like lonesome backyard dogs calling out to fire truck sirens.

"She mumbled a lot," I said. "I think she was upset about her movie."

"The one that premiered last night?"

"That's the one."

"In what way was she upset about the film?"

I knew why she had blasted that horror movie in the background when she called me. It was the last thing she had done before all the bullshit started. Before Juliette Fairchild scooped her up as though she were a shivering Chihuahua at a kill house. Before she was forced to see a shrink. Before everything she was and could have been became a potential headline.

"She said she wanted to forget it ever happened," I said, surprised at how quiet my voice had gotten.

Davila leaned onto the table, his chin illuminated by the glowing tablet. "About those photos ..." His gaze scanned my entire face, like a laser-eyed robot. "I do find it odd that the victim was found in an almost exact position as the photo you sold to *The Hollywood Express*."

There it was. "I sold several photos to *The Hollywood Express*. It just so happened that the ones they posted are similar."

"Still. Curious."

"The last time I saw Mallory was two nights ago, and there was no sign she was going to kill herself."

Keep it together, fairies.

"I'm not accusing you of anything."

"What is this, then?" I said, my throat clogging. "What do you want to know? What do you want me to tell you?"

Davila turned the tablet and showed me a photo. It was Mallory. Sprawled on the bed. Naked and mostly exposed. Arm tossed above her on the pillow. Her face was relaxed. Almost relieved.

What are the symptoms of a heart attack?

"What I want to know, Miss Westcott, is why this picture has everyone riled up like it was the risqué front cover of a magazine. As though it wasn't a photograph of a dead young woman, like the subject hadn't just swallowed a fistful of pills with the purpose of ending her own life. Tell me what makes it so special, Miss Westcott. Tell me why it isn't the fact that she's dead that makes anyone care, but the fact that the visual in this photo is so tragically erotic that we're disappointed it's the last we'll see of it."

The tablet trembled in his hands. A film of sweat covered his forehead. Deep in his eyes swam a haunting sadness. A tormenting polarization.

I didn't have an answer for him. He didn't need one. He already knew it.

When Davila left the conference room, I wasn't under arrest, but it didn't feel right leaving.

He'd left the tablet on the table. That photograph glowed on the screen. That photo from the scene, of Mallory post-mortem.

It was better than any of the photos I'd taken of her. It was pure. Honest. Raw. Not staged or posed, not backlit or filtered. It was the real Mallory Braun.

I don't know her at all.

FIFTEEN
Juliette

IT WAS A NICE SPA. Smaller than my usual spot—which meant the parking lot was three spaces deep, and the valet guy was a little shit who asked if I was worried about the zombie apocalypse shutting off the grid, leaving me no electricity to power my car—but it was quiet. I needed quiet.

Forgot About Dre blasted into my headphones when I felt a tap on my foot. Through the eyeholes of the glowing LED therapy mask I saw Hope. She waved her arms around. Mouthed something I couldn't hear.

"Twenty minutes," I said, my own voice muffled by the music. I showed her the digital timer attached to the mask.

Hope blinked. Looked like she might cry. I closed my eyes and pretended I'd hired someone who actually understood how the real world worked.

Twenty minutes later, I found Hope curled in a chair in the waiting area, teary face buried in her phone. "Oh thank God," she said, jumping to her feet. "What do we do? I don't know what to do. You have to tell me what to do."

"There's nothing to do." I made my way to the changing room, Hope at my heels.

"We have to do something."

"Why?"

"Well… I mean… Because, well, Mallory is dead."

"I know. I'm the one who found her." I dropped my robe to the floor and stood there, buck fucking naked. Hope stared through the fog in her eyes.

"Luke Connelly called me like a dozen times. I'll read you the last text he sent." She held up a phone wrapped in a shiny, rose-colored case. "He says, 'Tell her the cops are looking for her. At her house, at the office. They even contacted that bleeping bleep hole she used to call a husband.'"

Never trust a woman who doesn't curse. That was my first mistake hiring Hope.

"We should call her family," she said as I strapped on my bra. "I wonder if anyone talked to them. Do we know what really happened? I mean, you were there, but do you... you know... know?"

"I'm not the fucking coroner."

Hope cleared her throat and I turned to see her looking at me with those big eyes that seemed to be surprised by everything. I was never that innocent. I learned how to build armor the second I arrived in L.A.

"I'll call Luke," I said. "Wait for me in the lobby."

"Okay." Hope exhaled, as though she'd been holding her breath, and finally left me alone.

Luke screamed into the phone the second he picked up. Something about the cops needing a statement, and how could I just leave the scene like that, and he had to ride in a cruiser home and why did I have to be such an asshole to the girl all the time, and I turned off the phone and stuffed it in the bottom of my bag.

I didn't have time for Luke. I had two more days of opening weekend to get through, and the dreadful anticipation of the box office numbers. I was exhausted from the previous night's premiere. Mallory was supposed to have been with me, doing her part to sell her movie like she promised she would. She wasn't supposed to stay home and fucking die.

I needed a drink.

Driving down Ventura Boulevard I saw that goddamn poster on every corner, at every bus stop. I couldn't get away from that smug, sideways smile, like she was posthumously celebrating the death of my hopes and dreams. One poster had the eyes x'ed out with permanent marker. I almost laughed.

Gastro pubs and wine bars lined the street, filled with young people taking extended happy hours they couldn't afford. I slipped into a bar, sat in a corner booth, and did everything I could to pretend I didn't hear her name.

Riley Westcott sat across the table, my Irish mule hostage in her selfish, greedy fingers. I'd once Googled the force of a fist punch. 150psi. I had a chance to test the fact when I reconsidered the details of my assault. If threw the drink on her, I wouldn't go to jail. Whiskey was replaceable. Oscars were not.

"You killed her," she said. Or, mostly said. It was difficult to understand beyond the slur. "You fucking killed her."

Riley's eyes were so red they overpowered her irises. The hand that held the mule trembled, and when I reached for the cup, she reeled it in and took a gulp.

"That's a thirty-dollar drink," I said.

"You really are incapable of normal human emotions, aren't you?" Riley swallowed more. I motioned to the bartender. He purposely diverted his attention. "You had this whole fucking spiel about protecting her, and what happened? Huh? What the fuck happened?"

I leaned back and folded my arms. "I really don't want to have this conversation with you right now."

"Oh, okay," Riley said. "Should I reschedule? You available next Tuesday? Or will you be too busy hunting more young women to ruin?"

"Like you have any reason to cry about it. You barely knew her. You did what, two shoots with her?"

"Three," she said through gritted teeth.

"Not sure that one counts, but okay."

"It fucking counts," she said and slammed down the tin mule cup.

Riley existed in a world of emotional melodrama and it drove me insane to be around her for more than five minutes. I had put up with it for trade of her talent. She saw things in her subjects normal people couldn't.

"How did you know?"

Riley looked at me. Took a moment to answer. "How did I know what?"

"Those photos you took of her…" The words were in there somewhere, goddammit. "How did you know it was going to happen?"

"I didn't know."

"You took pictures of her looking dead, and twenty-four hours later, she was." My voice had raised, and people were turning to look.

Riley anxiously glanced around the bar. "The shoot was her idea. She was the one who wanted to look like a dead Hollywood star. Don't blame my talent for being able to capture how Mallory wanted to be seen."

"You went behind my back to shoot some kind of suicidal how-to." I was shouting. Patrons were definitely listening. "It was lined up. Everything was perfect. This movie is the highlight of my career, and now all anyone talks about is the fact that Mallory Braun is fucking dead."

Iced cocktail splashed my face before I saw Riley raise the cup. There wasn't much liquid to toss, but the action was the real insult. I let the whiskey and ginger ale drip down my neck.

Riley stared across the bar, heaving. "I don't know what happened. Mallory was messed up inside, but she wasn't suicidal. The cops are investigating like it's not just a suicide. Isn't that the vibe you got?"

"I haven't spoken to the police."

Her eyes popped open. "What? Why not?"

"I was the one who called it in."

"Oh," she said, and leaned back, eyes traveling all over me. The bartender finally arrived with a cocktail to replace the one I was wearing, and Riley motioned to him. "Put that on my tab, will you? The first one, too."

"That's generous of you," I said, but Riley didn't operate under the laws of generosity.

"Good luck with that Oscar, Juliette." She slid out of the booth, then looked back and said, "For fuck's sake."

SIXTEEN
Alice

THE DAY HAD BEEN flooded with everything Mallory Braun. She was everywhere. Fans on social media posted photos of her captioned #iLoveMallory and #TheBestDieYoung, as though her suicide were as heartbreakingly simple as a puppy dying of cancer. Internet articles did the best they could with limited information, but every single one of them said the same thing: no one saw it coming.

Was it truly possible that no one saw it coming? No one, not her friends, not her family, not those entrusted with the task of shepherding her?

I saw it coming. I was in the car right behind hers, taking note of the slight swerve, the tendency to brake too late, the abrupt burst of acceleration. I knew an inevitable wreck when I saw one.

That girl's face was everywhere I looked, and every time I was reminded of how false the representation seemed. I had sat across from her, listened to her voice, studied her anecdotes and nuances and none of it matched the version of her plastered all over Instagram. Could I have been the only one to foresee the conclusion, to anticipate the climax?

Once the kids were in bed, I downed half a bottle of wine and watched the eleven o'clock news on the living room TV where I could absorb every repulsive detail in high-definition.

"Mallory Braun, 25, was found dead in her Sherman Oaks home from an apparent overdose of prescription amphetamines," the reporter said. "Known as a cult favorite for her work in indie and offbeat films, Braun recently received Oscar buzz for her latest feature." The broadcast showed a brief clip from that horror movie that had captured everyone's attention, leaving out the best parts.

"This evening, hundreds of local Angelenos held a vigil in her honor at the Hollywood Cemetery, where some of her new movie *Between Broken Pieces* was filmed. We'll go live to the scene to join the crowd of heartbroken fans."

Matt entered as I filled my wine glass with the rest of the bottle. He had avoided me all evening, no doubt reeling with guilt over having masturbated to photos of a dead girl whose body had yet to turn cold. How would he fuel his libido now that his spark was deceased and rotting?

"She's dominated the news today," he said. "Any mention of your article?"

"That was the entire focus of the report from Channel 4." My throat was rough, tarnished by the wine. "These pansies are going for the tear-jerk effect."

Matt didn't respond, but turned up the TV volume as fans jostled for position at a local reporter's microphone.

"How has Mallory Braun's death affected you?" asked the reporter.

"Mallory was an amazing actress," said the first fan as she clutched her chest. "She had such an honesty to her. She was just so real in her movies."

A second fan grabbed for the mic. "She was so pretty. She had so much to live for. I mean, it's hard to imagine why she would do this. But we'll always remember her," he said, and held up Riley Westcott's Mallory-as-dead-starlet photo.

The alcohol wasn't working fast enough. My arm raised the glass to my lips at the same moment Matt moved to put a hand on my leg, and our limbs collided. Red wine splashed on the couch. I didn't care about the furniture; the kids had long-since destroyed everything valuable in the house. But did he have to waste the wine?

"Listen to me, hun," he said. "You are a good, kind person. This happened regardless of your influence. You have to believe that you had nothing to do with her suicide."

I whipped around. Was that contempt in his eyes? "I don't know why you feel the need to convince me of that."

"I'm just saying, you seem pretty shaken up about this."

Of course I was shaken. I had been witness to the slow burn, watched it unfold, recorded it all on my phone. How could I not be affected? For Matt to suggest that I had wrestled with the notion that the fault lie somewhere with my influence was atrocious. It wasn't my fault Mallory Braun killed herself. I was a reporter. An observer. Nothing else.

Distracting me from my doubts and fears had never been a skill of Matt's. More often he did the opposite, made me obsess over it, read too deeply into it, made me believe that those few pesky thoughts floating in my brain were there for a reason: to prove correct.

"I won't be able to sleep," I said. "I'll work at the office. Don't wait up."

I stood, swaying with intoxication, but I disguised it well. I had had a lot of practice hiding things from my husband, including how I loathed his attempts to lift my mood and preferred the sensation of being suffocated by a pillow. I needed a solid force and tremendous weight to challenge the vulnerability of my physical self.

Behind me, beads of sweat rolled down Trevor's smooth torso. Each of his thrusts shoved me harder onto the bed, my face deeper into the pillow. "It's your fault you're in this position," he said, breathless.

"It was a great fucking interview," I said into hypoal-lergenic down.

"You're right, it was. So stop crying about it, or I'll stick it in your ass."

I looked back at him, wondering if I could take it. Wondering if it were up to me to decide if I should. "What kind of journalist am I if I ruin the lives of the people I interview?"

"Once doesn't make a trend."

"It shouldn't have happened so soon. What did I miss? I sat across from her, I looked into her eyes, and still I don't understand why she did it."

"All right, that's it."

He pulled out. Plunged into the other hole. He ripped me open as I sucked him in, pulling me into depths of pain I hadn't felt in years, so why was I still obsessing?

"I see her face everywhere I look," I said.

"That's what happens to dead celebrities. They never go away."

"You're a fucking asshole."

"No, I'm fucking an asshole."

"I convinced myself that the interview was too bril-liant not to publish. That it didn't matter if it hurt anyone. Because it was the truth, right? I don't even trust my own conscience anymore."

Sharp pain erupted on my ass cheek, a split second before I heard the smack. Trevor leaned over, pushed his hand into the top of my back, and growled into my ear. "You may have been promoted to my boss, but remember, no one but me knows what a real piece of shit you are."

He spanked me again. When he spanked me a third and forth and fifth time I forgot what I was thinking about until the doorbell rang. Was it her, offering me one last glimpse into her soul before she floated off with red-cheeked cherubs into the afterlife?

"That's the food," Trevor said. He pulled out of me and I was left feeling empty and unsatisfied. Stuffing his over-sized erection into his boxer briefs, he waddled to the front door. I could hear no words spoken, just the patter of his footsteps returning, and the clatter of the visitor's shoes.

I was still naked on the bed when Juliette entered. "Alice, we need to talk."

SEVENTEEN
Fiona

"DID YOU PURPOSELY choose this place?" Dr. Lam sat in my chair, studying every detail of my office. First thing that morning, he'd met me in the parking lot. He didn't ask to take my seat. It was an act of assertion.

From the couch, the room seemed smaller. The lack of windows more apparent. "I got a good deal on the lease."

Dr. Lam sat up straighter. Made his eye line higher than mine. "You look like you had a rough time yesterday. Did you see any patients?"

"It was my day off."

Nodding, he crossed his legs. Forced a casual presentation. "When I saw the news yesterday morning, you were all I could think about."

"They're making too big a deal of it." I sat as tall as I could. Tried to level our eyes.

"Fiona, she killed herself."

"She wasn't suicidal. She was a recreational abuser. That was obvious the first day she came to see me."

"Did she admit to that?" he asked.

I had no recording of my first session with Mallory. He would have no proof if I was lying. "She came in specifically asking for drugs. I've told you that. I played you the clip."

Dr. Lam laced his fingers together in his lap. Took his time. Forced my anxiety. "Why don't you play the clip for me again."

There was something in his face I couldn't read. Excitement, maybe, but it didn't make sense to the context.

Still, I needed to prove to Dr. Lam that whatever happened to Mallory Braun the previous night wasn't suicide by way of mental illness. She was fine. She was a manipulator and a fraud, and she died because she didn't care what happened to her or anyone around her.

Pulling my phone from my pocket, I kept my eyes on Dr. Lam and pressed *Play*. Mallory's voice came through the speaker. The sound of it made me cringe.

"*It's not my fault I'm a celebrity. I just want to act.*"

Then came my voice. "*What makes you so stressed about being a public figure?*"

"*People just need to see me, that's what I've been told. Did you realize this room didn't have windows when you signed the lease?*"

"Why is she asking about the windows?" Dr. Lam said, laying his own path of observation.

"Everybody mentions that. Listen to the rest."

"*People expect a lot of me. All kinds of things. I want to give them those things, I do. I just need help finding the way to do it. That's what you have to understand, Dr. Shea. I have to give the people what they want.*"

"Wait," Dr. Lam reached out for my phone. "Let me hear that again."

I reeled in. "It's all the same bullshit, pretending how difficult her life is."

He stiffened. Uncrossed his legs. Leaned forward. "You can't hear it, can you?"

"Can't hear what?"

"Fiona, her voice is full of anxiety. The way it raises in pitch, the choke of her words, the struggle to speak that last line."

I gripped the phone. "If you could have seen her face, you wouldn't say that."

"The voice doesn't lie, Fiona," he said, still shaking his head. "Her voice sounds exactly as it did in the video, so I can make a pretty good assumption about what her face looked like when you recorded that."

I wasn't prepared for a surprise. "What video?"

Five times he rapped his fingers on his leg. He'd internally debated something—yet the decision was already made. Whatever he wanted to show me was loaded and waiting on his phone.

It was a video of the drug dealer's hallway, when Mallory showed up in that thin T-shirt and wet hair.

"*This is good stuff right here,*" came the dealer's voice. "*Gonna get me lots of hits. Come on, girl, give the people what they want.*"

Dr. Lam paused the video. "There. When he says that, 'give the people what they want,' see how she recoils?"

What I saw was someone shimmy for the camera. "I don't know why you're showing me this."

"Because this is the last evidence of Mallory before she was found dead." His voice was sharp. When he pressed play on the video, his eyes never left me.

"*I'm having a crisis, Dr. Shea, and I really need to talk to you. Please, Dr. Shea. I need your help.*"

A Ziploc bag of multi-colored pills flew into frame and Mallory caught it as I was heard saying, "*I know why you're really here. Now leave me the hell alone.*" Then the video cut to black, but not before a tear is seen rolling down Mallory's cheek.

"Fiona," Dr. Lam said in a controlled, quiet voice, "you gave Mallory Braun the drugs she used to commit suicide. Why did you do that, Fiona? Why?"

"She wasn't suicidal." It was the only cohesive thought in my head. "She just wanted drugs."

"She could have gotten drugs anywhere. Just like you do."

He was doing it again—making me feel blame for the manipulation of others—but I knew I was right. I got to my feet. To a higher vantage point. "Stop blaming me."

"I'm not blaming you, Fiona, but someone will."

"It's not my fault." I was suddenly next to the door.

"It's blinding you, and the only way you'll be able to protect yourself is by seeing what is really happening here."

"Stop!"

I burst through the door, not knowing nor caring what Dr. Lam's final impressions were. The stairs were long and treacherous and I had every intention of going home to find relief for the swirling in my brain, but there she was, in the parking lot. Alice Welsh.

She had company. Another taller, sturdier woman leaned against a white Tesla with her arms crossed. Dismissive. Possibly boredom.

"Fiona!" Alice waved her arm with more movement than needed to be seen. "We need to talk to you. It's about Mallory Braun."

I didn't have time to hide.

Alice approached me, hands held out and open. "I know there's a lot going on right now, and you probably spoke to the police, but we need your help."

Help. That's all anyone ever asked me for. But they never took it. Especially not Alice Welsh.

The other woman pushed off the car with a huff and grumbled to Alice loud enough for me to hear. "There's no time to play nice." She approached me with her hands at her sides. "Juliette Fairchild. I'm the one who referred Mallory to you. Like it did any good."

Alice whipped an arm out to stop her. "Easy."

"What," Juliette said with a shrug. "She's clearly not a good therapist if you're still fucking someone other than your husband."

Alice rolled her eyes. "Jesus, really."

"I warned you about needing that divorce advice."

"My marriage is fine."

I finally found the ability to speak. "What do you want?"

With a brief look to Juliette, Alice took another step. "Insight. We need to better understand what Mallory was thinking before she died. What would have caused it, why did she do it."

"Who gave her the fucking pills." Juliette added with a head snap.

I flinched, and did my best to hide it.

"If I do help you—and I'm not saying I will—what good will it do?" I asked.

The women looked at each other. Shared some kind of pre-established understanding. Alice pursed her lips and pushed out a whole lungful of air.

"We're going to prove that Mallory Braun's death was a set-up of her own making," she said.

Juliette tugged on the lapel of her undoubtedly expensive blazer, and added, "We're going to prove that Mallory set the whole thing up on purpose."

It didn't take much for me to understand what they were saying. "You're going to prove that she killed herself because that's what she thought the people wanted."

The women did their best to keep from smiling.

EIGHTEEN
Riley

PLASTERED DRUNK was probably not the best way to walk into a police station, but I didn't drive there. I wasn't bothering anybody. I was there to help.

I was certain I fooled the front desk deputy.

"I need to speak with Detective Davila," I said as slowly and clearly as I could.

"Uhhh …" the deputy said. He must have been mentally handicapped. That explained the reception job. "Davila's not available."

"I need to speak to him about one of his cases." I leaned over the desk and whispered. "About Mallory Braun."

His eyes went all wide as he put a hand on his gun belt. I worried he had been posted at the desk not for his handicap, but for having a loose trigger finger.

"If I can't speak to Davila directly, then I'll take his email address," I said. "It wasn't online. I looked, so don't tell me to Google it."

"We have a contact form on our website if you need to submit questions or concerns," the deputy said.

"You're not getting it. This can't go to some intern's inbox. This is top-secret stuff. Evidence that could make or break the case. Internal details for special eyes only."

I'd leaned in too far over the desk. He leaned back. Scrunched his nose.

I should have popped a damn breath mint.

Amateur.

"Are my eyes special enough?"

The tall, bald detective named O'Toole appeared next to me, taller and balder than I remembered.

"She says she has evidence for the Mallory Braun case," the deputy sputtered out, finally caring to help.

"I'm Riley Westcott. I'm a friend of Mallory's." A sharp coldness ran through me, and I shuddered. "Was."

Fuck. Why did I keep doing that?

O'Toole straightened. Literally grew two inches. "I can't give you Davila's email."

"Trust me, you want to." I pulled out my iPad and flicked on the display. On it were the remaining photos from my shoot with Mallory, the night before she died.

O'Toole squinted at the screen. "Where did you get those?"

"I shot them. With Mallory. That was my photo on *The Hollywood Express* website yesterday morning. You need to take them."

"And do what?"

"Keep them safe. Analyze them. Figure out if there's a connection. If not, great. If there is …"

I didn't want to tell the detective that it didn't matter whether the photos helped their case. Honestly, I hoped they wouldn't, because if there was a connection between my work and Mallory's death, then they needed to lock me up on the spot.

I couldn't look at the photos anymore. Every time I did, I wondered what hid behind those listless eyes. She'd been plotting back then. Everything was planned, with me as her first played pawn. I stared at those photos and wondered what went wrong.

Where I went wrong.

"Listen, if you don't collect these as evidence, I'll put them all over the internet, and then you'll never be able to do your job."

"Threats don't help," he said.

"Fine. You know what? Take the whole fucking thing." I held out the iPad. O'Toole stared from his absurd, towering height. As thought it were a hot plate, I shoved the tablet into his hands. "Just fucking take it!"

Knots filled my stomach as his long fingers curled around the edges of the iPad.

I couldn't let go. Phantom limb, or some shit. A grip so tight O'Toole looked down. At my wrists. Perhaps he wanted to shackle them. Perhaps he saw the scars. Perhaps he saw something else. Perhaps he thought I was full of shit.

And whiskey.

"You're presuming we're investigating foul play," he said.

I searched his face for a clue. "Aren't you?"

If I was completely off-base, he'd have shooed me out right from the start, grumbled something about leaving the dead to rest in peace, and why is it that people suddenly care about a person after they're gone, you greedy little shithead.

I let go of the iPad.

He held on.

My heart crumbled.

"Log this as evidence," O'Toole said, handing the iPad to the deputy whose oily fingers greased up the screen.

I knew, right then and there, he should have thrown me in the clink.

A vigil had been planned for that evening. I'd heard about it online. It was meant to be everyone's last chance to say goodbye to their beloved Mallory. It didn't matter that she'd only recently become a sensation. Her movie was doing well in the theatres because everyone saw it as her final salutation and wanted a piece of that special brownie. No one cared who she was, not really. They certainly didn't deserve a comforting hug while they cried during the final credits of *Between Broken Pieces*.

But I knew her.

I thought I knew her.

If I could just exist in my blissful world of ignorance for a little longer, maybe I could say goodbye too.

Bright flowers blanketed the sidewalk in front of Mallory's house. Cards with hand-written notes were ribboned to stuffed animals. Clusters of Mexican candles from the 99 Cents Only Store burned dangerously close to the hedge, most of the Virgin of Guadalupe.

Yellow tape was still strung across the front door, but anyone who visited Mallory's house knew the back door didn't lock. Some jackass broke it at a party once. Mallory never cared to replace it, and apparently, neither did the cops. No longer did a fragile young celebrity need to be safely tucked inside.

The glass door squeaked when I pulled on it, rattling the whole house. Were I a spiritual person, I might have believed it was Mallory saying hello.

I couldn't help but feel some kind of a lingering form of life. A piece broken off and left behind. Like the chipped edge off a ceramic cup. Or a diamond from the ring of a spoiled, careless trophy wife.

It didn't look the same. Didn't feel the same. Mallory was gone and her house had become someone else's. There wasn't anything left to say goodbye to.

There had to be. I needed there to be.

Each step up the stairs robbed energy I didn't have to lose. My whiskey-soaked brain sloshed in my skull like a tuber down a water slide. As I reached her bedroom door, I couldn't help thinking about the one and only time I had been granted entrance into the queen's room at the palace. Back then, I found her naked and glowing, eager and waiting.

It should have been me who found her. Not Juliette.

But she got there first.

Again.

The words caught in my throat as I tried to make sense of why Juliette stood in the middle of Mallory's bedroom.

"What the actual fuck."

Juliette turned away, her long neck twisting like a Red Vine. "How drunk are you, on a scale of one to ten?"

She'd ruined it. She'd ruined everything. She ruined Mallory, my friendship with her, my moment of grief. I craned to look to the bed, to the final resting place of the girl who should have been laying there alive.

I saw the photos.

A dozen of them. Some, the portraits I took of Mallory, the ones I handed to O'Toole as evidence. The rest, snapshots of Mallory the morning they found her in that very bed. My photos were matched with a corresponding image of the crime scene. The before and the after. A photographic one-two punch.

Disgusting. Beautiful. So perfect.

My voice came out as a low, slurring drone. "Juliette, seriously, what the fuck is this?"

Something rustled in the closet. Juliette glanced at it though the sides of her eyes. "Mallory asked you to shoot her like this, didn't she? Why? Did she give you some kind of prompt, tell you it was for a project, or for marketing? Was it a joke? Was she planning to prank someone? What were they for?"

Her questions were rapid-fire, ones I either didn't have answers for or didn't feel inclined to share. She'd lost her chance to rewrite the story of Mallory's death to fit into her own plot. She didn't get to keep fucking everything up just because she got there first.

The closet door opened and there was Alice Welsh, creeping out from behind a whole row of jackets and coats. The woman whose article played a cruel joke against my photographs. Beside her was Fiona O'Shea. The woman whose career choice did more harm than good.

A joyful collection of assholes.

Juliette jabbed a hand in her direction. "I'm not done yet." Alice stopped, but didn't retreat.

I wasn't surprised that Alice Welsh had been with Juliette for whatever twisted scheme they were in the midst of. Both had been dropped from the same sour lemon tree, into the same steaming pile of shit. What surprised me was that I couldn't definitively guess which woman was initially responsible for the lunacy.

"Just when I thought you couldn't be any more of a psychopath," I said.

Fury ripped through Juliette's face. "I want to know why you took these photos of Mallory! Just tell me what they mean!"

She lunged at me.

A bath towel flung out of nowhere and covered Juliette's head. She froze. The room went silent.

Beside me, Fiona had her arm suspended out. Surprised, like her limb had gone rogue.

Juliette pulled the towel off. "What the hell was that?"

Fiona's arm trembled. "If a snake gets loose, throw a towel over them and they'll stay put because they don't know which direction to go to safety."

Alice snorted, and Juliette threw the towel back at Fiona. "I swear to God, if I go to jail, I'm going to shank every one of you our first day down."

"No one's going to jail," Alice said.

"You are trespassing in a dead girl's house," I said.

"So are you," Juliette said.

"I'm here to pay my respects."

With a laugh, Juliette waved an arm. "Sure. Fine. Do your thing. Meanwhile, we are here to do the job of the cops and figure out why the hell Mallory decided to off herself the night of her premiere."

What a sick, heartless cunt.

"You didn't care about Mallory. You took advantage of her. You used her. You made her your puppet so that you could get your fucking Oscar. Hell, I wouldn't put it past you to have convinced her to kill herself so you could have this spectacular opening weekend."

Juliette flinched as though Fiona had thrown the towel again. "I would never wish death on someone in exchange for box office numbers."

"You might not wish it, but you clearly don't care either way."

I watched the muscles tense in Juliette's face. She was trying so desperately to hold herself together. "You make me sound like a fucking monster. Like you're not at all responsible, like no one knows you had a habit of taking photos of actresses while they played dead, like you didn't drug them and fuck them. You don't get to play martyr, Riley. For fuck's sake."

How dare she.

Alice took a stiff step forward. "Wait, is this not the first time?"

"No, it's not. She and Mallory had a whole collection. Way more than this."

How fucking dare she.

Juliette's eyes bored into me. Her hand had always been more playable than mine. It was exactly why I had lost Mallory and found her again, only to lose her for good.

I knew it would come to this. I knew she'd force me all in. How fucking dare she.

"How did you know about the other photos?" I said.

A smile snaked across Juliette's face, cracking the stone-molded exterior right through the middle.

"She sent them to me," she said. "The night she died, Mallory sent me every fucking picture you have ever taken of her."

NINETEEN
Juliette

As RILEY'S FACE DROPPED, I knew I had won. Mallory had been her little pussy puppet, but she was my golden egg. I wasn't about to let some new-age hipster like Riley Westcott over-cook my yolk.

"Why would she do that?" Riley asked, sounding like a terrified child.

"More importantly, when?" said Alice.

I waved her off. "Last night."

"Exactly what time? Check your email." Alice was doing that reporter thing again, prying with surgical precision. I dodged as she reached for my phone.

"Is that really important?"

"I think it might be," she said. "The cops were concerned about a timeline. Like something didn't add up for them. So if we can piece it together—"

"We might be able to take ourselves off the suspect list." Most days, I despised Alice Welsh. That day, she was the smartest bitch in the room.

Riley choked as she spoke. "I presume you all have alibis."

"I'm divorced and I live alone," I said. "I am not blessed with an alibi."

"Me neither, unless you count my cat." The sound of Fiona's voice was about as soothing as a feline in heat. Alice had me convinced Fiona would be helpful to the cause, but I didn't trust her. She spent more time watching than participating. It was aggravating.

"I was home with my husband," Alice said.

"Were you?" I said.

Her eyes got impressively sharp.

Riley shook her head. "The girl is dead, and you're blaming her for it."

"She wasn't suicidal," Fiona said suddenly.

"But that doesn't mean we killed her," I said immediately. "Because that would be absurd."

"There's not a thing about this that isn't absurd," Riley said.

"Our angle is that Mallory killed herself to make a point." Alice held up two photos. The subject was dead in only one, but God damn, it was hard to tell the difference. "We just happened to be a part of her statement."

"But she wasn't suicidal," Fiona said, eyes twitching between the three of us.

"Seriously?" Riley said. Her arms flailed. "What kind of a statement is she making by drowning herself in pills?"

"She never took drugs before you wormed into her life," I said, which made Riley flinch.

"You can't turn this on me."

"You told her I could get her medication," Fiona said quietly. "You had her convinced I could prescribe her pills, but I couldn't."

"Just because your fiancé offed himself, didn't mean she would also," Riley said.

"But she did," Alice said. So harsh. So heartless. I was starting to like the woman.

"It doesn't matter how she got the pills," I said. "What matters is that we didn't give them to her."

"Actually …" Fiona started, then drifted. I wanted to shake the words from her, but Alice went for the subtle approach.

"You can tell us," Alice said. "What happens in this room stays in this room."

"Except Mallory Braun," I said.

Riley's hands balled into tight fists, shoulders pulled up to her ears. She was moving into fight mode. Good. I'd been itching for a brawl.

Alice stepped toward Fiona. "It's important we know everything you know, Dr. Shea."

Fiona stared back at Alice. Nervously cowered by the door. If I'd had the skills of a psychologist who analyzed people's imperfections for a living, I would diagnose Dr. Fiona Shea as having Two-Faced Cryptic Compulsive Liar Disorder. She was hiding something. Something bad. Riley had eased off her fight stance, but she'd fired me up. I wanted to fight.

"Tell us what you know," I said, my voice louder than even I was ready for. Fiona glanced at the floor, to the towel at my feet. "Tell us what you fucking know!"

"Why are you yelling?" said Alice.

"I'm not yelling!"

Fiona's eyes started to water.

"Juliette, you can't lose your shit right now," Alice said.

"She's hiding something. She's a fucking liar."

"No one in this room is a steward of fact," Riley said.

"Then why don't we all have a round of Truth or Dare," I said. "Minus the Dare part. Because we don't have time for any more bullshit."

"I gave her the pills!" Fiona shouted so loud I actually jumped. Her teeth jutted out like a frightened dog. I eyed the towel.

Riley hissed. "You what?"

"It's not like I forced her to take them," Fiona said. "I didn't shove the drugs down her throat. I declared her mentally healthy the first time I met her. The only reason she came back was to get drugs. I just wanted her to leave me alone."

"So you gave her a handful of pills?" said Alice. She was a lot less defensive of the shrink.

"She was a recreational abuser," Fiona said. "There was no evidence of addiction, or even any need for medication."

"Are you kidding me?" Riley took a step toward Alice. Alice took a step toward me. "She wasn't a recreational abuser. She was barely a user, and trust me, I'd know."

"Oh for fuck's sake," I half-laughed. Half, because I'd voluntarily joined the band of lunatics.

"Mallory only ever got high when we were shooting. That's it." Riley's voice cracked, and it caught Alice's attention. Which caught my attention. I watched carefully as Alice's eyes darted to the bed, mind turning.

"What?" I asked. "What is it?"

She flicked her fingers at me. "Pull up that email. The one Mallory sent you."

I was reluctant. The email was my trump card. Not just a slice, but the whole fucking enchilada. I didn't know what I could do with it, and I sure as hell couldn't figure out why Mallory sent it to me, but I wasn't about to just hand them over.

"Oh, wait." Alice was looking at her phone. She made annoyingly graceful flipping motions with her thumb across the screen. Then flipped her phone around to show me the screen. "Someone already posted them online."

"What?" Riley and I said in unison. She followed up with an under-breath, "That slimy son of a bitch."

"She sent them to me. Only me. She said specifical-ly," pulling my own phone from my pocket, I read aloud, "Here's your grand finale."

"3:17 A.M.," said Alice, looking over my shoulder.

"One minute after she called me," Fiona said, and we all turned to look at her.

"What did she say?" Riley asked.

"I was sleeping. Missed the whole thing." Fiona's eyes shifted. Lying again, undoubtedly.

There was a sudden chill in the air. I didn't believe in ghosts, but even I had to admit there was a creepy vibe in the room, and I had been the one who'd touched a dead girl.

"Wow," Alice said, breaking the silence as she looked at the photos. "These are really good."

Riley inhaled. I didn't hear her release.

Alice turned her phone to Fiona, and asked, "What do you see?"

The question seemed to startle Fiona, like she didn't have any goddamn clue why any of us were there. When she squinted at the screen, I really had to question if Riley was the most intoxicated woman in the room.

"Her eyes are red," Fiona finally said.

I considered the tensile strangling strength of the towel.

"Look deeper than that," Alice said, a little too encouragingly. "Is she purposely making her expressions look so lifeless? Is it the drugs? Is it acting, or is it real?"

Ages we waited for Fiona to respond, but she just stood there, staring at Alice's phone.

"This is a waste of time," I said. "We're assuming Mallory set this up as some social experiment, but she wasn't smart enough for that. She was lazy and selfish, and she didn't care about the career she'd forced everyone around her to work so hard to create."

"She wasn't lazy," Riley said. "And she was fucking brilliant."

I wanted so desperately to whack Riley in the cunt. "You're just saying that because you don't get to fuck her anymore."

Riley stared at me, shaking her head. "You never listened to her, Juliette. You didn't care. All you wanted her to do was to be a pretty portrait in the background."

"Nobody cares about anybody's personal shit," I said loudly, because apparently no one was listening to anything I had been saying. "Mallory Braun's job was easy. So fucking easy. She didn't have to do anything, didn't have to say anything. She just had to do what I said. Show up and shut up. Play dead, for all I fucking care."

My voice echoed off the walls, and then was swallowed by the silence. It didn't matter that I couldn't retract the statement, because it was true either way. I knew from the moment I met the girl that she would be my undoing. If only she'd gotten rid of herself sooner.

As though reading my thoughts, Fiona shouted, "She wasn't suicidal!" and then a cop walked in.

TWENTY
Fiona

STIFF, ROLLED SHOULDERS. Shifting, rapid eye movements. Trembling hand hovering over his belt. Cocked and ready, like he'd stumbled on a pack of startled raccoons.

"Nobody move."

Riley was the only one with her hands up. Juliette pulled her elbows in, moving into a fighting stance. Alice had her sharp eyes all over the young cop, sizing him up.

"Fiona, the towel," Juliette whispered. She nodded to my feet. I was in no way prepared to pit a piece of terry-cloth against a gun. Juliette started to bend over, and the cop drew his pistol.

"Don't move. Just stay right where you are," he said. "What the hell are you even doing here? This is an active crime scene."

I caught Alice's eye. She had been darting them around the room—as though trying to remember every detail—until she caught me watching her. "We have something we need to tell the detectives," she said. "It's imperative we speak with Davila and O'Toole."

"Imperative?" the cop said.

"It means it's important." Juliette rolled her eyes.

"I know what it means," he said, clearly having wrestled with the word.

"We have some insight that we think might be of interest to the detectives regarding Mallory Braun's death." Alice chose her words carefully. Calculated. Passive embellishments. "Dr. Shea here is a clinical psychologist and she may be able to help break down what Mallory was thinking the night she died."

The cop stared at Alice. Blinked four times. Then turned to me. "You're Dr. Shea?"

"Yep," I said with a half wave. Juliette rolled her eyes again.

"You know why Mallory Braun killed herself?" he asked.

Riley—not having been part of the conversation that took place prior to our arrival at the house—dropped her face in disappointment. She knew what was happening. I had been cornered by Alice Welsh and Juliette Fairchild in the parking lot of my office building while they built their case: Mallory Braun died in the performance of a lifetime.

Finally someone else saw what I had tried so desperately to communicate to others—Dr. Lam especially. Eight months had passed since my fiancé died, and I was still begging to be heard. Still fighting to be taken seriously.

And then two women showed up and asked me to speak the truth. I had never felt so understood in my life.

Riley sighed. Purposely loud. "She knew we'd all end up in her bedroom."

"What does that mean?" The cop scrunched his face.

Juliette stepped forward. "It means that if you're going to take us in for questioning, you might want to do it before we blast our insights all over Twitter."

With that, the cop waved us through the door. Just before I'd passed the threshold, something on the ground caught my eye: a torn piece of a business card, with my name on it.

The ride to the police station was a blur. We were stuffed into the cruiser—Riley up front, me squashed in the back-seat with Alice and Juliette as my flanks. No one said a word the whole way. Bodies were stiff. Eyes grazed the hills beyond the window. Alice tapped her fingers against her thigh in a repeating pattern. Even the cop kept quiet. I caught his eyes several times through the rearview. He would squint and then quickly look away. His best attempt at intimidation.

Once at the station, we were led to a conference room with floor-to-ceiling windows and a long conference table too small for the oversized space.

Riley was first inside. She mumbled to herself. Alice and Juliette spent more time looking at each other than anything else. I entered last, eyeing an extra large flatscreen set up on one end of the room.

Detective O'Toole stood by the windows, wearing a button-up shirt that did nothing to disguise his muscles. Beside him, a lean mustached man thumbed through an iPad. I swallowed down my fear.

"Ladies," O'Toole said. "Sit anywhere you'd like."

Juliette and Alice sat across from each other. Optimal position for eye contact and subtle silent messages.

Riley skipped the chair next to Juliette and slumped in the third one. She jabbed a finger toward the other detective. "Hey, is that my iPad?"

"The L.A.P.D. thanks you for your donation," O'Toole said. The other cop gave him a stern side-eye. It was easy to tell who was in charge.

I hesitated in the doorway. Made myself too obvious. Attracted too much attention.

The mustached one spoke up. "Dr. Shea, my name is Detective Davila. I understand you have some insight into Miss Braun's psychology the night she died. Please, take a seat."

O'Toole's face remained stern and calm. During our last meeting, I told him I didn't have anything helpful to share about Mallory, and I worried he would hold it against me.

"Dr. Shea," he said. I trembled at the deep tone. "Sit."

I slumped into the chair next to Alice. She motioned for me to sit up straighter. I did.

O'Toole addressed us. "To answer your first question, no you are not under arrest. To answer your second question, yes we are investigating the death of Mallory Braun as a possible case of foul play. No, that does not mean murder."

"Then why the fuck are we here?" Juliette said. "None of us killed Mallory."

"I just said…" O'Toole took a deep breath. "Listen, you're not on any suspect list. We brought you here because we have some questions. The behavior that all four of you have displayed is… interesting."

"Suspicious interesting?" Riley said.

Davila stepped forward. His movements were sluggish. Dark skin surrounded his eyes. He needed sleep. "This has been a rough couple of days for us. For you too, I imagine, since you all knew Miss Braun in some capacity. There's no bringing Miss Braun back to life, but I would like to avoid this situation happening again."

"You don't think there will be copycats, do you?" Alice's voice was softer than normal. She was practiced at playing passive.

"It's not copycats we're worried about," Davila said. He reached for a remote on the table.

The flatscreen turned on and showed the photo that everyone had been talking about: dead movie star Mallory Braun. The fake one. Riley turned away.

"6:00 A.M. Saturday morning, *The Hollywood Express* posted an article which featured an interview with Mallory Braun, written by Alice Welsh," Davila said in a factual tone. "The article was accompanied by this very photo, taken by Riley Westcott."

"Is your plan to spurt shit we already know, or does this have a purpose?" Juliette said.

O'Toole puffed out his muscular chest. "Ma'am, I suggest you shut up and let the detective talk."

With a glance at Alice, Juliette sank back in her chair.

Davila hardly made notice of the interruption. "The interview referenced in the article was conducted on Friday afternoon, after a series of press junkets and hours before the movie premiere for the film *Between Broken Pieces*."

O'Toole added, "We are trying to determine the timeline between that interview and the moment her body was found."

Alice jerked around in her chair. "Why does the timeline start at the end of the interview? That's a little specific."

O'Toole nodded once. "Yes. It is."

"Dr. Shea," Davila turned to me. "Had you read the article?"

I shook my head. "I don't need to."

"So you're basing your assumptions about Miss Braun solely on your personal interactions with her?"

Something about Davila threw me. Passive aggression. Or, aggressive obsession. "They were professional interactions, and I'm not making any assumptions. It's all based on my knowledge and experience as a clinical psychologist."

"And what experience is that?"

Detective O'Toole was using his direct questioning technique, but the casualness was gone. It was possible he knew more than he let on. It was possible he knew what happened to my fiancé.

"I'd seen this kind of behavior before," I said. "It's common among new actors who haven't yet figured out how to separate their public and professional personas. Mallory knew that her actions got attention. She thrived on it. As she became more well-known in the industry, she found what people liked about her and set out to exploit it."

Alice nodded, trying not to smile. Juliette leaned back, arm tossed aside. Riley folded her arms across her chest and pouted, but stayed quiet.

"You knew she wanted to exploit it," O'Toole asked, but it wasn't really a question. His tone was firm. "You knew she wanted to use you for prescription drugs, so why, Dr. Shea, did you allow her to do it?"

O'Toole clicked the remote and the screen changed to a video of security footage aimed at home in a neighborhood marked by cracked asphalt and harsh yellow streetlights. Mallory appeared in the frame, heading for the sidewalk from the house. In her hand, she carried a Ziploc bag of mixed pills. Suddenly—from across the street—I appeared and rushed up to her.

There was no holding in my gasp of surprise.

"Oh Jesus, what is this?" Juliette asked. "Are those the drugs she took?"

"She followed me," I heard my voice crack, but there was nothing I could do to ease it. "She followed me to the dealer's house."

"And you gave her the pills," Riley said slowly.

My heart thumped in my chest. "I realized my mistake. That's why I went back, to take the pills so she couldn't blame me."

Alice's voice came at me from the side. A slow hissing of words. "You were afraid of what she'd do with them."

"No. I didn't know what she would do with them."

Riley was harsh and loud. "She swallowed them, that's what she did!"

"She was not suicidal!"

Juliette threw her head back. "Jesus, with this again."

"But you went back." Alice kept asking. Kept prying. Slowly. Methodically. Painfully. "You went back because you believed it was possible that she would use the pills to commit suicide."

"You knew!" Riley's voice rattled the floor-to-ceiling windows. "You fucking knew she was going to do it!"

My heart rattled uncontrollably in my ribcage. I had to clench every muscle in my body to keep it from shaking me apart. That wasn't why I went back. It wasn't. It was the same deception. Just like last time. Mallory was going to ruin me. I wouldn't be tricked again. She was a sneaky, conniving liar. That's what she was.

She wasn't suicidal.

She wasn't suicidal.

She wasn't …

TWENTY-ONE
Alice

Fiona sat so still I wondered if she had turned to stone. It had been my idea to bring the therapist into our plot, an epic fuckup that was my fault. Even as her patient, I couldn't speak for the quality of her talent, so why did I feel so inclined to trust her? I had hoped she'd bring legitimacy to our argument that Mallory Braun had none of the signs of someone planning to commit suicide, or of someone who would self-medicate without restraint. Hers was a death planned, premeditated, orchestrated with such fine precision that those of us who predicted it were still left stunned and confused.

She'd had her doubts. Dr. Fiona Shea second-guessed her decision to let Mallory go home with the bag of pills that directly led to her death. What changed her mind?

I looked up to see Davila watching us. Judgment radiated from his eyes. If I was going to get out of that police station in one piece, I had to stick to the plan.

"According to the interview by Mrs. Welsh, Mallory was unusually self-aware," Davila said. "You describe her as a confident, sometimes cocky, young woman."

"That's true," I said, as I subtly rolled my chair away from Fiona.

"She didn't ask for help, or hint at wanting to get out of the business?"

"Mallory knew she was good at her profession." My chair hit the table leg, marking the furthest I could get from the therapist.

"And she never spoke of any emotional distress or depression?"

Juliette answered for me. "All she wanted to talk about was fucking on-camera."

"She knew her power lay in her sexual allure," Fiona added, but nothing that came out of her mouth sounded sincere anymore.

"How does that translate into ..." Davila had a hard time saying it. "How does sex beget suicide?"

"It hits all the same neurons in your brain," Riley said. Eyes drooping, she stared at the table as though wishing to melt into it. "Sex and violence, it's all the same to your senses. Releases dopamine. Gets the adrenaline running. That was the thing about Mallory..." Riley inhaled. "She made violence sexy."

"It's why she was in all those horror movies," Juliette said, nodding, suddenly in agreement with the woman she seemed to most despise. "People liked watching her have sex. They liked watching her be chased and mauled. They liked watching her die."

O'Toole motioned to Juliette with the remote. "You mean, like this?" He clicked a button, and the TV screen showed more security camera footage, this bit of Juliette on Mallory's front porch at night. She'd pounded on the door. Shouted something.

The Juliette across the table from me buried her head in her hands. "Oh fuck."

The video switched to show the backyard, where a naked woman lay face down in an internally lit pool. A classic Hollywood homage. Juliette crept into the back, looked directly into the pool, then turned around and left. Seconds later, the woman splashed and came up for air. It was undeniably Mallory Braun.

My eyes stung as I stared at Juliette, head on the table, face buried in her arms. I wondered if I stared long enough whether I would burn a hole through her sleeve.

It didn't make sense. Juliette had been adamant about keeping Mallory tucked safely under her wing, protected from all those pesky predators who wanted a bite of the tender flesh of such succulent prey. How could Juliette fail to mention that incident? Who exactly was she attempting to mislead? How did I read the whole thing so fantastically wrong?

O'Toole paused the playback. "The video was time stamped at 9:35 P.M. Friday night, five hours before the victim was presumed dead."

"What exactly brought you to the house, Mrs. Fairchild?" Davila said.

Juliette raised her head, and spoke with a soft tone used by women who didn't want to be heard. It sounded like she was faking an accent, and badly. "She wasn't at the premiere, so I went to her house to see if she was okay. I found her in the pool, and then …"

"And then you walked away." Riley's voice was gritty. She glared at Juliette with the sort of glowing hatred that might lead to passion-induced manslaughter. "You found her unconscious in a pool, and you fucking walked away."

Juliette jabbed her finger at the screen. "She wasn't unconscious. It's on the video."

"You didn't stay long enough to know that."

"I heard her splashing. And I left because I had a premiere party to get to."

"Jesus. You are a heartless animal," Riley said, slumping down in her chair, as though she wasn't the one who had cinematically imagined Mallory as a dead girl. Which was worse?

I turned to Davila. His steely expression was startling, but I couldn't afford to waver. I needed to leave that place with my dignity intact. "Do you think it's at all possible Mallory knew Juliette was at the house and purposely put herself in the pool like that? You saw how she looked up when Juliette left, right?"

Davila and O'Toole exchanged a glance. Had I hit on something they hadn't thought of, or maybe, something they had wondered themselves?

"And why follow Fiona to get drugs?" I said. "This is L.A., you can get drugs anywhere. But instead she stalked her therapist and then walked away with a bagful of pills. It doesn't sound like suicidal behavior, does it?"

"It doesn't sound like the behavior of a psychologically sound person, either," Riley said, "despite how her shrink would have us all believe."

Fiona hadn't moved an inch. I wondered if she was still breathing.

"If you believed she was unstable, perhaps you should have said something to her in person, Miss Westcott," Davila said, to which O'Toole did his thing with the remote.

In a clip from security footage outside a cottage-style house, Mallory approached a door and knocked. A few seconds later, Riley answered. The bag of pills was in Mallory's hand. She held it up. Riley said something, then closed the door, leaving Mallory alone on the steps. The porch light turned off.

"You're fucking kidding me," Juliette growled. "You're blaming us for ignoring the signs, when you had the perfect opportunity to stop her."

Riley stumbled over her words. "I was exhausted. And pretty high myself, if I'm honest. I didn't know where she got the pills, and I didn't think she'd take them. She only takes them when we shoot, so she can have that certain look for the camera."

"Maybe she just wanted company," I said. "Someone to talk to. To hang out with."

Riley erupted, saliva spurting from her violently flapping lips. "She didn't want to 'hang out.' She wanted me to shoot her. Goddammit, I got the shot I needed, she didn't need to keep it going. I had already made my point, people knew I was the best at photographing her. She wouldn't listen. I told her no one would care about more of the same old shit, and the only way it would be interesting again is if she were actually fucking dead."

Riley's last words bounced around the room and she sunk back, letting all the air out of her lungs. White-knuckled and tense, Juliette's gaze flickered over the tabletop. Fiona wheezed beside me, on the brink of crying.

The evidence against our argument was alarming. If we were there to prove that Mallory's decisions were her own, we certainly had a lot to show just how hard she was nudged to make them.

"There's one more," said O'Toole.

Eyes landed on me, but I wasn't as worried as they were for me. There wouldn't have been a video of me handing Mallory drugs, or spying on her at the house. I stayed home that night. I had my alibi. But as I watched the detective click another button on the remote, something inside me twisted sideways. The screen changed to a screenshot of a Twitter feed. My Twitter feed.

"Remember this tweet, Mrs. Welsh?" O'Toole's voice lifted, practically singing. "Funny how you forgot to mention you'd read it before. 'If anything happens to me, be grateful that @AliceWelshReports has the key to all my secrets.'"

"And then," Davila added, solemnly, "at 3:20 A.M., minutes before Miss Braun's presumed time of death, there was this eloquent response."

O'Toole moved to click the remote again, and I turned away, my left eyelid twitching as I did. No amount of blinking could subside it. That was it. I had hoped the damning evidence had disappeared, but when I heard the gasps of the other three women, I knew it had survived to live in infamy in the empyrean of the internet.

Davila's voice spoke my own, damning words. "@MalloryBraun, I will revel in your secrets long after you are gone."

My ears flooded with the sound of pulsing blood. They couldn't think …? Could they?

"It wasn't meant to be cruel, or suggestive," I said. "And I deleted it as soon as I learned she was dead."

Davila's shoulders slumped over. "You told her that her secrets would outlive her. That you would outlive her."

"She wasn't supposed to die so soon." My voice shook. My whole body trembled. I didn't know how to make it stop.

"She was dead only minutes later."

"You can't blame her death on me," I said, hating how my voice screeched. "If that's what pushed her over the edge, then she was well on her way there before that."

"Clearly." Davila placed the iPad on the table. On it was my interview. If I could take those words back I could clarify some things, make sense of all the loose strands, paint Mallory as the maker of her own fate, not the fragile puppet dancing to the forceful tug of strings.

"So what now?" I asked, each word struggling to free itself from my choking throat. "Are we under arrest?"

After several agonizing moments, Davila said, "No."

"But here's the thing," O'Toole said, "you four are here because you wanted to prove it was Mallory Braun's fault that Mallory Braun is dead. In police work, we call that a red herring. So what does that make you ladies?"

I had no idea what that made us. I still didn't know if that meant Mallory planned her death for the purpose of making a show of it. I still didn't know if I was a purveyor of her suicide. Was it really possible that my stupid Tweet pushed her to do it?

My mind went back to those photos, the collection created by the brilliant Riley Westcott, the ones Mallory sent Juliette moments before she died.

The photos had Mallory in a variety of clothing styles, against diverse backgrounds. None of them featured that strange, deliberate smile she wore in the poster for *Between Broken Pieces*. Instead, the Mallory Braun in those photos stared into the camera with a distinct listlessness, halfway between bored and comatose. It would have been off-putting, had the subject not been so distinctly captivating.

She made you want to know why she didn't care that she was laying on the steel rail of a train track. She made you want to know why she lacked any vulnerability being mostly nude in a crowd of people. She made you want to know why she was unafraid to be surrounded by a dozen hypodermic needles and straight razors.

And then I remembered. The end of my interview with Mallory. I had listened to that damn recording so many times I had it memorized:

"I'm a placeholder. There are a thousand other girls like me wandering L.A., looking for someone to capture them and put them in the right slots. And when the mold shifts and the slots take a different shape, those girls go back into the slush pile. We're all closer to losing our place in the mold than we realize. That's why you have to solidify yourself before it's too late."

That's what she did. Mallory Braun solidified her place in the mold.

Davila sat in the chair between Riley and Juliette. "While investigating Miss Braun's death, we interviewed quite a few of the people in your inner circles. Family, coworkers, friends. There's one thing that was common among all of them. Not a single person was surprised we were investigating your involvement. They all believe that, as long as the four of you continue doing what you do, Mallory Braun won't be the last to die."

My chest felt heavy. I couldn't believe someone would say something like that about me. Who was it? Who would toss me out like a drunken late night dollar store purchase? Trevor? It had to be Trevor.

"Tell me who," I said. My mouth was so dry it was difficult to speak. "Tell me who thinks I'm so fucking terrible that I'd let a young woman die."

Davila held up his hand. "Mrs. Welsh—"

"Tell me!" I sprang to my feet. The chair clattered behind me. "Tell me who, because whoever it was doesn't know a goddamn thing about me."

"It was your husband," O'Toole said. "Actually, he called us."

The heaviness in my chest threatened to suffocate me. How dare he. How dare Matt sweep me under the bus like that, how dare he presume he knew anything about Mallory or what I knew of her. How could he assume anything about what happened between Mallory and me in that hotel room when he had refused to even read my article?

I needed to play him the recording. Then he'd hear it. He would hear her words, straight from her mouth, in her voice. Then he would know who Mallory Braun really was.

I burst from the conference room and clicked his name on my phone. A video call. I wanted to see his face. I wanted to see the guilt in it, I wanted to watch him apologize, to beg for forgiveness.

It took an ungodly seven rings before he picked up. "Alice?" It was dark where he was. I could barely see his face, but there were voices in the background.

"Fucking hell, Matt!" I screamed into the phone. "Are you trying to ruin my career?"

"Kind of seems like you're doing fine at that yourself," he said, his voice flat.

"It's not my fault she killed herself. The cops even said so."

"Well. Good for you." Someone shushed him, and Matt started moving.

"Where the hell are you?"

"I'm at the movies. Watching *Between Broken Pieces*. You should see the theatre, it's packed." The screen turned around and I saw hundreds of people illuminated by the projected light. A couple of them waved.

My blood boiled. Heat radiated from my face.

"So that's how you want to play this, huh? You're going ruin my life so you can have more time watching your big-screen girlfriend?"

The camera was back on him again, showing he was at the theatre door. "What are you talking about?"

"I know you're into her. I know Mallory Braun turns you on."

"Jesus, Alice, she doesn't turn me on. Especially not now."

"I've watched you get excited by her."

His face was serious. Almost sad. "Alice, I got excited because you got excited. This energy burned inside you whenever you talked about her, and it was hot. I thought you were getting off to her. I just didn't realize you got off to the thought of her self-destruction."

For the first time in my life, I didn't have the words.

"I know how you work, Alice. You think you're this truth seeker, hell-bent on revealing the darker side of humanity, when you're right in the fucking middle of it. That's how you know where to look for it. That's why you're so good at predicting it. Not because you know how to think like the worst us, but because you are the worst of us."

Matt had made his way back into the theatre, and I could barely hear it over the thumping of blood in my ears: her voice. The camera turned once again, but this time to face the movie screen.

There she was, Mallory Braun, in her brilliant but ill-fated film, sprawled in the bed of the character she'd just seduced, laying out an anecdote I imagined coming from the girl herself:

"You never really know a person. You can stare at them day after day and have no idea what their souls look like. You don't even really know your own. Look in a mirror and it's still wrong, it's all backwards. But if you're brave enough to shatter that mirror, that's where you'll find the answers. That's where the truth is, in between all those broken pieces."

GOING WITH THE FLOW

Gabi Lorino

SEPTEMBER

THROUGH HER WINDSHIELD, Sara could see a boxy beige hospital with giant square glass windows reflecting the odd dark clouds in the sky. Unfortunately, they weren't rainclouds. The outside temperature on her dashboard read 105 degrees.

If only she could make it to the shade of the crisscrossing overpasses ahead! Then, she'd get temporary relief. Exiting at the 134 would be crowded, but maybe the Holly Drive exit would work. From there, she could take the back roads home. Not that she knew them, but her GPS system could figure it out.

Grey and white ashes flew gently through the air like snow.

Isn't there a Morrissey song about this?

A few ash flakes landed on her windshield. Reacting, she pulled on the lever to spray fluid onto the windshield and wipe off the dirt with the wipers, but the pump groaned and no water was sprayed. The wipers pushed a few ashes off her windshield.

"Bet we're out of fluid again," she said absently, not realizing she'd spoken aloud, kind of like the way she yelled, "Really, asshole?" to the pushy Audi driver that had cut in front of her and then skidded to a stop five hundred feet later to sit in this mess.

Sweat dripped down her sides even though the air conditioner was on full blast. The AC worked better when the car was moving. Plus, the fumes from the other cars were awful; that meant her windows should stay up. Under her hood, the compressor rattled and sputtered like a tiny motorcycle being driven around in circles on top of the car battery.

She glanced at an old Toyota truck to her left, rust-orange in color. The driver, an older Mexican man, had his windows down and apparently didn't have the option of running the air conditioner. They exchanged weak smiles.

"I get it, buddy," she said aloud. "This is not fun."

She shook her head when she realized she was talking to herself again, then fumbled for her 'pop-star headset,' paired it with her phone, and scrolled through her contacts.

"Power on. Battery high. Connected," the headset spoke into her ears.

She looked for someone who wasn't in rush-hour traffic like she was, someone who wasn't dealing with end-of-the-week heat-wave insanity in L.A. *The heat makes people so angry*, she thought. To her right, a hillside with bleached clay supported a few green trees. The rest looked barren and bald.

The cars in front of her eased forward, as did she in her car, though the shade of the overpasses still seemed so far away.

In the Cs of her address book, a name popped out: Cassandra. Cassandra, who lived in a house she could afford in Florida, was probably luxuriating in proper central air conditioning at home at that moment, or maybe at a Happy Hour somewhere.

It was worth a try. Sara hit the call button and heard the phone ring.

"Sara?" Cassandra asked. She sounded winded.

"Yeah, it's me. What are you doing?"

"Walking off my week. Seemed better than self-medicating."

This was their code word for inebriation in all its glorious forms.

"Why would working out be better than self-medicating?" Sara asked.

"Can't afford new kidneys. Gotta take care of the ones I have."

As usual, Cassandra was an anchor in a sea of bullshit. Her matter-of-fact tone comforted Sara.

"God, I've missed you," Sara said.

"You can come back any time," Cassandra countered.

"It's not that easy." Sara shook her head.

"No? You know the offer still stands. I'd make room for you, if you need a place to land. And the rent's cheap."

I haven't taken her up on it, though. Yet.

"They're talking about making me permanent," Sara said. "They asked me to name a salary the other day."

"Wait, am I having déjà vu?"

Sara laughed. "Yeah, this happened with the last job too. Maybe they asked me to name a salary to keep me motivated until they run out of funding for my position. Annual contractor migration begins before the holidays."

"I don't know what to tell you. Maybe just go with the flow," Cassandra said.

"Ha! You would *never* take that advice," Sara laughed.

"Just because I would freak out if someone told me to go with the flow doesn't mean it's bad advice. Here's more. Change is good! Keep reaching for the stars!"

After she shook her head and laughed, Sara asked, "What's going on with you?"

Cassandra sighed. "Work's fine. House is fine. Still driving the same car."

"Preaching to the choir. What else? Anything?"

They shared stories of family dramas, career highs and lows, relationships attempted and gone wrong.

Sara smiled as she eased her car into the shadows, which seemed to lower the temperature by fifteen degrees. She saw smoke plumes rising from a mountainside on fire. It was too far away to confirm, but the 210 West had to be closed. Hence the insane traffic from eventually being herded from five lanes down to one or two. The air conditioner compressor sputtered and she flipped it off, felt the oven-like heat for about four seconds, then flipped it back on.

"How's living with Duncan?" Cassandra asked.

"Who? I live with a roommate, amiga."

"Oh I thought… well, sorry to hear that. Or am I?"

"You're not so brokenhearted over it," Sara said with a lilt in her voice.

"Thank goodness. Ha. You're so funny."

Once the off-ramp was available, Sara hung up. According to the phone display, they'd spoken for an hour and fifteen minutes.

What a relief it was to drive fifteen miles per hour! It was even more exhilarating when she could shift into third gear, twisting and turning through the foothills to get to her home sweet home. The fire nearby perfumed the air with a scorched smell. She needed water and the relief of being away from the heat. Sara was almost home.

She would have loved that modest yet overpriced two-bedroom-one-bath apartment more if she didn't have to share it with her former boyfriend and current roommate, Duncan, but that wasn't something she wanted to explain to Cassandra. She tried not to think about this as she gathered her bags and headed for the door of the sparsely-furnished abode.

"Sara!" Duncan said, his blue eyes glinting as he opened the front door. Duncan stood six foot, two inches, with an impeccable jawline and wavy brown hair. For his career, Duncan used an old family name, McAllister, even though he was clearly Hispanic. He was gorgeous, objectively speaking.

"Home from work?" she asked. They tried to remain cordial at home, though it helped that they both were gone a lot.

"I got some great news. Was hoping you could celebrate." Duncan beamed at her.

Sara aimed a measured glance at him, as if to ask, "What's your game, buddy?" He wasn't usually this friendly. In fact, he looked eager for something.

I hope it's not my body, Sara thought, then stifled a laugh. She was terribly out of shape, and there didn't seem an end in sight to the heavy load she carried at work. Unless she could figure out how to run on a treadmill and crunch numbers simultaneously, her fitness level was going to stay stuck at the low setting. While her once-flat torso had gained a soft outer coating, Duncan remained buff. He had to. For work. Besides, their chemistry had gone from so-so to meh months before, part of the reason for the breakup. She suppressed another laugh.

"What's going on?" Sara placed her work bag into a closet near the front door and hoped to God she wouldn't pick it up for the rest of the weekend.

Duncan, who had retreated to the kitchen (which was the size of a walk-in closet), flashed her a broad smile as he stirred the taco meat on top of the stove with a wooden spoon. "The miniseries got picked up. Rehearsals start right away, and filming next month."

"You're kidding! Which one?"

"The one set in Seattle about the internet tycoons. I'm playing one of the leads."

She smiled. "Duncan, that's fantastic!"

"Thank you, thank you very much. Here, fill up a plate." He motioned toward the taco shells and stovetop covered with browned meat and warm refried beans, then pointed to the table with all the toppings in little bowls.

He never went through this much trouble when we were dating, Sara thought as she grabbed a plate and filled it. *I won't question dinner, though. I freaking deserve it after the week I've had.*

There was a flurry of walking past each other, grabbing a drink or utensils, and getting everything on the table for this odd dinner together. *I won't miss this tiny kitchen*, Sara thought. *I need to look for a new place.*

She plopped into a chair and shook off her shoes, took a long sip of water, and sighed. With the air conditioner humming nearby, she was starting to feel human again.

Duncan sat across from her and bit into his first taco. She followed suit. Between bites, he mentioned, "It's set in Seattle, but we're filming in Canada."

"Eh?" Sara said.

Duncan looked at her blankly.

"It's a joke," Sara explained.

"Oh, right!" He turned on his thousand-watt smile again. "We'll be filming for two months, which is kind of rough timing for the lease." Duncan turned down the corners of his mouth and opened his eyes wide.

Meanwhile, Sara ate voraciously. "Great tacos," she murmured.

Besides, she needed a moment. She knew that face. It was that you-need-to-do-something-for-me, I'm-so-wonderful-that-it'll-be-your-pleasure-to-help-me-out face.

Sara didn't know where he got this sense of self-importance, but it was like he'd majored in it in school.

"Thanks, Sara. Listen, I need to leave it to you to handle the rent while I'm gone."

She dropped her taco and chewed, scrunching the space between her eyes in a way that would give her wrinkles sooner rather than later according to her aesthetician. Staring at him, she swallowed hard and said, "Rent's two thousand a month."

There was that charming smile again. "I'll be away," he continued.

"Paypal," she responded, wiping her mouth with a disposable napkin. "Number Goddess Sara at Gmail dot com."

"And I won't be back until the holidays."

"Wait, that's beyond our lease. What's your game, buddy?" It needed to be said aloud.

He shrugged and aimed what she knew to be a fake grin her way. He was an actor and she knew him. Knew who he really was, probably too well. And, judging by the direction of this conversation, not for much longer.

"I just need a chance to catch up on some bills," he said in a let-me-explain-this-because-I-see-the-big-picture-and-you-don't tone. "You've had it so easy. Your contract's lasted–what?–a year? And here I've been struggling."

Indeed. Struggling at the gym to do more reps maybe.

"It's your responsibility to pay your bills," Sara said in a snarky tone that matched his. "What I earn has nothing to do with what you owe or what you're responsible for."

Sara's dinner curdled in her stomach like sour milk. There really was no such thing as a free lunch. No such thing as a free dinner, too, not from Duncan McAllister, actor and professional leech.

"Can you really be so selfish that you can't take care of things while I'm gone?" he demanded, tapping his fist on the tabletop. "Would you really leave me hanging like this?"

"You think I'd leave you hanging?" Sara yelled. "After you tell me you're leaving town for a few months, and you're just going to leave paying the rent to me?"

"I didn't say I wouldn't pay it eventually," Duncan snapped. "I just need some time to get caught up. I thought, because your job is so secure, that you could take the reins for a while. It takes a while for my paychecks to start."

"My situation isn't that secure," Sara began.

Duncan rolled his eyes and murmured, "Pobrecita."

That really pissed her off. "No, I'm serious. Funding gets cut and I go. I've been there a year and I'm not permanent. What does that tell you? I'm disposable."

"Sara, you make good money." He pointed at her across the table.

She shook her head. "That's irrelevant. That's what I need to float from one job to the next. Just like you. Only it takes me a lot longer to find a new one." She considered her urge to hurl bowls of taco cheese and sour cream at Duncan's head and realized she was being childish. Then again, so was he.

He jumped up from the table, grabbed his keys, and opened the front door. "We're not done talking about this," he yelled. "I'm sure, sometime when you're more reasonable, that we can figure it out."

She glared at him until he walked out the door and slammed it shut.

OCTOBER

Sara took to wearing sheath dresses—they hid her weight gain the best—under coordinating cardigan sweaters as the weather moved from sultry summer back down to the double-digits. Footwear ranged from sensible plain flats to bright pumps, depending on how much confidence she thought she needed when dressing for the day. Her swipe cards hung from a purple rhinestone lanyard, and she made an effort to wear coordinating jewelry with each outfit. She wanted to look sharp at work, no matter what.

It was best not to bring problems from outside into the office. Sara kept all office talk to recipes, outings, and travel plans for the upcoming holidays. There was no sense in being a Debbie Downer. In fact, given the vibe at 'home,' work felt like an oasis of calm.

"I'm a little afraid to try that pumpkin cookie recipe you gave me," Miranda, the woman in the cube near Sara's, said after they exchanged morning greetings. "Afraid I'm going to eat them all!"

"What a coincidence. I'm afraid that it's going to be a while before I can work off last year's cookies," Sara quipped. "So I'm kinda afraid to start baking. It's still warm outside. Doesn't seem right somehow."

"Now you're talking," Miranda said. "I'll buy that excuse till I'm at the grocery store again and thinking about what I want to get."

"Thank God my shoe size never changes," Sara mumbled as she put her laptop into the dock, booted it up, and reviewed documents over the two-monitor spread. She had chosen red pumps for the day, worn with a black sheath and thin white cardigan.

"But you're fit," Miranda said.

Not as fit as I was, Sara thought. She clicked on the calendar function in Outlook and saw the grid of her day ahead, with appointments blocked off and notes to herself about preparation. It seemed like everything to do with project management was trying to hold onto eighty-seven threads at once without letting any of them get tangled.

At least seeing those organized chunks of time soothed her analytical mind.

Analytical. That word rang a bell. About a week before she broke up with Duncan, he'd confessed to his mother in Spanish that she, Sara, was too analytical. She wasn't creative like him, and he didn't think she'd ever understand him.

They were together, sitting in the same room, when this conversation took place. Little did he know she understood Spanish. Though she felt her chest flush, she kept her face still as his sister talked to her about her job. Sara and Duncan's sister pretended to ignore the conversation between mother and son as Mama patted Sonny Boy's hand and said what a shame, because he was such a genius.

Sara cleared her throat, shook her head, and looked around herself at the rows of cubicles. There was no need to reminisce about that doomed relationship. Rather, it was time to make the revisions to the Business Continuity Plan that the round-table discussion had revealed, though it seemed that this company allowed the people who bothered to attend the meetings to set policy; it was never clear what the organization did or didn't do to follow up. But no matter, this BCP was on a deadline and who was she to question what they said?

Next came the meeting for deploying a new antivirus software. The first attempt had shut down various functions throughout IT, and the vendor still didn't have an explanation as to why. Maybe the second deployment would go smoother? There was no telling, though she'd bet it would wreak the same type of havoc again.

William, the IT guru who sat catty-corner from her, walked in with his motorcycle helmet under his arm. He fit the tall, dark, and handsome stereotype given to California guys. Sara didn't lust after him, but rather enjoyed the view.

He greeted everyone in the area. Sara smiled at him and looked back at the document on her screen. She tapped at keys to include the updated information in the BCP, then sighed and hit save when an Outlook reminder popped up at a quarter-hour before her first meeting of the day.

As she gathered materials from her desk, she overheard William's conversation with Carlos, the programmer who sat next to him.

"You rode your bike on the Five? Here?" William asked.

"Yeah, man. It was pretty sketchy." Carlos was quiet.

"Man, you shouldn't be out there on a bike during rush hour." William sighed. "The way I see it, you've got a second chance at life now, son. Make the best of it."

Carlos choked out a laugh and said, "Yeah, I'm not doing that again."

Sara laughed as she pulled her laptop off the dock, smiled at the guys, and walked to the meeting room.

That was one thing she'd had to get used to after moving to California. You didn't call the interstate I-5, like you called the main interstates back east I-75 or I-95. Instead, the roads were "The Two," "The Five," "The Ten," "The One-eighteen," and so on. It sounded ridiculous at first, but eventually she was able to say it with a straight face and put the thought of Saturday Night Live's mock soap opera, *The Californians*, out of her mind.

The meeting room consisted of a big screen on one wall, whiteboards on another; its door and other 'walls' were translucent sage green. Sara snapped on a light and noticed that the whiteboard was covered with writing from a previous meeting. A quick glance around the room told her that there were no erasers nearby.

"How 'bout working *that* into the budget?" she said aloud, to no one, then pulled out a zipper bag containing an eraser and dry-erase markers (because most rooms didn't have them supplied) and scrubbed the whiteboard clean. "I bet that's the only thing we finish today," she muttered.

By ten o'clock, no one had arrived. Typical. Her East Coast training had fallen so far by the wayside that it was now out of sight. Meetings happened whenever people wandered in. That was the first of many things she learned about working in California.

Though she made her best effort never to browse on her cell phone during meetings, she picked up her phone and looked at the message that caused a green light to blink.

Ah. The apartment-finding app she'd installed sent her a message about a nice studio apartment in Silver Lake for $1,600 per month.

Maybe I should live in an RV, she thought, then shook her head. How were apartments in town so expensive? And who the hell could afford them? Trust fund babies? Computer engineers?

She could rent a room; that would mean paying $700 or so per month instead of $1,500. Because she had time, she tapped out a quick email to someone on Craigslist offering a room up by JPL, NASA's Jet Propulsion Laboratory:

Employed professional in need of a room November 1. Quiet, no pets, and not very many possessions. I am a contractor and unsure of the length of my current employment. Contact me via email if I am considered. Thanks for your time.

Joachim, a business analyst, poked his head in the door and greeted Sara, who snapped back into business mode, hooked up her laptop to project onto the big screen, and led the meeting. Others who trickled in were brought up-to-speed thereafter.

The day turned into a blur of remote meetings attended by screen and headset, and in-person meetings in which one person clamored for more time to get something done, or shrugged about some task that should have already been completed; another colleague checked his phone obsessively and jumped up to report to the CEO's office; and many rabbit holes were explored. Sara's eyelid twitched by 1:30 P.M., when she realized that she hadn't eaten lunch, so she pulled a Think Thin bar out of her purse and enjoyed the few bites full of peanut butter and chocolate.

It's funny how eating these makes me think about being thin rather than being thin. I've really got to look at the label one of these days.

She was guzzling some water from her aluminum water bottle when her boss, Mario, passed her desk. He was a large man, what clothing stores would call 'big and tall,' who'd played college football for UCLA. Mario was known more for his exploits on the field than his managerial prowess.

"Sara, I haven't had time to send a meeting request. Can I see you at two o'clock, my office?" His deep voice boomed throughout the cube-filled area.

Sara nodded. "What do I need to bring?" she asked.

Mario gave her a half-smile. "Just yourself."

Perhaps another software deployment was wreaking havoc on various systems. Mario seemed tired. Either that or upset.

Sara brushed the crumbs from her lap and took in the expanse of papers on her desk. Perhaps she could leave the office after her meeting with Mario and get all the little tasks that nagged at her done in the privacy of her own place. Shit, anywhere else would be less chaotic than that cubicle farm, where people either yelled into their desk phones or put their damn phones on speaker to attend remote meetings.

Her grey attaché bag was the perfect dumping ground for all the papers on her desktop. She clipped the stray papers to a clipboard, slid it in, and added her laptop beside it.

"Time to leave work and get the real work done," she muttered as she walked to Mario's office, slid open the translucent sage-green glass door, and sat in the chair across from him.

It was a small office, closet-like, with whiteboards littering the two real walls that had notes scrawled on them referring to deployments, projects, and potential vendors. Wood-grain cupboards hovered over his work area, and UCLA memorabilia cluttered the wall and desk.

Mario hung up his phone and folded his hands together. "Sara," he began, then looked down. "As you know, we employ contractors to keep our finances flexible. I fought for you, I really did, but unfortunately we have to end your contract."

"Oh. My," Sara said as she brought her right hand to her heart. Though a gale force wind had just blown through her solar plexus, she sat still and pursed her lips. She had to appear calm, no matter what. There had been that contractor, Elena, who cried in a conference room for a couple hours after she found out that her contract was ending. Sara vowed that she'd never be that person; she wouldn't make a scene or cry or get upset if or when they let her go. This was business, not personal. She'd been hired to work on a contractual basis and she'd fulfilled the duties related to the contract. Never mind that this place had kept her on staff for a year past her official contract's end and asked her to name a salary a month before because it seemed she was so instrumental to their success.

I'm out of shape and stressed out, working my ass off trying to prove myself, and this is my reward? Seriously? This is happening again?

Her stomach felt sour. Sara wondered if she would be nauseous.

Mario looked at her, then blinked.

She needed to engage with him and find out more.

"Was there anything I could have done?" she asked. "Why did you ask me to name a salary before?"

Mario shifted in his chair. "Everyone's pleased with your work. We've really benefited from having you here. It's just—" Mario's hands went up into the air, and he sighed as he brought them back to his desk. "We're over budget with payroll, and upper management won't approve any more permanent employees. In fact," Mario said, lowering his voice, "most if not all contracts will end before December. CEO's orders."

Sara sighed. Being dismissed had been inevitable. She'd become 'always the contractor, never the permanent employee' for the past six years and this routine was getting very, very old.

Maybe she should've left L.A. when the first job didn't work out, but at the time that seemed like she wasn't giving her new West Coast life a chance… and though she had posted for many permanent jobs since then, she only received calls from headhunters with contract work.

She took a deep breath and stared at Mario. "When will the contract end?"

"We can keep you on until the week before Thanksgiving. After that, the higher-ups have pulled the plug."

Never mind that the contract would take her just three weeks into living somewhere new, and she couldn't afford to give up those weeks, those hours. She needed every bit of money she could get her hands on. Her thoughts strayed again. The phone always rang in January, but what about the six weeks in between her last workday and New Year's?

Sara nodded. "Okay. Let's meet and talk about what needs to be done between now and then. How about Monday at our weekly meeting?" She couldn't force a smile, but she did manage to make her voice sound normal.

Mario smiled and visibly relaxed. "Sounds good, Sara. You'll stay on until the end?"

She pursed her lips together, closed her eyes, and nodded. Then, she stood and moved through the office as if on auto-pilot, wishing colleagues a good evening, laughing at their assessments of traffic on the main roads, and walking to her car.

It had become a windows-down kind of day. Sara invited the breeze to blow stress and uncertainty off her shoulders. She took deep breath after deep breath as she drove down the back streets. The rare clouds in the sky blocked the sun from patches of the San Gabriel mountains as dusk crept closer.

She didn't go straight home. Instead, she found a parking spot near a frequent haunt of hers and texted her friend Robin, whom she knew from two or three jobs back. Their similarities were striking: the same haircut (classic bobs); nearly identical career paths; and a love for what used to be called alternative music. A bond had formed that allowed them to stay in touch once their work paths diverged.

But Robin, who was a California native, had a reasonable mortgage on a small house she'd bought nearly twenty years prior. Robin also had a husband. And so, while they could empathize a great deal about their professional lives, their personal and financial lives were miles apart.

Sara pulled on the bar's heavy wooden door and walked into the main area. A bartender stood behind the L-shaped counter polishing glasses and joking with a couple who sat at the bar.

Sara joined them and ordered a bottle of their finest sparkling water.

"Nothing harder?" the bartender asked.

"I'm waiting for a friend. We'll see," Sara said.

Robin appeared not much later, and they each ordered a glass of Chardonnay. They moved to a booth in the corner to speak privately.

After plopping down onto the vinyl and shrugging out of her olive-drab jacket, Robin looked over at Sara, tapped her hands on the glossy wooden table, and asked, "What gives?"

"Week before Thanksgiving, I'm out," Sara replied.

"Damn. Damn, damn, damn," Robin added, hitting her hands on the table with each 'damn.' "You were so close to getting off the merry-go-round of contracts. Weren't you?"

"Yeah, I thought."

"Are you upset?" she asked.

It was a fair question.

Did Sara want to do her current job indefinitely? No, she didn't.

How did she feel about this, then?

"Okay, confession time. I'm relieved, even though it's kind of like being dumped."

"Is that all?" Robin laughed and raised her glass. "Every time I see you, you're stressed out, telling me how much work you have and how so many things get in the way of what's supposed to be done and all the chaos of working there." She touched her glass to Sara's and said, "They had to let you go. You weren't going to leave otherwise. Though let's have a moment of silence for those sweet, sweet benefits you didn't get."

Sara sipped her wine and smiled. "You're damn right. I wouldn't have left, offer or no. It's the best money I've ever made."

"Yeah, but at what cost? Tell me, Sara. What do you want to do? What do you *really* want to do?"

This question couldn't be tackled easily. If what she'd trained to do for a living, and what she'd done in her career so far, only warranted three to twelve-month contracts anymore, then her career focus needed to change entirely.

Next, she had to consider staying or heading back east. Her brain worked like a database as it sifted information and feelings. West Coast equaled big dollars (earned and spent), freedom, anonymity in the big city, a feeling of endless options and opportunity. East Coast equaled better stability, fewer dollars (earned and spent), familiarity, connections, and a heightened sense of deadlines, rules, and decorum. Both offered friends, fantastic staycation opportunities, and great food… but she could only live and work in one place at a time.

After taking a gulp of wine, Sara set her glass down. She decided to be vague in her response because she didn't want to broach the topic of 'maybe I should move back east' with her California friend. "Honestly? I want to get in shape, but that has nothing to do with work."

"So what? You'll have plenty of time. Take December off. Something new will come in the new year. Work out. Get outside. Enjoy! But think about what you want out of your work, next time."

Sara shook her head. Was it worth asking for something she didn't think she could get?

"I want balance. Enjoying what I do at work, and having a life outside of it. And just once, I want to hear back from places where I can dig in and stay, where I can set goals and aim higher and feel like I have some control. I'm tired of this bullshit."

"Yeah. Me too. What about money? Are you okay?"

"Not sure of where I'll be November first or what the next place will cost. Short answer is I don't know. But not in dire straits. Haven't had much time to spend money this year."

"My place is tiny. I wish I could help," Robin said.

"Don't worry about me. I've made it through other changes before. I can make it through this one."

"Haven't you though. So what's the story with Monkey Man?"

Monkey Man was the nickname Sara gave Duncan after he grew a goatee. He hadn't figured out yet that it wasn't his best look, and she wasn't about to tell him.

"Still leaving his goatee clippings all over the bathroom sink," Sara said, and laughed.

"Is he still trying to get you to store his stuff for him in your unit?"

Sara sighed. "*Trying* being the operative word. He needs to find some new unsuspecting woman to shack up with. That seems to be his new project."

Robin's face fell.

"Oh, but think of all I've learned this year. I've gained so many experience points," Sara added.

"Did he bail on the rent?" she asked.

"No. We paid the last month's rent when we moved in. I forgot about that. Now, what happens to our bills, which are in my name, and the cleaning deposit remains to be seen. No matter what, though, it's money well spent. I've already kissed it goodbye. Hence my big stupid smile." Sara clenched her teeth together in an ugly expression, and Robin laughed.

"To next year," Robin said, raising her glass to Sara's.

Sara responded in kind and touched her glass to Robin's. "To next year!"

They finished the wine and walked a block to have dinner at Chipotle, then went their separate ways.

In the hopes of earning a good reference from Mario, Sara threw herself back into work and noticed that her eyelid twitched more, not less, in response to this final deadline.

One week before the move-out date, Sara came home to a nearly-empty apartment. He'd been vague, and she knew he'd disappear sometime, but he didn't provide any warning. Duncan was gone along with most of the furniture. Her shelves remained, covered with her things. There was no table to work from anymore, no couch for watching TV, but her TV remained on the floor next to the computer modem.

"Thank you, God," Sara said aloud as she noticed the blinking lights on the modem. He'd probably laughed at the thought of leaving it behind and sticking her with the whole internet bill, not realizing that she needed it for more than 'networking,' as he called it.

A glance into the kitchen told her that all the dishes were left behind, and therefore hers to pack and move—or give away. This made sense, as Duncan was a mama's boy and dishes were 'women's work.' He'd probably forgotten they were there.

That wasn't so bad. Maybe she would have time over the holidays to learn how to cook in that cast iron skillet he'd used to make taco dinners.

NOVEMBER

DUNCAN HAD ALWAYS said that things fell into place, and she wanted to believe this would apply to her own life too. Regardless, Sara was surprised when she didn't end up in a motel.

When Brian, the welder/Uber driver from Altadena, answered her inquiry to rent a room a few weeks prior, he had asked her one question before meeting her: *Can you commit to staying at least two months?* She quickly agreed. That would take her through New Year's Eve.

She teared up when she first saw the room. It had a big closet, a plain queen-sized bed (no more sleeping on an inflatable mattress!), and a boxy wooden dresser. There was also a TV in the corner of the room, which Brian said could go if she didn't want it. She said, "No, let me keep it. I'll use it." Hers could stay in storage for the time being.

There was far more to think about than cookie recipes as the holidays drew nearer, but Sara tried to keep everything light at work. When it came time to say goodbye to her co-workers, she did her best to talk with them, enjoy the vignettes they told, and accept the praise and good wishes for her future. She realized, as she handed Mario her badge and company-issued laptop, that she was starting to forget everything already: passwords, programs, apps, details of the job, names of her colleagues, everything. It was as if unnecessary info had to be purged from her memory in order for her to figure out her next steps.

She passed by a sea of faces on the way out.

So many Jennifers, Julies, Carolyns, Christophers, Mikes, and Craigs. Just like at the last job, and the one before that. Everything changes too often anymore. Commute, location, agency, colleagues, tasks. Everything.

She came home from her last day on the job, poured a glass of wine, lay back on the bed, and stared at the ceiling. After an Epsom Salt soak, Sara began to manage her next project: herself. It didn't offer typical compensation, though it would be a satisfying and extremely important endeavor.

Project Sara required things to be assigned to manageable categories. All her past positions and choices and future goals were pieces of a puzzle. What would that puzzle look like when it was finished? What was Sara's Big

Picture? What steps could she take to bring her closer to the life she'd envisioned when she left Tampa for L.A., lured by a better opportunity than the one she'd left behind?

Back then, Sara had envisioned a blossoming career, a cute house in Rossmoyne, a dog… and let's face it, a husband and maybe a baby.

Her first job in L.A. became less secure when the firm was bought out, and she pushed herself to find new work before the layoffs hit. Thus, the carousel of contracts began.

The man situation turned out to be nothing to write home about, and she couldn't manage a dog with her work hours, so at age thirty-seven, she still didn't have a dog.

Put that in my Big Picture, Sara thought. *A life stable enough to include a dog.*

Sara exercised daily to gain strength and to stop her runaway thoughts. Her feet pounded pavement through the leafy neighborhood lined with pine trees; around the track at the nearby recreation center; and on the paths that went into the San Gabriels, where from one direction all you could see was wilderness, but if you turned around, you could see downtown L.A.

Cassandra called and texted Sara frequently after Sara confessed that she'd been let go, but Sara wasn't sure what to say to her friend about her invitation to move back to Tampa.

"I'm pretty paranoid," Sara confessed over the phone to Cassandra as she walked through a leafy, shaded park. "Would people see me as a failure? Like I couldn't make it in the big city?"

"That's ridiculous," Cassandra said. "Fact is, times have changed. It's hard to get permanent full-time work anymore. You rock at your job no matter what."

"Thanks. But how will I know what to do next?" Sara asked.

"You live in L.A. Don't you have a guru you can ask?"

"Ha ha, very funny."

"Have you tried meditating?"

"What's that? Medicating?" Sara laughed.

"Well if you had a guru, she would probably tell you to stay in L.A. because it's, like, totally awesome," Cassandra said in a 1980s Valley Girl accent.

"Right. Robin would want me to stay, because it is! And she complains about her friends moving away so they can buy houses and stuff."

There was a pause as Sara reached a split in the path where she had to choose a direction. One was bumpier, and one smoother and less shaded. She chose the sunnier path.

"Of course, I'll have to dodge stoned drivers if I stay," Sara said.

"Hardly an issue overall. They're mostly on Xanax out here," Cassandra said.

"And housing is tough. I can't imagine I could ever buy a house here."

"That's true a lot of places, though. I couldn't afford my house at what it's worth now."

"And what about my love life? Future dating options?"

"Nothing to brag about here, amiga," Cassandra said. "But I don't know about there."

"There's so much to think about."

"You were always so good at making lists."

Sara thought for a moment, and a glimpse of the parking lot came into view. She could keep walking and talking, or hang up with her friend and head over to the car. She chose to wind down the conversation.

"Look for the signs. Reach for the stars! Keep a dream journal!" Cassandra teased.

"*You* keep a dream journal." Sara laughed.

Sara walked across the grass dappled with light that filtered through the trees and took in the scene. People played with dogs inside the gated dog park nearby. She found a bench where she sat and emptied the dust from her sneakers, then put them back on.

The choice at the split in the path had been an easy one, but that decision only affected her daily fitness walk. Major life decisions carried more weight than that.

Later that afternoon, after showering off the dust and sweat, Sara brewed a cup of tea, walked to the back porch of her rental, and sat on a lawn chair. She could hear the trill of nearby hummingbirds and see an occasional flash of shiny red feathers. Though the sun was setting, feathery clouds were visible in the darkening sky.

Clearing her mind wasn't possible, so she tried imagining being in a Tampa backyard instead. How would she feel if she were there? She remembered the cawing of blue jays and the distant clanging of wind chimes, then remembered (and smiled) at the memory of the local supermarket, Publix, giving out football schedules at the cash register. She and her nerd friends used this information to know when to avoid traffic near the stadium, but she suspected most people used it for more obvious reasons, such as planning barbecues.

The way the air felt was different there, too. Come summer, there would be flashes of lightning in the sky and thundershowers. She laughed out loud as she thought, *Good news is, I still know how to drive in the rain.*

Cassandra's most recent text had read:

I'm postponing the next game night until January. Too many obligations between now and new year's. Want to come?

Then she'd added an emoji of a happy face with nerd glasses.

Do I want to come? I'd have to say goodbye to Robin, which would be no small matter. We would probably just be email friends after that. But do I want to try something different? New year, new everything? Dear God, yes!

It was time to trade earthquakes for hurricanes, to take a chance on where she used to live and learn how it had evolved since she was part of its work and social ecosystems years before.

Sara lost herself in a daydream of being welcomed back into the East Coast fold while she sipped her tea and the sun set.

When it was dark, she roused herself from her reverie, walked to her room, and pulled out a notebook and pen… because it was time to make a new list.

SALT IN THE HELL MOUTH

Cody Sisco

FAIR WARNING: it's never a good time when the Hell Mouth opens.

I've seen it happen so many times. I've heard the gut-wrenching rumble. From Redondo to Pomona, Anaheim to Ventura, once in Bakersfield—I won't be going there again—and more times than I can count within the L.A. grid-and-noodle streetscape, darkness explodes and blots out the sun.

I try to be there when the mouth opens. We have "demonic detectors" in every neighborhood—our network has the best coverage—giving me one to two hour's notice. Sometimes it's not enough. L.A. traffic is the worst.

This morning my brain is de-fogging slowly. Events from last night replay in my mind, nightmare visions of blood and gore, the tang of smoke and sharp knives. Sobs. In my line of work, you'd think the screams would get to you. Nope. It's the sobs that give me shivers and make me want to crawl into a hole and plug my ears.

My little clay gargoyle starts mewling. I pick it up and the voice on the other end—I've giving up trying to picture what a call center on the "otherside" looks like—tells me we have a situation. It doesn't matter how foggy slow I am, I have to get in gear.

The rideshare car picks me up ten minutes later.

Yes, I rideshare. It's not that I'm a fan of the gig economy. I get "rewarded" per demon vanquished so I understand the stress of the hustle. But my "rewards" are spiritual-redemptive so there's no way I can afford a car payment.

You might think a demon hunter would have a magical teleportation device or at least a fancy helicopter that could reach the scene fast. Well, this isn't a Hollywood movie and I've never had anyone offer me a gazillion dollars. My progressive friends are like, you should write a grant proposal. They start talking about 501c somethings, which I now know are *not* a type of jeans, and they seem to miss the point that since there's no legal recognition for what I do, anything contract, finance, or government-related is a no go. Besides, you don't want a bureaucracy involved in demon hunting. It would get... messy. Demons infest bureaucracies for lunch and eat them as dinner. What do you think happened in the 40s?

Never forget, they said.

And then what happened? Cambodia. Rwanda. Srebrenica.

You've heard of these places. You think you know what happened. Some innocent bystander bullshit, or a clash of nations narrative, or some other dogma. You want to know what really happened? I'll tell you, but you won't remember—it's the Hell Mouth. It makes us forget. That's what makes *me* special. I remember. When everyone else, or nearly everyone, has a demonic encounter, which can range from steamy to unseemly to sadistic, they always forget. It's like a veil draws down and their memories—poof!—they disappear. Even if you've had your fifth encounter, you don't know how to deal because it's your first time, again and again. The scars add up.

Luckily, most people never pop their demon cherries. Nor do they rideshare with a chatty driver all the while worrying that they're too late, that hell is literally spilling over, and they are the only ones who can stop it.

This isn't me feeling sorry for myself. This is me explaining what it's like so you're prepared. Remember.

My rideshare stops in one of those neighborhoods where people live their entire lives hustling to make a living and probably never see their account reach a thousand-dollar balance. These are my people. When I get "rewarded," this is where I go, to spread the "rewards" around, to prevent the Hell Mouth from opening in a place like this.

Today it's already too late.

Getting out of the car, I'm hit by a wave of dry heat. The air feels both hollow and filled with something like static electricity but a thousand times more powerful. My ears ring with a high pitch like the last unending death cry of a tortured angel. I smell blood and rot. The Hell Mouth is ripe.

None of these sensations are real in a measurable way, but they are real for me. Cosmologists take for granted that every place in the universe obeys the same natural laws, that time—as measured by the distance light travels in a vacuum—moves constantly forward, and that mass and energy are equivalent and interchangeable.

So. Much. Horseshit.

I long ago made peace with the illusion that I'm a three-dimensional animal imbued with consciousness by virtue of the density of the brain tissue in my cranium. Whatever we are—holographic intersections of higher dimensional forces, simulations in a cosmic multiversal computer, a dream reflected in the cornea of a goddess sleeping with one eye open—we're not aware of what we are. My greatest fear is that when any one person, or alien, hits on the truth, the whole thing will collapse like a house of cards upset by a fretful toddler. There's a theory of inflationary instability that says the laws of the universe could fluctuate, anywhere, for the briefest of moments, and that change, which is incompatible with our reality, could spread instantaneously and bring about the end of everything. What if that instability originates in a Hell Mouth—a spiritual black hole here on Earth? If it was going to happen somewhere...

My ears are burning. A thing is here that doesn't belong. Demonic emanations don't coexist well with our normal lives. That's why my senses are going bonkers. Some people feel it; some people choose not to. Most just don't remember. Remember.

The street is blocked off at the intersection. Police cars are parked across the road at angles that announce something bad is going down. Their lights flash meekly under the bright morning sun.

Cops can't do shit about what's wrong here.

I'm sweating. There's no cool marine layer. 100 degrees might not be the high today; we might go higher to infinity, to inferno. I feel bad for them in their uniforms for a second, and then I'm reminded that I'm too late and yet I still need to hurry. As usual, all I can do is damage control.

When you're a curanderx, you see things quickly and clearly. You've had years of seeing layers of gender painted on peoples' bodies through clothing, mannerisms, and makeup. You've had years of practice looking past all that to the heart of truth. You see the truth because you don't take it for granted.

I see that here, today, someone has died horribly. The house at the center of the commotion flares magenta in my vision. Problem is, the infection has already spread. There are two police officers interviewing a woman on the sidewalk who sobs between her answers. One cop nods, listening. I can see on his face that he's trying to keep it together, but this crime, this time, there's something that bothers him, he's seen too much, or too many of these scenes, and her pain is his pain and he's doing his duty, but fuck if this might not be the last straw. He's human. I don't worry about him.

His partner is possessed.

Infected. Compromised. Whatever you want to call it. His face isn't shocked-slack; it's frozen. His gaze moves from person to person, he keeps an eye on the scene, he asks the right questions. But something has taken hold of him and will only get stronger. I wish I could exorcise whatever has him, but that's not how all this works. I meant it when I said I was too late. There's nothing I can do for him.

I move deeper into the scene. There might be someone here I can help.

Sidebar: you probably want an explanation. What's a curanderx? Who the hell am I? What am I doing here?

Short answer: I'm a healer.

Long answer: the day I was born my parents took a look at my genitals and decided they had a girl. They were wrong. I'm not a being that fits into any box that's already been devised. Binary sex assignment and fixed gender identity are as much overused and abused vestiges of patriarchal legacy kingdoms as the House of Lords, colonial racism—whose wombs matter?—and bride prices still being paid in backwaters of global progress toward gender enlightenment. I can do whatever I want with my genitals using what biology, my imagination, and a consenting partner allow, and it's none of anyone's business. In the meantime, I call myself a curanderx to anyone with an open mind, and everyone else can call me by my chosen name: Salt.

I am the salt crusting the tears of the survivors. I am the salt that returns to the earth within the bodies of the fallen. I am the salt that turns demon blood to stone.

Caution tape, a waxy sulfur yellow like the blood of demons I've not yet petrified, blocks my way. There's a man *in extremis*—I think perhaps he's a friend of the family—chasing away onlookers, yelling in a strained voice that crackles. He's seen the body of the victim, I think, and it's breaking him, the imprint of it.

Neighbors who have wandered over to see what's going on catch his eye. He lopes toward them, eyes bulging, spit flying; he'll turn himself inside out screaming, "You want to watch this shit! You want to watch!?" The neighbors turn away, slink back to their houses. He spots me, eyes widening, for I've ducked under the tape, and he comes at me.

I hold up a hand and whisper when he's close, "I'm here to help."

No magic words. No silly conjuring gestures. Just the truth.

Magic is a question of spirit, of making the world take note and respond. It's about being receptive and therefore received. The spirit travels in sound and voice. I can see that he's heard me because his coiled, angry, desperate tension eases. His shoulders slacken. His rage doesn't dissipate, instead it's eclipsed by a deep indigo mix of despair and hope, twin sentiments: the classics. These I can work with.

"Can you take me to the door?" I ask. "You don't have to go any further. I want to help."

It's funny how I know things without knowing. Sometimes I say just the right thing without thinking about it. And it's always something lame, never brilliant. It's just *right*.

The specific history of trauma is etched on his face: he wishes someone had been with him, had walked him to the door, had been next to him when he went inside to see whatever was there, had taken his hand at that moment.

He wishes he hadn't been alone. In all the panic and chaos, he realizes, right now, that he's not alone anymore. I'm here.

He takes my hand gratefully, and I see in his gait and gaze a little boy, his spirit scared and sad, the child inside all of us who most times stays nurtured in the mature over-growth of our experience, except all that has been ripped away. That's what demons do—they tear at our self-con-ception, they eat our confidence for breakfast, trample our ideas of a moral universe, and suckle on disillusionment.

Demons have been busy these last few hundred years. They migrated to L.A. along with its colonizers, displac-ing the local demons who previously only had hunger, plague, fury, and jealousy to work with, and a limited flock to tend. Now their ambitions are boundless. Disillusion-ment. Self-deception. Spiritual vapidity. They can't open their mouths wide enough to feast on our frailties.

They need us to think we're weak. That's why I can't take a day off. I can't not make the trip when the gargoyle cries out and the "otherside" issues my marching orders. That's why I'm holding this man's hand, a stranger, and why he's comforted. Because we are strong. And I'm going to close the fucking Hell Mouth today. No question about it.

We approach the front door. Back on the dust-streaked sidewalk, the woman being interviewed by the police of-ficers watches me like she knows me and her head nods a little. The policeman with the heart gives me a half-smile. The demon-haunted policeman stares blankly.

A tremor of fear and doubt climbs my spine. The neighbor-man stays on the threshold as I go inside. He can't see again what he's already seen without breaking.

The hallway is carpeted. Two open doors lead to bed-rooms. Pictures crowd the walls. School portraits.

Photographs of the dead, when I look at them, appear as high-contrast, pixelated distortions—brightest sun and moonless night. A girl with braids and ribbons, smooth shiny skin, wide oval eyes displaying wisdom and wry humor. She could be the next Oprah, I think. Other school portraits show a young boy with a goofy grin and thick glasses. He would grow up to be a charming nerd, my type of guy, someone who can play basketball one day and then do karaoke in drag the next. The contrast and grain on these photos have been cranked up to heaven. Two victims, then.

I wipe tears from my cheeks. This family deserved more than what it got. Years of dreams cut short scream at me—there will be no more pictures to add to this crowded tableau.

The hallway opens to a living room and, beyond, a bar with two stools, a kitchen. The living room is where it happened. Crime scene photographers are busy, stepping gingerly around two figures wrapped in white on the floor. The mother is in the kitchen. She put the white tablecloth over the bodies, reaching for ritual comfort.

There's a war inside her. The Hell Mouth opened beneath her and tried to swallow her whole. She is in the process of being devoured. I can see her fighting back. She knows how to be strong. She knows what it is to never give up. But this is too much, isn't it? A life of fighting real-world demons doesn't prepare you for the otherworldly. What do you do when "stay strong" and "keep living your life" don't work anymore? When everything has been so cruelly taken?

I move a chair to sit and face her. A grief counselor has been talking to her, ineffectually, because she cannot hear. She's inside the mouth and is only aware of the hot rush of foul air enveloping her. I take her hands, which feel cool to the touch. Good. I begin talking, telling her about the Hell Mouth, in words she can understand. The counselor leans in and listens as avidly as an overachiever on the first day of classes. I tell the mother that she doesn't have the luxury of forgetting. She'll remember. Like I do. Someday she'll be doing this work. Like I do. Because we cannot forget.

The oppressively loud silence that wraps her like a smothering blanket begins to unravel. With each blink of her eyes, she comes out of her shock, slowly, uncertainly. For a brief, sublime instant, she forgets what's happened, listening to the shouts outside.

I realize with a heart-thumping gestalt, hearing chaos gyring from the depths, that we're in far deeper trouble than I imagined.

The front door bangs open down the hall behind me. I hear heavy footsteps, rise to my feet, and turn. The possessed policeman is coming toward me, eyes like congealed blood focused on me. He knows what I am.

"You shouldn't be here," he says.

The woman is gaping, her eyes squinting because she sees half the truth and it terrifies her, as it should. I put my hand on her shoulder, as much to draw strength from her as to provide reassurance. We're in this together. A circle of two, a stronger ward than one alone, I tell myself, because this has gone sideways fast and I need to believe I'm prepared for it.

When a demon takes over, all the faculties and knowledge of the host are still there, subsumed in a hateful miasma, available as slings and arrows in their arsenal. Demonic possession is like a cosmic magnifying glass, polarized to amplify only the worst attributes. Paranoia, malice, envy, and nihilism crowd out mercy and love. The result is a being so twisted and foul that most people can't truly see it. They see someone having a bad day. They say, "Oh, she's a real piece of work," or, "He must have been provoked." The excuses flow because we don't want to believe the monster is already inside the house.

"Come with me," the policeman says. His fingers lightly stroke the butt of his handgun.

Full disclosure: I've never taken a self-defense class. I don't have fancy killer instincts like Buffy the goddamn vampire slayer, whom I would phone in a heartbeat if she would come running.

I am vulnerable. Big Man with the gun probably has a dozen ways to take me out and there's nothing I can do with my slender body to stop him. I've got one trick up my sleeve and I can't use it yet.

"She's a friend," the woman says. "She can stay." I don't correct her about my gender. Ain't nobody got time for that while the Hell Mouth gapes. Besides, I'm still, belatedly, deciding between *xe*, *they*, or my own invention.

"You're in shock," the policeman says to her. "Your children are lying on the floor in the other room with their heads bashed in and she entered the crime scene to take advantage of your state. Ma'am, look at your children."

His words have their intended effect. She looks and it's like a spell smothers her. She's not speaking up for me anymore.

"I'll go with you, voluntarily," I say. "Look, I'm cooperating." I hold up my hands and smile without parting my lips. A pressure is building slowly, so very slowly, at the back of my throat, in my chest.

He grabs me by the shoulder and hauls me roughly through the living room. As I step past the children's bodies, a tear slips from the corner of my eye. The mother's grief pours out on the floor, sweeps over their forms, and moves on. No comforted ghosts. No ethereal resonance. They are gone, gone, gone.

The policeman stops me at the end of the hall, next to a bedroom door. The angry neighbor-man comes in through the front door; he's lost to the Hell Mouth now; I didn't do enough. Like a prisoner being handed off, he grabs my arm and pulls me with him into the bedroom and shuts the door. The children's room. The policeman stands outside, a sentry.

"Renounce your connection to the otherside," the demon in the neighbor's body says. Maybe he smells it on me, an assurance that there's more to this world than pain and suffering. "You cannot fathom infinity."

This might sound like gibberish, but it's not. Human languages aren't suited to expressing extra-dimensional imperatives. Some concepts don't translate. What's happening is he's trying to diminish my human self and take over, make me another soldier in his demon army. Waves of hate, revulsion, and bile batter me. I hate him, lose sight of his essential humanity, and suddenly I'm an iota less human. He disgusts me, and so I lose some of my capacity for empathy and compassion. He's winning and my truth is fading.

The details of his coercion shouldn't be shared. Some of it is psychic, some is physical. You don't want to hear it all; hearing it would change you. The highlights reel includes hair torn from my head, clothes ripped and laying on the floor, insults hurled at my naked body—and it's the insults that sting the most because demons *know* our insecurities, the things we don't tell our closest friends, our hopes, our shame. The physical abuse is bad, but I don't cry out. I know he won't kill me—they want converts, not a body count. He stops short of leaving me disabled. They're not *wasteful*.

The neighbor-demon is surprised in the first twenty minutes to still be struggling to chalk up a win. After the next hour, he's enraged but also impotent. There's nothing more he can do to me. He's run out of ideas. Demons aren't known for invention.

From my place on the floor, doubled over after a particularly brutal kick in the ribs that probably didn't break them, I see his shoes: grime covered high-tops. The black denim of his pants has long faded to a dark gray. The hem of his left pant leg is coming loose; a lone thread the color of fake gold trails behind his shoe as it impacts my shoulder with a *thwack*. He kicks me again in the face and my teeth cut across my inner cheek. I taste blood. That'll be a bruise to carry for a while.

He breathes in, swells, breathes out, is diminished. He's panting, angry, desperate. I wonder: if he thinks he can't convert me, will he decide to kill me? And how much time do I have left in this world? These disembodied thoughts are a sure sign I'm in shock. I mumble a weak prayer to an ebony-skinned goddess of compassion with eyes made of pulsars—she must exist somewhere in the multiverse as I've imagined her—to give me time and strength. I feel a little better. The light limning the window shade has dimmed. Time has gone weird in this room. We're getting closer to dusk. The Hell Mouth, as strong as it has been this day, is on borrowed time. I just need twenty real minutes, and then I've got this.

The demon drags me from the room across the carpet with my head locked in his massive arm. He smells like man-sweat, a turnon, and sulfur, a major turnoff. The sulfur thing is funny really; an alchemical nuclear reaction that consumes oxygen, hence all those mystical weirdos across history obsessing over the Philosopher's Stone, the number 666, and odd geometrical shapes. They were onto something but never really figured it out. Should have asked more women to join them, would've discovered the truth that way. I'm close to passing out.

He lifts me up in front of him, his tightening hands seal my esophagus. I can feel my lips turning blue; this isn't figurative or hyperbole or my spooky curanderx perceptions. You try getting choked and see what I mean. Blue lips, and swollen. Fuck, if I pass out, I'll be helpless, and choking like this keeps me under their power. I've got no combat skills, but I've got to do something.

The house is empty. This is good. The bodies have been removed, the survivor-mother relocated. The Hell Mouth has expanded, but its center, emptied of people to sustain it, has begun to wither.

I reach up and gently press my fingers against the demon's jaw, trying to reach the man inside. Static electricity, literally a stream of electrons, zaps him lightly. This isn't a magic trick, I just lucked out. Or maybe my otherside friends finally decided to step in. In any case, his grip loosens, I twist, slink to the floor, and look up.

"Save yourself," I say.

His eyes widen. "My god, you're hurt!" he says.

A clash of wills manifests as gelatinous thunder. His mind quivers from the strain of reasserting itself while still inhabited by a foreign force. To an outsider, it would look like he's having a seizure.

Through cracked lips and a bloody mouth, I begin to sing notes as ancient as the first animals in the ocean, perhaps older.

A low hum at first is all I can manage. A crooning. I interrupt myself to say, "I'm here with you. You can win this fight," and continue to sing.

I see a note of thanks in his eyes right before he slumps down, unconscious. My lullaby accompanies his rest.

On weak knees, I rise. In the hallway, scanning through envelopes laying undisturbed on a side table, I learn that the mother's name is Clarissa Davis. That could be helpful later. Right now this Hell Mouth needs to close. I stumble to the kitchen and fill a glass of water to soothe my throat, washing some of the mouth blood away. I'm battered, but I'm standing. I can do this.

After making my way outside, I see police cars at the curb and police tape warding off the curious. The street has reopened to traffic. I sing on the stoop for several long hours—moonrise after midnight brings me renewed strength—a continuously varying tune that sounds sad, resigned, and weak in my ears, a human-eternal hybridized song that pushes against the breach, and eventually seals it.

Now to deal with the aftermath. Otherversal and malignant soul invaders need to be expunged. I will rideshare to the police station. I know what to expect. It will be strangely quiet as officers go about their business. A nearly inaudible hum will vibrate my teeth. Some demons arrive in weakened states and wither when their hosts' emotions shift. Others are strong and crafty and know how to sustain themselves. I already know I'm dealing with the latter. I know I'll find the demon at the precinct, making a mess. What I don't know is whether I can be loud enough to drive it out.

CHROMOSOME CIRCUS

Amy Sterling Casil

Macadam's Circus had played out their week in Fontana, forty miles east of L.A., when Joshie the Clown found Little Bear. Joshie was packing up the VR headsets in the Tokyo Tank trailer when he heard whimpering. He patrolled the rows of gummy plastic chairs until he found the source: a boy in a fuzzy blue sleepsuit, huddled in the next-to-the-last seat in the back. The hood was pulled tight over the kid's head. He looked to be about four, and he stared up at Joshie with still brown eyes.

"Hey, don't be scared," Joshie said. He put on his best clown grin. The boy shrank away and tucked his chin into the suit.

Montego Bay, Macadam's hulking lead carny, came up at that moment. "Another lost kid," he said. "Better call the cops."

Joshie said, "I don't know, Monty. Look at his clothes."

The sleepsuit was smeared with yellow streaks of dried mustard. Joshie caught a whiff of sour child sweat as he loosened the knot at the boy's neck which held the hood tight. He pushed the soft fabric away from the boy's forehead to expose short, luxuriant golden fur.

"He's a freak," Montego said.

Amid the fur were two delicate pointed ears. The boy growled deep in his throat as Joshie touched the tip of his right ear.

"No point in calling the cops, is there?" Joshie put his arm around the boy and lifted him from the seat. The boy made little hooting noises as he nestled his head into Joshie's white and red striped ruff.

"Wonder if he can talk?" Montego stepped into the aisle. Montego was a normal, in the sense that his powerful chest and arms as thick as the average woman's waist were paid-for modifications, cosmetic only, as opposed to Joshie, who'd been born a clown, his nose ending in a tip the size and color of a ripe apricot. Joshie's most embarrassing disability was hidden beneath his red satin gloves: he had only three spatulate fingers and a thumb on each hand.

"Hootie-hoo! Hootie-hoo," said the boy.

"His parents must be real winners, dumping the kid here," Montego said.

Joshie shook his head. "Where else?"

Montego fingered his chin. "You got a point," he said. Then, his face darkened. "You're not thinking about keeping the kid?"

Joshie stroked the soft fur on the boy's head. The small legs tightened like a vice around his chest. "Maybe," he said. "You know what? I think he's a little bit like Gyla."

"Wrong color." Gyla was the silver wolf girl and her fur was all over her body. Montego crossed his arms and his bulging muscles tensed until it looked as though they'd leap from the skin. "Don't be stupid. Macadam will be royally pissed if you keep that kid."

The boy squirmed and Joshie got a whiff of the fur on his head. It was silky, but it smelled dark and oily, or maybe it was only the filthy smoke from the burning tires. "I know somebody who does child welfare in L.A. County. I'll call her when we get there."

Montego squinted at him. "Yeah? Well, maybe so. You'd better call her."

"Sure, Monty," Joshie said, grinning with his big red mouth. Montego cracked a smile and waved him off.

Joshie left the Tokyo Tank trailer and started across the lot, his big red shoes flapping and crunching in the pulverized blacktop. He started toward his own trailer, then paused a moment.

The boy said, "Hot! Hootie-hoo!"

"Yeah, I'll take you to see Gyla," Joshie told him. His heart skipped a beat at the thought of her, and he pushed the feeling away. Gyla could never, ever have any interest in Joshie other than friendship. He'd told himself that a million times. Gyla was beautiful, even though Gyla was, like Joshie, and like the kid, and the majority of the people of Macadam's Circus, a freak. A virally-produced genetic accident, sterile, a sport, a loser. The big man, Macadam, had scales. A fish man. Gyla had silver fur, a heart-shaped face and golden eyes.

Joshie crunched his way around the back of the trailers to Gyla's, which was pink, freshly painted, with a nice white awning over the door. The kid was getting heavy, and he was hooting loudly in Joshie's ear by the time he knocked on the door.

Gyla wore only her bright blue G-string when she answered. Joshie tried to look at the pictures on her wall and not her breasts when he came inside.

"What's this?" she asked. She was buffing her silvery fur with a soft brush, the kind they made for horses. She looked curiously at the boy, who kept his face firmly pressed into Joshie's ruff.

"I found him in the last row in the Tokyo Tanks," Joshie said. "Look at his head."

Gyla smiled and petted the boy's head lightly. "Don't be afraid, little guy," she said. She gave Joshie one of her sharp, hundred-watt smiles and his cheeks flamed under his greasepaint. "Hey, you're just like me. Want to come to Auntie Gyla?" She held out her arms, and the boy hooted harder. Joshie grimaced, because the kid was hooting right in his ear. His floppy cauliflower ears were more sensitive than average ears, and even though his rainbow wig gave some protection, it didn't make any difference when someone was making noises that loud, that close to his eardrum.

Then, the boy started to scramble against Joshie, his little feet digging like knives into Joshie's ribs. "Hey, easy," Joshie said, but the kid had already leapt away, into Gyla's arms. She grabbed him and stumbled.

"Gyla!" Joshie stepped forward, but she wasn't upset, she was laughing. She fell back on her blue velour couch with the boy, who was hooting fiercely and tugging at her silver fur, wherever he could get a handful of it.

"Yeah, you are like me, little guy." She looked up at Joshie amid her wrestling with the child. "He's pretty dirty," she said. "Need to give him a bath."

Joshie nodded and sat on the edge of Gyla's dressing chair. "That's what I came for."

Gyla deftly began to unzip the boy's sleepsuit. "You'd better calm down now," she told him. "Auntie Gyla's going to get you cleaned up." The boy squirmed, joy obvious in every movement of his small, wriggling body, and tried to bury himself in Gyla's stomach.

"Help me out Clown Boy," Gyla said. She was laughing.

Joshie got up, careful not to flap and break something with his big, ungainly feet, and held the boy around the waist as Gyla got him out of the suit. Save for his face, the child was covered completely in curly, golden fur.

"He looks like a teddy bear," Joshie said. Better than a clown, he thought. Even fish men like Macadam were better than clowns.

They got the boy into Gyla's clean, peach-colored bathroom and Joshie ran the water while Gyla poured pink bath crystals in the water. "See, it makes bubbles," she told the boy. He flapped his thin furry arms and gurgled.

Like a baby, Joshie thought. He wondered if the boy's parents had even tried to talk to him, or if they'd done as so many had done, treated the little freak kid like a pet. He seemed like an animal, but there was intelligence in his dark brown eyes. He splashed in the water, and giggled, just like a regular kid.

Gyla leaned over the tub and her perfect round, furry breasts looked so lovely that Joshie forgot to breathe for a moment. The boy splashed, and where the water hit Gyla's fur, she was dark and oily-sleek. Joshie sat on the toilet seat and bit his lip.

"Scrub his back, will you?" she asked. Joshie's hand trembled and he grimaced as he took off his glove. He didn't want Gyla to see his ugly hand. He grabbed a soft brush with a wooden handle and worked suds into the boy's fur.

Then, the boy reached over and pulled the glove from Joshie's other hand. "Clown, clown," he said.

Gyla gasped. "Hey, he can talk!"

"I guess so," Joshie said. He tucked his hand in the pocket of his striped satin pants.

Gyla's delicate face grew serious. "You're going to call someone about him, aren't you?"

Joshie shrugged, then lathered the boy's head, careful to keep the soap out of his eyes.

"He is like a little teddy bear," Joshie said. He had a sudden reverie, picturing a little white house with a picket fence, a mailbox, a revolving sprinkler in the front yard, watering a perfectly-trimmed green lawn. He, Joshie, sitting in a swing on the front porch, and Gyla next to him, in a blue and white checked housedress and a white apron. White slippers on her tiny, furry feet. They were swinging, and the boy was wearing checked Bermuda shorts, running through the sprinkler, laughing.

"You'd better call someone about him, Joshie," Gyla said, a little more firmly this time.

"I know someone in L.A. who helps kids like this," Joshie said.

"Well good," Gyla said. She got a star-shaped sponge wet and began to dab at the boy's face. "He's a nice kid, but how would you take care of him? You don't know anything about kids."

"Yeah," Joshie said.

"Even though you did come from a normal family and all," she said.

"It wasn't all that normal," Joshie said.

Gyla's eyes narrowed. She bared her teeth. "You don't know, Clown Boy. You don't know nothing about it, being in a home."

Gyla, like most of the freaks of Macadam's Circus, were jealous of Joshie, who had lived with his parents until he was eighteen, in Orange County. He'd gone to school with normals; he even had his high school diploma. It had been hell, he tried to tell them, hell until he went to Clown College and discovered that there were whole societies of people like him, some of them even worse off than he, though in his heart, there was nothing worse than being a clown. But most of the freaks had been in homes, dorms, going to school all together. Their hurts were different from his, and even with Gyla, trying to talk about being a living clown in the endless purgatory of a public high school was like trying to explain sand dunes to an Eskimo.

"Please," the boy said. Joshie and Gyla both leaned over the tub. Gyla's ears pointed forward. "Please wanna stay," he said. "Like you." Then, he looked up into Gyla's face. "You pretty. Like you best."

"Aw, jeez," Gyla said. "Can you believe it?"

Joshie pictured the house again, then, as Gyla brushed against him and he felt her warm, damp fur against the back of his hand, he shuddered. He guessed he could find that social worker's number. She'd been a friend of his parents. His father, mother, it had been duty more than anything, keeping Joshie. The looks of disgust on his mother's face, when sometimes he came into a room and she hadn't been expecting him, or the beaten expression that his father had worn, for years. A man who had wanted a son… who had instead gotten a clown. And the arguments. Late at night. Accusations. The virus came from sex, that was one thing everyone knew. Joshie's mother and father had invested a lifetime in accusing each other of being the one who'd picked it up, the one who'd contributed the tainted egg or sperm and made Joshie. He remembered one of his father's parting shots: "I'm just thankful you won't make another one like you, Josh. You won't be getting any girls pregnant." Joshie had thought for a long while his father had meant that Joshie was too ugly for anyone to make love with him, and the bitterness was almost palpable, but after a time he realized that his father had been talking about sterility. All freaks were sterile.

Maybe the white house with the picket fence (which was Joshie's house, until age five or so) was not such a good idea.

Gyla insisted on making a bed for the boy on her blue velvet couch.

Joshie curled on the floor under a soft satin quilt that Gyla had sewn by hand. He listened to the boy's soft, contented breathing, and also to Gyla, who moved restlessly in her sleep, and who moaned, and with each moan, Joshie could not help thinking of going to her bed and forming his body around hers, then running his hands up and down her lean, furry flanks, stroking the soft, round breasts, but he willed this thought away by gazing at the boy's perfect, smooth little face, the way the fur curled away from his forehead in the moonlight and glinted off the tips of his small, pointed ears.

He did look like a teddy bear, Joshie thought, and at that moment, he decided to call him Little Bear. He told Gyla in the morning, and she agreed, while sipping coffee, that it was a fine name, very good, until they got to L.A. and Joshie called his friend from the child protection office.

The next day about four, they got to Long Beach, and everyone was grumbling because Macadam had picked a new spot for the circus, in the looming shadows of the huge waste conversion plant. It had been an oil refinery at one time, but as there was little oil left, it had been refitted for waste conversion. It was raining and the lights of the plant shone dimly through the fog. If Joshie squinted the right way, he could picture the high steel spires as the turrets of a castle.

"You're going to call?" Gyla had borrowed some clothes for Little Bear, who'd cooed and hooted as she'd dressed him. He was eating a corn dog in Gyla's trailer while Joshie stared out the plastic window at the waste plant.

"Yeah. Guess I'll use Macadam's phone."

"Good," Gyla said. "Why don't you go now? Before they come and get you to help set up. I've got to fix my costume. I'll watch him." She gestured at Little Bear, who grinned. His T-shirt was smeared with grease and fried batter crumbs. Mustard streaked the fur around his mouth.

Joshie found the social worker's number in the pocket of his green army jacket, the ugly one with sleeves long enough to cover his hands.

Probably, the number wouldn't work. He considered returning to Gyla's trailer and telling her that he hadn't been able to reach the child welfare woman. No, he couldn't do that. He walked across the muddy yard to Macadam's.

Macadam was eating compressed soy pellets from a plastic container, pouring them directly into his mouth, then crunching them like peanuts.

"Hey, Joshie!" Macadam's head was slick and oval, hairless, greenish-white and delicately scaled. He had epicanthic folds around his eyes, and thin lips the color of spoiled knockwurst. Joshie had once watched Macadam lift the rear of a trailer out of the mud. That had been in Fresno. Macadam hadn't even gotten out of breath.

"I need to use the phone," Joshie said.

"Sure," Macadam said, his mouth full of pellets. "Heard about the kid."

Montego Bay had doubtless shared the story. Joshie now knew he had to make the call. The house with the white picket fence faded to a pinpoint, then blinked out. "Yeah, I know a lady who can take care of him."

"Should have called the cops back in Fontucky," Macadam said. Macadam had a derisive name for every town, and Fontucky was his for Fontana.

"Didn't want him to be taken to a home," Joshie said. He went to the phone and picked up a pencil, then began to punch the numbers.

"Where the hell do you think he'll end up? Little bastard's better off there anyway." Macadam wiped his lips.

Joshie didn't bother to remind Macadam that he'd grown up in a house, with parents.

Someone answered the number with, "L.A. County Special Services."

Joshie asked for the woman who'd been his mother's friend, Claire Brigham.

"She's not with us any longer."

"I needed to talk to her, it's a special case," Joshie said, feeling nervous twinges in his stomach.

"She's retired. What was your name?"

"Josh Petersen. She was a friend of my mother."

"Mr. Petersen, anyone here can help you. Do you have a child for placement?"

"I, uh," Joshie paused. Macadam was leaning over, listening in. "I might know of someone, yes. Mrs. Brigham is still in the area?"

"Yes. Look, is this about her volunteer work?"

Joshie heard rustling papers. "Sure," he said.

The woman gave him Claire Brigham's number and he clicked off and punched the numbers as quickly as he could, struggling with the pencil in his clumsy fingers. He turned so Macadam couldn't see his face, and he heard the big fish man chuckling. Laughing at his hands.

The number rang a long time before someone picked up the phone, an older woman, laughing. "Look, if you're trying to get Pizza Pirates, I guarantee this isn't the right number."

"Mrs. Brigham? I don't want Pizza Pirates, I wanted you," Joshie said.

Macadam said, "Ha!" and began rattling the drawers of his desk.

"I'm sorry, I can't hear you," the woman said. Her voice was a mature woman's light tremolo.

"This is Josh Petersen. Maybe you remember my mother, Shirley?"

There was a pause on the other end of the line. "Yes, I do remember. You're the son, the one who…"

"I'm the clown," Joshie said.

"You got that right," Macadam interjected. Joshie's face grew fiery.

"Well, how may I help you, then? Is your mother in trouble? Has something happened?"

"No, nothing like that," Joshie said quickly. "It's just that, well, I'm with a circus now, a real circus. I'm a clown. And there's been something come up."

"I'm glad you found a place for yourself," Mrs. Brigham said. "Not many can say that."

Joshie turned to stare at Macadam, who was filing his nails to a point. He always kept them like that. Macadam had four long, slender fingers on each hand, but they were webbed. Maybe there were worse things than having only three big fat fingers.

"We found a boy abandoned yesterday, in Fontana. We're in Long Beach now. He's…"

"He's a changed child," Mrs. Brigham said.

Joshie had never heard that way of saying it before. He decided that he liked it. "He's got the virus, yes," he said.

"And you wanted to find a placement for him." Mrs. Brigham laughed, but not happily.

"Yes. We…I can't keep him."

"No," she said. "No, of course you can't. Well, you got me here at home, so you must have heard I'm no longer with the department."

"I did. I was calling because we don't want him to go to a home. I thought maybe there'd be somewhere else, something else."

"There are no families for children like this," she said.

"But maybe something better. Isn't there something that can be…"

Mrs. Brigham paused. "There is something, but it's only for the children with the greatest potential. I've been involved in a project for some time. It's called High Haven. In Lake Arrowhead. Maybe you've heard of it?"

Joshie hadn't. "High Haven?" It sounded wonderful.

"It's like a camp, only year-round. Run all by people who've been changed. Privately funded."

Joshie's heart leapt. Something like that, for kids like Little Bear? "That's what I want," he said.

"It's not that simple. This boy has to have some support system outside of High Haven. People who care about him, and a place to go when he turns eighteen."

Joshie's mother had packed his things and put them in a large cardboard box on the front porch on his eighteenth birthday. "I see," he said.

"I'll have to come see the boy, meet with him," Mrs. Brigham said.

"We're in Long Beach," Joshie told her.

"Quite a drive. I'm not sure I can make it."

"I'll pay for an electric cab," Joshie said. He thought of his meager stash of money. Macadam fed them and housed them, but he paid wretchedly. Still, his money should cover it, providing Mrs. Brigham didn't live very far away. Her number had been from the San Fernando Valley.

"That's very nice of you," Mrs. Brigham said.

"We're here for a week. When can you make it?"

"Tomorrow afternoon, most likely." She asked for directions, and laughed when he told her they were in the shadow of the waste plant. Awful area, she'd said. Of course it was. Those were the only areas where Macadam's Circus went.

When Joshie got off the phone, his heart was light. He could hardly wait to tell Gyla about High Haven. Somehow they'd work something out, convince Mrs. Brigham that there was a, what had she called it? A support system for Little Bear. Gyla would help, he knew it.

Macadam had finished filing his nails and was rearranging his desk. "Heard you talking about High Haven," he said. "Let me tell you kid, it's a ripoff."

Joshie bit his lip. "What do you know about it?"

"It's all a scam, Clown Boy. Ain't nothing up there. Didn't I ever tell you how lucky you were to be working for me? At least I pay."

Joshie put on his gloves. "Yeah, you told me," he said.

"Look, maybe I should just call the cops. That kid's gotta be in a home."

"Don't do it," Joshie said. His heart was racing and he couldn't fathom the expression on Macadam's face. "Don't you do anything like that. I'm taking care of the problem."

Macadam leaned back in his chair. It squealed from his weight. "You know what? After you screw this up, you'll be back, Clown Boy. It's me who takes care of all of you here. Don't forget it."

Joshie didn't trust himself to say anything else, so he just shook his head and stumbled from the trailer. He'd only gone a few steps when Montego Bay came trotting up.

"Hey, I've been looking for you. We've got to get the Tanks set up, and the Abominable Snowman." It was drizzling rain and Montego's hair was slicked down over his forehead.

Joshie was still shaking from the run-in with Macadam. "I—I wanted to tell Gyla I've got something great set up for Little Bear. I mean, the kid."

"No time," Montego said, then he grinned. He didn't seem to notice that Joshie was breathing like a bellows. "That's good news about the kid. Calling him Little Bear, huh? If he was a little older, you might get him set up as a clown. Think of that, did ya?" Montego grabbed Joshie's arm and led him away.

Joshie had no choice. He slapped the seats up as quickly as he could, and checked the VR connections, which had always been his job. His fingers were clumsy, but his

AMY STERLING CASIL

brain wasn't, and no one knew the system better than Joshie. Montego then had him brush down the animated Abominable Snowman, which required little coordination, and check the dry ice bays not once, but three times. One of them was stuffed with wads of blue and orange chewing gum and sticky used cotton candy cones. Grumbling, Joshie scooped out the mess. Then, finally, Montego released him with a sharp slap between his shoulder blades that took his breath away.

Joshie rushed to Gyla's trailer. It was already so late, nearly dusk. He bounded up the steps and tried the door. It was locked. Maybe she'd taken Little Bear to get something else to eat, or to meet some of the other performers.

"Hey, Gyla," he called. There was no answer. Joshie went to the window, where the lace curtains Gyla had sewn on a windy night on the road between Escondido and El Centro were drawn. The lace was filmy, transparent, and Joshie could see shadows within.

Gyla was inside, moaning, and a man was behind her, a large man with slender, webbed, long-fingered hands, stroking her breasts in slow, circular motions.

"You hairy little whore," Macadam said.

Joshie watched Macadam's big, sleek, scaly body through the lace as he did barbed things to Gyla, and he listened to her soft moans and Macadam's wet grunting. Then, Joshie turned from the window and with a sudden, sharp pain deep in his gut, he bent near the steps and vomited.

Thunder crashed and it began to rain, and he headed for the clown tent. At least Little Bear had not been in the trailer. Little Bear had been somewhere else, and for this tiny thing, Joshie was very grateful.

Little Bear was in the clown tent, sitting on Hunny the Pig Girl's lap.

She turned her smiling pink face to Joshie and said, "Gyla asked me to watch him. He's a real sweetie, isn't he?"

Little Bear saw Joshie and went, "Hootie-hoo! Hootie-hoo!" Then, he flapped his arms like wings.

"Come on," Joshie said, and he grabbed Little Bear, roughly, under the arms, and began to carry him off.

"Hey, something wrong, Joshie?" Hunny the Pig Girl's face was full of concern. Her small eyes were as wide as they could get.

"Nothing," Joshie said. "Thanks a lot, Hunny." He retreated to his trailer, where he tried to interest Little Bear in some cheese doodles and a game of go-fish with a crumpled deck of cards. Little Bear began to cry.

"Want my lady," he said.

"Aw, damn," Joshie said. Then, he remembered his balloons. He filled balloons and made animals for Little Bear, who cooed and hooted madly as he put a balloon hat on his head and pinched and squeezed the bright yellow rubber until it popped. When Little Bear tired of balloons, Joshie got out his makeup kit and made a sweet, smiling clown face on Little Bear, who sighed in wonder, then rubbed the red and the blue into the white greasepaint until his face turned into a pink and purple abstract work of art.

Joshie took Little Bear to get a bowl of soup and some crackers in the mess tent, then returned to the trailer. After Little Bear, who talked when he wanted to, begged and begged, Joshie allowed him to paint his face, or rather, smear greasepaint on with his soft little fingers.

"Like your nose," Little Bear said. "Funny."

"Yeah," Joshie said. "Real funny."

"Not sleep with lady tonight? My lady?"

"No, Little Bear," Joshie said. He turned away and Little Bear hooted softly. "Lady wants to be by herself."

Joshie tucked Little Bear into his own narrow bed and drew his rough green Army blanket around his neck. Little Bear complained about the scratchy wool so much that Joshie got out an old padded ski jacket and draped it over his small body. He took the blanket himself and sat in the folding chair by his card table, staring out the rain-streaked window.

Whenever Joshie closed his eyes, the image of Macadam bending over Gyla, kneading her soft, furred breasts, came to him like a cheap Polaroid snapshot. So, Joshie kept his eyes open and stared, a dry, empty feeling in his stomach. From time to time, he thought of what Macadam had called Gyla, and his stomach turned.

Joshie's only experiences with women had been of a business nature, quick, rough and dirty. And the women had never looked at his face, never. And he still recalled the chill shudders of some of them, when he'd touched them with his ugly hands.

Gyla had seemed to enjoy Macadam's hands, with those awful pointed nails, the webbing between the long fingers. Still, maybe he'd threatened her. Macadam was like that. Several women had left the circus, suddenly, in the middle of the night. All Macadam's doing, Joshie knew. But Gyla had been moaning, soft and pliant. Willing.

No one had ever moaned that way with him. Joshie put his head in his hands and rested his elbows on the unsteady card table, and thought, bitterly, that maybe Gyla might like to be hurt. He looked at his stubby hands, and wondered if he could hurt with them.

The next day the circus was open. Joshie had three shows. He made Little Bear up like a tiny clown and instructed him to sit quietly in a slat-sided red wagon and smile at the people as they came by. Little Bear hooted and cooed at everyone.

"He's darling," a woman in a leather bodysuit said. "Look at that little teddy bear clown." Children pointed at Little Bear and Joshie and giggled.

After a while, the clowns were finished and the acrobats came out. Gyla rode a unicycle and danced with hoops to delicate piano music. A hush came over the crowd when she came out in her pink costume, a little risqué for the young ones, with her pink G-string and a couple of patches over her breasts. But the circus got away with it because Gyla didn't expose smooth flesh, merely sleek, silver fur.

Joshie held Little Bear on his hip and worked quietly along the edges of the crowd, handing out neon plastic flowers to the kids. Joshie never talked to the crowd. He mimed everything.

"Look at that girl," a woman said softly. "She looks so strange."

"But she's beautiful," came a little girl's voice. "Her fur is so shiny and silvery. I wish I could dance like that."

"No, you don't," the woman said. "Don't say that, honey."

"Mama, she's pretty," the girl insisted.

Joshie stroked Little Bear behind his furry ears.

"We enjoy the circus, dear, but we don't want to be like them," the woman said.

Joshie could not bear to listen any longer, so he moved on. At last, the show was over. Macadam came out in his gleaming green suit, the bullet-headed fish man, and bade everyone a safe trip home after enjoying the sideshow.

Gyla caught up with Joshie and Little Bear on their way to the clown tent.

"Hey! I missed you last night. Hunny told me you picked up Little Bear, and I waited for you all evening," Gyla said. Her tiara was crooked. Joshie reached over and straightened it.

"Sure," he said. "I bet you did." Couldn't she see him trembling?

Gyla stopped. "What's wrong?"

"Nothing," Joshie said. "Let's get something to eat. Look, that woman I told you about is coming today. She might take Little Bear."

"Really?" Gyla grinned. She tried to link her arm with Joshie, but he pulled away. She caught his eye. "Joshie, what's the matter?"

"Nothing's the matter," he told her. She looked so beautiful, in her tiara and satin costume. Of course she wanted Macadam. He had the money, and he was powerful. Joshie didn't blame her, not at all. Probably, it had been going on a long time. Macadam's hands had been familiar, knowing, as they ran along her slender body. "Let's get something to eat and we can talk about Little Bear."

"Sure," Gyla said, still uncertain. She walked silently with them into the tent.

Gyla fetched soup and crackers for she and Joshie, and another corn dog for Little Bear, along with plenty of mustard and napkins. She fussed with a napkin at Little Bear's neck while Joshie talked. It was better to talk about Little Bear. Better to talk about anything except Gyla.

The words rushed out. "Her name is Mrs. Brigham. She's coming this afternoon. She's older, didn't want to drive all the way out here. I told her I'd pay for her cab."

"That was sweet," Gyla said.

Joshie cleared his throat. "Look, she told me about a place called High Haven, up in the mountains. Little Bear could go there, if he's got …what did she call it? If he's got a support system."

"Oh," Gyla said. "I think I might have heard of it."

Joshie kept on talking. "We've got to convince her that Little Bear has some kind of home base here with us. Otherwise, I don't see as if he has much of a chance. After all, he doesn't talk very well. The noises, the crazy flapping. We know it's from how he was treated."

"Bad," Gyla said.

"Yeah," Joshie said. "Very bad. But I don't think Mrs. Brigham cares about that." Little Bear was gnawing on his corn dog and hooting happily. Joshie paused and wiped mustard from his chin.

"I have heard of this place," Gyla said. She crumbled a cracker into her soup. "It's run by people like us. All of them. Only… only they have educations. And money. And they care." Gyla stirred her soup.

"Where'd you hear about High Haven?"

"Somebody told me about it. Not in a nice way."

Joshie started to touch her delicate, furred hand, but he saw his big, ungainly red glove. Gyla liked sharp nails, webbed fingers. Not a baggy clown glove with only three fingers and a thumb.

"Seems to me that place takes money," Gyla said. "Donations and such. Maybe they'd be more likely to take Little Bear if we agreed to send money each month." Her head hung down now, and she was watching the crackers softening to white mush in the hot soup.

"Maybe," Joshie said. "I got the impression Mrs. Brigham meant that the kids needed to have a place to go after they turned eighteen and had to leave this High Haven. Like, a job and a home and such."

Gyla brightened. "I can ask Macadam. He likes the kid. He…"

"No!" Joshie shoved his soup away so hard that noodles and broth splattered over the table. "You damn well won't."

Gyla stared and started to say something, but Montego Bay interrupted.

"There's a woman here," he said. "Says she's here to see the kid."

Joshie leapt up and grabbed Little Bear. "Come on," he said. "There's a lady who wants to meet you. She's very nice, I promise."

Gyla followed, and Joshie didn't dare stop her. He couldn't chance upsetting Little Bear before Mrs. Brigham had a chance to talk to him.

Mrs. Brigham was outside the clown tent. She was a small, neat woman with a man's fishing hat pulled tight around her ears. The corners of her eyes crinkled.

"Josh Petersen? I didn't recognize you. You've grown up."

"They call me Joshie here. Joshie the Clown."

"Ah," Mrs. Brigham said. "This must be the boy."

"We're calling him Little Bear," Gyla said, stepping forward.

Mrs. Brigham smiled. "You're another friend, then?"

"I'm with Joshie," Gyla said. Joshie held Little Bear tighter, and Little Bear began to squirm and hoot.

Mrs. Brigham extended her hand. "I'm Mrs. Brigham. Do you know your name?"

"Little Bear," Little Bear said.

Mrs. Brigham tried again. "Yes, I've heard that, but do you have another name?"

Little Bear shook his head and said, "Hootie-hoo!" Then, he flapped his free arm, instead of taking her hand.

Mrs. Brigham looked questioningly at Joshie. "Has he done this as long as you've had him?"

Joshie paused, then decided there was no reason for lying. "Yes."

"It's called autism of change. We see it in many changed children, especially those who've been neglected."

"Autism?" Joshie remembered hearing that word, it was something like retardation, or craziness.

"No, not to worry. It's not like classic autism. It's responsive to treatment and training. In fact, most outgrow it."

"If they go to a place like High Haven," Gyla said. Joshie thought that she looked like she wanted to cry.

"Yes, if they go to a place like High Haven." Mrs. Brigham crossed her arms and studied Gyla. "You've heard of High Haven, then?"

Gyla nodded. "Listen, I want you to know that Joshie and I are committed to Little Bear's future."

Little Bear scrambled so hard against Joshie's side that Joshie had to put him down. Little Bear ran immediately to Gyla and buried his face in the fur of her stomach. Gyla stroked the back of his head and kept talking. "You take donations, don't you?"

"I'm not precisely associated with them," Mrs. Brigham said. "You'd have to speak to the staff. All High Haven staff are changed."

"I like that word," Gyla said. "Better than freak, or differently-abled. What I wanted you to know is that I make good money here. Good enough, anyway. I can afford to send money each month for Little Bear, if that's what you want."

Mrs. Brigham shook her head. "Donations are welcome, but High Haven is more interested in the human side of things."

"But I'm not human," Gyla said.

Joshie stepped between them. "Please, just talk to him," he said. "Can you do some tests here? See if he's … how you said to me…if he's got potential?"

"I'll come back another day," Mrs. Brigham said. Little Bear let go of Gyla and ran to Mrs. Brigham and held her leg. She looked down and tentatively stroked his head. "That's all right, Little Bear. I'll come back with some friends and we'll play games, okay?"

Joshie didn't know whether to cry out in anguish or relief. "Can't you take him? Take him now."

Mrs. Brigham shook her head, slowly. "No, I'll have to get some help for this. He obviously doesn't talk much. We have different tests for that. I'm not qualified."

"I remember," Gyla said. "I've taken all the tests. Little Bear is smart. And he's young enough. If you take him to your High Haven, he's got a chance." Joshie saw now that Gyla was crying. "You can have as much money as I earn. I don't care, just so long as he has a chance." Then, Gyla looked up at Joshie, straight in his face, and opened her mouth as if she was about to say more, but instead, she turned on her heels, in her delicate white slippers, and ran away, toward her trailer.

Joshie stood silently a while, then collected Little Bear and pressed his face into his ruff. "I'm sorry," he said to Mrs. Brigham. "She was raised in a home. Most of them around here were. She's…"

"Bitter," Mrs. Brigham said. "I can understand that."

Joshie examined her broad, honest face. "Are you coming back?"

Mrs. Brigham looked at her shoes, which were practical brown brogans. "Yes. I'll call some friends. They'll come back with me. Give me a couple of days."

"All right," Joshie said, because it was all that he could say.

Then, Mrs. Brigham walked back across the damp, packed dirt lot to her waiting cab. She hadn't asked Joshie for any money. He called after her and asked about the money, but she waved him off.

"Go and talk to your girl," she called. "I'm thinking right now she needs a friend, Josh."

"She's not my girl," Joshie said.

"My lady," Little Bear said in Joshie's ear.

Joshie knocked on Gyla's door with his red-gloved clown hand. He and Little Bear waited a long time before she answered.

"She's not going to take him," Gyla said when she opened the door.

"Hey, don't say that," Joshie said. "She's coming back with some other people, in a couple of days."

"I've got some money," Gyla said. "I can get more."

Macadam's money. Joshie put Little Bear down on the blue velour couch, more roughly than he should have. Gyla had been crying, and her golden eyes were red. Joshie wanted to feel sorry for her, but instead, here she was talking about Macadam's dirty money.

Little Bear ran to Gyla's bathroom.

Gyla rubbed her eyes, and Joshie heard the water running. "He wants another bubble bath," she said.

"Mrs. Brigham doesn't care about money," Joshie said. "You heard her."

Gyla bent over and unhooked her bra. Joshie had to look away, and she walked around him and sat on the blue velvet couch and crossed her legs, then rubbed her eyes.

"Everybody cares about money," she said. She crossed her arms behind her head and thrust her chest out at him.

Joshie sat in her dressing chair and fiddled with her combs and brushes. "Everybody doesn't care about it," he said. "Or selling themselves."

She gasped, a little gasp, then her face hardened. "What are you talking about, Joshie?"

He slammed the big brush down on her dressing table, then picked up one of her blue fringed bras that she had flung aside. He held it up. "This? How about your good friend, Macadam."

"He's not my friend," Gyla said.

"Yeah?" Her silky round breasts jutted out at him.

"One of us is going to have to go in and check on the kid," she said.

"You do it," Joshie said.

"All right." She stood, then sauntered past him.

As she walked by, Joshie reached out, with his awful clown glove, and grabbed her waist.

She gave a little cry, then said, "Joshie, don't play me that way. I like you too much."

He pushed her from him. "You don't like me," he said.

She ran her hands over her hips, then turned toward the window. "No," she said. "Maybe I don't. But I like your face."

Late afternoon light streamed in through the lace curtains and fell across her slender shoulders. She turned and straightened her G-string.

"Tell me that again," Joshie said. His voice sounded strange and rough.

She turned back and she was smiling. "I've always liked your face, Joshie."

He leaned forward and he touched her side, gently now, and stroked the soft fur.

"Hunny will watch Little Bear," she said. "I'm sure she will."

"That's not the right thing," Joshie said.

"Oh, yes it is," Gyla said. Then, she bent over and put her hand on Joshie's cheek and kissed him. Her fur smelled of sweet powder, like a baby. Her little tongue flicked in his mouth and Joshie felt the trailer spin around him.

Then, just as quickly as she'd kissed him, she pulled away and went to the bathroom. "Hurry up, Little Bear," he heard her say. "You're going to visit with Hunny tonight." Then, Joshie heard Little Bear's squeal of delight.

After the arrangements were made and Little Bear was left safely with Hunny, who'd been thrilled at the honor of keeping him, Gyla came to Joshie. His fingers played over Gyla's soft fur.

Gyla caressed his face, lightly touching the tip of his nose, and he hated it at first and wanted to turn away, but she would not let him.

"You're so gentle," she said, over and over.

Joshie, his heart slamming in his chest, ran his fingers over her thighs, feeling as though he would cry each time she cried out. And she did not shudder at the touch of his hands, his clown hands.

"My beautiful girl," he told her. "Beautiful Gyla."

Late in the evening, as he lay beside her and cradled her in her soft, sweet-smelling bed, she began to talk.

"I can get a lot of money," she said, and he put his hand on her cheek to hush her, but she turned, and kept talking. "They all give me money. Lots of it. But I'd never take it from you, Joshie. I care about you."

Joshie remembered Macadam, bending over Gyla, handling her so roughly and coldly. It had enraged him, but now, he felt only sadness. If Gyla had been a normal girl, she never would have had to endure something like Macadam. Joshie couldn't think that Macadam was "someone."

"That place," Joshie said. "That High Haven. Maybe they wouldn't just take kids, Gyla. Maybe there'd be a place for us."

Gyla laughed. "No, I don't think so," she said.

"I meant it," Joshie said. "We can at least try."

"This place was freedom for me," Gyla said. "Can you understand that? To you, it's just a job."

What did she think he was? Where else would he earn a living, with his clown face and ugly hands and feet? Joshie ran his fingers along her flank and said, "I'm no different from you."

"Oh, yes you are, Joshie. You're a human being," she said.

"You're a human being, too," Joshie said. "Don't ever think you're not." Macadam's ugly words couldn't be how Gyla thought of herself. He stroked her back gently, until she fell asleep. Curled beside her, after a time, Joshie slept.

The next morning, he woke to the patter of rain on the roof of the trailer. Gyla was gone.

He dressed and ran out, in search of Gyla and Little Bear. Macadam greeted him beside the clown tent.

"You've got an appointment this morning," Macadam said.

"What? I'm looking for Gyla and Little Bear. The kid." Joshie rushed past him, fighting the desire to drive his fist into the big man's scaled gut.

"The boy is in my trailer. Lady says she has full payment for you and the boy to go to a place called High Haven." Macadam laughed. "I hear it's real nice up there."

Joshie stopped. "Where's Gyla?"

Macadam picked at one pointed nail. "She's taking a break."

Joshie rushed at him, his heart pounding. He grabbed Macadam's jacket. "Where is she?"

"She's fine, clown. Don't worry about her. Your ticket has been punched." Then, Macadam raised his arms and pushed Joshie away.

"You'd better not have hurt her," Joshie said.

Macadam shook his head. "I'd never hurt her. She's very special to me," he said. His eyes were hard and blind-looking, like a shark.

Joshie ran past him, to the trailer. He would grab Little Bear, then find Gyla, and they'd all get out of the circus. That was the right thing, he realized. The little house with the white picket fence. Gyla in the swing beside him, and Little Bear playing on the lawn.

When Joshie reached Macadam's trailer, Mrs. Brigham was there with a tall, red-haired man and short, dumpy woman in a caftan. Little Bear was playing with a set of colored blocks behind Macadam's desk.

"You're a very fortunate man, Josh," Mrs. Brigham said. "Someone has endowed you and Little Bear."

Joshie looked between the man and the other woman, then at Little Bear. "I don't understand."

"You and Little Bear will both be going to High Haven. Little Bear will start preschool there and you are to be trained as a cook."

"Cook?"

"Yes, I'm afraid it's the only opening they have right now."

"What about Gyla?"

"She's staying," Macadam said as stomped into the trailer and pushed the blocks aside to sit at his desk. He smiled down at Little Bear with his shark-like smile.

"I won't leave without her," Joshie said.

"I'm afraid you have no choice," Mrs. Brigham said. She was still wearing the fisherman's hat. "The person who gave the endowment has stipulated that it's just you, and Little Bear."

"Then, just take the boy," Joshie said. "I'm not leaving without Gyla." He glared at Macadam, who merely smiled and toyed with the drawers of his desk. Macadam's nail file glittered on the desk. It had a sharp point, and Joshie was closer to it than Macadam. He could jump, grab it, hold it to Macadam's scaly fish throat.

Mrs. Brigham moved close and said very softly, so softly that Joshie might not have heard, had it not been for his over-large, sensitive ears, "Just come with us and it will be all right. Trust me."

Joshie nearly gasped, and he looked between her and the letter opener. Macadam's neck… he was so close. Little Bear threw a block, and said, "Hot!"

Joshie decided he would have to trust Mrs. Brigham. "I'll be back for Gyla," he told Macadam. "You can count on that."

"Right," Macadam said, grinning. "You frighten me, Clown Boy."

"Let's go now, son," the red-haired man said. He leaned over, and Little Bear scooted farther behind the desk.

"Come on, Little Bear," Joshie said. He squatted, and Little Bear looked up from the blocks, then reached for him. Joshie picked him up, feeling the familiar weight.

The woman in the caftan beamed. "You'll have a lovely time at High Haven," she said.

Macadam laughed as they left the trailer.

They walked toward the chain-link fence which surrounded the circus encampment. The waste conversion plant loomed overhead, spumes of white effluent smoking from its stacks. "Go ahead," Mrs. Brigham told Joshie. "Get in the van."

Joshie held Little Bear close. "You must think I'm crazy. I won't leave Gyla. Never."

"Just get in the van," Mrs. Brigham said.

The red-haired man stepped forward. "There's no cause for alarm," he said. The woman in the caftan patted his arm.

There was a driver in the van, and he opened the side for all of them. The others climbed in, and Joshie turned, looking back on the collection of circus tents and trailers. The sideshow lights flickered in the early morning light. The door to Macadam's trailer swung open, and he leapt down the steps.

"Please," Mrs. Brigham said.

The red-haired man pushed Joshie halfway into the van. "Didn't think he'd figure it out this quickly," he said.

Joshie looked around, confused, then the woman in the caftan and the red-haired man both forced him inside. Gasping, Joshie grabbed Little Bear as the red-haired man buckled them in their seat.

Mrs. Brigham slid to the front, then turned to the driver and said, "Get going." Macadam was close enough that Joshie saw the gun in his hand.

"Let's hope he's a poor shot," the red-haired man said.

"Oh, he's a circus freak," the woman replied. "Not a professional."

Macadam crouched. Joshie bent over and tucked Little Bear's head into his chest. He heard popping noises, then dull whacks, and a few high, whining noises.

"He is a poor shot, isn't he?" the red-haired man said.

Joshie was completely huddled now, his breath coming in gasps. "You people are out of your minds," he said. The van jerked and threw Joshie against the door.

The red-haired man laughed. "You can sit up now. We're well out of range."

Joshie sat up and turned to see the circus lot fading in the distance. Little Bear curled against him, and he held him fast, then grabbed the red-haired man's shoulder. "Gyla's back there with Macadam. He'll kill her!" Joshie dug his fingers hard into the man's shoulder.

The red-haired man smiled. Joshie at first didn't understand when instead of replying, he reached with his free hand and tugged at the red hair. It peeled away to expose a perfectly smooth, white scalp. "I'm a clown too, friend," he said.

The woman in the caftan leaned across the seat. "And I'm porcine," she said, and she removed her face in one neat piece to show a round little pig snout and a pink rosebud mouth underneath it.

Little Bear said, "Hootie-hoo! Hootie-hoo!" From the back of the van, Joshie heard a tearing noise. He turned and saw the carpet covering lifting up. Joshie fumbled with his seat restraint.

Then, Joshie saw a pair of pointed gray ears above a delicate, heart-shaped face.

Mrs. Brigham was trying to say something. "I didn't think Macadam would figure it out so quickly," she said. "I'm sorry, Josh."

Joshie barely heard her. "Gyla," he whispered. Little Bear struggled to escape the seatbelt. His feet dug into Joshie's thighs.

"I gave them money to pay Macadam," Gyla said. "It didn't work out just like I'd thought."

Little Bear said, "Hootie-hoo! Hootie-hoo!"

"It worked out fine," Mrs. Brigham said. "You have a good friend in that man Montego Bay."

"Money doesn't matter to us," the other clown said. "But it mattered to Macadam."

"Even with the money, Macadam still tried to keep her," Mrs. Brigham said.

The blood was rushing in Joshie's ears. The other clown, the pig woman, they were so confident. Powerful. Gyla leaned over the seat and took Little Bear. Then, she kissed Joshie on the cheek.

"I love your face, Joshie," Gyla said. "I love your hands."

"Hootie hoo!" Little Bear shoved his furry head hard between the seats. Just for this one moment, Joshie paid no attention, except to Gyla's velvet fur, even when the tears stung his eyes and ran along his big clown nose into the short, soft fur of her exquisite face.

❧

LITTLE WOMAN

Cody Sisco

"The thing you have to remember," Liz said as she stirred her cocktail with a pointed pinky nail, painted black like the rest but grown long and shaped into a threatening talon, "is that men are always trying to put you in a box." She raised her hand, tilted her head back, and sucked the liquid from her finger like a worm from momma bird's beak. "This drink is giving me life!" she cried.

I was enjoying a glass of Albariño, wondering not for the first time if Liz was unstable. But it was good of her to meet me out. Our booth at the Coiled Serpent was far enough away from the throbbing and warbling speakers that we could actually talk. Lasers cut through artificial fog above our heads.

On the ride over, looking at the searchlights marking the half-marathon's course down Hollywood Boulevard, I'd realized I maybe had mild culture shock after returning from a month in Europe. Add to that a sleepless night and a long day at work, and I was rapidly approaching burnout territory after one day back on the job. I wanted to reverse course and think only of the warm inland valleys of Galicia, where grapes produce fine vintages despite the Atlantic moisture that fogs the coast. Real fog, not this machine-made lung trash filling the club.

I was deliberately trying *not* to think about what my coworker Sal had said today, but Liz kept prying. His words came back to me with their sly indirectness, complimentary objectification, and undermining doubt: *You can let loose a little. Clients want to see your curves.*

Had he really meant what he said or was it a one-time slip? Never one to wonder too much about the origins of good or bad human behavior—I had disavowed Catholicism and never looked back—I said, "Forget him. What do you think *I* should do?"

"Record everything."

"That's illegal."

"Who's to say what's more illegal, recording or harassing?" Liz said. "Look, Jen, I'm not saying use it in a court of law. I'm just saying, if you've got the verbatim record, tit for tat, write it down, share it with someone—with me, for instance. It's evidence if things ever get really bad."

"I don't want it to get bad. It's bad enough already. 'Clients want to see your curves?' He didn't say *he* wanted to. He's so... so..."

"Sleazy. But in a charming way. And in a way that makes you doubt if maybe it's you who has the problem, not him." She placed her surprisingly warm hand on mine. "Jen, I get it. I know the type." She squeezed and released, then pushed up her sleeves, making her rainbow-colored ceramic bracelets go *clack clack clack*. "It's the friend of a friend who corners you when no one's looking. Or finds a way to rub up against you because it's crowded in the elevator. Or ruphies your drink. Or rapes you and says you were begging for it."

I groaned in disgust.

She went on, "They're all the same guy. What I'm saying is, watch out. It's not going to get better."

"That's bleak."

"That's life."

And on that terrible note, we clinked glasses. "Fuck men," I said, meaning it.

That was probably the moment the curse was sealed.

☽

I'm not a witch by practice or by lineage, as far as I know. Maybe I'm not really a witch at all. But I've come to appreciate the power of magic.

There are forces swirling around us, animated by our actions, that we mostly fail to perceive and understand. Until they are illuminated. I heard that once at a modern Wicca lecture. Concepts, and, by extension, words, are the fuel that powers magic. A long-haired lady who never wore makeup, never dyed her hair, and never cinched her curves into a tight bodice said that a flock of birds once delayed a plane from taking off just long enough for Homeland Security to track down a red flag no-fly-list end-runner and remove a group of terrorists before they had a chance to hijack the plane. Where did those birds come from?

She also told the story of a woman who said she picked the winning lottery ticket because her fingers led her to it, despite her brain trying to pick out a different one. Forces, and concepts, act on us without our volition, mostly. So she said.

I laughed it off until I was acted upon big time.

☽

It was a normal day at the office, meaning my phone was ringing while I watched angry emails flood my inbox. Through the window, I saw children scamper toward the tar pits while their parents tried to keep up and watched as a glitzy gray-haired couple slowly approached LACMA's secret entrance for big donors, ready to sign over ten million bucks because it was important that the poor have culture too, if not an exclusive VIP-only door.

Sal in his flapping gray blazer came by, asking if I had a minute. "Of course not" was the answer.

"Only a minute," he insisted, "I need to show you something."

I went to Sal's office. Halfway there I realized I'd forgotten my phone, and that this interaction would be off the record.

Oh well, this will be over quickly, I told myself.

It was cool and minty moist thanks to some gadget under his desk. I'd heard him boasting about his top-of-the-line humidifier to the other guys in the office, but he never said anything about it in front of the ladies. He didn't want to seem prissy—he was that type. Anyway, the air was cool and calming in his office and I did relax a bit being away from my computer. I wagered that he had some new online sales widget that let him cyberstalk potential clients. He's excellent at bringing in random creative directors desperate to spend money on our services.

My hunch was not wrong. His monitor displayed a spreadsheet representing a hot pipeline of dollars, enough to let us all earn our bonuses by mid-year. But there was a catch. We didn't have enough staff to manage all the projects. We needed to tap our freelancers, which is why he wanted me. I managed those relationships.

"Nice. Okay," I said, "I get it, we're going to be busy. Send me the staffing request forms and I'll start reaching out."

He gave me a cold, hard stare. "I'm not filling out a single form."

Sal had a vague accent that didn't really fit his southern European heritage. It sounded more Colombian than

Italian and the way he said "filling" made it sound almost like "feeling." I could tell he wasn't "feeling" the "extra" work required to compile the staffing requests, and I understood his frustrations. If we could all be just a little more flexible and nimble, we'd get a lot more done. That was fine, but the boss wanted structure, processes, checks and balances, and accountability, and so for me to act on a staffing request required a form that Sal was going to have to "feel" out.

"Sal, I can get started on the profiles, but to put a concrete offer out there, I need the details. I need the form. We'll make it happen quickly, okay?"

His shoulders were bunched up. I could see the strain he'd been carrying and his fear of the mountain of work avalanching toward him. He needed someone to share the burden with.

Then that cold stare came back and I wondered what it meant. My arms were crossed, not defensively, I hoped. It was his mint humidifier chilling the air. I valued our relationship, even if sometimes it veered toward inappropriate, and I thought maybe I had my guard up too much and maybe that was the odd tension between us. But I didn't unfold my arms.

"You're always looking for ways to solve problems, Jen," he said. "I appreciate it."

He reached out and patted my arm, then slid it down and gave my elbow a squeeze, not realizing that he had actually just nudged my boob with his hand.

I realized, then, looking at the smug leer on his face, that he did realize, and he knew that I knew. His hand was still there, squeezing, nudging, fixed tight, not letting go.

I froze. He was testing me: what he could do to me, what I would say, how I would react. The pressure of his knuckles was arousing and for all the wrong reasons—I felt violated, I felt desired, I felt I should scream or push him away, I felt like I could be someone who breaks all the rules and falls in love with a man who harasses me—if only it wasn't this particular man who was middle-aged and looked worse for wear, sad and frumpy, rather than exotic and suave. I could forgive the right wrong man and trust that he would never do it to anyone else, only me, because I was that irresistible.

I knew these thoughts were bullshit because the truth was harder, clearer, and unavoidable: he was a predator and I was stupidly doing nothing, being easy prey. It was disgusting. It was everything I feared. It was just awful. It was the worst.

I wanted to disappear.

And I started to shrink.

Literally.

I noticed what was happening because of the shocked expression on his face and because we were no longer eye-to-eye. I looked up at him, close enough to feel his hot agitated breath—he must have had pork for lunch—and he loomed over me, scanning the room because he didn't see me; I'd vanished.

More to the point, I'd shrunk to half the height of a Barbie doll.

I stood on the outstretched palm with which he'd gripped me, and, when his hand recoiled in fright, I managed to wrap my arms and legs around his finger. I hung on for dear life as he plunged his hand into his pocket. At least my clothes shrank along with my body.

The world went dark, there was a jangling of keys, the musty smell of privates, and everything undulated. He rubbed his big sweaty palm against a truck-trailer-sized semi-erect penis that strained against his underwear. I cowered among the loose change and keys.

His booming voice said, "Jen? Jen?"

So he didn't know I'd stowed away in his pocket. Well, I wasn't going to tell him. I stayed quiet.

"Okaaaaay?" he said with an uncertain laugh. "Chicks, man."

Ohhh, if I could reach up and smack his face!

He moved around his desk and sat down. Beneath me, the pocket fabric was like a trampoline. I was pretty sure I was standing on a testicle.

For a moment, I thought about jumping up and down to make him howl—I could bring the pain!—but I didn't want the attention.

It wasn't easy to stand. The fabric above pressed me down. I lay on my back, reluctantly, and had one of those maybe-if-I-close-my-eyes-this-will-all-turn-out-to-be-a-dream moments. Nope.

So what does one do?

They never discussed this scenario in my self-defense classes. They advised us to use an aggressor's moves against him. Of course, that didn't apply when he was the size of a building. I thought about making a report to HR. Supposing I could make it back to my computer, I'd have to execute some pretty epic dance moves to type out a message. I'd be lucky to manage, "Help me, I'm literally a tiny woman," and the truth of it was, no one was prepared for a situation like this. How could they be?

You probably won't agree with my choice.

I went home with him.

I understand why that was problematic. But from my point of view, I didn't just shrink randomly: there had to be a reason. Something about my relationship with Sal had led to me becoming the tiny dancer in a known chauvinist's pocket. If I was going to undo it, I couldn't undo it alone.

It was that type of insight that started me thinking that perhaps I had a bit o' the witch in me.

The rest of the day involved me planning my comeback, humming Queen B's *Lemonade* tracks, trying to ignore the disgusting sounds and smells of Sal's bodily functions. I have nightmares to this day of those horrible hours.

Around midnight, I emerged from his pants pocket and climbed to a place on his bedside table to sit and think. In the dark, I played mute unwilling witness to Sal's pre-slumber antics from my perch behind his Skymall alarm clock. Turns out he didn't get the raise we'd all suspected he did and he was whimpering over his bank balance. Anyway, he finally closed his eyes and snored, spread-eagle on his back.

I extracted a single, jagged key from his keychain and held it like a rock star guitarist ready for a solo. Call me Joan Jett. Call me Kelley Deal. Call me Sheryl fucking Crow. I could do this.

Feeling ready, I threw the key onto the bed, leapt and picked it up again, and climbed over the hills and valleys of a velour bedspread. The ascent onto his chest and the challenges of lugging the key with me had my heart beating so hard it thundered in the quiet room. With a deep breath, I made the final climb onto his cheek with key hoisted and yelled.

"Wake up, you asshole!" My voice was cartoon-tinny, not at all menacing.

His eyelids sprang open and he looked around frantically. It was semi-dark; the only light came from a billboard's glare spilling through his blinds. That was my bad. I should have turned on the light, though that would have been challenging and now it was too late.

"Right here, Sal. It's Jen. Don't even think about moving or so help me I'll pop your left eye and lodge this key in your brain."

"What? What the hell, Jen? Why are you Barbie-sized?"

"You are going to choose your words very wisely or never breathe easy through your nose again. Got it? I want an apology."

"I can't hear you. What?"

"APOLOGIZE!"

"I'm sorry. Jeez. What happened to you?"

"You can do better than that, you giant sack of smells! You jerk! You asshat, useless jerk!" Of course, by this point, I realized I was talking nonsense, but I was still so mad at him, I couldn't choose my words. I felt light-headed and struggled to maintain my balance. "*Why* are you sorry? I want to hear you say it."

"I'm sorry I… I mean… we didn't get to finish our conversation?"

"You assaulted me! Boob grabber! Male chauvinist harasser!" This went on for a while as I used every word I could think of. He seemed to be catching more of my words. He got the picture, he said, interrupting, but I wasn't done.

"Malfeaser!" If there was any magic word, that might have been it, arcane as it was. Whatever triggered the process, I started to grow. His skin was oil-slick under me and my balance became precarious.

"Ow!" he shouted. His breath didn't blow me away as much as it would have seconds before. I was standing over his face, at least one foot tall, brandishing the key and threatening him in a voice that sounded less silly now that my vocal chords were longer.

I felt the blood rush from my head and I let loose a primal scream of anger. My head bumped against the ceiling. I'd grown much, much bigger.

My bare feet would now only fit at least size twenty shoes and there was barely room on the bed on either side of him—I knew I could never again find a nice-fitting pair of Miu Mius and nearly wept. I had to stoop and put a hand against the wall to steady my weak legs—blood didn't seem to be filling my head as much as it should. Why were my clothes in tatters when before they had shrunk? I now understood why the Hulk was always so angry; the world doesn't make any sense! The key was a tiny piece of metal. If I wanted to hurt Sal now I could do it with a foot. He would choke on my big toe.

"Jesus, Jen. I'm sorry. I thought we had something."

"Rapport, it's called. Trust! And you violated it."

"I didn't… I didn't mean to. It just happened and then I didn't know what to do. Damn, you must think I'm such an asshole."

"You *are* an asshole. You just didn't know it."

"I'll do whatever it takes to fix this."

"Look at me! How are you going to fix this?"

"You look great, really stunning—"

"Sal!" I raised my foot over his face. I wasn't looking forward to the feeling of his skull imploding, but if he said another goddamn sexist word…

"Jen, please, I'll do anything."

The anger drained out of me. I collapsed onto the bed, sitting, nearly bouncing him out of it. My body felt unfamiliar and I didn't think I was quite as big as I'd been a second ago. Barbie-sized me had been pretty stable. Big me seemed to be all over the map in terms of size.

He pulled the covers up to his neck, a modest gesture.

"Maybe if I retrace my steps…"

To the Coiled Serpent!

First, though, a bit of clothing.

Sal cut a hole in his blanket and I wore it as a poncho, a short one that showed off a lot of leg. He also found some bungees that I used to belt a sheet beneath my pelvis. Leaving through the door of Sal's room, by lying down and squeezing myself sideways, gave me a few scrapes. The door to his garage was extra-wide, thankfully.

Soon I was riding on top of his car in a humiliating position, legs splayed wide and bent at the knees like I might give birth at any moment. My hands gripped the rear window edges, my back arched, and my boobs reared like some trashy dame on a 50's paperback porno.

In the dark side streets on a Monday, I was driven through the neighborhood like the lead float in a Grrl Power parade. When we got to Hollywood, people assumed I was some kind of viral marketing ploy. I pretended to be animatronic, turning my face away from onlookers and telling Sal to hurry up so I wouldn't show up on TMZ.

When we arrived at the Coiled Serpent's parking lot, I rolled off the passenger side and found myself to be bigger than ever. Sal went around the corner to the front entrance. I stepped over a fence into the back patio of the Coiled Serpent and almost smooshed a couple of goth women smoking.

"What the fuck!" one yelled, more angry than scared.

"Sorry. My bad." I shrunk a bit. "So sorry." Shorter, shorter.

"Better watch your ratchet ass," one goth girl said.

"She's the size of a blimp," the other commented.

I stepped on a garbage can and flattened it. They rolled their eyes. I shrank a few more feet.

As I waited for Sal to open the door from inside—the handle was too small for me to operate—I said, "Sorry sorry sorry," but I didn't shrink much more so I figured that wasn't the magic word after all.

Once inside, now only about seven-and-a-half feet tall, I had to scrunch down to avoid snagging my hair on lights and pipes running along the ceiling. I sat on the dance floor, holding a bottle of gin, tipped my head back, and took a shot.

Sal came over and waggled his eyebrows at me and the gin bottle. "So, what's the plan, Jen?"

People were staring, but in that Hollywood insider way where they don't want to be seen looking unless you're someone *very* famous, which is why I loved this place. Had loved it. In my current state, it wasn't so great.

I thought about my situation. "I cursed men, I think, and then it came around and bit me." I sighed. "I release you men from your curse."

Nothing happened.

Sal said, "Maybe we should light a candle?"

I pointed to the booth where I'd sat with Liz, a small candle guttering at its center. He brought the candle back and placed it in front of me.

With the bottle in one hand, and another on Sal's shoulder, I said, "May everyone be treated with respect and empathy, and justice meted to those who deserve it, be they men or women." I closed my eyes and swigged a small sip, then, suddenly feeling my mouth full of burning gin, I did a spit take all over Sal. He frowned and winced.

"Sorry," I said.

"I guess we're even," he said. "You look—I mean, you seem to be nearly the same height you were yesterday."

"Not nearly. How am I going to explain these extra inches?"

"Stretching racks on Melrose? Yoga? Or say it's your secret. Everyone in L.A. has one."

"We shall never speak of this again, or I will cast a spell on you."

He twitched his nose, left-right-left, and then went to pay the bar tab.

The hair rose on the back of my neck and I turned around, expecting to find someone watching me. There was Liz, standing in a dark corner, wearing a Stevie Nicks-styled black lace skirt and an electric-blue satin blouse like from one of those 80's music videos. Her frizzed-out hair was buffeted by the blast of a smoke machine.

Liz, the mentally unstable friend, with that weird pinky gesture last time we were here, in the Coiled Serpent. I wanted to smack myself in the face but decided to save the gesture for her.

I stalked over to her. "You did this! Didn't you?"

Her white teeth, rimmed by her black-lipsticked mouth, shined bright in the club's emerald laser beams. "You own him now," she said. "He's your puppy."

"That's not what I wanted! You should have asked me."

"I was sticking up for my sister. We're in this together." The smug smile on her face made my eyelid twitch.

I pushed her into the wall. "You shrunk me to about six inches!"

"Huh?" Her brow scrunched and she looked at my bare feet. "Oh. Ohhhhhh."

"Yeah, oooohhhhhh. I've been about six different sizes in the past hour."

She pouted. "I don't see how one of my spells could have done that. A shame, really."

I sighed. The gin bottle in my hand felt like it weighed fifty pounds. "Come on." I led her over to the table in the corner. Sal looked at us quizzically and I waved for him to join us. "Jen, this is Sal. Sal, *this* is the person you don't want to mess with." I wiggled my nose. He quivered like a frightened rabbit under her scowling gaze.

"Let's all just try to be nice," I said, "and figure out how Liz can help us make our bonuses this year."

Liz brought out her phone. "Let me see, I think there's a spell in here somewhere for equal pay. With a few tweaks…"

NEGRO IN A HOT TUB

Andre Hardy

THE DAY BEGINS with me realizing I am sore. My legs, butt, lower back, even my torso feel like I've been in a professional football game. Which is something I know a little bit about; once upon a time, though not for long, I ran with footballs for money. Presently, my soreness is the result of sitting for hours upon hours in writing workshops. I am smack in the middle of a ten-day residency learning to write good stories—like the one you're currently reading. I had no idea that workshops could make one's backside so tender. The soreness spurs me to comb the residency schedule for free time. Next thing you know, I am off to the Hollywood-Wilshire YMCA for a hot tub, steam, and sauna.

The Hollywood YMCA is a venerable old building listed on the National Register of Historic Places. Constructed in the early 1920s, the architectural motif is Spanish Colonial Revival. Boasting a magnificent courtyard of red clay tiles and delightful queen palms, the exterior oozes with the charm and character of a Spanish villa. And as you might imagine, being in Hollywood and all, the doors have witnessed a steady parade of human characters. The infamous Benjamin "Bugsy" Siegel, when he wasn't busy killing people, used to pound the heavy bag there. Think about that. A fit hitman? Lord have mercy.

Integral to my story are the handful of men who've been members for longer than I have been alive. It is not unusual to see a muscular, ninety-plus-year-old man swaggering through the locker room naked. Which I happen to find totally awe-inspiring. Not the naked part, necessarily, but the idea of being in the gym at ninety-plus.

Typically, I pay homage to the old dudes by engaging in their favorite pastime, storytelling. They tell. I listen. My hope is one day the secret of longevity will slip. In the interim, however, I am happy to hear their stories. And man I've heard some doozies.

One time, a guy who was an Ohio golden gloves champ in the 1930s—he'd come to Los Angeles by way of Vegas where he'd thrown fights for the mob—told me about the day George Clooney got his lip busted on the basketball court. Apparently, the pre-famous George was a pretty good hoopster but a feisty, foul-mouthed competitor. And, as feisty, foul-mouthed men tend to, he got into a brouhaha with the wrong guy. "Whamo!" the old boxer told me, punching the air with his gnarly fist. "The guy hauls off and socks him one, right in the kisser."

I arrive at the Y from my residency a tad after two. The parking lot is promisingly empty, and after making my way through the courtyard, past the check-in desk, I settle in a nearly empty, almost silent, locker room.

"Thank God," I whisper to myself, "all the old dudes are gone."

I love the old dudes. You know this. But after five straight days of considering plot and character, I do not need more plot and character. I need sensory deprivation. Meditation. Breathwork. And everything is going according to plan. I slip on my trunks and head for the Natatorium, prepared to soak my glutes in relative quiet.

Ah, but it is not to be.

☉

Natatoriums are noisy by nature. The walls are hard. I expect the ricochet-splashing of languid afternoon lap swimmers. What I do not expect is the abrasive, bombastic voice that attacks my ears. The voice emanates from the hot tub across the room. I look. What I see sweeps me into the fairytale orbit of alternative facts.

It is just before Christmas 2016. Like everyone else in the universe, mainstream media has been bombarding me with images of vajayjay-grabbing white men. Said images land on me, a Negro, as somewhat nightmarish. Sort of like Jason Voorhees emerging from graveyard fog, fresh blood on his knife, whistlin' Dixie. So, it makes sense that my mind could be playing tricks on me. For, standing in the middle of the hot tub, I swear, is the aforementioned, vajayjay-grabbing archetype of which I spoke. I am struck nearly dumb. Not because I'm into (so-called) celebrities or anything like that. Hell, turning a blind corner a bit fast, I'd bumped into Russell Brand a few weeks earlier in Whole Foods. Almost knocked my man flat. After his very British, "Excuse me, Mate," I nodded and kept moving like he was regular ole' Joe The Plumber. My shock has to do with the pussy-grabber's wreck of a body. I whisper aloud, "Sweet baby Jesus, clickbait is real."

☉

Ah, clickbait . . .

At the risk of sounding long-armed, lanky, and perhaps slow-witted, I confess to being a sucker for the stuff. Yes, I know, it's base entertainment. But I find it irresistible as a heapin' helpin' of fried chicken & biscuits, collard greens, and watermelon.

I've grown a particular fondness for any headline that mentions Walmart. The one that reads, "*You're Not Going Believe They Wore This To Walmart,*" is always good fun. Good fun because I considered it hyperbole. "That has to be photoshop," I'd mutter, click and grin. "Will you look at this here," I'd smile, laughing out loud. And so, on I'd go: clicking, ogling scantily clad, big-boned women who couldn't be real. I willingly played into the idea that Walmart had them in spades. Ranging from big-boned to very big-boned, proud American women with patriotic tattoos on their rolls-and-rolls of flesh. Every now and then, whoever designs the stuff adds a hillbilly or two.

Once there was a tough guy wearing an NRA cap, his mullet resting nicely on the shoulders of his sleeveless white t-shirt. He had that frontier, square-jawed, colonizer look about him—that look makes me nervous, by the way. But I kept clicking. And I'll be goddamn if the shocker wasn't… wait for it… that he shopped in short-shorts! And his goddamn junk was loose! Photoshop or not, that one had scared me straight for a good while.

❧

Now I'm eyeballing the admitted vajayjay grabber, shaking my head. The official narrative has him standing 6' 3" and weighing a respectable 239 pounds. But what I see looks like, dare I say, his clickbait photos. He is nowhere near the strapping figure the official narrative claims. I give him 5'10" max, which is still respectable in my book. The discrepancy is his weight. I've mentioned my old job of running with footballs for money. Well, because of that, I have a dead-eye, sniper-like skill of quick physical assessment. The pussy grabber is 275, at least. And sloppy at that. My momma might say, "Ooooh, child, he done went a few biscuits too far."

I hate myself for judging, but I've started and now I can't stop. It's the mainstream media's fault, I tell myself. Their ceaseless propaganda, like God, is ubiquitous and turning me into a world-class critic and expert complainer.

I notice his midsection is pear-shaped and the color of Pillsbury biscuit dough, which creates a freaky, creamsicle contrast against the orange tint of his face. And his belly, well, it's rather beefy, I mean, compared to the lean, left-handed basketball player he intends to replace. It screams late-night burgers binges. I shake my head again suspecting double quarter-pounders, fries, and chocolate shakes have got hold of him. Sort of how clickbait and this goddam story have got hold of me and won't let go. I pause, with a chime of revelation. "Oh my god, his loose skin is just like those big-boned Walmart women," I whisper.

And what masterpiece his hair is. It is maybe a little thinner, a little more orange now that I see him in person. But, it is diligent about the work of concealing his forehead and bald spot all at once. What is remarkable, however, is how it remains stiff-as-cement despite the steamy humidity. Somewhere in the back of my mind, I wonder how that is even possible. I'm thinking about hairspray when I see his hands. And I'll be damned if they aren't the teeniest tiniest little things I've ever seen. He uses them, in a way that seems familiar, to accessorize his pompous bloviation.

☙

I have entered a strange new world where truth and make-believe are one in the same. It has created a hot tub predicament. And I'm not quite sure what to do. For years mainstream media has bombarded me with stereotypical images about myself. Yeah, I know it's propaganda. Still, sometimes I get confused. For instance, whenever I wear hoodies, I find myself suspicious of my right hand, wondering if it might steal money from my left pocket. With that in mind, who knows what stereotype could be triggered if Tiny Hands starts using foul-mouthed, locker room talk? And he may need Jesus to save him if I hear anything about all Mexicans being rapist. Hell, I haven't forgotten that, sans the white hood, he carried a metaphorical torch, evoking hate toward the Central Park Five. He wanted to burn those innocent boys. I'm afraid if he starts that divisive, racist rhetoric in my presence, he won't be seeing Sambo, Coon, or good ole' Stepin Fetchit, who was television's favorite Negro, back when America was Great. Lately, I've noticed Nat Turner, Huey Newton, and Malcolm X rumbling in my bones. Philando Castile's murder did it. I've finally had enough.

"You better head back to campus before there's trouble," I mutter, shake my head, and shuffle toward the door.

However, before I reach the Natatorium's exit, I think better of the choice. Something about leaving feels like losing. Like letting my ancestors down. As if the German Shepards that bit them, the hoses that sprayed them, the spit in their faces, the clubbing, the lynching, and rapes was all for nothin'. They did that for me, I remember. "Besides," I say to myself, "you've got four years of this B.S. in your future, big fella. You may as well get some practice in controlling the savage, pistol totin', thugged-out Negro you are programmed to be."

I listen and decide to take a chance.

❧

Tiny Hands stands in the middle of the hot tub swaddled in pure white steam bubbling off the surface. He blocks the path to my favorite jet, a strong one on the end that massages real good. I step in, navigate right past him, apparently unnoticed. And I'm not being sneaky or anything like that. He just can't see me.

As soon as I sit down and exhale a long, relaxing breath, Tiny Hands says, with a confident grin, "I just finished my book. I talked it over with a guy in publishing last night. He thinks I'm onto something big—gonna sell millions of copies."

Well, well, well, I think, perking up. Isn't this a pleasant turn of events?

Tiny Hands is talking to a big, hard-bellied Russian I've seen around the gym before. The Russian, I've always suspected, is one Bad Hombre. Some kind of Hollywood mob king slash internet pirate. I know because I've seen him and two other guys speaking Russian. Whispering, looking over their shoulders, and whatnot. And everybody knows Russia never sends us their best. But that's not the point. The point is the Russian smells a deal and is listening carefully. But now so am I—sheepishly ear hustlin' the conversation while chastising myself for always being so goddamn judgmental.

"You are disgraceful," that ubiquitous, docile, Negro voice says to me; the one I hate who's always singin' about the sweet bye-and-bye. "Tiny Hands is a good writer. You wish you were a good writer. Give the man a chance. I'll bet he's the nicest person you'll ever meet. Shameful, you are very shameful. Sad."

You should know that I love, love, love words. Merriam-Webster's *Word of The Day* podcast is like pecan pie with thick crust and vanilla ice cream. Words like cavalcade and vicissitude and crepuscular give me a rollercoaster thrill. And, man, words strung together by masters like Dickens, Jay-Z, Hemingway, Kendrick Lamar, or Walter Mosley are just like, *wow!* With that brand of love, I open my heart to Tiny Hands' story.

He rakes my nerves talking about how smart he is. "Just brilliant," he says. "Everybody tells me my ideas are sensational."

Bad Hombre nods then cuts a glance at me. By then I have slid myself along the hot tub's great wall, and they are positioned right in front of me in steamy waist-high water. It is obvious I am listening. Obvious I am yearning to talk story. But Tiny Hands does not appear to see me. I am an Invisible Man.

"I've built a massive company, okay. Incredibly massive," he continues. "Now I'm going to use my business smarts to make lots of money selling books. It's hard to believe as brilliant as I am that I never thought of this before." He grins high and mighty. "It's the most incredible idea ever. Revolutionary."

"Oh my God," I mutter. "These idiots have scripts."

I think he's heard me because he pauses. Looking in my direction, though, he gazes over my head, pondering, staring off into the future. After a beat, he turns to Bad Hombre with a rising grin, and says, "You know, I'm thinking this could be the biggest return on investment in the history of business. It only took me a month to write the book!"

Total sacrilege, I think. Nobody writes a book in a month.

Bad Hombre seems to hear me think. He glances at me and sees my eyes have narrowed and I am frowning.

Then Tiny Hands confuses us both. "I'm looking for a Chinese translator," he says. "Know anybody?"

This time Bad Hombre holds my eyes. His thick Russian brow is heavy with questions. But hell, I don't know what to say. I shrug, turn my palms up and mouth, "Chinese translator?"

"There are what, a couple billion Chinese?" Tiny Hands says flippantly. "After I translate the book I'm going to self-publish, put it on Amazon for two, maybe three, maybe even six bucks. I'm going to make a fortune."

Bad Hombre asks, "Your book… tell me what is it saying?"

Tiny Hands scoffs, waves his hand, "Saying? The words don't matter. Chinese will buy anything with my name on it. What matters, you see, is *The Art of the Deal*. And this deal is Picasso." He adds, "I own several, you know."

"Lots of money this deal?" Bad Hombre asks.

Tiny Hands beams with good fortune. "And there are no more black guys counting my money anymore. I had this one guy, so lazy. But it's not his fault, because laziness is a trait in blacks. Now all I've got are short guys in yarmulkes."

The racist insults roll off his tongue with such nonchalance it takes a moment before they register. But finally they land and I stew with his disrespect for words. Yes, being called lazy burns. Especially when my ancestors worked cain't see-to-cain't in the fields pickin' cotton. But there is something more bothersome about him saying "words don't matter." I can't take anymore and, off the wall, I fly. My two fists are raised like judgment day.

I have stood by before, watching as they occupied Wall Street, watching as they protested the Dakota Access Pipeline; always watching. Not this time, though. I think, profoundly: First they came for the words, and I did not speak out. Then they came for the paragraphs, and I did not speak out. Then they came for the books, and I did not speak out. Then they came for writers, and there was no one left to speak for me.

Guessing by the terror in his wide eyes, Tiny Hands has finally seen me. An angry Negro sprung from the shadows—like he'd been warned—to harm his innocent white body. As we stand there, our eyeballs locked together, I sense another goddamn predicament.

If I touch him, I am going prison. Probably for a long, long time. But when the world finds out why, I'll be recognized as a literary martyr. And that seems like a good thing. I envision millions of book-loving Americans marching on my behalf—chanting that I should be free. And in a profound historical moment, broadcast live on mainstream media, I will stand before the court shackled and collared like my ancestors. My last words before being converted into a widget in the Prison Industrial Complex will be those of Dr. Charles Johnson. I will say, "The health of a culture can be measured by the performance of those who speak and write its language. So am I wrong, then, for busting Tiny Hands' lip?" A hush would fall over the courtroom. And then…

Eh, it sounds like fun.

But I have a workshop starting in an hour.

And everybody knows traffic in Los Angeles is no joke.

❧

© 2017 by Andre Hardy. Previously published in Lunch Ticket and Tribe LA Magazine. Reprinted by permission of the author.

NO VACANCY

Bonnie Randall

LUKE LEANED against Della's door. "You never told me you were psychic."

She jerked 'round, the velocity whishing the plants on her desk and making their leaves wave in the sunlight, casting shadows that crept on the floor. Luke edged back, feeling childish for doing so—yet also somehow safer for having moved out of their reach.

"Who told you that?"

Her tone, like cracking ice, made guilt squirm in his belly. Lovely Della. His dear friend. She looked so... caught. Still—"Does it matter?" All these years they'd been colleagues, Luke had never been able to pinpoint *what* was different about her, only that something was. He'd never met another therapist who could, with such immediacy, peel back the nuances of a patient's years-long pathology. Or nail, with unerring accuracy, the origin of problems as proficiently, or as rapidly, as Dell. The word *unnatural* had occurred more than once yet always he'd ushered it away, rebuking himself as uncharitable (not to mention melodramatic), and as most certainly shameful; to label Della 'unnatural' was nothing more than professional envy he could not deny.

Or at least it had been until his sister got sick. Then *stayed* sick. Now, as desperation and confusion grew daily,

Luke found that he clung to the word *unnatural.* Clung and hoped. Because whatever had happened—and was still *happening*—to Mich…? It was unnatural too. So if Della could help, if what he'd always darkly guessed at was true…?

Finding out had been easier than he'd thought. One night (and a few whispered promises) with her estranged sister confirmed what he'd always suspected.

Unnatural. Psychic.

"You… you slept with my *sister?"* She stared.

He blushed, yet what she said struck him; he'd expected her to deny anything psychical. Maybe even become indignant. Instead here was a full-blown display of her abilities. Then—"When?" she asked softly. "When did you sleep with her?" And this too was jarring. He'd been fully prepared for anger. Even disgust. Not…*intrigue.*

"I'd really rather not go into details." He plucked lint from one cuff, an attempt at nonchalant that in no way made him less aware of the incredulity—and (aha!) *there* was the hostility!—on her face.

"You don't want to go into details," she echoed. "Right. I'm quite sure you don't."

His gaze bopped, looking everywhere, *anywhere,* to avoid the serrated chill in her eyes. It landed upon a notepad at her elbow, one she'd been writing on as he'd approached.

700. Seven hundred. Numerically, and in script, the number seven-hundred covered the page, at the bottom becoming mere scrawls with what appeared to be frantic question marks tacked behind them. Reading it—*Seven hundred!?*—Luke edged back like he had when the plant shadows had bitten at his feet.

Della rasped, "H-how? How did you meet my sister?"

"I…" He pulled his gaze from *seven hundred,* surprised by how unwilling he was to look away. Something about it... He shook himself back to the question. "She came to me," he said, and childishly yearned to cross his fingers, dilute the lie. Della's sister had *not* exactly come to see *him;* she'd shown up looking for Della here, at the clinic, but she'd been so... well, so enchanting that, amazingly, he'd forgotten his own broken sister for a moment.

Then that moment had become too great an opportunity to pass by. Was Della psychic? Her sister could confirm or deny, and even in the heat of the act he hadn't known if he was a bad friend, a bad person, or just human and hurting and horny, and now...

Now guilt kept gnawing at his belly and he wondered what all Della could 'see'.

"It's a shame about your birthmark," she said, dry.

His face lit, heat that felt high school. He shook his red cheeks away. "I... I need help, Dell. My sister, my Mich. She—"

"Michelle is still struggling?" Instant thaw; at once Della became the therapist, the friend, he knew. Luke unwound, yet... 'struggling'? As far as euphemisms went it was a big one: Mich had been fine—*better* than fine—when she'd jetted off to L.A., *"For the stars, Luke! I've been commissioned to paint for the stars!"*

A lifelong dream realized; recognition from the Hollywood icons she'd worshipped ever since they'd been kids. But then... psychosis. Catatonia. Ever since she'd come home she was unable to paint anything except for one startling picture, a canvas that froze him from inside out. *"Whatcha painting, Mich?"* he would ask, and if she responded at all, it was with the only word she'd said ever since he'd brought her home from downtown L.A.

"Razor." Grated out because her speech had become so sporadic it was now only growls emitted amid small sprays of spittle: *"Razor, razor, rayyyyyzzzuuurrrr..."*

Post-traumatic stress disorder. That's what he'd told Della and the rest of his team during their monthly self-care conference. But PTSD… that was a weak euphemism too. "She paints," he whispered. "But… not like this—" He pointed to a piece on Della's office wall. "Not anymore."

Della regarded the painting. He did too, and the old familiar swell of pride in his chest made his heart ache. Only Mich could make dust motes (of all things!) look beautiful. Here she'd captured them sailing up, transfiguring into stars in the sky.

One look at that painting and Della had been smitten; to her it was a depiction of healing—broken people transcending from dust into stardust.

Mich, however, had been fantastically wounded by this interpretation. "It's supposed to be *movie stars*, Luke," she'd told him privately. "People who go from bland… to *royalty*."

Royalty? He'd rolled his eyes. Sometimes Mich's Hollywood obsession was a little much. "A sale is a sale, isn't it?" he'd replied.

Her shrug had been dismal.

Now he wondered if she'd ever paint anything as whimsical as dust motes again. *Razor.* The word zinged in his ear. "She… paints the same images over and over," he murmured. "Dirty water. Bloody towels. A straight razor—"

"—that looks like it belongs in an old-fashioned barber shop."

It was startling to have the image plucked from his head, yet also a strange sort of relief to be heard. 'Heard'. Whatever the hell she was doing.

Della reached back, hand blindly settling on that sheet of seven-hundreds she'd written. "Time," she said, raspy. "Therapy."

"It's been nearly a year." Almost to the day since he'd caught that flight after receiving a phone call from a volunteer in a soup kitchen (a *soup kitchen?* What the *hell?*): *"We have someone here who says she's your sister. She keeps screaming your name."*

When he'd arrived Mich had been fully psychotic, yet the staff in that skid-row soup kitchen, used to whackos and derelicts, had barely shrugged at her wild ravings of, "Razor! There's a razor! I made a razor! Oh *no!*"

Luke, however, had been shocked beyond speechless. "Wh-where are her clothes?" he'd finally managed to ask, as his sister, his lovely, appearance-conscious sister, had shoved fingers into a rat's nest of hair, shivering in nothing but a sleep shirt, ankle socks, and, he'd hoped, underwear.

"This is how she showed up," murmured shelter staff.

He'd struggled to keep his game face on as Mich unraveled before him. He recalled crouching before her. "Should we go back to where you were staying? Get your things?"

She'd screamed as though dipped in boiling oil, and the staff member, compassionate, placed a hand on his shoulder. "Her things probably aren't even there anymore, Doctor. Where she was…" His face screwed up, easy to decode: wherever Mich had been staying was a fleabag.

And this baffled Luke still. Mich had means—and expensive tastes to go with them. *What* the *hell* had she been doing in a place that looked, when the cab he'd then hired rolled past it, like a once-worldly hotel now gone hostel? A 1920s relic coughed up on skid row?

And why had Mich screamed and clung to him, tears soaking his shirt, until the place became a mere pinprick, obscured by palm trees and a clutter of street signs in their rear window? "She had—*has*—a white streak in her hair now," he told Della, a bare whisper.

"Lucas, you *know* sometimes trauma imparts leavings on the body—"

"Really, Dell? Would it also leave a damn scar from the base of her neck to her buttcrack?" This he'd observed, in utter shock, when he'd examined her, not like a brother, but like the doctor he was.

"What did *she* say happened?"

He looked her in the eye. "That she got cut up when she tried hiding the razor."

Della swallowed, audible. "Yet there was no blood on her sleep shirt or underpants."

It stunned him, again, how accurate she was. A psychic. Good God. In med school, and certainly during his psychiatric rotation, he'd routinely assessed psychic claims as schizophrenia, or some other Cluster A disorder.

And now look at him, considering the ethics of it. The integrity, or lack thereof, of a counselor who practiced therapy upon clients all while knowing she could read their damn minds.

"I have never hurt a soul with what I can—and sometimes can't—do," Della said starkly.

Yet had he, with no otherworldly talent or ability, hurt someone? Wasn't he hurting her, a *friend,* right now?

"And you need to understand: psychic ability, it's… a talent. And like any talent, there are limits. For example, an impressionist painter who tries art deco—"

The old hotel he and Mich had passed splashed up in his mind and as it did he swore he could hear the pretentious *clink!* of champagne flutes. The breathlessness of affluent, ambitious chatter.

"—and fails spectacularly," Della went on. "Or the classic pianist who just can't play boogie-woogie. Talent has limits, Lucas. Even a great vocalist can't sing *every* song."

He digested this silently, grinding his lip between his teeth and wondering—did she know why he'd *really* approached her? Hell, *outed* her?

"Yes," she said. "I do."

"Wow," he said, and knew he had no right to feel pissed off. Still—"For a vocalist who can't belt out every song, you do a mean a cappella."

She didn't flinch. Instead she pinned him, eye-to-eye. "Understand something," she said.

He felt his face become hot.

"If I can read you—or *anything*—unerringly, it's because you, or they, let me." She paused. "And if I *can't* read something other than a few murky spatterings? It's because it *won't* let me."

A chill marched up his spine, and with it a word out of nowhere: *Prophecy.* He shooed it away. "Where I want us to go," he began but Della gazed beyond him.

"Black and white portraits," she announced tonelessly. "Glamor shots. Glamor queens."

This came out free-association, as though she was looking at a Rorschach inkblot he couldn't see. Nonetheless, what she was 'seeing' made sense. The place he wanted to take her, its doors had opened in 1924 right next to old Hollywood, and in its heyday, class and beauty had strolled its corridors wrapped in fur stoles and pearls.

Glamor queens. On the surface this impression was accurate, but...

But Luke had always sensed something more, something dark that crept within all that old-school Hollywood glamor. Something sinister seeping beneath all the sensuality and enviable sophistication. 'You're only as sick as your secrets' was an old therapy maxim, and it made his skin crawl when he applied it to vintage Hollywood. So it was hard to explain—or even accept—that the era enchanted him too. And while he could not discern precisely why, what he did know was that the affinity for it made him feel unclean in the same way that his own occasionally eager anticipation to hear a client's recount of lurid trauma made him feel abhorrent and deeply ashamed. For the secrets in the shadows of all that glam beauty… he got the sense they were very traumatic, and very lurid indeed. And that was partly why he now believed—"Something happened there, Dell. Where Mich was. And now…" Now that razor in her painting. The blood-stained towels. That murky, dis-colored *water*…

"Lucas," Della imparted softly. "Would *Mich* want you to pursue this?"

No. This came viscerally. But that old hotel, its affluent chatter, it said, "Yes."

Della frowned. "I can't tell if you're lying."

Nor could he.

"I want to tell you no."

Hope flared. Want to didn't mean *would.* "Then… why don't you?"

"Because—" She flashed a look over her shoulder. *Seven-hundred.*

A shiver cut through him and he glanced to see if she had an open window.

"Because, Lucas, I care about—"

Their eyes caught, and for a heartbeat it seemed that everything he'd never had the courage to say was at last spoken between them.

"—because we've been friends a long time." She looked at the floor.

Yes. They had.

"And…" She raised her head. "And because of your hair."

He frowned.

"That white streak you say Mich has. You've got one too. Right down at your scalp. Your hair… it's bone white."

❧

He waited for her at the airport, half-convinced she wouldn't show. When she appeared with an overnight bag in one hand and an iPod in the other, his knees turned to water.

"How's Mich?" she asked briskly.

Painting. Always painting. And now she'd added a new element to the canvas. Two words that sent screams through his skin.

No Vacancy.

"I-uh-I hired a homecare nurse for the weekend."

She nodded. "Your streak is whiter."

"Yeah." He knew.

Her lips tightened. "And you're ready to be my guide?"

"Yes," he answered, for this had been Della's only, yet unyielding request: that their travel was to be done without revealing destination nor any other geographical detail. *"Because this will be hard enough without wading through any confirmation bias prior knowledge will instill in me."* Hence the iPod and earbuds looped through the strap of her carry-on. The contact case and solution she now wrestled out of her bag. "I'm going to the washroom to pop my eyes out," she said, grinning at her own joke.

He couldn't.

"Wait for me outside the door. Without lenses, I'm blind."

Blind. An inexplicable chill skittered across his heart yet he said nothing, just waited then led her, noting that she did not so much as glance at her boarding pass when they passed the clerk at their gate. And when she took her seat on the plane, she pooled the wires for her earbuds on her lap alongside a tidily folded black blindfold. "For when we land," she said, then opened her purse, extracted an elasticized eye-mask too. "For here on the plane," she said primly.

He grinned and she scowled but he didn't care; the eye-mask had ruffled frou-frou on its hem, so *not* Della, and it had been so long since he'd laughed, the sound was both foreign and—"Vacant," he said.

Her gaze quickened. "Pardon?"

He shrugged, a little embarrassed. "I-uh-I was just thinking how anything funny—it's been vacant."

She said nothing but her hands trembled as she fitted her eye-mask on. "This way I'll just look like I'm sleeping instead of flying blind."

Blind. He cast the word away again. "And you plan to wear a *blindfold* when we land? How do I explain that to a cabbie?"

"You don't. You rent a car, cheapskate. And as for the blindfold—do you want accurate answers or not?"

No. You do not. Luke stiffened. That thought, its voice—it sounded like Mich, the *rational* Mich, the one he'd known and loved before the west coast made her crazy. *I miss you,* he thought, and tried to picture her the way she once was.

The old hotel she'd fled from splashed up instead, a torch of light warming its every window and inside all the beds turned down, flea-bitten bedclothes folded back and awaiting a guest. *Ghastly.* His insides recoiled. His fingers, however, reached. He gripped the armrests, shaken by the ungoverned yearning. By that inexplicable damned enchantment. "I only want answers for Mich," he whispered.

But as the plane taxied down the runway he could not tell if the flutter in his belly was dread… or excitement.

◑

Della arrowed up as they began their descent. "Lost?" Her hands fisted on the armrests. "Lost?" she asked again, and her face, locked and listening beneath her frou-frou, was tense. Then—"No," she breathed. "You're not lost."

"I'm here, Dell," he said, and a chill met his flesh when he took her hand.

"Yes." She nodded. "I'm cold 'cause it touched me. Where-ever we're going… it just rested its hand on my shoulder."

And did it hold a bloody towel? Wash with dirty water? The thoughts jittered wildly and he held fast to her hand. "Did… did it say anything?" God. It was humiliating to even entertain such lunacy. Could a building *really* say something?

"Yes," she said and, still masked, looked in the direction of his face. "No Vacancy. Do you know what that means?"

The title of Mich's strange picture. That's all it could be. 'Cause really—No Vacancy? That dump hadn't celebrated a night of No Vacancy in years. Although… He pursed his lips. "Maybe it's threatened," he said. Maybe it was trying to suggest there was no room for them if they came. He smiled. *You **will** give me back my sister, you hellhole.*

Della hesitated, then, "Yes," she said faintly. "Maybe."

◑

With her hand in the crook of his elbow, Luke led her down to the belly of the airport, where the rental agencies lived. "I got us a Lexus," he said, once he'd filled out the forms and attained the key.

"Huh," she replied, as he tucked her into the passenger seat. "I've never ridden in a Lexus and now I can't even see."

He grinned a bit. "You'll see it on the way back."

She fiddled with her seat belt. "Sure you don't want me to drive?"

He wondered if she knew he rolled his eyes at this droll little joke.

"Yes," she answered, a smile crouching in her voice. "But only 'cause I know *you,* Lucas, not because I'm psychic." She bounced one leg and it hit him then; the jokes, the twitching—she was nervous. "And isn't it just like you to drop extra for a Lexus?" she prattled. "I've never known anyone with more champagne tastes."

Right. Wait till she 'saw' where they were going. He hit the gas over L.A.'s labyrinth of freeways, and joined the glut of traffic headed downtown, hands growing greasier and greasier on the wheel.

"You're keyed up," she said as he emerged into the downtown core.

He glanced sideways. "And you're not?"

Blocks ticked by. "I'm wary," she said finally, and as the streets became thick with wanderers, the homeless, and addicts, she said, "Lucas? Are we lost?"

Lost. That word again. A siren bawled past, and up ahead Mich's soup kitchen squatted on the right like a shabby promise.

"Are we stopping here?" Della asked, and sounded so hopeful he nearly *did* stop, call this entire quest off.

"Not yet," he said tightly, and his hands curled on the wheel, muscle tension answering and becoming stiff in his shoulders. A parkade butted off on their left, and he turned into it, paid and pulled into a stall. "We'll have to walk a couple blocks," he said, grimacing at the warzone of dead coffee cups and fast food wraps strewn over the pavement. At rags that once had been clothing, scattered hither and yon.

"Spent glamor," Della said quietly, then climbed out of the car. "Elbow?" she asked.

God knew she needed one here, blindfolded or not. He squired her down a bruised sidewalk where more garbage, rank smells, and people milled, several catcalling upon seeing her blindfold: "Hey, man! What's *your* game?" Others, though, were interested only in scoring a sale: "Up? Down? What's your fix, bro? How 'bout the lady?" Tiny glimpses of product were flashed by quick hands, little bundles, brown and white.

Luke kept walking. Della murmured, "Street people."

"Yes," he said and guilt chewed him, bringing someone like *her* somewhere like *here*, drifting through clouds of cigarette smoke, weed skunk, and blasts of sour body odor, stains on the air.

"Hey!" One street person pointed, mouth gaping in toothless wonder. "You guys making a movie? You filming a *movie?*"

Luke picked up the pace, Della's phrase *confirmation bias* buzzing in his ear. Movies. Stars. *Mich.* His head hurt. *Why here?* He tried wiping his new shoes clean of the filth from the sidewalk then froze, a scatter of yards from their destination, unable to tread even into the shadow the old structure cast.

It's just a building. Yet his feet still cringed like on that day when Della's plants had cast those strange, creeping shadows.

She, at his elbow, said, "Lucas? What's wrong?"

No Vacancy, was the answer he longed to give, the haunting title of Mich's strange canvas. *There's no vacancy here. We need to go.*

"Lucas?" she repeated, but he ignored her, caught instead by the old hotel looming in wait, light winking from a few of its windows, and old wrought-iron fire escapes twisting up each of its sides.

Luke's gaze climbed those treads, reached the height of the building where a sun-beaten sign blared off one side: **LOW DAILY WEEKLY RATES.**

The advert, now vintage, was once a boast of affordable decadence for the intrepid cosmopolite. Now… now it was nothing more than a sleazy come-on.

His eyes tracked back down. Surely this old place *had* once been elegant—but now its handsome red canopies were mere pock-marks over windows which… some lit, most dark, reminded him of that street person's toothless smile.

Still and in spite of it all, a sign o'er the front entrance gleamed in shiny defiance, the once-golden glitz of old Hollywood.

THE CECIL HOTEL

Luke shuddered and, "Seven hundred," Della's voice wobbled as it broke in. "Lucas? What's that number from?"

Seven-hundred. As in her handwritten, ever frantic, *seven-hundred*? Or… his gaze raced back up to that vintage sign. Below **LOW DAILY WEEKLY RATES… 700 ROOMS**.

His shoulders twitched, imagining that many eager dwellings, and as he pulled his eyes from the sign he felt oddly threatened.

"Lucas?"

"It's… just a number on a sign," he lied, mouth chalky and feet forcing them forward, shuffling up the scabbed sidewalk to The Cecil's front door.

Brass shone on the other side of the window, and when they crossed the threshold chandeliers glittered while marble gleamed at their feet. Art deco. Retro decadence dialed straight out of somewhere like *The Great Gatsby*.

"I taste champagne on my tongue," said Della.

Luke considered this. Had *that* been what had seduced his champagne-tastes sister? The illusion of opulence? But… how could her artist's eye have not seen that it was all merely façade? This lobby, a false front like the myriad movie sets in this town, did nothing to belie that outside the bricks were all crumbling. Didn't erase those iron fire escapes, snaking up fifteen floors—surely their very existence revealed the hotel's past-due status? Even that beaten sign on its side—weekly rates, for God's sake! How could Mich have missed all the… what had Della called it earlier?

"Spent glamor," she answered.

Yes. Faded glory. So… *Why here? Mich, of all places you could have stayed… why **here**?*

And its appearance didn't even account for the *history* of the place. He shuddered, glancing beside him. Della had become as still as the building itself. Was *she* attuning to its history?

"There are bodies," she whispered, and tilted her head back as though she could see over their shoulders, back out the front windows. "They're falling out of the sky."

He whirled and—*What the **hell**?* First one shadow then another indeed seemed to hurtle down from the sky, each crashing into the ground. *Confirmation bias,* his head jabbered, for surely he was not seeing what Della could see. Yet those crashing shadows… *they're Los Angeles,* he thought wildly. 'The Angels'. Because suicides here, scores of them, truly had sent bodies swan-diving from these old canopied windows, bodies that could well appear to be angels, falling out of the sky.

"Are you okay?" she asked.

"I… sure." He kept his hand on her elbow, led them further inside. "Mindful," he said. "The floor's slippery."

"With blood?" she recoiled and he glanced at her sharply. Joking again?

She wore no smile. No expression at all.

"No," he answered faintly. "Polished marble."

"Yes. And blood," she whispered.

He looked down. The floor, clean and gleaming, had a compass rose laid into the marble at the center of the atrium. *Just in case you're a **Lost** Angel,* he thought, again wildly, and deposited Della in the center of it.

"Wait here," he said, then hurried to check in.

The front desk was one more tribute to yester-year: brass columns, a marble counter, and a bank of old-school pigeon-holes, glossy black and holding bona-fide retro lock-and-tumbler keys. "I have a reservation," he said to the desk clerk.

"We know."

He gaped, yet the clerk, a California blonde tricked out in a vintage bellhop's uniform—brass buttons, pillbox hat—regarded him blandly. "When you called you said you'd be traveling with a blindfolded woman."

Ah. Right. He felt his face flush as he glanced back to where he'd left Della.

She stood immobile mid-compass, like a lovely wax sculpture, blindly waiting.

Blind. That goddamn word was making his insides blanch, and when the clerk said "Oh, look! You have our resident artist's room!" he whipped back around.

"*Pardon?*"

"Room 1013. That's our Resident Artist's Room." Her flawless face folded into a squint. "You didn't know?"

No. He'd just known that 1013 had been Mich's room. But 'Resident Artist's Room'… her commission to the stars had been *here*? *This* had been contract she'd boasted of?

"Your key," said the clerk, and passed him a small, narrow envelope, *1013* written in pencil on one side. "And the elevator." She directed him, two practiced, pointed fingers. "Welcome home," she said, then beamed.

Luke quelled a shudder, yet *cast member*, he reminded himself. Everyone in L.A.—hell, even employees in the kiddie theme parks—considered themselves 'cast members'. So none of what they said was real dialogue, they all simply spoke off a 'script'.

"Sir?" A young black man with cherub's dimples and tricked out in the same vintage get-up as the clerk, approached him with aplomb. "Help with your luggage? Easy to get lost in this grand, old place."

'Grand'? And seriously? Dimples or not, this guy's face was pitted with meth sores, and the skin on his hands had faded to a dead sort of gray. *Might want to stop using, friend,* Luke thought, and wondered—did The Cecil routinely recruit staff from the denizens of street folk outside? "I can manage," he said.

"As you wish." The bellhop beamed, but his grin struck Luke as sad. God, what a terrible gig this must be. "Welcome home," the young hire tacked on.

And what an abhorrent tag line. This place truly had no clue. Reclaiming Della off the compass, and eased by the warmth of her elbow in his palm, Luke turned them in the direction of the elevator, just down the hall.

"Film projectors," she said suddenly and, down the wainscoted hall, the lone elevator opened, a mouth for no one.

"There are film projectors here, aren't there?" Della's gestures were vague. "They… look old." Her mouth made a moue, then—"Olivia de Havilland?" she said. "Judy Garland?"

"*They've* been *here*?" Though… why doubt it? This place once genuinely was what it masqueraded as now.

"N-o." Her reply teetered out, slow. "Well… maybe. It's their *era*—it's been here." She paused. "It still is."

No. This, stubbornly. *My **sister's** here.* "The elevator," he muttered, and tried steering her.

Her feet cooperated, but barely, then she halted altogether beside a Greek revival bust, all seductive curves and blank eyes. "Blind," she blurted.

He jolted, half horrified by her accuracy, half fascinated.

She looked troubled. "The word blind—it's like 700. Lucas, *do you* know what it means?"

He had a guess, spun from research he'd done on this place, yet even as he debated how to say it, he looked into the statue's blank eyes and, "If I tell you what you're next to it might clear it up," he said instead.

"Okay," she agreed, but sounded unsure.

"There's a bust—well, a whole statue, really. Between you and the elevator, a Greek revival relief and her eyes—"

"No." She flicked an impatient hand. "It—*she's*—lying."

He gaped and reflexively edged back.

"She's only a symbol. Blind," Della repeated, and her mouth worked. "Remember 'blind', Luke. It's important. Real important."

Nodding, and mindful of the statue that now seemed to smile, he jabbed the elevator button to rise.

The door slid open like an awakening eye. *Blind,* he thought, shuddering, and led them inside. *Did* The Cecil have eyes that he, even *without* a blindfold, could not see?

"Yes," said Della.

He flinched.

"I don't know what question you just asked, but whatever it was—the answer is 'Yes'."

No Vacancy!

He leapt. Where the hell had *that* come from?

No Vacancy! Again, this time plaintive and fully recognizable. *Get out!*

But, Mich, he tried calling back, and the elevator shut them in, swept them up.

෩

The numbers over the door glowed and dimmed, floor-to-floor as they climbed, and at Four they lurched to a halt. The door stuttered open to a wall, robin's egg blue, white wainscot in glossy contrast. Luke blinked. Downstairs the same style had been apparent—the wide wainscot, wide baseboards, and regal crown molding—but in the lobby everything had been black with gold. So now, with the colors—perhaps each floor in this place was some sort of quaint nod to the bold geometry and garish colors of the art deco age.

"Yes, sort of," Della answered and before he could be taken aback by her unsolicited response, a young man, sniffling and in pseudo army fatigues, slunk into the elevator with them.

"Which button?" Luke asked, but the kid waved him away, and as he selected his floor his cuff rode up to reveal track marks, blister red, staggering up the inside of his arm.

Luke's brow hopped and the kid jerked his arm down, face awash with pink shame. Yet when their gazes clashed his mouth still jerked, a cautious little smile that reminded Luke of the way a leery dog would lick the hand of a stranger, uncertain whether it was about to be cuddled or kicked. "Hey," he began, but 'are you all right?' was lost as the door coughed open on Five (canary yellow this time, same glaring white wainscot) and the youth scurried out, steps somehow in consort with his track marks, crooked and lacking direction.

They re-ascended and Della said, "What floor did we just leave?"

"Five."

"Five," she whispered. "There was an overdose in the hallway there once. In the sixties. A man—well, a boy, really."

Gooseflesh broke out beneath Luke's dress coat. That kid who'd just left. Had he been flesh and blood? Or—

The elevator *schunked* to a stop as '10' lit above, and the door burst open to tomato bright walls. "Oh!" Della jerked back as if she could see the red shock.

"Del—" he began, but she lifted her chin.

"Well, don't *you* look like you just opened an artery?" she said.

An internal bath of chipped ice flooded Luke's chest.

"Let the games begin," Della said softly and kept her chin up, offered her elbow. But then—"Wait!" She fell still, head cocked.

Luke's breath locked somewhere mid-throat as a sliver of smile found her face. "Are you... are you playing peek-a-boo?" she asked.

A cold draft assaulted his spine.

"No." She shook her head. "Not peek-a-boo. Hide and seek, right?"

The elevator door, still gaping (how the hell was it still open and gaping?) allowed Della to peer sightlessly inside, to the front left corner where battered floor buttons were so faded that some were rendered to just mere indentions. "Look," she said. "She's hiding there, in the corner."

The crawling cold crept on his backbone, and when he glanced nothing was in the corner save a smudge of red that may or may not have been his eyes, adjusting to the light. Still, the shape—slim shoulders in what could be a red sweater—struck him as something like a visual whisper; indiscernible, yet audible. And definitely human.

"Stay away from the water." Della spoke into the sanctum. "Run far, far away from the water." She paused then, like she waited. "She won't listen," she said quietly, then lifted her face, peered blindly toward his. "What floor are we on?"

"Ten," he answered and pulled the key with its old diamond-shaped key ring from the envelope that read 1013.

The Artist-in-Residence's Room.

Della remained on the cusp of the still-open elevator, and Luke stared at it. What was wrong with the damn delay on the door? Unless… a slinking certainty crept into his mind. The old place was reading Della's inertia, it knew she had second thoughts. Beads of sweat popped upon his upper lip. She couldn't back out. Not now. He needed her. *Mich* needed her. "You said this place was trapped in another era," he said lightly, the first thing he thought of. "Incredible, how you know that."

"How I *feel that*, you mean." She paused. "And you feel it too."

He glanced at the décor. Reproduction? Or…

"No," she said. "Not reproduced. It… like a transparency. The past overtop of the present, the present overtop of the past. Both are here, Lucas. Past and present."

Future too. The thought popped quickly, another stark startle of certainty.

He kicked it away. This was no unworldly time warp. The décor was just a cheap hustle, an effort to sell effect. All one had to do was just look close at all this supposed opulence and see it was all only bright matte colors. And the glossy white trim, it was all chipped and blackened from countless fingers—

"Not fingers, Lucas. Those stains are from shadows."

He quaked and her earlier word—*transparency*—licked his ear. Transparencies—shadows that used to be people? Or people who were somehow mere shadows…? He shook himself, angered by a play on words that felt… well, like trickery. What the hell *was* this old dump, anyway? Better yet, what was it still trying to be?

A riff of Bible verse slithered forward to answer, the Book of Matthew: *'A tomb beautiful on the outside, but inside filled with dead men's bones and wickedness.'* A bolt of adrenaline wracked him, and the urge to dive back into that open, waiting elevator was so strong his legs twitched. Yet—"Mich." Her name left his lips for the hundredth time. The thousandth. *Why were you here?*

"You *know* why."

There was a thread in her tone, accusation. Luke squirmed from it.

"In your heart you can see this place just like me."

No. Again he glanced at the elevator. Again he thought *Run!*

"Champagne flutes," Della intoned. "Cigarette holders. Martinis with iced gin."

"There's nothing like that here," he croaked, yet his eyes roamed reflexively, *eagerly,* and the compulsion to immerse himself in that world, to be aware of it, be *part* of it, to uncover every dark, depraved nuance he'd always sensed there… *No!* He snapped himself back. *That's not who I am!* That's only who this place was trying to trick him to be.

Nonetheless, juniper pungency, gin, persisted in his nostrils, and when he glanced down he was rolling a cigarette between index finger and thumb. "Hell!" he exclaimed, and threw the cig.

The worn carpet absorbed it, and as it faded from sight, "Hell?" Della echoed, then her voice slipped back to monotone. "Beautiful, big-eyed women," she said and her eyes, protected by the blindfold, still somehow beseeched him, large and guileless. Then when she said, "Drop-waist dresses. Feather plumes in their hair," Luke didn't know if he was hearing her or seeing it as at once her clothing began switching out, pearls, hose, and headbands, a rapid-fire costume change not unlike a yesteryear Hollywood starlet.

"You're—" *Scaring me? Beautiful?* All was lost as she gushed—

"And the *men*."

Luke's breath caught as, down the corridor, a gentleman—*Wait, that's me!*—clad in black tie and hair glossy with Brylcreem flashed a slight and ironic smile before disintegrating into the shadows.

"Dreams." Della moved in a slow circle. "They're hoping here. Dreaming here."

A cast of characters stepped out of that yawping elevator only to evaporate one by one as Luke clung, enchanted, to the image of flappers whose dresses dripped with beads. To wise guys wearing fedoras and wide collars.

"There are people here," Della whispered. "Hundreds and hundreds of people here. And they're not just dreaming, Luke." She swallowed, a rasp. "They're craving."

"Craving?" he sounded skeptical, but inside, something said *Yes!* "Craving what?"

"Eminence," she breathed. "Fame. Immortality." She faced him then, eyes still buried beneath her blindfold, yet once again boring into him. "And they have it. Immortality. Just not… not the way that they'd wanted." She reached out then, ran an unseeing hand down the white wainscot bisecting the hall, fingers kicking up a small cloud of grime. "I'm sorry," she said softly. "That the dream you starved for, *whored* for, turned into this nightmare."

Luke stared. Would the hotel respond?

The narrow hallway, its scarlet walls, began to gently close in then expand, like a bellows bloated with breath or—

"With blood," said Della. "This place… it's like a parasite that soaks itself in despair. In agony. In *loneliness*."

That little junkie down on the fifth floor. His tepid smile had been lonely, no question.

"That's where we are," Della declared. "In a place that bathes in rage and despair. A place that devours dead dreams."

Dreams. Mich's dream of being commissioned 'by the stars'. His gut lurched.

Della faced him, blind. "You feel it, too. You're no psychic, Lucas, but you feel it too."

"Yes." He nodded.

"It's a hotel."

"Yes," again.

She nodded too, visibly orienting. "When we deplaned I said 'Lost'."

And ever since he'd repeated it silently, over and over.

"You need to know, Lucas—I didn't mean lost as in could not find their way." She looked at him, blindfold still in place. "They're not lost *literally*. They all know *exactly* how to get where they're going."

"They?" he said and the cold returned. Made him shiver.

"Lost as in lost cause," she said. "Unrepentant. Unredeemable. After all." She paused, lifted her chin again. "They don't call this city *Lost Angels* for nothing."

He started, but quickly reined himself in. "The translation is actually '*The* Angels', Della, not '*Lost* Angels'. Don't you know Spanish?"

"Don't *you* know colloquialisms?" she retorted. "And what part of *psychic* do you not understand, Lucas? And let me tell you something else: where-ever... whatever hell-hole this is that you've brought us to—we're on a fool's errand here. Lost means lost be it literal *or* figurative, and there's nothing it will allow you to find here. You can't out-smart a... a parasite that's a century older, and a hell of a lot hungrier, than *you*."

"But Mich—"

"Was seduced by whatever big lie was downstairs in that lobby. 'Cause there was one, wasn't there? A big lie?"

Old-school Hollywood was downstairs in that lobby. The seduction of glamor and opulence. A stage set like so many others in a city that proudly, even smugly, called itself 'Tinsel Town': all show and no substance.

"Except there *is* plenty of substance," Della corrected. "Every floor, all the walls, every beam holding this place up... blood-soaked bones, Lucas."

He flinched, yet... melodrama. Surely that was just melodrama.

"Of *course* it's melodrama!" she snapped. "Why do you think this place has clung to its glory-days era? Melodrama was always what worked for it *best*."

The bright walls, their white wainscot, even all the bold, round mirrors that faced the open elevator upon every floor... *Eyes that **your** eyes can't see.* Luke shifted, un-easy. "So what... what do you think that it wants?"

"I told you: immortality."

It had already been standing a *century.* "Doesn't it have that already?"

"Well..." She shifted, one foot to the other. "It has history—do you know its history?"

"I do." Once Mich had come home, his research had been ruthless.

And so had his need to sleep with the lights on for many nights after.

"How about you?" he asked. "Can you see… do *you* know its history too?"

"Impressions," she muttered. "Not details. I… I just know this place has never been Disneyland."

Something purred. *Did* something just purr? He had to be getting caught up in his own melodramatic confirmation bias, yet could not help but look up as if he could see through the ceiling, all the way to the floors where at least two serial killers had called home.

"Welcome home," that cast-member desk clerk had told him and now, neck tingling, he pondered Della's outburst. What *were* the odds of so much violence and hatred and tragedy to have happened in one distinct spot?

"The hungriest people have the most succulent souls," she whispered, then shook herself. "Sorry. I have no idea where that came from."

A shiver seized his face and forced it 'round to look down the hall. Room 1013. He held up the key as though Della could see. "Mich's room, Dell. Mich's *mind.* I want it back."

"It won't let you have it."

She was right. The instinctive part of him—the psychic part *every* human had, remnant from caveman days when the body needed to know how to sense a predator—it said run.

And so did the open elevator, which seemed to be gaping in defiance to this place, practically begging them to hop back in and escape, make the right decision. Run.

So do it. Run. Yet when he opened his mouth, he said, "Can't we just *try?*"

"You won't win."

"Why?" Christ, he sounded like a petulant child.

And she must have thought so too for she grasped him, albeit blindly, by both lapels and shook. "Listen," she hissed. "Use your *head*. Beyond this hotel, consider this whole city, this whole *area*. Does anywhere else you've ever heard of know compulsion, or seduction, like *here*?"

No. In fact the notion of 'Hollywood dreams' was such a cliché it was now an unfunny joke.

"Los Angeles *inhales* people's dreams, Lucas. Eats their delusions of grandeur. This city… this city sells hope better than the slickest mind-control cult on the planet."

She wasn't wrong.

"But it does even more than that, Luke, and that's where, *spiritually* where, things get dicey. L.A.… it's known *worldwide* as a place capable of making identity, geography—even *time*—shift. It's been doing it, and being downright worshipped for it, for *decades*. So do you really think that's not powerful? Think that ability, shifting time, shifting identity, hasn't permeated right down into the *soil*? It's become a part of what an old hotel like this can now do all on its own. From trait to state, therapist. You *know* this stuff."

Of course he did—as it applied to people. *People* adapted and assumed traits. But *places*?

"What's stronger than hope, Lucas? What's stronger than a craving?"

He had no answer.

"How many times has this city—this *hotel*—heard the words 'I'd do *anything*'?"

An electric vein of sensation crackled down the vestibule, erected the hair on his arms and—God help him—the excitement robbed him of breath.

"There's a whole lot of power when a whole lot of people are hungry for promises a place like this has no intentions to keep," said Della, and darkness oozed down the hall.

Still—"S-some people here—in L.A.—they're successful," he said. "They're stars."

"Are they? The children who snort coke at cast parties when they're barely twelve? The A-listers who submit to group sex, anal sex, *any* unwilling sex just to become overnight sensations? How much of the glitter and glam that the public licks up is only air-brushed perversion, Lucas? Degradation that you and I make a living *healing* people from?"

Souls cast into bottomless wishing wells. Hadn't he always thought that himself? Especially about old, classic Hollywood that had been borne a mere stone's throw from here? *This place bathes in despair.* Yet—"Not all—" he tried again, but his desperation died upon her pitying smile.

"You want to tell me something pure can come out of a place that tells lies for a living?" She clucked her tongue. "Have you ever, in your practice, seen someone come out of a relationship with a psychopath who's not emotionally and psychologically mutilated?"

No. He had not.

Dark cold floated around them, and in it Luke recognized an action he knew, an action he had perfected down to an art. Listening. Someone (something?) was crouched silently and listening with unmistakable attentiveness— much like a therapist would do. Rolling his shoulders he shifted, wanting to somehow chase it off, yet… he fell still and attuned, in a way he supposed Della attuned, to the listening. It was patient. Wise. More sensations he knew. More feelings he'd *exuded.* A flash of respect he could not control burst inside and he rapidly rejected it because what the hell was this? Mockery? He turned a circle in the corridor like a boxer. *Screw off!* he sneered.

The listening—and the patience—ensued. Then Della spoke:

"A place like this," she said, "—and there's more than one in this area—they're like batteries. They drain every hope, every dream… and they're *clever,* Luke."

The listening. The wisdom. He was certain, in that moment, that she had no idea exactly *how* clever.

"They'll show you what you want to see—until you see and do what you'd never, not even in nightmares, believed you'd see and do."

A piece of history hurtled to the forefront of his mind; a rag-tag group of young hippies seeking peace in a commune out in Benedict Canyon. Living there happily until their leader compelled them into blood-soaked butchery just a handful of miles away in Beverly Hills.

Then, more recently, there was Mich, his Mich, screaming incoherently in that soup kitchen: *"There's a razor he's got a razor get that **razor**...!"*

You'll see and do what you never, not even in nightmares, believed you'd see and do.

"Mich," he whispered. What *had she* done with that razor? "Why her?"

"Why *not* her?" A twist of smile screwed Della's mouth. "Why not *you*?"

Artist-in-residence. His mouth went to grease and *Drawing what?* he asked the listening quiet, but The Cecil, still patient, did not answer.

"And some cannibals feed off human flesh to survive, but others, like here? They do it because they crave the *flavor*."

The darkened cold now laughed and a rush of vomit jellied in Lucas' stomach, shot up his throat. He swallowed it back, spitting, and trying to reorient.

The décor waxed and waned wildly; the present, the past, and he wondered—*had* time folded over on itself here in The Cecil? *Was* this campy art deco style not really a reproduction but instead a *reaching*, from backward in time?

"Lots of things warn folks to stay away from this area, Luke." Della's voice had fallen dead quiet. "Even the land this city sits on—it's called a fault, did you know? Now consider that language. A fault. Could that mean *at fault*? And if it does, do we even need to wonder why all of Heaven's Lost Angels once landed right here? The Universe *planned it* that way, and yet…" Her face fell, mouth inverted under her blindfold. "Yet here we are, an adoring public who *worships* the people this city creates."

As had Mich. So proud to be commissioned by the stars. And now that beautiful, gifted part of her had been… well, if he was understanding Dell right, it had been inhaled by this place. Locked up in Room 1013. He gazed down the hall. "Just… please, Dell. Let's try."

"You'll lose, Luke. This place… you told me you could feel it. So you know it holds trump. Blind," she tacked on then, spontaneous like before. "Have you figured out what it means?"

"No," he said, and kept his eyes fixed, down the hall. "Della, please."

Her feet parted, one butted up against the still-open elevator, the other pointed toward him. She was going to refuse. She was going to rip off her blindfold and dive back into that elevator which, relieved, would hustle her back downstairs and spit her back out in the lobby where she'd see that compass rose and know exactly what direction to run.

And then he'd have no hope of ever fixing his sister. His throat closed. Burned.

Della sighed. "Take my hand," she said.

Shadows swam up the hall and led them down to Room 1013.

☾

The painting was the first thing he saw, and when he cried out Della grabbed him, hands patting. "What?" she said. "What's happened?"

"It… there's a picture. Mich's picture." The original of the still life she repeated now, except… "*Lovely,*" he breathed. A period piece straight out of 1924, it was unlike Mich's current efforts (which had degenerated into little more than manic tossings of paint upon canvas) and instead a true reflection of her photo-realism skill: a razor, gleaming silver, angled atop a fluffy white towel and nestled beside a rich puff of white shaving cream. A crystal vase of cream colored roses stood off to one side and Luke stared at the picture, transfixed, until his gaze hit the brass placard at the bottom, the title.

Welcome Home.

A bolt of adrenaline cut through his belly, and Della said, "The razor. Lucas. Is the razor in that painting?"

His head bobbed and he forgot that she could not see him.

"I'll take that as a yes. Lucas, listen to me."

Her words and tone registered, rapid-fire, yet he only paid scant attention. *Mich.* His gaze roamed the canvas. *What **was** it about this painting? What did it do to make you not Mich?*

"We need to get out of here, Lucas, are you listening? Cut your losses. Let's leave."

Leave? And "Losses?" he hissed. "This isn't a poker game, Della, it's my *sister.* And just because *you* were okay giving up and cutting out on *your* sister doesn't mean that I am!"

"My…" She jerked back. "My sister told you I gave up and cut *out*?"

"Well, she certainly told me that you two don't talk anymore!"

"We don't…" A small, grim smile grabbed her mouth. "Well, that's certainly true. We *don't* talk. Yet how interesting that you thought it was me, and not *she*, who cut contact."

Once again brick red heat seized his face. Still— "She's… sexually relaxed," he said. "You're… not. I thought maybe the rift was about values."

"Oh, Lucas." A wasted sort of laugh shook her throat. "In the space of a first meeting she slept with you, and you with her, and that makes you both *sexually relaxed* instead of plain old indiscriminate?" She shook her head. "And regardless, our sexual mores—or lack thereof—are not why she stopped speaking to me."

"Oh?" His breath waited somewhere between throat and gut.

"I'm psychic," she said. "Unnatural. Unclean."

Unnatural. That had been *his* word.

"And as for my sister…" Della drew a big breath. "Lucas, she stopped speaking to me a lifetime ago and then… then she died."

No. *No.*

"And I *know* I should have told you as soon as you brought her up. I knew agreeing to any of this was wrong, even depraved, but…" She snagged his gaze, large eyes pleading. "But I lost my sister too, and I thought maybe by her appearing to you she wanted to reconnect with me. That I… I could reclaim her the way you want to reclaim Mich."

"Dell—"

"I'm sorry, Lucas. I'm *sorry.* It was a dirty secret to keep and the filthiest sort of lie by omission, and I guess I should have *known* it was all just a projection, just a damn *movie,* but still…" She wept.

"Dell," he said again and reached for her, but the room tilted. He weaved, and a thought—*time folding over!*—

whished in and whished out and his feet jumbled together and he stumbled, striking a hand out to the bed so he wouldn't fall.

When he righted himself, the room glowed.

"What?" he said.

All the paint was brand new. And the grime and the stains on the carpet and bedspread… gone.

"Wh-what?" he repeated. "How?"

"Lucas?" Della's voice seemed to project from somewhere other than where she was standing. "I… I can't undo the blindfold."

Orienting, and teetering a little, he searched for her.

His breath caught. Of course she couldn't undo the blindfold. He regarded her and heat he could not help, heat he'd always felt, welled inside. Trussed up like that on the bedspread (chenille, he believed the soft fabric was called) in a black slip and with all her black hair cascading… her image called to mind Vivien Leigh. Elizabeth Taylor. Every classic calendar girl he'd ever seen: creamy skin and soft, vintage lingerie.

"Lucas." She sounded breathless. "I can see what you're seeing—and that's *not* what you're seeing. I'm still standing here by the wind—oh!" She shrieked and, distantly, he heard a clatter—like a hip or knee had just jostled a table. "Oh my God, someone just *jumped* from this *window!*"

"Della," he chided and stooped to where she was tied, ready to at last kiss her plump mouth, taste its rich, dark lipstick. "Wait." He drew back. "I should shave first."

"Lucas, no!" she cried and, *"There's a razor!"* he heard Mich say.

He blinked. Why, yes. There *was* a razor. There'd been a razor waiting here all along. Grinning, he reached out and Della babbled, "L.A., Lucas! It's capable of making identity, geography—even time—shift!"

Indeed. And how handy. He placed his hand in the portrait.

Mich yelled, *"He's got a razor get that **razor**…!"*

"Lucas!" Della, shrill, strangely still did not sound anywhere near the bed where she was tied up.

"Luke!"

Was she crying? Dimly, he heard someone—or something—whisper *Despair.*

"Listen to me: there's a young Asian woman waiting out in the hall. She's crooking her finger because she's ready to play hide and seek with you in the elevator!"

Yes, well perhaps she was bored. Maybe lonely. "I'll get there, honey. All in good time."

"*No*! You don't *understand!* Th-there's an addict too. A kid who tells me you smiled at him. He's wearing a green army coat and he's waiting for you to come talk to him down on the fifth floor!"

Yes, of course he was waiting. That poor kid needed a therapist. And now… here he was. Luke exhaled, relaxed for the first time since they'd arrived. Helping people. It had always made him feel right at home.

Welcome Home. The painting. That desk clerk. Now he understood. He was *home.*

"No, Lucas! Stop! Listen! It's greedy. It took Mich but she wasn't enough. It knew it could get you here too! It kept her so she could call out to *you.*"

How clever. And now—"I'm here," he told it, and pulled the roses out of the painting too.

They smelled divine.

"Lucas, *please listen:* 'The hungriest people have the most succulent souls'. I understand what it means now.

It means you'd do anything to find Mich, restore Mich, and now *look where you are!*"

Yes, look where he was: a luxury hotel in the most glamorous city in the world. About to bed a blindfolded Della who looked like a starlet ready to play sex games. "I just need to shave." He took the razor, ambled into the bathroom.

Indoor plumbing and scalding water. This place really *was* modern.

"Lucas!" Della called and, strangely, that black bellhop from downstairs appeared behind him, a reflection in the mirror.

"Hot shave, sir?"

Luke bestowed him the razor. "Why, certainly."

The bellhop tilted Luke's face back with one hand, positioned the razor with the other, and leaning close, rested his mouth on Luke's ear. "You'll see and do what you never, not even in nightmares, believed you'd see and do."

Then a red wash jetted out before them, the same blaring color, Luke thought dimly, as the gaudy paint out in the hall.

◑

Della's throat was raw from screaming by the time someone came, and she had no clue how dark the night had grown once police arrived and a detective untied her, took her blindfold off.

She scampered off the bed, recoiling from its spread—picked-clean chenille; threadbare and soiled with long-standing stains. "H-how?" she croaked, astonished that her wrists truly *had* been trussed up and now hurt from being tied behind her back.

Capable of making identity, geography—even time— shift.

The detective, a woman, read her face. "You don't remember him tying you up?"

"N-no." *'Cause **he didn't.***

"He never talked about suicide?"

"Never." Not out of the confines of discussions regarding their patients.

"Had he been depressed?"

Depressed? No. But sad…? She clawed through her own sadness, her own *horror,* and, "Yes," she whispered. Lucas *had* been sad. Despairing, to be precise. His sister, his best friend, had been ripped away. Then dangled here, a carrot on a stick.

Or, more aptly, projected here like a damsel in distress upon a glam silver screen.

And had she too not played a role in this movie from Hell? Revulsion scurried on her arms, making the skin feel like it bunched. "W-where… what's this place called, anyway?"

The detective's brows hopped. "You don't know?"

Della shook her head, so cold she was sure the movement might make her crack.

"It's The Cecil on Main, Della. Do you know it?"

Yes. And no. She knew it the way a rape victim knew her assailant—intimately, yet unwillingly. Obscenely. "I do now," she whispered and her sixth sense prickled, drew her gaze to the hall.

A crowd hung there, both visible and not visible. Among them a killer leered, a pentagram scrawled upon one of his palms. The little Asian woman who'd been hiding in the elevator quivered there too, and when their eyes met she gave Della a small, melancholy sort of wave.

Della returned it and saw, to the Asian woman's right, a circa 1940's beauty, her lovely face marred by a macabre smile carved, ear-to-ear.

Black Dahlia whispered her psychic voice, and as that wrecked face nodded, Della noted others, dozens of others, some bodies stabbed or strangled, others wrecked and ruined by the crush of velocity upon pavement. Lost angels. Hunting dreams and finding nightmares. Despairing then hurling themselves from some of The Cecil's seven hundred hungry windows.

Hours ago Luke had asked himself a question she'd heard: *What are the odds of so much violence and hatred and tragedy to have happened in one distinct spot?*

Normally, Della knew the chances would be mathematically absurd. But here… "Dead dreams are delicious," she whispered. And this place, like so many others on a fault, *at* fault—"It soaks itself in despair," she said, and was not unaware that the Detective beside her did not disagree. "And the desperate, the *hungriest*—they have the most succulent souls."

The hall crowd nodded gravely—some even sadly—then began drifting away.

The detective had kind, knowing eyes in a gentle black face. "Della," she said. "We'll need to go to the station, take your formal statement, but afterward—is there anywhere we can take you? You… really shouldn't stay here."

But part of me will. For as much as this place devoured dead dreams, she knew it delivered them too. She could traverse the globe and The Cecil would stay with her—just as it had stayed with Mich in that painting.

The painting! She wrenched around, looking for the canvas, and, "That?" she burst.

At best, the picture was a nonsensical still-life: a towel, some white feathers, and a white glob of—ugh. Was that supposed to be whipped cream? Was this picture some sort of hat-tip to a sex game? Could *that* be why Luke had imagined her all tied up and wearing that bizarre old full slip with its pointy-breasted brassiere? Repulsed, she looked away, past a vase of dead roses, and said, "There's a soup kitchen, a shelter. It's just a few blocks awa—"

"I'm familiar." The detective nodded. "But surely you don't want to go *there?*"

And be surrounded by sleepless people, noise, and chaos to carry her through this dark night? God, *yes*. She nodded.

The detective, clearly reluctant, nonetheless guided her toward the hall, raising an arm as they passed the bathroom where tomato-bright splashes startled the walls, a seeming homage to the red strokes of color painted out in the hall. "No need to see that," the Detective murmured, yet as Della shuffled past she looked anyway.

A bright glint, a stainless-steel razor, winked from atop grimy grout, and alongside it more feathers, like the ones in the painting, drifted slightly as she and the Detective passed by. Wait. She halted. Those weren't feathers. *"Your hair, Lucas,"* she had said, and he'd lifted a self-conscious hand, covered the white streak she'd first noticed when he'd recruited her for this horror.

Now here was his white hair on the floor. *And* in that picture; *not* feathers, but hair. A piece of him this place had laid claim to… then immortalized upon canvas as if it laughed up its sleeve; its own stylized version of a voodoo doll.

"Told you this place was already immortal."

The whisper, wry, seemed to come from Luke's mouth, slack and shocked there on the floor. Della's feet froze adjacent to his—stiff, twisted, and still encased in their stupid-expensive five hundred-dollar shoes. *Because I don't know anyone with champagne tastes quite like you, Lucas.* Tears rushed to her eyes.

"Never mind, Dell. Just go. 'Cause it's blind the same way the angels are lost. So hurry now. Go."

She listened, locking his voice with her while she delivered a proper statement, and keeping it close all the way back to the soup kitchen shelter down on skid row where she gratefully accepted a cot from a volunteer who scrambled to make her feel welcome.

Welcome home.

Shuddering, she sank to her little threadbare mattress, its shabby bedclothes having been placed in her hands and smelling strongly of bleach and fabric softener. Cuddling them, she called up a search on her phone, Luke's voice a gentle guide in her ear. *"Blind, Dell. You told me to remember that it was important."* Shaking, her fingers stroked keys. **CECIL** she typed + **BLIND**

The search kicked back immediately: **Cecil (male name), meaning: Blind**

A course of cold tided through her and again she heard Luke, his voice sounding the way it did when he was moved by his most wounded patients. *"It's blind the same way the angels are lost, Dell."*

"Yes," she breathed. "Meaning it's blind by *choice*." The Cecil… blind by choice to every abhorrence and perversion and crime ever committed in its endless rooms, for in exchange for all the despair and broken dreams it inhaled, it in turn gave carte blanche to each eternal resident, allowing all the sin and debauchery and murder they could gorge on—thus creating an endless feedback loop of destruction and pain to devour.

The Lost Angels are all blind by choice.

She wasn't sure if that was still Lucas, or just her own psychic mind and, shivering, she pulled her legs up, tucked them close, grateful beyond reason for this little threadbare island here in a buzzing shelter bathed by a glare of fluorescent lights beneath which nothing could hide and no shadows could rise up to become people.

"Hey lady."

A skinny black man approached with a smile, his face cherubic, like… an angel. Della looked away, to the couple of cold, condensation beaded bottles of water dangled between his callused fingers. He offered one over. "Looks like you can use this."

She croaked a thank you, and he plopped down beside her, a tiny cloud of dust puffing up from his clothes.

"You just came from The Cecil," he said.

Her gaze sharpened.

He shrugged. "I hear things." He chugged water.

She watched him, her own bottle sliding down to dangle next to her crossed ankles.

"That place is baaadd, baby. *Evil* bad."

"You've been there," she said, neither statement nor question, and her hands grasped the water, gauged its temperature.

Liquid nitrogen cold.

"I have," he agreed.

She glanced at him. "How'd you get out?"

A hunted look briefly flitted through his eyes and, "I run," he whispered, cocky grin crumbling. "I run but I… I always go back."

She nodded, working hard not to shiver.

"Don't go back, baby." He rose. "No matter who calls, and no matter what it is they might say—don't go back."

"I want to," she whispered starkly, a confession she'd barely allowed herself as she'd run over that compass rose in The Cecil's grand lobby and felt it spinning beneath her, direction out of control.

"Uh-huh," he said again. "I know you do. We *all* know you do. Just like we all know that if I was talking to you *there* and not *here*…" He found her eyes. "Then you'd stay." He turned then, started walking.

Her gorge rose. Clots, blood and brain, were matted in his hair. The back of his skull was all shattered.

And he was wearing an old-fashioned bellhop's uniform.

"Keep runnin' baby." He did not look back. "Keep runnin' till there's no rooms left."

No rooms? She frowned, then… **700 Rooms.**

A puzzle piece clicked into place.

"*What does it want?*" Luke had asked.

"*Immortality,*" she'd answered, so sure.

Yet—"*It already has it,*" he'd replied and… he'd been right. The Cecil *was* already immortal.

But… "It's also greedy." She had told him this, but now… now she married it to **700 Rooms**, to No Vacancy, and when she did she at last knew—"It wants—"

"Honey?" A shelter employee crouched before her, did an immediate double take. "Oh! Someone's already been here with water. But—" He frowned, slid the bottle from between her lax fingers.

It was no longer bone-chill cold but instead tepid. Slightly warm.

"Let's trade," he said brightly, but his face was a wash of distaste. "Yours… you haven't *drank* any of this, have you?"

Della looked. The water in the bottle was murky. Tinted brown.

She paints dirty water.

A stench she could smell permeated through plastic and she inched back. *Capable of making identity, geography—even time—shift.*

Yes, 'cause that water had been clear and cold when it had been offered. *Snake oil,* she thought, and searched through the crowd.

The black bellhop raised a rotting hand from where he stood beneath a glowing red EXIT. "Still rooms, baby." He smiled. "Still vacancy."

Nodding, she again could hear Luke: *"What does it want?"*

A flash of **700,** first seen psychically, then seen whole as she'd rushed from The Cecil.

700 ROOMS

"No Vacancy," she whispered. No Vacancy like the angels who weren't really lost and the eyes that had been blinded by choice. The Cecil had told Luke No Vacancy, but it hadn't been to warn him away.

"It was an invitation," she announced, and wondered—which room was he in right now? Still 1013? Or visiting the killer way up on the 14th floor? Maybe playing hide and seek in the elevator? Or... or perhaps he was counseling that sad little junkie down on the 5th. The Cecil, after all, *was* home to so many.

And blind to all the dark things they liked to do.

Della shuddered, wrapping her bleach-leavened blanket about her and curling up tightly on her little cot. How long would it take the hungry Cecil to at last fill all **700 Rooms**? How many more years would pass, and how many desperate L.A. generations would bury broken dreams before The Cecil would at last be sincere when it whispered, in a compelled visitor's ear, **No Vacancy**?

WILD IRISH ROSE

Gabi Lorino

DONALD'S BEEN AROUND. I can tell by the way I catch myself smiling like I did when we were courting all those years ago. One day, I was in my lazy chair when his voice boomed through the house: "Rosie, now, how're you doing, my love?" I turned to look for him but I didn't find him anywhere.

The next night, he walked through our back door, plain as day, wearing his faded O'Shea's Irish Pub shirt and olive-drab work pants. "Won't be long now till it's time to go on our trip, love," he said as he strolled through the room. I nodded at him from my lazy chair and held out my hand, but he never took it. A second later, when I had the wherewithal to look around, he was gone again.

"Donnie. Where are you off to?" I asked the four walls surrounding me. "Where are we off to? California?"

We always wanted to go. It was like a poor person's version of Hawaii, although the only people we knew who went to Hawaii were servicemen during WWII. Of course, none of them were there on a pleasure cruise.

California's endless poppy fields, its beautiful coastline, and its deserts were things we saw in pictures and on TV. Once in a while, the Weather Channel would run a feature about a California aquarium or resort or amusement park, and Don would say, "Well now, would you look at that? It's time for our California dreaming again."

We got married in the fall, then worked hard through the pub's busy season. We were supposed to be off to Los Angeles for our belated honeymoon, to dine and dance at swanky clubs like the movie stars did, when Memorial Day rolled around. But by the time business slowed, I was pregnant with Baby Number One.

Back then, doctors didn't know what they know now. We probably could have flown there and back with no damage to the baby. But my doctor was unsure, and I was a bundle of nerves, so okay… I played up my frailty. I told Don we absolutely couldn't go. Doctor's orders! The baby's life was at stake!

Of course, the pregnancy turned out fine, as did the one after that. Patrick and John—those were our boys. Donald Patrick was the first one born, the image of his pa with that white-blonde hair. Beautiful baby. We called him Pat from the start. Then came John, but we always called him Jack. He was dark-haired like two of his grandparents, but with blue eyes like mine.

My happily-ever-after was filled with noisy boys, messes, endless cooking, and housework in addition to running our pub. But as the years wore on, I wanted a break from other people for a while… and a comfortable retirement.

At first look, Donnie called this development and its golf carts and its senior-centric activities and amenities 'indulgent.' I argued with him, asking why not spend the money on the place we'll be most days? Once we retired and moved into our new, comfortable home, I continued to be voice of reason, the one who kept us home when we could have been out traveling before my knees and his heart gave out. "It just isn't practical," I argued. "We have everything we need right here. Everybody's here. Our doctors are here."

Instead of visiting California then, we opted for expensive flooring in the kitchen with that tile that looks like hardwood when we replaced the original floors. Don insisted that it be a dark color, like we had in the pub and his childhood home before that.

Now I have this wonderful flooring, but we never stepped foot in California. I suppose I could console myself with memories of Don, but that seems a bit hollow, too.

◐

"It wasn't all shamrocks," he said, at the end. We were in a sparse hospice room painted mint green, surrounded by low lighting, linoleum floors, and a glass door between us and the rest of the world.

"Donnie, how could you say that?" I asked, squeezing his hand.

He moaned, and I released my grip.

He took in a labored breath. "It was a good life. But I got tired of fighting."

"But we haven't fought for ages."

Pat knocked on the glass door. He and Molly had come to say goodbye to him. They both looked grim and serious, and I decided to give them a moment alone with Don.

I found myself hovering just outside the door, going over what he'd said. Tired of fighting? How was he tired of fighting? For years, we'd lived in our community, spent time with friends, relaxed in our easy chairs and watched TV. The biggest drama of our later years happened when a hurricane threatened or one of the grandkids hit some milestone, but now that they were all done with school, there wasn't much excitement tied to them.

What had there been to fight about? I thought everything ran smoothly! Of course there were adjustments to be made when we married, when the kids were born, and when we retired, but other than that, it seemed fine to me.

Don's ragged breathing continued for another hour. A parade of grandchildren followed, and then Jack and his wife Cheryl arrived. Each arrival displaced someone at the bedside, to keep Donnie from being overwhelmed. It was as if they'd choreographed how to do this.

I thought back on his drinking, which he never stopped, and his smoking that he'd given up twenty years before. Maybe if he had done less of those things, he wouldn't have been on his deathbed so soon.

Wait. Hadn't I told him not to do those things? Besides, the things I told him to do were for his own good! He didn't always listen to me, though. Maybe that was what he meant about fighting.

Eventually I made my way back into his room, sat down, and took his hand. His breathing slowed until it stopped. I held his hand until it relaxed. After kissing him on the temple, I left the room.

The beep of a heart monitor slowed and then stopped. My Donnie was gone.

I don't remember the rest of that day. Somehow I arrived home, and the family wanted me to stay over with Pat and Molly, but I wouldn't do it. (Don't you love how in some families, there's a debate for what one person ought to do? It always ends the same. That person's going to do what she's going to do and there's no need for your debate about it, thank you very much!) I wanted to be home, where I lived with Don, where we dreamed of Ireland and California and all those wonderful places we didn't go. Where I had spent the last twenty years with him, enjoying our retirement, cultivating new friendships, laughing at the local gossip.

At first, it shocked me how quiet it was there. I spent weeks crying and talking to myself, then I switched and talked to Donnie (because he could hear me, right?), asking why did he have to smoke for so long, why did he have to drink so much, and why was he gone?

The only answer I got was in a dream I had a few weeks after he passed. He smiled broadly as he walked through a village with stone walls built like a maze around thatched-roof buildings. Tall grasses swayed in the breeze, and in the distance, the ocean crashed onto a sandy beach. Three laughing men accompanied him.

I woke to a peaceful, happy feeling. He was in a good place, with good people, whoever they were and however that afterlife stuff worked. I smiled whenever his name was mentioned after that dream; my crying had ended.

⊘

The years sort of cascaded after that, one after another. Turn around and it was Christmastime again. Damn, was it really time for another birthday? Over and over, the world turned. Sun up, sun down. Somehow I ended up the only grandmother on Earth with grandkids ranging from ages twenty-five to forty, all of them unmarried. (It's crazy! They act like I'm some fossil from the Stone Age for wondering why they haven't taken care of that already.)

Meanwhile, some things didn't change, except everyone got older, day after day. Though I complained about it mightily, the transition to a single-income household wasn't too traumatic, and most everything here still has a lot of use left in it. Luckily, the last roof we put on our house still holds.

At some point, Pat and Jack tried to talk me into leasing a room to another old lady as some sort of Golden Girls setup, but I vetoed that suggestion even though it had been approved by the O'Shea Family Committee. "It's my house, boys," I told them.

The yammering went on. "We worry about you. We don't want you to be alone all the time."

It's like they have no concept of how peaceful my life has finally become, and how I want to keep it that way!

Not that I'm condoning the fact that my granddaughters live alone. They're at the place in life where they ought to be having babies! I did my time, and so should they!

But for me, a life on my own is my reward, isn't it?

Well, isn't it?

I made one last attempt, after Donnie was gone, to get to California. My friend Barbara and I went to the AAA office and made reservations for a guided bus tour through coastal California, taking a detour inland to see the poppy preserve in bloom and a few spots in Los Angeles. It was going to be awesome! We trolled the racks at the SteinMart on weekdays to get our wardrobes ready for the big trip. I even bought a new sweater! (Haven't done that in at least a dozen years! No need for it in Florida. Who buys sweaters when it's not for vacation?)

Anyway, Barb and I were excited—so excited, in fact, that when I attempted to talk to her on the cordless phone while I dragged the garbage can to the curb, I fell and broke my wrist. Our gab session about what day trips to book turned into her hanging up and calling 911 while I writhed in pain on the hot driveway. My neighbor Manny saw the commotion and came over to help me, too. Thank goodness.

Oh, the pain was excruciating! I honestly saw stars! I was about to lose my mind for the minutes it took for

EMS to take me away to the hospital. Minutes that felt like hours.

The pain-worse-than-childbirth finally ended with some heavy painkillers. I could sleep after they repaired my arm. I was given strict orders to take it easy once I was discharged and come back for therapy once the cast was off—what was it, twice a week? All the time, it felt like.

Since I couldn't manage my luggage with a messed-up arm or get out of physical therapy appointments, we cancelled the trip. Barbara was disappointed, but I was completely resigned. California had always been out of my reach; with or without Donnie, it didn't matter. It was best if I didn't try to go there again.

Once I returned home from that hospital ordeal, as I sat alone with my thoughts (which was the absolute last thing I wanted to do!), I thought of Donnie. I thought of all the adventures we wanted to have, the exploring that he wanted to do but didn't.

I had always worried about the future. I wondered if there would be enough money to see us through to the next month, and the month after that. What was it about me that made me feel like everything that wasn't getting taken care of right away was an emergency? There was the business, our business. Our boys and the boys' families too. Always something going on. That worry, that need to feel like I had things under control, it stayed with me for ages… until Donnie passed, and my friends started dying.

Few things put life into perspective like losing a loved one, or in my case, lots of loved ones. It's like we all start out on the same bus, rolling along for miles and miles. When we reach a station, some people exit while others climb aboard. At each stop, the door swings open. Some come, some go.

When we were younger, and the people who departed were old, it made sense. Now that we're the old people (and half the people I knew ten years ago aren't on the bus with me anymore), it's different. Now we're the ones lining up to exit at the next few stops.

My worrying and fretting turned out to be for nothing. I could've ended up with half of what I have now and still be all right. I've finally realized that all you need throughout life is enough, and when you don't have enough, that's when it's time to get creative. Besides, it's not like you can take anything with you!

Another lightbulb went on for me, regarding Donald. It became clear that we didn't fight in our later years simply because he didn't want to anymore. I would swoop in with my worry-talk and my arguments about being practical, and he didn't have the energy to change my mind. It was as simple as that.

I thought I was taking care of him and making sure we'd always have enough, but really I was disappointing him. I didn't mean to, but I'm sure I did.

I hope he's forgiven me.

❧

"Rosie, old girl, they're playing our song."

Donnie says this while I'm cooking scrambled eggs in the kitchen as the radio on the granite countertop plays an instrumental version of *Do you know the way to San Jose*.

I don't bother looking around to find him, because I figure that I won't catch a glimpse. "Donnie, I can't even pick weeds in the garden anymore. My knees won't let me. Do you really think I could make it out to the West Coast?"

After turning the burner off, I stagger over to a chair near our heavy wooden table. Suddenly I'm feeling nauseous and tired. I'm overcome with a need to rest even though I woke up just an hour before.

"I'll take you there," he says. He's sitting across from me wearing a maroon sweater that makes his hazel eyes look dark brown, and he reaches out a hand to touch mine.

He's here again! I don't want to believe it, but I do. Part of me knows that he's passed, just as part of me knows he's here with me now. Habit takes over and I reach my hand over to his in one of our oldest, most familiar gestures.

I can feel it! I can feel his hand the same as I did countless days across this very table, before he was gone. Even stranger, all the aches I felt a moment ago have vanished. My fatigue has given way to a happy, energetic feeling.

"Donnie, it's you! It's really you!" My heart gallops, and I feel an irrepressible smile form on my face.

"Let's go," he says.

I can't contain my happiness. I ask, "Where are we going?"

"Anywhere you want," Donnie answers.

My eyelids feel heavy, though it seems I can see whether my eyes are open or not. There is a comforting warmth surrounding us, and soon a bright white light takes over the space where walls and pictures and floor and furniture once were. There's only us, linked together, smiling at one another. We neither sit nor stand; we float.

I feel a love I haven't known for years, a lightness in my being, an all-encompassing happiness, and I know, just from being near Donald, that he feels the same.

All the worry and pain I ever felt, or held onto, has vanished. My Donnie holds no grudges against me. We are both perfect and whole again.

The light intensifies; it is both calming and brilliant. And finally, somehow, the essence of who we are manages to meld with the light. It feels like a whole new beginning.

ENDLESS SUMMER

Jude-Marie Green

WE ALL GO DOWN to the sea, Annie, Duane, and I. Annie surfs. She digs on the big waves and the small waves, but mostly she likes the sand and the water. Duane goes for the scenery, as he calls it, and he gets as turned on from the guys pumping iron and glistening with oil and sweat as from the blonde perfect women in bikinis wearing roller blades.

"You never watch them, Kim," he says to me. "You should check out those muscle beach guys, you could get lucky."

He's joking. I hope.

I like the scenery too, but my view is up. The hot sun beats down on me, slantwise in the morning and edgewise in the afternoon, and I keep that boiling star to my back. I'm looking for the things that fly.

Yes, the seagulls and sandpipers are adorable in a clumsy way, but I'm not a bird watcher. The bright-colored kites spin, buffeted by the salt wind, and I stare at them, but they aren't the main attraction. I look for the planes; well, sort of planes. I search for the other things.

Duane and Annie make a joke of it, say I'm searching for flying saucers, but I look for points of refracted light coruscating off the fins of a cigar-shaped rescue vehicle.

My people won't send a whole ship; they'll send a small snatch and grab job. I *hope* they'll send one.

Duane brings me a soda, sloshing ice, and plops down next to me on the sand. I blink the sundogs out of my eyes and take the cup with a lotion-greased hand.

"Seen anything green yet?" He smiles at me lopsided. I'm not attracted to Duane, but sometimes I want to brush the coarse mane of sun-bleached hair off his forehead. When he smiles at me like that, I want to touch him.

"Annie," I say, joking. Her surfboard, one of the stubby ones, is green and white, and she wears those colors under her black neoprene bodysuit.

"Yeah yeah," he says, then sucks on his soda. The air rattles through his straw.

We both look out at the breakers where Annie and a dozen other surfers are lined up, waiting for a good swell. We can just make out their dark silhouettes; Annie is the small one near the middle, because that's where she always is. The sun burns out any identifying details and leaves the surfers democratically identical shadow black silhouettes. The people on the beach who care will be wowed by a good ride, not by the rider. A swell develops behind the line and some of the surfers begin to paddle. Annie isn't moving; she's waiting this wave out. She probably timed the swells and knows a better one is coming up soon.

I shade my eyes and look over their heads. There, something flashes on the sharp horizon. All my muscles tense and hairs rise on my forearms.

Duane gasps. For a moment I think he sees it but he's still watching the surfers and Annie has spilled off her board. She'll be fine, she always is. I stare at the horizon again but see nothing.

Stiff cool breezes presage sunset. Particles of sand are blown in undulating ripples, seeking and finding entrance in my clothes, coating my skin with a grime that stinks of fish and salt. Summer night on the beach and I feel fine.

Duane and Annie and I sit around the brick pit, feeding sticks of firewood to the flames. I dream that maybe we're assuaging some minor god's desire with our burnt offerings of marshmallow and hot dogs, the god of the evening sand perhaps. I smile. My eyes burn a bit, both from watching the sky and from the smoky heat of the fire, and my smile brings involuntary tears.

Annie passes a soda can filled with something a bit stronger than soda. I slug some down, then wipe my face with the back of my arm, then pass the can along to Duane.

It's time for me to begin. I hold the steel-string guitar like a pillow across my lap and fiddle around with the pegs. They don't need much tuning.

"My favorite movie is 'Endless Summer,'" I say, plucking a high-pitched chord. Annie and Duane sigh. Since I've known them, we've watched that movie almost every night, 42 times, on a dvd that Duane bought specially for me. I want to surf but I'm too clumsy, too tall, too old to learn. Boogie boarding isn't enough but it'll suffice when the urge gets too strong. But boarding doesn't channel that wild surf urge the way the music does, the music that somehow combines with the waves and shakes me up. Every time.

"Steve-o plays the best music ever," I say, jangling up a mix of notes.

Steve-o is a surf music god. Sometimes his band performs on the pier of the next beach over. I haven't seen him yet, but he's sure to take the stage sometime this summer. Listening to his band play the live sound would be the highlight of my visit.

I don't rave about Steve-o as much as I want. Annie isn't a fan of instrumental surf music, and Duane's tastes are so channeled that he likes some of Steve-o's tunes but not others. He won't listen to a live performance because Steve-o might sing; he hates Steve-o's voice, but digs the instrumental stuff. He's got the tracks, the ones he likes, ripped to a portable music device which he attaches to his ears whenever he doesn't want to talk.

I like the honest sound of a live music experience. Nothing I've ever heard is better than good musicians working out the chords of a wailing song. There are other good surf bands, like the Insect Surfers, who play surf music with a rock feel; or the Mermen, a jam band in San Francisco who improvise and extend the tunes; but Steve-o is my favorite. He's the original. His tight music tugs at my viscera. I picked up the radio broadcast – why *yes,* we are listening – and followed the music here.

"I talked my captain into stopping here," I say.

"The ship's crews are built of friends and family. Our journeys are far too long for strangers, we can't chance being so far from home port and learning we hate one another. The down side," and I grin because I love that phrase, "the down side is that we can sometimes influence the crew to do unreasonable things. Like setting down on an interdict island just because the music is so good. My captain, my lover, he did this for me, he sent me here to appreciate and collect. He ran the interdiction for me."

Duane and Annie have edged closer to each other, their hips touching. They think it's high romance that my lover did this for me, to please me. I strum something sweet I composed just for them, something alien and off-pitch according to Duane but romantic according to Annie.

"He set me down here, clean landing area, the beach at midnight, and he promised to pick me up again in a week."

I wipe my stiff fingers down hard on the strings, a harsh jangle.

"I watched his ship go up in the sky and I watched it explode. The interdict police shot him down.

"The landing ship disappeared in a pinprick of light, but the community ship exploded like Fourth of July fireworks. My comms all went dark."

I start a single-pattern arpeggio on the strings, running through the chords, a beginner's practice but comforting.

"And then I found you two." I stop playing and wind my arms around the guitar's cheap birch body.

Annie unwinds her arms from around Duane and puts a little distance between their hips.

"You can couch surf with us as long as you want," she says. "Until your ship comes back for you."

Duane stifles a snigger and she digs her elbow into his side, ungentle. Duane still doesn't believe me, but he does like my story. And my playing. As usual, he has his recording microphone pinned to his T-shirt and the red light is on.

"Can you play 'Wipeout'?" he asks. He knows the answer, he's asked the same thing for the last four weeks.

"'Wipeout' is best on electric guitar," I say. "But I can play something for you."

I swing into a standard surf riff. Duane and Annie seat-dance a bit, getting into the sound. After a few minutes I stand up and begin playing my own compositions, like I always do. Other people who've been tending firepits start to wander over. I'm developing a regular audience.

My music builds from the whisper and thunder of waves hitting the beach and the sounds of deepest space. Deep space doesn't sound all sterile and cold, by the way. Whale songs are more like it. I've heard the birth of stars in recordings of whale song.

After a while people are dancing and a couple other acoustic guitar players have joined me; someone has bongos and tries to keep us honest with a good steady beat. The firepit burns high and I'm grooving on the salt wind chill and the heat of the open flames and the emotion of people having a good time. I'm grooving on music that I love.

A while later the fire has burned down and people have moved off, nighttime silhouettes as they leave in pairs and groups. No one is alone.

Except me.

I stop playing when Duane and Annie start for their apartment, a tiny place just steps from the beach. Sand scrunches under my feet. They open the door but don't bother turning on the lights. Their bedroom door closes behind them. I collapse on the futon, a green stained mattress in a wood frame. I'll shower in the morning. For now I take comfort in smelling like beach and fire.

I dream of home. I was born and grew up in an urban center in the midst of a continental land mass, but my life revolves around my community ship. I don't yet have children in that community, but I have parents, siblings, lovers past, lovers future. The captain is my current lover by lottery and we like each other more than usual. He likes my music, which grates on the conservative crew's ears and won't earn me a place on the education board. A visit to the world that produces this music and throws it away into space like gifts to the universe, I whisper in his ear when cuddling him, a research visit will complete my apprenticeship and confirm my worth to the ship's community. We can navigate around the interdiction police, I brag. We do that all the time.

He agrees. He loves me.

I awaken with the sunshine full on my face, this world's sun a yellow flare that warms me through.

I killed him. Him and my entire community. The interdict police shot them down, as per protocol, but I'm responsible. I understand the policy, put into place after we extended a friendly hand once to a vicious civilization. I accept those consequences for me. I did not count on those consequences for him.

Of course I'll be rescued. Sooner or later they'll send a pod for me; they surely can't leave me here. This place is isolated for many reasons. I studied before I came here, I've done my best not to trip on any of the traps here, I haven't said, 'take me to your leader,' I haven't exposed my physiology to official scrutiny. I never thought I'd be here for longer than a week. But soon, my comms will chirp and I'll know it's time to leave.

I might have time to say goodbye to my friends, I might not. The rescuers will hand me over to the interdict police. I'm not sure what will happen then. I imagine I won't like it.

We head out to the beach after a quick breakfast of yogurt and fruit and coffee.

I swim. I entertain a few children by building an enormous sand space ship which the tide erodes away. I lie in the sand and watch the seagulls and pigeons fight over discarded food. In the long afternoon, after the sun has slid across most of the sky, I think I see what I'm looking for above the horizon. Something flashes through shades of green.

I think I hear my comms chirp. I glance at the receiver but it's dead black still. Could I be hallucinating? Could desire have deranged me? The answer of course is yes, but I don't think I'm insane.

I could be wrong. The sun beats on my head. I pick up my guitar even though it's not dark yet and strum something harsh and fast. My comms chirp again and this silvered link to my ship and community that Duane thinks is a broken watch lights up, glows.

I'm not sure how much time I have left but they will find me soon. They track me through the comms. I cannot remove the comms, though right now I'm tempted, but the only way would be to remove my hand and then I wouldn't be able to play the guitar.

I put down the guitar on my beach towel and run into the water. I'm not a strong swimmer but I like to ride the waves, body-surfing. I'm afraid. I swim out to the biggest breakers, out by the surfers, and slide towards shore on the curls. The water is like space, riding the waves much like popping out of the airlock and riding the ship's skin.

After an hour my muscles are loose and I'm exhausted, in a good way. I walk out of the water.

Two men are standing next to my beach towel. They're dressed for the beach, flowered swim trunks, Hawaiian shirts, zoris, sunglasses. I'm afraid all over again and my muscles tense into hard ridges. I walk up to them and wait.

"Someone sent us a demo," one of them says. "Is this you playing?" He presses a button on a hand-sized recorder and I hear music, my music, compressed and somewhat tinny but identifiably me.

"Yes, that is me," I say. These aren't my people. I'm still dealing with the shock of relief when they make the offer.

"Steve-o's playing tonight at the pier and he wants you to stand in," the other guy says. "Can you handle a Fender?"

I should say no. I want to stand in with my hero's band and play the best surf music in the world; I can play a Fender electric guitar, Stratocaster, wah-wah, reverb. But my comms glow. I'll be rescued any minute. I don't want to commit to something this important if I can't follow through.

"You bet," I say.

They tell me where I need to be in two hours, just after sunset, and while we're shaking hands Duane and Annie walk up. They're excited but don't say much.

I remember Duane recording my firepit sessions.

"Did you send them a recording?" I say.

Annie blushes. I've never seen her blush; I'm surprised I can see that heat rise on her tanned cheeks. Nonetheless, her face burns. We stare at her. Duane frowns just a bit.

"I knew I was missing a session," he says. "I guess it's okay. Ask next time.

"I guess you need to get ready," he says to me. "I'll grab recording gear."

I feel his upset and I know why. He tried to sell my story to the tabloids but they didn't bite. They didn't even answer his letter. He hopes to get some money for the story; maybe he thinks he'll get some money from the recordings. Having a permanent houseguest is an expensive proposition; he's said this to Annie when he thought I couldn't hear.

I hope they find some way to profit from the music.

I shower, using too much hot water, too much soap, too much shampoo. I don't know what the interdict police will do to me. The few stories I've heard are grim, without a definite end; people just disappear. This bit of grooming, a long cleansing in a tiny apartment's even tinier bathroom, might be the last I ever experience.

We walk along the palm-tree-edged sidewalk in the dark blue evening. I point out stars to Annie and Duane. They've asked me before to point out my home star, but I can't see it from here, it's hidden by time and distance. We get to the pier a little early. The crowds are already milling, waiting for the king of surf music to come out on stage. A warm-up group is playing and they don't suck. The audience dances, gyrating in counterpoint to the high-energy sound of lyricless surf music.

Steve-o's roadies come out to greet us. Duane and Annie refuse back-stage passes; they want to sit up front so they can record the show. Of course they don't mention that; recording a live show is technically illegal, and Steve-o is notorious for not allowing recordings. I ask the roadies to help my friends find good seats, then I move backstage to where the group is setting up.

They don't let me talk to Steve-o. I don't care; it is his music I love, the sounds he can coax from his silver-stringed guitar, not the man himself. I fondle the heavy Fender guitar they've given to me, heavy maple lacquered to a high gloss, the name, Stratocaster, curling along the peghead.

A band member, an older man with long silver hair and a van Dyck beard, works his way over to me.

"You're not the star," he says, and I grin. "You won't get a solo, so don't even hold your breath. Just try to keep up, okay?" He sneers at me like he doesn't think I should be here.

Probably I shouldn't.

I'm so excited I'm not sure I can keep my fingers on the strings. I hope that I do. I don't want to fail my hero.

The warm-up band finishes its set and clears the stage. We move out front. The van Dyck beard guy positions me near a tube amp on the left side of the stage. He jacks in my Fender but doesn't turn on the amp. I reach down and switch it on.

I wish I could see Duane and Annie but I can't see anyone who isn't on the stage. The lights blind me. There's some patter between the band members and then someone announces over a loudspeaker, "Ladies and gentlemen, the event you've been waiting for! Steve-o and the Newtones!"

Steve-o waves his arms over his head, his fingers making the shaka, hang loose sign. The audience cheers. The band swings into the first number, an oldie I memorized long before I set foot on this world, and I easily follow along. My fingers add trills all by themselves and I see band members throwing glances my way, but they're going with it.

Steve-o is a master. He commands the stage, strutting back and forth like a rooster, slamming through his numbers and making the audience scream for more. I watch from my tiny x-marked spot on the stage and I play this loaner Fender guitar and I'm glad that Duane is recording this.

There's a break between the second and third number and van Dyck beard saunters over to Steve-o and shares some words with him. I can't hear what they're saying. Steve-o shakes his head mournfully, and then it's time to play the next number.

During the bridge in the third number Steve-o points at me.

I know what this means. I edge forward, up even with Steve-o, and follow along with his chords. After a few moments he backs away and lets me take off.

I'm soloing with my hero's band.

The song is another oldie and I've built riffs for this which I've practiced over the years. I launch the trills I composed and the crowd growls its appreciation, its love. I'd never considered how much the crowd's love must affect the band; the energy and smell of sweat rise up to sting my nostrils. I respond by playing chord combinations I've composed on the spot, new ways to highlight the rhythm of this song. I'm cool, I'm jamming, my fingers are hot and the strings vibrate.

The crowd roars.

I get to a sweaty place and let the song swing out of the solo and back into its more familiar rhythms. Steve-o steps up to the front mic and leads applause for me and the crowd adds clapping to its roars. My head is filled with light. Someone is pulling my elbow towards my x-marked spot and I back up gratefully.

The hand on my elbow doesn't let go when I get to the spot. I strum the Fender and glance at the roadie. He's not a roadie. I know this even though he's wearing black jeans and a Hard Rock Café tee shirt.

"Time to go," he whispers to me.

I turn off my amp and a feedback whine flares over the band's music. I see Steve-o grimace but he keeps playing. I put the Fender down on the stage. Goodbye, Annie, Duane, I think. Goodbye beach and music. Goodbye summer.

❧

UNQUIET BAGGAGE

Cody Sisco

MAYBE I'M A GHOST? I don't know. That seems so typical.

I know I'm not an echo, a resonance, a specter, or any of the other terms thrown around by people who don't know anything about the dead.

What I am is a collection of chopped-up body parts tossed in a suitcase and carried onto the Gold Line by my husband. My murderer.

At least he's not carrying me in a leaky sack.

It's really not fair that I ended up this way. When we met in high school Michael was the sweetest, though sometimes he would punch walls and his sweat always had an angry shine to it. But he also said things like I was his moon and stars. He wanted to pamper me. Pamper is a funny word for a fifteen-year-old to use. I ate it up.

Michael was my bae, my boo, my lover, and my husband.

Now, years later, he's my killer. The sad part is that I'm sad *for* him for killing me. The *sad* sad part is that I'm also sad that he's going to get caught. Ghosts can be many shades of sad, it turns out.

You can't just bring a suitcase full of body parts onto the Gold Line and expect to get away with it, I want to yell at him. But he's not listening to my advice, my emanations, or whatever. He's making shifty eyes at everyone on the train. That black lady has his number. She's going to call the cops as soon as he's not staring her down. Same with that white beardy hipster with the square-framed glasses that look like they're made of popsicle sticks. Meanwhile, I can smell the homeless guy two seats down. I'm a dead guy in a suitcase and *he* smells bad. Fuck L.A. sometimes.

I'm not glad I'm dead, per se, but I don't mind that much. There's something better on the horizon. I'm waiting for something and it's going to be good and glorious.

The train car wobbles and whines its way slowly through South Pasadena.

My death comes at a bad time in my career. I rocked social media. I could tell you all the trending hashtags, engagement tricks, click-through ratio targets, and the keys to maximize discovery. Michael thought I was a fucking wizard.

I'll be honest: I didn't get with him because of his brains. He had a fire inside him that is so rare these days, so sexy. Everyone is so, totally, yeah, like, whatever, like chill and stuff. Why get upset? Why get excited? Why not go to sleep one day and never wake up?

Michael was always the opposite. Everything got to him. The good and the bad. I brought home a silly little cupcake one day that said, "J + M = LOVE." He cried.

He cried a lot today. I don't know if anyone else on the train can see it, but me—being incorporeally and weirdly perceptive in my specter-form—I can see salt tracks on his cheeks. He was crying as he chopped me to pieces in that abandoned restaurant. It's not that he didn't love me. It's that his heart wasn't made for the long haul.

I'm genuinely curious how he thinks he's going to get away with this, what he thinks comes next. Say he buries me somewhere. My guess is Eugene Debs Park. He'll probably carve our initials in a nearby tree, which is how they'll find my body. Keep in mind he's only got a garden trowel stuffed in with me, so it's not like he can dig very deep. If he buries me and goes home, then what? He'll never recover. He'll miss me so badly. He'll want to pamper me. But I'll be gone.

It actually is sad when I think about it, in a distant, *hey, did you hear about that dead guy in a suitcase*, kind of way. Maybe I'm in shock. Oh my god, that's exactly what a ghost is, isn't it? Something bad happens, creates a shock, and then the ghost just somehow sticks around. Poor specter can't move on because—shocker!—he was chopped up and stuffed in a suitcase. This wasn't supposed to be on the gay agenda.

Michael stands, preparing to get off in Highland Park. This suitcase itches. I can feel his discomfort, the shakiness in his arms and legs, but he can't let go of me. I can't let go of him either.

He drags my pieces off the train, boards a bus, and then gets off again at… Home Depot?

I picture him dragging me through the aisles. Or maybe propping the suitcase in a shopping cart, my pieces dripping, leaving a trail that follows him around the store as he searches for a good shovel.

But no, and this is the weird part, he doesn't go into the store: he lurches around the parking lot until he finds a spot next to the pillar supporting the 110 where it vaults over the river and tears through the Elysian Park hillside. I can see pavement soaked in motor oil and beds of stained cardboard boxes, covered in pigeon droppings. Shit, this is depressing. I thought he would go to the park or maybe just the river and get on with it. What the fuck are we doing here?

I want to leave. I want to go somewhere with… with… a beautiful vibration.

I'm alone now while he walks over to the day labor crew and barters for something. He wants—oh, God!—he wants lighter fluid and matches.

This is so pathetic. The least he could do is blow torch me and leave nothing but ashes. His plan won't work! I'll be turned to bits of bone and charred flesh while he weeps, thinking about how stupid he is. I thought maybe he'd come out of this—I don't know—*changed* maybe. Ready to give himself over to a grander plan: atonement, confession, redemption, that whole thing. No, he's a failure. It's embarrassing to watch.

It's dusk now. What few people come and go are clustered near the bright orange signs and the well-lit areas. The taco truck chugged away an hour ago.

This end of the parking lot is abandoned. He opens the suitcase, but he doesn't remove my pieces.

He splatters my remains with flammable liquid. Good and wet he's got me. Now he's fiddling with the matches, but he's shaking so badly he can't do it. This is the worst, twisted, sexual replay anyone could imagine. Finally, he gets one lit and in the flare I see he's crying again. There are two very clean tracks down his face, which is otherwise grimed by the terrible, no-good day he's having. Will he go get a taco on Fig after this? My one hope is that he doesn't end himself by walking into traffic or jumping off a bridge. His silent tear-stained company is too much right now. If we could talk, specter-to-specter, I might lose my mind.

Despite my snark and doubts, the flames are having a powerful effect. Maybe it's the ritual of it. Fire is an ancient and profound thing. I try to manifest before him, looking as I did in high school, innocent, his moon and stars, so he can see what he's lost. If I could show myself to him as an old man, I would give him a gut punch. That's what galls: all those years… I won't get to find out what I could have become.

I give up. I'm better off free.
Goodbye, Michael, husband, murderer, failure.
I'm going to a place in the universe that sings.

DRY BONES

Dario Ciriello

CHAPTER ONE
Roberto

November 2016
Hillsborough, NC

I WAS TEN MINUTES from home when the call came through from 626, my old area code. It would still be light there; here, the night was dark, and I was coming up to the frost hollow where the road dipped to the Eno River. There'd been a patch of black ice there that morning, and I slowed way down as I took the curve.

I didn't know the incoming number, but I took the call. In spite of everything that had happened, I still missed the San Gabriel Valley. Maybe someone there missed me.

"Sanchez," I said.

"Roberto?" A woman's voice.

It took me a second to place it. Leticia, my ex's mother. "Leticia?"

"Yes. How are you, Roberto?"

"I'm okay." I said it mechanically, trying to keep focused on the road. Though she'd always been at least polite to me, unlike her asshole husband, Laura's dad, we'd never really been close.

"It's about Laura, Roberto," she said, before I could ask.

A shadow I knew too well swept my heart. "Tell me," I said, bracing for whatever was coming.

Laura'd gone missing nineteen months ago after setting out on one of her habitual hikes. After a year, I filed for and was granted a default divorce.

"They found her body," said Leticia, with a hitch in her voice. "Tuesday of last week. The police came to the door this morning. I thought you would want to know."

Tuesday last week. Today was Friday, November 11. I did the math. They'd found the body on the Day of the Dead.

The dense sycamores arching over the narrow two-lane almost met overhead, like I was driving a dark tunnel under blackness. I'd expected this call for the better part of two years. I'd never expected repulsion to be its accompanying emotion.

"They're sure it's her?" I said, gently accelerating up the rise towards home. The tires had stuck around the bend, the lethal patch of ice melted in the day, I guessed.

"They just identified her from…" She choked up, then went on, "From dental records."

I was silent several seconds. Ahead, the lights of Hillsborough twinkled. My mouth was suddenly very dry. "Where?" I said. "What happened?"

Her voice seemed far away. "Up in the hills." She paused. I waited, hearing her soft sobs. "They're doing an autopsy."

I nodded absently. "The hills. Of course," I mumbled. I turned right on Lakeshore without thinking, heading for the Brewpub. "Going up to Mount Lowe, right?"

"Yes, at the campground. It rained hard last week."

It's not the bullet you're watching for that gets you. My concern had always been for the teens and tweakers and gangbangers who hung about the abandoned estate grounds at night. Laura'd told me that once in a while, walking to the trailhead, she'd glimpse a tent deep in the undergrowth where the old estate had stood. *Laura, the place is dangerous. At least don't go up there at night. Please.* Instead she'd died at the Mount Lowe camp, the site of the old tavern.

I shook my head. I couldn't understand how the rains would factor in. "Wait, was there a mudslide? How did she die?"

Her voice faded in and out, breaking. "They don't know, maybe the rains exposed the body." More sobbing. "I have to go, Roberto. I just thought you should know."

I swallowed. I'd stopped in the middle of the road without even realizing it, an accident waiting to happen. I pulled over to the side and killed the engine.

"Wait. Have you… has someone actually ID'd her?" I said it as gently as I could.

That got full-on hysteria. Finally she said, "There's nothing, Roberto. Just bones. Bones."

There was nothing else to say. I thanked her and gave her the best words I could.

When I got home I'd look at flights. Right now, I just wanted to drink.

Laura

October 2014
Altadena, CA

I knew the scar for what it was the very first time I saw it.

We were in Roberto's car heading up Lake for the open house, and I knew three things right then: that the scar cutting up the foothills towards Mount Lowe was the line of an old railway; that something of dream and magic had existed at the end of it; and that we were going to buy the house we hadn't even seen yet.

The San Gabriels beckon tall and wild behind Altadena. Most days they're blue-green, but the sun can paint them orange and the winters white. Even climbing up the long, slow grade of Lake Avenue, most people don't notice the line of the old tracks until it's pointed out to them. There's a tangle of paths and trails up on those sleep slopes, and the scrub is a blotchy maze over that fine, sandy soil.

We'd been in the house two months when we took our first hike up into the foothills. Or tried to, in any case. It was a hot weekday noon, absent the early morning or evening complement of hikers. Without a clue about the trailheads in the Cobb Estate, we scrabbled and scrambled our sweaty way up a loose, sandy wash, slipping in our tennies in the dry yellow dirt until we reached a bench at the intersection of what I would later call the balcony trail, because it cut horizontally across the lower skirts of the hills.

Looking up at the increasingly rough and uncertain scratch of dry orange runoff, Roberto frowned. "I'm not sure about this," he said.

I took his hand and squeezed it. I fished out the vape pen I'd loaded with Purple Kush and took a puff of the heady, aromatic bud. "Come on," I said, passing it to him, "it'll be fine." It's possible the spell of the place was already settling around me, too late to stop even if I'd wanted to, which is questionable. Everything has its price, and wonder and magic don't come cheap.

Roberto took a deep breath and made a face. Ten minutes later he was sprawled on the dusty, rutted ground, cursing with a broken ankle as I dialed 911. That was the first and last time he ever went up there.

A few days later, I was back at 7:30 A.M., smarter and better prepared. I'd read up on the trails up to Echo Summit, and discovered that access was through the Cobb Estate, which I hadn't even realized was public land. I wore my hiking boots and carried a day pack containing food and ample water. The forecast was for a high of ninety-some degrees, and I planned to be home or at least on the way down by then.

The marine layer had come all the way in that night, and when I arrived, a small cluster of hikers was assembling in the early morning cool outside the gates to the old estate. A brief conversation gave me all I needed to know about the trailheads. I entered the abandoned property alone, politely declining the offer to join their group for the hike. Nature, for me, was always best enjoyed solo, and I never understood the appeal of hiking in large, chatty groups. An ex once called me solitary and catlike, and I had to agree.

I'd not gone more than a few hundred yards before a memory of early childhood burst on me unprepared, capturing my attention so completely I had to stop.

We were at the ruins of Tulum on the Caribbean. I'd just turned three, but my father, his travels interrupted by my unexpected arrival, couldn't wait any longer to pursue his interest in ancient sites, and had persuaded my mom I was old enough.

I remember the heat, and scrunching my little eyes up before turning away from the brilliance of the bright Caribbean water just below the ruins. Mom pulling the brim of my straw hat lower over my face as I began bawling. An ice-cold lemonade bought from a vendor and a spell sitting in the shade of a nearby palm placated me, and my mom took my hand and coaxed me back out onto the path leading to the ruins. Dad was nowhere to be seen.

We started up the steep steps of the pyramid of the Castillo when a veil settled over my sight and I felt my hand slip from hers. I slumped to the rough stone of the steps and lay semi-conscious for some minutes. Back in our hotel in Valladolid, the local doctor, a small, thin man with bright black eyes and an infinitely sad expression, pronounced me a victim of heatstroke and recommended a day's rest. My father didn't hide his irritation.

The real show, and the first intimation of my close-ness to the world beyond the veil, came two days later at Chichen Itza. Without warning, the world seemed to go flat as I lost all sense of depth. Bright day turned to shud-dering night flickering feral red and laced with smoke. I was on my back, gazing up at a waning moon half-hidden behind rags of cloud. Around were hundreds, and the thick jungle air pulsed with excitement. My nostrils filled with sweat and the coppery scent of blood, and I knew the un-forgiving black edge of obsidian as a thing of everyday use.

I woke back in the hotel, and this time the same sad doctor advised my parents to take me home. Years later, my mother told me he'd confided in her that it wasn't the first time he'd witnessed such a case. That some very rare peo-ple—though never, in his experience, children—seemed psychically sensitive to ancient sites, succumbing to faints and visions. "In truth, I have always suspected it to be au-to-suggestion," he told her. "But a child this young… "

Back in Santa Barbara, the business was forgotten. But my parents never took me on a trip to archaeological sites again.

I looked around. The old Cobb Estate had its palms and cacti, and the roads and walkways were themselves re-turning to nature as weeds and roots reclaimed the stone paths and the few remaining foundations and terrace walls. But the resemblance to the Mayan places stopped there.

No dark jaguar gods were worshipped here, no beating hearts cut from living flesh with gleaming obsidian blades.

A pair of tall palms swaying high from amid a jumble of smaller trees and undergrowth caught my eye. Something slipped within me, and the early morning quiet yielded to the sewing-machine chatter of what could have been an engine. I caught a glimpse of something deep red and shiny moving slowly along the pebbled road beyond the vegetation, the half-glimpsed shape, maybe, of a stately vintage automobile. The word *Packard* slid through my mind. Then the vision was gone.

I stood, startled, for a long moment. I wasn't prone to psychism, and never had an episode since that forgotten weirdness in the Yucatan. I'd always—perhaps as a result of my dad's frustration at having his hobby so inconvenienced, I saw it now—taken a hard line on the topic of the paranormal. So…?

I smiled. The sad doctor's auto-suggestion, of course. I'd just remembered that childhood experience and been thinking on the Estate's history, and my psyche had delivered. I shook my head and walked on.

I didn't take the long trail that day. Instead, and in the days that followed, I explored every yard of the old estate until it was as familiar as my own home. Like a cat, I somehow felt I needed to know this small territory well before venturing far afield.

My web searches had only turned up a few pictures and limited information about the Cobb mansion in its glory days, but as I explored the property, a picture of the place gradually built in my mind's eye.

The estate had been home to a lumber magnate and his wife, passing at his death to the Pasadena Masons. Later it became a nunnery; the property was finally bought as a speculative investment by the Marx Brothers. In the late fifties, the home, by then in a state of advanced disrepair, was demolished. After a period of uncertainty, a gift from a wealthy donor supported by a number of smaller contributions from local residents enabled the city to acquire the land and keep it open for public use.

With the ruined estate as the anchor for my excursions, I took to exploring the multitude of shorter trails and paths that crisscrossed the area. I mostly shunned other hikers. But during the few encounters I had, I was more than once told that the estate had a reputation for being haunted. I smiled inwardly at this. The grounds, to my sight at least, were home to some few lingering impressions and eidetic images. It was the ruins of the White City, and most of all the tavern far above, that were haunted, and the ghosts I met there would upend my life.

I set off on the Sam Merrill Trail to Echo Mountain early on a Friday morning in early November.

Among the many things that astonish about the sprawling plain of concrete we call L.A. is the deep silence and peace to be found only short way up into the foothills, as though the metropolis stretching out below were just a projection, or a model seen through glass. I became aware of this just a few minutes into the sparse, low woods along the lower portions of the trail. There was birdsong, and the lightest sigh of air in the leaves as the sun began to climb.

There were other hikers ahead and behind me, and I stopped more than once to let some group by. The strength of my resentment at their presence took me by surprise: it was all I could do not to snarl. Digging for the cause of this, I found myself taken by a strange sense of belonging, of knowing this terrain. But rooted as I felt in space, I had the sense of time sliding uncertain and unmoored, and myself a compass looking for my temporal north. I shook myself free of these odd notions and resumed my upward progress.

I paused at a small, south-facing promontory a mile or so up the trail. Sat in the dry yellow dust, I drank water and ate half of one of my BLTs as I took in the view. The marine layer had burnt off, leaving the morning unusually clear. The cities and hills of the L.A. basin extended in every direction. Off to my right in the middle distance the downtown buildings punched up tight and sharp, their vertical reach dwarfed by the infinite horizontality of the city. Far off I could see the ocean; farther still, way off to the southwest, what had to be one of the Channel Islands.

I reached the site of the old resort on Echo Mountain in the late morning. The day was warming, and I was glad of the level ground. In a profound silence I walked the last few hundred yards. The tracks of the old funicular railway had run along here, I was sure, an impression confirmed moments later by a giant cogwheel and sections of cable set beside the now-broad trail, along with a number of heavy carriage axles and wheels. From not far ahead I heard voices raised in what I couldn't imagine was anything but banal and social chatter. I sighed and trudged on.

As I stood in the open space where the resort once called "the white city in the sky" had stood, I tried to picture the Echo Mountain House hotel as I'd seen it in the black-and-whites I'd viewed online, complete with mustachioed Victorian and Edwardian gentlemen striking poses, and their ladies with their elaborate hats and graceful parasols. It wasn't hard. But the mental image brought with it an undercurrent of unease. Behind the brilliant white paint and the festive air of the visitors and guests was something uneasy, a shadow of ruin. The chatter which a minute ago had so disturbed me faded, leaving me to face down a rising fear. It pulsed and radiated from the ruined concrete and cracked stairs of the old foundation, bubbling up from the dry dirt to coalesce into an invisible, hostile fog.

I forced myself to breathe. The day around me remained bright; beneath my feet the ground was steady and reliable. But the sense of looming danger was strong, and it took a great effort of will to not let it overcome me. My heart was straining in my chest, and my feet wanted to turn and run.

I walked up to the person closest. Solitary or not, talking to someone would anchor me, bring me back to Earth. I didn't know what was going on, why this was happening, but I wouldn't give in the irrational.

He was tall and young, maybe thirty, with thick dark curls, and handsome to the point of hot. Something about his clothing, the off-white slacks, the cut of his shirt, was oddly retro, but I was too preoccupied with combating my rising panic to think on it. His tan boots were dusty and looked as though they could have told some stories.

The man turned to me as I closed on his personal space. He was a full head taller than I, well over six feet. He cocked his head and gave me an odd half-smile as if to say, *Do I know you?* His eyes took me in head-to-toe before fixing on mine for a long moment.

"Beautiful, isn't it?" I blurted out. Inane, but I was the one who'd made the approach. And scrambling for words at least gave me something to keep my mind off my crazy panic attack.

"Until the next deluge," he replied. His face split in the most boyish smile and he stuck out his hand. "Jack."

"Laura," I said, grasping his palm. His grip was gentle and warm. Something shifted inside, grounding and centering me.

Jack nodded slowly. His gaze flicked briefly over my shoulder, as though checking something in the far distance before returning to me. His eyes narrowed; his expression had turned serious. "Are you okay?" he said, touching my arm lightly.

I swallowed. The panic, thankfully, was dissipating. My heart slowed, my breathing deepened. "Yes," I said. "I'm fine. I don't know..." I looked around. "The climb, perhaps. I should probably have some protein."

He gave a small nod. His booted foot scraped at the ground. "A few years ago, we could have ridden the railway up and gotten a good meal up at the tavern." He grinned.

I laughed. "Quite a few years."

"You should see it," he said. Something behind me caught his eye again, and his face became preoccupied, distracted. I turned, shading my eyes, unsure what I was even looking for. An infinity of hazy sky hanging over the metropolis's cities and hills filled the view beyond the low steps that once led to the hotel.

I turned back to Jack. "I wonder—" I began. But he was gone.

I looked around, searching, my eyes sifting the fifteen or twenty people scattered around the site. But Jack had vanished as though he'd never been.

❧

That night, I felt the most intense sexual stirrings I'd known in many months. When Rob came up to turn in, I was deep into my book. But when he climbed into bed and kissed my cheek in that awkward way of his, it stirred me like he'd spent twenty minutes on foreplay. I was suddenly horny as hell.

I turned and wound an arm around his neck, kissing him hard. My fingers curled in his hair. Overwhelmed by my ferocity, perhaps, he sank back in surprise. His hand slipped under my tee at the back, but by then I was tearing at his shorts and climbing on top of him.

Rob didn't know what hit him. He went along for the ride, surprised and a little stunned-looking—I don't think he could have stopped it even if he'd wanted to. After, as we lay close, getting our breath back, he squeezed my hand. His eyes were half-lidded and heavy. "Wow," he murmured. "Just, wow. I don't know what got into you, but whatever it was, hold onto it."

I smiled as he slipped into sleep. What could I say? I did know what had got into me. It was Jack.

CHAPTER TWO
Roberto

November 2016
Altadena, CA

I LANDED IN BURBANK at 9:30 on Saturday night and took an Uber straight to Phil and Anne's house. Phil and Anne were our neighbors for the two years we had the house on Poppyfields Drive; we'd bonded hard and fast, and they stuck with us through the escalating difficulties of our marriage and saw me through the anguish of Laura's disappearance. We'd stayed in touch by phone and email since I moved east.

We hugged. After unpacking and freshening up, I joined them in the living room. Anne had laid out cheese and cold cuts, raw veggies and apple slices. Phil poured us a fine Chardonnay and we toasted our reunion, despite the circumstances.

"So, do you know anything more yet?" asked Anne, as I filled a small plate. I'd not eaten since leaving Raleigh, and I was famished.

I shook my head. "I have an appointment at the sheriff's office, and then I'm going to the funeral home."

"We read about them finding... finding Laura," said Phil.

"Right. Last week." I started in on the cheese and apple.

Anne put her hand gently on my wrist. "I know you need to see her, hon."

Phil nodded. "We had heavy rains for days. Made a mess up in the mountains."

Anne gave me a gentle smile. "It's awful. She was so lovely, that gorgeous red hair..." She shook her head. "We did admire how you moved on, Rob, but I'm glad you'll have real closure now. That's always a good thing."

Phil nodded. "You can use my car," he said. "Anne can drop me at work and pick me up tomorrow—it's not far out of her way." When I tried to decline, they insisted. "Do what you need to, and just let us know if you're going to be late. Anne's got dinner covered, so we'll just see you back here whenever."

Lying in bed an hour later, I thought about the whole closure thing. My life had moved on, but a big part of me hadn't, was stuck here. Would Anne's *closure*—I'd always mistrusted the word, with its New Age/Pop Psy overtones—change that? Yeah, I should allow for the possibility. But the damage was deeper, and stranger, than I even admitted to myself.

The rot started with Laura's very first hike up into those damned hills, the day I went back to work at JPL with my ankle in a cast. At first, I thought she just enjoyed the exercise and views, but I soon began to see it was more than that.

In the following weeks, Laura's occasional pot use became habitual and heavy as she developed what was starting to look an obsession with the foothills and the Mount Lowe area. She was drinking more, too. Sometimes she didn't get home till after dark. At first she was apologetic. Maybe because I didn't push back—should I have? I'll never know, it wasn't my way —she was soon doing whatever she wanted without apology or explanation.

Soon, though we spent less time together, the time abruptly became more intense. Our sex life, which had fallen off a lot in the last months, began to sizzle. This confused me, since Laura seemed in other ways to be drawing away from me. We hardly talked. When I tried to engage her, she seemed distracted. Sometimes she didn't even answer me; she was always stoned. But her lovemaking became aggressive and demanding to the point where she'd leave me feeling I'd been ravished and drained by some blank-souled succubus rather than the warm, playful creature I'd married.

It was in March, just weeks before her disappearance, that I found out about Jack, and the visions.

Laura

March 2014
Altadena, CA

A hard, late-season rain provided the opportunity I wanted to get up to the site of the old Alpine Tavern under the shadow of Mount Lowe without having to worry about crowds. I finally had an open calendar; guessing the weather would deter most people, I loaded my backpack into the Subaru along with a lightweight tent and everything I needed for a couple of nights and called Rob at work.

I'd wanted to go up there for a long time, but something—holidays, annoying social and family engagements, visiting friends from out of town—always seemed to conspire against it. Also the campsites were limited, and on a first-come, first-served basis.

It was a Tuesday, and we'd talked about going to a movie that night as an attempt at a date. It was near noon by now, and Rob wasn't happy about my canceling. I knew my growing absorption with the mountains and the past weighed on him, but he wasn't the type to fight, he just stuffed his resentment. It was his way of loving me: he could take it, so he did. It suited me.

Oddly, he'd just the previous night tried to engage with me about my fascination with the old ruins on Echo Summit and Mount Lowe. Rob talked about how Pasadena and Altadena seemed to be a center for mysteries and oddballs. "Take Parsons and his weird cult thing. I mean, the guy founded JPL, for God's sake, but he was crazier than a sack full of cats. He…"

I tuned him out, more interested in the Netflix series I was trying to watch. Rob took the hint. He paused, gave me a crooked smile, and left me alone.

Maybe I should have felt bad, but at the time it hardly mattered: I was already drifting beyond his emotional orbit and becoming a stranger even to myself as other, older, forces began to move me.

I left the car near the gate on Chaney and hiked in the five or so miles up Mount Lowe Road. The road was broad, and I splashed my way through puddles and gritty mud from the night's downpour. Heavy cloud cover threatened more, but the rains had washed the air clean, providing cinematic views over the city and way out to the ocean. I took it leisurely, and arrived in mid-afternoon at the trail camp by the site of the old Alpine Tavern.

My hunch had been right. Not a soul was there to disturb the profound silence. With luck it would stay that way.

I pitched my tent and arranged my pack and sleeping bag inside. The trestle picnic tables were dark with moisture, and the pungent stink of wet ashes hung around the firepits. I clambered around the terraces trying to discern which of the sections of stone wall might have been part of the old tavern. Occasional breaks in the cloud cover brought ghostly wisps of steam from the pebble- and pine needle-strewn ground.

There was a small stream nearby. I'd brought six pint bottles of filtered water, enough for my short stay; if I came again I could travel lighter and just filter water from the stream.

On the near edge of twilight, I wiped down one of the picnic tables and set up my single burner camp stove. The sun was settling into a band of dark cloud off to the west; no spectacular sunset tonight, just a quiet dimming into a grey twilight. I fetched out a soup packet, along with a pack of dense rye farm bread and a little jar of butter, filled a pan with water, and set it on the burner. Not one to abandon all the civilized comforts, I'd brought a bottle of wine and my vape pen. As the water heated on the hissing stove, I sipped at my wine and took a good hit of the weed.

Later, well-fed and wrapped in my warm jacket, I turned down my LED lantern and sat in the deep dark, listening to the night sounds and looking out over the galaxy of lights of the cities below. The sky had cleared and the moon wasn't yet up. I lay a tarp on the ground and stretched out flat. The star fields populated and deepened. I watched as a satellite paced its way through the constellations, and soon caught the brief flash of a shooting star.

A soft crunch off to my right startled me. I sat up quickly. A few yards away, a tall, man-shaped piece of night moved in the starlit dark.

I scrabbled in my pocket for my flashlight, heart halfway to my throat, thoughts flying in scatter of unnamed fears. Being stoned and buzzed from the wine didn't help.

"Who's there?" I yelped. I had no kind of a weapon, and whoever was there was just a couple of long strides away. If they were going to hurt me, I didn't have a chance.

My hand closed on my flashlight and I wrestled it out in a rising panic, thoughts redlining like an engine screaming between gears. The light came on, the beam bouncing off ground and stone walls and tree branches as I scrambled to my feet in rising panic. The light found his face just as the unseen intruder spoke.

"Laura?" he said. "It's Jack. Remember me?" His voice was quiet, calm.

I stared, but didn't see. Or didn't see *him*, only the writhing shapes of my terror as my mind struggled to get my perceptions in order and my adrenaline-charged senses rightside up. My heart jackhammered at my chest and my legs trembled.

His features snapped into place in the wash of white light. The thick curls, the full, sensual lips, the boyish look. His dark eyes met mine, staring right through the brilliant beam as if it weren't there.

It was a moment before I could speak. Then, "Jack?" I whispered. Later it occurred to me that the fact of knowing him should perhaps have made me more rather than less scared. But his calm, something in his look, the warmth that seemed part of him, felt somehow reassuring. "What... I mean, how did you...?"

"Find you?" A disarming smile. "I just asked, and here you are."

I stared at him blankly. *"What?"* I shook my head. He shrugged.

"Wait," I said. I swung the flashlight beam and stepped over to the picnic table where I'd set the lantern down. I turned the knob, and white light reached out to swallow the nearby dark.

He walked into the pool of light. Jack was tall, and carried himself well. I was high and more than a little jittery from the adrenaline that had come with my panic at his appearance, but something in me welcomed his arrival. I sat on the bench, back to the picnic table, and gestured for him to join me.

"Thanks," he said, and sat at what seemed the right distance—not close, not far. He leaned back, elbows on the table, long legs outstretched, and looked up at the sky, considering the night.

I should have been terrified, alone up there, miles from anywhere, with a complete stranger. But his presence seemed entirely natural, as if we'd known one another for years.

Jack's gaze lowered and he turned to me. "Sorry if I scared you. Coming out of the dark like that."

I smiled. "I did panic for a moment. You startled me."

"*Pan* is the root of the word *panic*." He gestured to the surrounding darkness. "Devil or God, he rules in the wild places."

I blinked. "I'm sorry?" My heart jumped again. I really wanted—*needed*—to believe this man wasn't crazy.

He pursed his lips. Then, in a soft voice, he recited,

Thrill with lissome lust of the light,
O man! My man!
Come careering out of the night
Of Pan! Io Pan!

"We've become so straitjacketed in our cities that we need the wild places to recharge," he went on. "Too many rules. The harder society represses our true natures, the wilder and more dangerous we become. Pan is our deliverer."

His eyes burned into the darkness, and he was silent for a long moment. Then, "Got some of that Mary Jane?" he said.

I'm sure my surprise showed. But, "Yes. Yes, I do," I said, with a smile. I reached into my jacket pocket and handed him my vape pen.

He held it up, turned it, puzzling over it. He put the mouthpiece between his lips.

"Here," I said, "press down on the button and inhale."

He took an experimental puff or two, then a long draw before handing the pen back. He nodded. "S'good," he hissed, holding down the vapor before releasing it in a long stream through his nostrils.

I took a deep drag, then another, and set the pen on the table. "So what brought you up here, Jack?"

"You did." He grinned.

That struck me as funny, and I giggled. "Come on, really."

He looked around. "This was quite a place," he began. "Ye Alpine Tavern. My parents brought me up here as a kid, and I came up a couple more times before it burned. In the summer they had an orchestra. The tennis courts were just over there," he said, with a wave.

I gave him a look. "Come on, Jack."

He turned to face me again. The lantern light glimmered in his eyes as they bored into me. I felt weirdly exposed, and not in an unpleasant way. I shifted my legs a little, unable to look away.

"This place is ancient history to you," he said. "Not to me." He reached out, resting his hand palm upwards on the bench between us. To my astonishment I took it. His hand was warm, almost hot in mine, and I felt a flush of heat deep down. My body felt deliciously heavy from the pure Indica smoke. I wanted touch.

He held my eyes, unmoving. "What do you think brought you here, Laura?"

I shrugged. Play along, why not? He's sexy as all hell. "I'm guessing that you did?"

"Babylon," he whispered.

I opened my mouth to ask what he meant; before I could speak, he squeezed my hand and said, "You should come and visit the Parsonage. I have a room or two empty."

I burst out laughing. I edged closer on the bench, never letting go of his hand, and set my other on his outstretched thigh. It seemed the most natural thing in the world. "For one, I'm a married woman," I said. "For another, if I'm hearing you right, you're a time traveler. Now, how's that ever going to work out?"

"Let me show you," he said, and pulled me into a kiss.

CHAPTER THREE
Roberto

November 2016
Altadena, CA

THE MORNING was bright, the foothills hard-edged and green from the season's early rains. I went first to the local sheriff's office and spoke to Brianna Davis, the officer who'd handled the case when Laura's body was found. She was a tall, sinewy woman with bright blue eyes. I couldn't stop looking at them: I'd never seen a black person with light-colored eyes before. Going by her amused look when she had to ask me a second time if I wanted coffee, I suspected Davis was used to it.

She returned with my coffee and sat opposite me. Her desk was crazy tidy, with the few items on it sitting dead square to the keyboard at its geographic center.

"The remains were found by a pair of hikers," she said, "just below one of the picnic tables. People sit and pass by there all the time. We have no idea how they got there, or why nobody noticed them before." She shook her head.

I frowned. "I heard there'd been a rainstorm. Could the rains have dislodged the body?"

She snorted, more in incredulity than humor. "That does happen, sir, especially if the body's been buried in a shallow grave. There's no chance of that here."

I couldn't understand it. "So I understand… " I took a breath. "The remains are far gone. How could she just show up there?"

Davis nodded. "That's the question, sir." She looked at a random spot on her desk and tapped a finger against her notebook. "We're hopeful the autopsy will provide answers. Right now all we have are questions." Those blue eyes came up and skewered me. *Do you have a question?* They said.

The one I'd been avoiding. "How bad," I heard myself ask, "is the body?"

Davis nodded again, watching my eyes as if holding my hand. "Just bones, sir. Dry bones."

"You're absolutely certain it's her?"

She frowned and tapped her finger some more. It was several seconds before she replied. "According to the dental records. Yes sir."

I arrived at the funeral home a bit before eleven. I signed in and was directed to a chair. A few minutes later, a chubby man in an expensive suit arrived. Used to dealing with family of the deceased, by his gentle manner. I told him I wanted to see her.

He nodded. "You understand, Mister Sanchez," he said softly, "the body's fully decomposed. Are you quite—"

"I'd like to see her," I repeated.

It was cold in the small room with the coffin. The man set his hands on the edge of the lid and his eyes flicked up to me one last time. When I nodded, he lifted the lid in a smooth motion.

There were sharp bumps and protrusions under the immaculate white linen covering her. They stopped about where her waist should have been. Something inside me came undone, like I was watching a movie, or standing behind a camera.

The chubby man lifted the fabric at her head.

The skull that peered up at me was a weathered, mottled grey-brown. It was flaking in parts, delaminating like slate. I'd never seen an actual human skull, but it didn't look like any of the pictures you see, all bleached white and smooth. I tried to superimpose Laura's face on it, to fill those huge round sockets with her eyes, to replace her pert little nose, to stretch full lips over the grinning teeth. Impossible. There wasn't the beginning of a way to bridge the gap.

Floundering in a tide of conflicting thoughts and feelings, weirdly disconnected, I placed my hand on the clean linen over what may have once been her shoulder and said my goodbye. It was the best I could do.

Laura

Jack's heart beat under my palm. We lay close and naked in my little tent, his strong hand caressing my back as I lay contentedly, my head on his shoulder, my leg crooked up over his. The cool night air, so still in the cozy pocket between the gossamer tent walls, felt good after the heat we'd generated.

We'd spontaneously combusted with a passion so sudden and fierce that he'd taken me right there at the picnic table, my hands braced against the rough wood, my jeans puddled around my ankles as he entered me from behind. When our breath returned, we slipped into my tent and smoked more pot before fucking again, leisurely this time, laughing and giggling as we explored and pleasured one another in the confined space. I was half afraid the tent might collapse around us, but somehow it stayed up through our lovemaking.

I stroked my hand over the fuzz of hair on his chest. "Really," I said, "where are you from, Jack?"

"Space or time?" he said.

I giggled. "Either, or both."

"Pasadena. It's January twenty-six."

"What year?"

"1946."

Between the wine, the pot, and the intense sex, I was in a dream. Nothing about any of this was real. And yet the pebbles beneath the bag and the thin plastic of the tent poked into me; there was a wet spot under my hip, and the bristles on Jack's chin scraped against my cheek as he turned to kiss me.

I shelved questions on the calendar issue and focused on the now. "Why here? What's special about this place? Or the White City ruins, since that's where we first met?"

"There are resonances in these mountains, and they draw people. There's a reason they built on this precise spot. This particular set of resonances surfaces in the Verdugo woodlands, too, and at the Parsonage. I've drawn and mapped it. But they're strongest here."

"Wait, stop." I had a half-dozen questions. *"Resonances?"*

"Elemental ones. Fire and Air."

I stared at him. "The Alpine Tavern was destroyed in a fire."

"Yes," he said. "Fire and storms leveled the White City. Laura, does *Babylon* mean anything to you?"

I shook my head. "I don't understand anything you're saying." One minute tender, romantic, delicious, the next a crazy man. I ought to have been scared; I was the opposite.

He tensed and his head came half up, as if listening. The tent walls shook in a sudden gust, and I felt a chill. I thought I caught a strain of violins, but it had to be the wind.

He kissed me quickly and rose. "Laura, I have to go. Come back? Promise me?"

"What?" I sat up. Oh!" I slapped the ground with both hands as I felt myself fall. Like a hypnagogic start, but I was wide awake. My hands went to my head, as if to steady it. "When? Wait! Who *are* you, Jack?

Jack was kneeling, his head bent awkwardly under the curving tent wall as he buttoned his shirt. He already had his pants and boots on. I couldn't understand how he'd done that.

"Tomorrow," he said, clambering out the tent fly in a half crouch.

"Wait!" I called. But when I looked out a second later, he was gone.

☽

When I woke in the chill of pre-dawn, I struggled to convince myself I hadn't just dreamed the whole episode. I pulled on jeans and my fleece, slid my feet into boots, and staggered to the portapotty.

My body told me I hadn't dreamed anything: a woman knows when she's been ridden hard, and I had, no question. Roberto and I hadn't had sex in at least a month; my enthusiasm and passion after meeting Jack the first time had carried us through a few weeks before fading to nothing. And I could tell from the way my tongue felt that I'd done some strenuous kissing; Roberto and I hadn't kissed in forever. He'd never liked kissing much.

I put water on for coffee and sat at the picnic table as I waited for it to boil. Jack had said to return today, but there was no way I could stay up here another night. I'd promised Roberto I'd come back; given how things seemed to be sliding between us, he wouldn't have taken well to my staying a second night. Oh, he'd have tolerated it, but I couldn't ignore all my feelings of guilt.

Closing my eyes, I felt Jack's lips on mine, his strong, gentle hands exploring my body, his fingers playing me like a flute. He was warm, irresistible… And I knew nothing about him.

I made coffee and began to pack my things. I rolled my bag, folded up and stowed the stove and eating utensils, and took down my tent. With everything packed and strapped to my pack, I took a last look around, smiled at the memory of last night, and started back on the trail.

How he'd happened up here, I couldn't imagine. He'd come seemingly out of nowhere, without pack or gear or anything. He could have been camped close by, just out of sight. Someone with good woodcraft could move very silently. I remembered my cousin Kyle showing me how to stalk deer that time he'd taken me hunting up near Three Rivers. We didn't get a deer, but when we surprised a four hundred-pound boar in the undergrowth it was only Kyle's speed and skill, shooting from the hip as he swung up his rifle, that had saved us from serious injury or even death.

If I knew anything about Jack, it was that he was a man. Not a ghost, not a time traveler, but a solid man, warm flesh and hot blood. And wherever he'd come from, it wasn't 1946. All the weird stuff about elementals and Babylon was crazy, and yet it had clicked somewhere in my subconscious, as though touching on things long forgotten and buried deep. I had to know more. Between my curiosity and the way he'd stirred my body to a pitch of desire I hadn't felt in years, I had to see him again.

CHAPTER FOUR
Roberto

November 2016
Altadena, CA

I GOT BACK to Phil and Anne's a little after noon. and crashed hard. I still hadn't caught up from Friday night's drunk, and there was the jet lag. But the emotional haymaker of seeing Laura's remains, I hadn't even started to process that.

Of course, things I'd been too tight and broken to discuss even with friends before I left—or ran—came out in the course of dinner. Something inside me had shifted, like a boulder slowly starting to roll, and I talked more and more freely than I had in a long while.

"I'd never have suspected she was having an affair," said Anne. "You think you know someone…"

Phil poured us more wine. "I mean, we could see there was some friction between you two now and then but, hell, what couple doesn't have that?"

Anne nodded. She turned to me, cocked her head. "So who was he?"

I sipped my wine. Without a prepared reply, what could I say? Because I didn't even believe the truth myself. I told it anyway.

"Someone else who worked at JPL," I said.

"Seriously? Did you know him?"

"Not exactly. But I knew *of* him."

☽

March 2015
Altadena, CA

I walked into the living room. Laura was binge-watching a sci-fi series I had zero interest in. Her vape pen was on the couch beside her and the room smelled pleasantly of strong bud.

I lowered myself onto the sofa beside her. She gave me a quick smile and returned her bloodshot eyes to the TV.

"Babylon?" I said. "Elementals?"

Laura looked up at me. For a moment she was startled. Then her surprise turned darker. "What the fuck?" she said, and hit the PAUSE button. "Are you going through my browser history?"

On the screen, an HD explosion froze in mid-bloom, the shockwave hurling a silhouetted figure in the foreground into the air.

"Whoa," I said, backing up. My laptop was in the shop and we'd never had an issue sharing. "You left the browser open. Just curious. I didn't know you were interested in magic and cosmic forces."

She bit her lip. Trying to guess, I could see it. Had I just looked at the open tab, or dug into the history?

"I was curious," she said. "Someone was talking about it and I wanted to know more."

I nodded. She'd been in all afternoon since returning from her hike.

She reached for my hand, squeezed it. "I'm beat. Let's order out. How does Thai sound tonight?"

"Sounds good," I said.

When we were done with dinner and she was hitting the vape again, I said, as casually as I could, "So just how did this magic stuff come up?" Crazy, but it took all my courage to bring it up again. I've never liked confrontation. It's just so much easier to say nothing. But I had to know.

"Mm," she said, and began to release the vapor slowly through her lips. She offered me the pen. I shook my head. She set it down on the table.

"I met a guy on the way down and we hiked together for a while. He was telling me about all that stuff, seemed really into it. He said the foothills had some correspondence with Babylon and the elements. I didn't understand it but it was interesting."

I nodded. "And the Babylon bit?"

She grinned, totally baked. "I didn't ask. I think he was a little crazy."

"But you hiked with him anyway? I thought you hated talking to people when you're in nature."

"He was nice," she said. Her palms spread and her face hardened. "Fuck, Rob, why the third degree? I was only talking to him!"

"I'm sorry, I'm just curious." It was true, but I was also scared, and I didn't know why. "What was his name?"

"Jack. His fucking name was Jack, okay?" She grabbed her vape pen and stalked off into the bedroom.

☽

Laura

My anger didn't last. Or rather, something stronger took over.

I pulled Rob out of the kitchen, where he was halfway through making a sandwich, dragged him into the bedroom, and pretty much ravished him. At first, he tried to protest: I slapped him hard across the cheek and told him to shut up as I pulled his pants down. After that, he was putty in my hands. I fucked him shamelessly, taking, taking. Whether it was fear or something else, he lasted far longer than seemed possible. The fact he eventually came at all was of no concern to me.

When I woke the next morning, Rob had already left for work.

☾

Tomorrow was Thursday. I'd already missed "tomorrow," and if I wanted to see Jack again I needed to get back there quickly. Would he come, though? What if he'd shown up today and found I wasn't there? Would he give up? He didn't seem the giving up type, but he'd left in such a sudden hurry I wondered if he had other obligations and restrictions. Like a wife, maybe. And kids.

And now I had a problem, too. Since Rob knew I'd met someone on the trail, would he be suspicious of my wanting to go back there at once? I could handle him, but some part of me that seemed to be flickering on and off was throwing up guilt flags. To hell with that.

I'd need to get up there early. Very early. Now the weather had settled, the five campsites up there would fill up fast, and you couldn't reserve them—it was first come, first served. I supposed I could always set up a tent a little way off the site, somewhere a bit hidden.

That afternoon, I restocked my backpack with food for three days and a half bottle of tequila, ready to leave in the early hours. If I parked the car and started on the trail at dawn, I'd easily be at the tavern site by eight-thirty. Unless the camp had today filled with hikers staying more than one night, which seemed extremely unlikely, that would guarantee me a spot.

I worried stupidly all day over how to handle Rob. In the end, I decided to stay close to the truth: that I was fascinated both by the Alpine Tavern site and by the suggestion the place had magical properties. I downplayed Jack's role. Just a passing hiker who'd come on foot all the way from the Cobb Estate and was returning on the trail.

Rob didn't try to stop me—he wouldn't ever—but he was unhappy as I've ever seen him. Even distanced as he was from his emotions, our recent closeness had left him more open and vulnerable than he might otherwise have been. Nothing I could do about that. I'd needed him, and he got something out of it.

That night though, I raped him again. And I mean raped. He hadn't wanted sex, actually looked scared at first, but his resistance quickly collapsed in the face of my desire and need. After, he was quiet. Looking back on it now, part of me winced at how cold I'd been in using him like that. But a more dominant part of my changing psyche didn't give a shit.

Once we'd been in love. But from the day he'd broken his ankle in the sandy wash at the top of Lake, some tectonic force of the heart had driven us irrevocably apart until we drifted free from one another like two lonely island continents. His nature was to repress his feelings, if he was even in touch with them. For myself, I wonder now if I ever truly had any.

Now, an ocean had formed between us. In truth, as long as I got what I wanted, I didn't much care.

I arrived at the Mount Lowe camp before eight to find it empty. The air was still cool, but I was glowing from the hike. I was glad I'd worn shorts.

I set my pack down on the same spot I'd camped at before and took my coffee over towards the lookout. The city spread and sprawled between canyons and up hills, its only boundary the ocean to the south and west. A dirty, crazy place home to seventeen million souls. There was art and industry, rot and beauty, wealth and squalor, birth and death, love and hate. Every possible thing a human might do was being done down there every minute of every day. People were being born, going to school, dancing, fucking, getting married, overdosing, sitting in traffic jams, making movies, being fired from jobs, going to AA meetings, giving birth, getting killed.

Would Jack show up? How long would I have to wait? I took a place at the picnic table and began to read.

Several hikers arrived as the day progressed. At one point there were probably two dozen people there, none of them Jack. I kept to myself as much as I could. Some tried to engage me; I was polite but didn't encourage them. They soon drifted away.

People were so doggy in groups. I always preferred cats.

By early afternoon, all the camping spots were taken. My mood sank. Even if Jack arrived, that meant no privacy. I was totally keyed up with a hundred questions and, I couldn't deny it, a burning desire to have him. I contemplated moving my tent off the site and a few hundred feet into the nearby scrub. Would anyone care? I didn't think rangers checked the site... at least, I'd not seen one. I puffed on my vape pen and put the decision off till later.

The sunset over the ocean was spectacular. It was also a lonely one, as Jack hadn't showed. I left the tent where it was and skulked off onto an outcrop of rock a few dozen yards from the campground. Some part of me knew that Jack, if he turned up, would find me wherever I was. I didn't consciously believe he had powers, but my heart knew he did.

The other campers had spread out over the picnic tables. They weren't loud or in any way obnoxious, but I resented their presence with a passion. I crawled into my tent a little after nine and drank and smoked myself to unconsciousness.

CHAPTER FIVE
Roberto

March 2015
Altadena, CA

I GOT HOME to an empty house. I'd been feeling sluggish and weirdly drained all day, and couldn't stomach lunch. Finally hungry, I picked myself up a pizza on the way home. I plated a couple of slices, took a beer from the fridge and went online.

I'd got my own laptop back that afternoon. I ran a new search on Babylon; there were pagan and Christian sites and wacko ones, as well as a couple of irrelevant book reviews. And then, scanning down just below the fold on a site which talked about the Goddess Babalon with an 'a', I came across the sentence, *Crowley's work is the catalyst for Jack Parsons, who was as passionate about Magick and Thelema as he was his pioneering work as an engineer and rocket scientist.*

Jack. Jack *Parsons*. And Babalon.

I'd heard the name, of course. You couldn't work at JPL and not know of Jack Parsons. In his short lifetime—he died young—Parsons had been a druggie, libertine, occultist, purveyor of home-brewed nitroglycerin, and rocket engineer, often all at the same time. He was also, along with a small handful of others, one of the founders of JPL.

It had to be a joke.

But why would a complete stranger approach my wife on a hiking trail and start talking about elementals, and asking if she knew about what had apparently been a ritual to summon a Goddess, some aspect of the Divine Feminine? Unless Laura, in her stoned stupor, had riffed on a casual mention and built a few odd words or comments into something it was never intended as. Perhaps she'd even misunderstood a mention of Jack Parsons as the hiker's name. None of it made any sense.

I read the article through in something like a fever. There were references to the "Scarlet Woman", the "Mother of Prostitutes"; to Kali and Lilith and the Black Isis, whoever she was.

I fetched another beer and dug into site after site. An hour and a third beer later, my head was on fire with knowledge about Parsons and the Babalon working; an aside of weird came in the form of a ton of detail about his mentor, the black magician and self-styled *Great Beast,* Aleister Crowley, and the discovery that Parsons's close collaborator was none other than L. Ron Hubbard, who would go on to found the Church of Scientology.

Even after reading all that, I'd have laughed the whole thing off but for one detail: the repeated mention and undercurrent of intense sexuality both sacred and mundane. Sex magic was the big thing for Parsons and his group at the Agape Lodge. A long poem in Parsons's *The Book of Babalon* concluded with the verses,

Her mouth is red and her breasts are fair
and her loins are full of fire,
And her lust is strong as a man is strong
in the heat of her desire,
And her whoredom is holy as virtue is foul
beneath the holy sky,
And her kisses will wanton the world away
in passion that shall not die.
Ye shall laugh and love and follow her dance
when the wrath of God is gone
And dream no more of hell and hate
in the Birth of BABALON.

❧

Laura called me early Friday afternoon to tell me she was staying another night. "It's so beautiful up here." Her words tumbled over one another as she spoke. "I hiked the East Trail today up Mount Lowe. I wish you could see it, Baby. The views. It's amazing."

Something in her tone was off. Could just be she was high and excited. I debated saying something about what I'd discovered in my searches but thought better of it. "I'm glad you're enjoying yourself," I said, though I wasn't. I didn't know what I was feeling, what to think, how to handle her. I hated drama. And my wife, always strong, knew it.

I let her bubble and effervesce a bit longer until she ran out of things to say. Had she met Jack up there? Was she even up there? It crossed my mind to ask her to snap a selfie and send it to me, but I didn't want to deal with the blowback. For all the emotional connection we had left, she may as well have been on the moon.

❧

Laura

On the second night, Jack showed.

I'd returned to camp ravenous. I poured myself a shot and chewed on crispbread and cheese as I heated water. I broke open two packets of dehydrated mac and cheese, stirred them into the hot water in the pan, and stalked off beyond the picnic tables to get away from the other campers. I sat in the loose grey dirt on the edge of an escarpment, looking out over the urban sprawl far below. I sipped at the bottle and vaped away as night drew the dusky edge of her veil over the city, and lights twinkled on across the valleys and up the skirts of the hills.

Stars had begun to seriously emerge when there was a movement to my right.

He wore a dark trench coat, and his hair was longer than last time we'd met. I set down my pan of food and scrambled to my feet to greet him. "Jack! I was afraid you wouldn't come."

We hugged, and I rose on tiptoes to kiss him. We stood there for a moment, connecting like hot wires, currents arcing and pulsing between us. The world went away for some moments.

We disengaged and sat. He smiled and pointed to my food. "Smells good. Don't let it get cold. Got a drink?"

I reached into my pocket and handed him the half-bottle of tequila. He took a pull and passed it back.

"A lot has happened," he said. "How long's it been?"

"Three days." I chuckled. "For me, at least."

He nodded, looking out over the city. I spooned mac and cheese into my mouth, trying to sort through the questions I had, wondering where to begin.

Jack spoke first. "I want you to come to the Parsonage," he said. "There's someone I want you to meet."

"The Parsonage?" He'd mentioned that before.

"My house," he explained. He pointed to somewhere in the mottled sprawl of concrete and green in the middle distance. "It's not too far."

I laughed, remembering his joke about being from 1946. "In space or time? Either way, I'd love to." I took a swig of the tequila and spooned more of the cooling food into my mouth. I leaned against him. He was warm, and very solid.

He stroked his chin. "That's the thing. You need to know I'm serious."

I shook my head. "I don't understand."

Jack put an arm around me and reached for my spoon with his other hand. Digging into the pan, he helped himself to a big mouthful of mac and cheese. "Mmm, good." He wiped his mouth with the back of his hand. "I'm not from here, Laura."

I opened my mouth to make a joke, but something about his look, the way he said it, gave me pause. In that instant, it was as though my sight cleared and I really saw him for the first time. A number of things which somehow hadn't registered before—the cut of his clothes and boots, the fact that he was wearing a shirt and tie under his trench coat—these things came into sharp focus as if I'd had my eyes shut until that moment. In that instant, I knew.

My chest tightened, and ice formed in the pit of my stomach. I began to tremble.

Pulling back from him, I said, "Th-this is a joke, right? You're not serious."

"I'm very serious." He gave me an address on South Orange Grove and made me repeat it. I stuttered, seized by some strange, unfounded fear. It felt so good and right to be here with him, but at the same time something was very off, like the point in a strange dream just before it spirals into nightmare and madness.

He squeezed my hand. "Relax," he said.

I tried to speak, but my heart was pounding so hard I could barely think. The pot, it had to be. Somebody had spiked it, fucked with it.

There was the soft crunch of movement in the gravelly scrub just down the slope from us. My fear ratcheted up towards full-blown panic. Jack's head snapped around and his eyes bored into the gloom below.

His long legs unfolded, and he was pulling me to my feet. Noises came out of the dark, something heavy moving down there in the night. Jack placed his body between the edge and me. "Back to the tent," he said, pointing to the campsite.

I hesitated, terrified, confused. My feet had grown roots.

The noises below grew closer, moving upslope. In the darkness, something snuffled and snorted. Jack frowned. Abruptly, he made a strange, stiff-fingered hand gesture, spiraling his open hand towards me, and spoke a word I couldn't understand. Then, "Go," he said, shooing me away. "Write down that address and come soon. I'll be waiting."

I didn't need to him to tell me. Adrenaline spiking, my legs churned and propelled me forward in an access of unreasoning terror. I ran back into the campsite, knocking over a folding chair someone had left out, and dove into my tent.

I didn't see Jack again that night.

❧

When I got home a little after noon on the Saturday, Rob was waiting. He was anxious and confused. I was frustrated and confused. He wanted to talk. I needed to fuck.

I pushed him down on the floor and started to tear off his clothes. He tried to resist but he was never one for force, whereas I had no scruples. I took what I wanted, and drew it out like a fine thread, raping him again and again, focused only my need and hunger, until I was sated. I fed on him, body and mind. When I finished, he was asleep in a second.

He woke three hours later. Whatever I'd become, I was halfway myself again. I pulled him close on the sofa and drew the blanket over us.

"I'm sorry, Baby," I said. "I don't know what got into me." I shook my head.

He nodded. There were questions in his eyes, a mass of them. He was pale, his eyes too shiny, as if he had a fever. He looked awful.

I smoothed his hair and kissed him softly. "Can I get you something? Soup?" I put my palm to his forehead: it was clammy and hot. "I hope you're not getting sick."

Limp in my arms, he closed his eyes as though just keeping them open was an effort. "Soup," he said.

As he ate, a little color returned to his face. He said, "What you're doing, Laura. It's dangerous." He looked at me as though waiting for a reaction.

I didn't have a reaction. I was only half listening, thinking about the address Jack had given me. I wanted to go right now, but what could I say to Rob? He couldn't stop me, but some part of me still cared enough to stay. I would go in the morning.

Rob lowered his eyes and ate more soup. Whatever he'd been about to say, he kept to himself. Or maybe he'd entirely forgotten.

CHAPTER SIX
Roberto

March 2015
Altadena, CA

THAT SATURDAY NIGHT was the last time I saw her. She left Sunday morning, saying she had some errands to run and might have brunch with her sister. I didn't argue. I'd slept eleven hours and was still feeling weak and listless. When I tried to think why, I couldn't remember. I had coffee, read a little, then slept again until early afternoon.

At three-thirty she still hadn't returned or even called, so I texted her. No reply.

After a couple more tries I called her sister, Alex. Alex hadn't seen Laura or even heard from her since early in the week.

I reported her missing the next morning.

The police couldn't find any GPS signal from her phone, but they found her car two days later. It had been abandoned on Chaney Trail Drive by the Mount Lowe Road gate. There was nothing unusual about the car.

They conducted a search along the trail and up at the campground. The search was expanded to the surrounding areas; dogs and a helicopter were brought in. After two weeks they gave up.

She'd vanished without a trace.

Laura

March 2015
Pasadena, CA

The street number Jack gave me, 1003, didn't exist. Where I'd expected a house, there were a number of condos fronted by palm trees and low-maintenance landscaping. I wandered around, puzzling over this, convinced I was missing something. I pulled up Google Maps on my Phone, and it confirmed I was in the right place.

Had Jack given me the wrong address? That seemed unlikely. It was possible I'd misheard him. Maybe it was 1013 or 1030.

I was just debating ringing some doorbells when, like that time in Chichen Itza, I had a moment of dizziness and my world went suddenly flat, all depth and perspective gone. The street lurched and slid around me.

I stumbled, caught myself. The daylight was gone. The condos were gone, as was my car. I stood in a quiet, darkened street facing a large, craftsman-style home. The front door opened and a woman hurried out towards me.

Or so I thought. But as the figure entered the dim circle of light cast by a low streetlamp, I saw that what I'd thought was a dress was in fact a white robe, and that the person hurrying towards me was no woman—it was Jack.

He began to say something. His lips were moving, but there was a roaring in my ears. My sense of depth and perspective stuttered again. Jack had almost reached me, but as my confused vision tunneled in on him he began to recede. Frustration twisted his features. The last thing I saw before the vision faded was his mouth working as if he were shouting. He raised his arm and pointed north and up, back towards the hills. He was telling me to return to the tavern ruins.

☽

I reached the Mount Lowe Road gate a little after 10 A.M. My pack was still in the trunk, along with a half case of water. I considered taking the tent, but something stopped me. Not something, but some scrap of conscience which, even in what I now understand was a crazy, half-possessed state, wouldn't let me completely abandon Rob again. I'd already done enough damage. It was very clear to me, without knowing how or why, that I'd in some way drained him, taken his life force. I hadn't wanted to, but I was very afraid of what I might do to him next time.

But a stronger part of me—and I was positively vibrating with strength and purpose today—didn't care. I wasn't going to call or notify him. I'd go up to the ruins, and Jack would be waiting. We'd talk, make love, and I'd be down by nightfall. Rob, if he was home, would just have to look out for himself.

I unstrapped my tent from the pack and dumped my camp stove, pan, and cup. I still had a couple of protein bars in the front pockets. I threw in a half-dozen pint water bottles, shouldered the much lighter pack, and set off.

This time I didn't slow or dally to take in the views. My legs pumped and my feet moved, my focus almost entirely on the tavern ruins, on seeing Jack. I twice reached into my jeans pocket for my phone, intending to text Rob, and twice drew my hand away. I'd see him tonight. And then I'd talk, explain, reassure him, tell him I loved him. Because I did love him, and in this moment I understood that I wanted to go back to him, wanted us to be as we were. But first I had to do this.

In those dusty morning miles up to the ruins, a strange peace settled over me. It was strange because I very clearly wasn't myself, and should have been terrified. In fact I *was* myself, but also another, harder, forceful being, a woman who gave no quarter and took no prisoners. She knew what she wanted, and nothing would stand in her way. Laura was along for the ride, unable to separate until we met with Jack again. Then Laura would return home, and everything would be settled.

☽

He was there to greet me as I approached. And so was the past.

It was night again. But instead of the flat, gravel- and pine needle-strewn campground, what loomed ahead was a stone and timber structure. Yellow light streamed from within. Tables and chairs stood outside in the cool shade of the pines. Above the steps to the main entrance, a quaint inn sign with the name "Ye Alpine Tavern" swung in the light breeze. Scattered groups of men, mostly, stood on the narrow terrace in front of the building, talking and smoking. A burst of laughter came from inside, where some kind of celebration was taking place, the whole underscored with the tinkle of ragtime piano.

Even as Jack came up to me, I stood, transfixed, not breathing. I was riven, split in two. Part of me couldn't believe this was happening; another part, the hungry, cold one, accepted it and strained with impatience.

Jack swept me up in a bear hug. "Finally," he said. A moment later he was leading me by the arm away from the tavern, away from the people and light. "Come on, we don't have long."

"What's happening, Jack? Where are we going?" As I said it, a jolt of the same unreasoning, visceral fear I'd experienced just two nights before sent a chill through me.

We went another couple of hundred feet, following the pale gleam of the railing as it wound around a curve and into the dark. Jack glanced into the gloom below. He turned to me, hands extended.

"Take my hands," he said. "Just look into my eyes. Whatever you see or hear, don't let go, don't turn. Can you do that?"

A small, scratching sound in the gloom below sent a tremor of fear through me. The night closed in around me like a fist and there was ice in my gut.

"Laura!" He seized my hands, his eyes burning into mine. "Look at me!"

I nodded. The night turned suddenly cold, and I had the sense of a desert plain capped with an endless canopy of stars. There was a rushing, like wind, which built to a roar, though no air stirred. My heart slammed against my ribs. I began to shake.

Jack's face was gleaming with sweat, and it was only the strength of his grip on my hands and the energy pouring from his eyes that kept me from running or collapsing in a faint. Someone was intoning what sounded like verse, and I caught snatches of it through the rattle and screech of the wind.

"…in radiant mortal flesh…"

The wind howled, though I couldn't feel it. A burst of chattering, gibbering noise, and dark wings beat in the night as something coal-dark and monstrously heavy flapped by.

"…death and hell are at her back…"

And now the air did stir, and the wind tore at me with icy fingers, turning and wheeling with us at its center. Something was rearing at my back, I was sure of it. I trembled with terror, with the wind, and now Jack was shaking too.

"What are you doing?" I screamed. I tried to let go of his hands, to run, save myself, but his grip was iron.

The wind whipped at his hair. "I'm taking you back, Laura. You belong with us. It's foretold." His eyes burned into me as he shouted out those final lines,

"And dream no more of hell and hate
in the Birth of BABALON!"

The world came loose and slewed around me. A woman's laugh, cruel and malicious, tinkled like splintering glass. I cried out as Jack and I were both swept up and careened, tumbling, into night and dark.

Roberto

April 2018
Hillsborough, NC

Three weeks after returning from my visit to Altadena, I received the report from the Coroner's office.

Apart from the dental record, a follow-up comparison of DNA extracted from her teeth with her dad's DNA confirmed her identity beyond doubt.

Still, the verdict on Laura was inconclusive. Her skeletal remains showed no signs of trauma or foul play. There was no reliable dating method for remains of "intermediate" age once decomposition had run its course, but the forensic examiner concluded the weathering on the bones and their extreme fragility was "consistent with the exposure to sunlight, dehydration, freeze/thaw and wet/dry cycles one would expect in the location where they were found."

However, there was one very reliable indicator of the age of Laura's remains.

Her right femur and patella, as well as her left ulna and the small bones of the hand had been partially enclosed by tree roots. The tree had grown through the chest area, shattering and dispersing the majority of her ribs. Tree ring measurement indicated "with a high degree of certainty" that the remains had been there for at least sixty-seven years, or since before 1949. Why nobody visiting this very popular site had ever seen the exposed skeletal remains over such a long period of time remains a mystery.

The coroner's report didn't speculate on the discrepancy between the time of her disappearance and the apparent age of the remains. It seemed that question should bother me, but when I tried to dig at it my mind just skittered about. In the end, I let it go.

About Jack Parsons and the Babalon working, quite a bit is known.

Parsons died on June 17, 1952, in a freak explosion while cooking up a rush order of fulminate of mercury for a film company. One theory held he'd been the target of an assassination at the order of Howard Hughes, and the Pasadena criminologist investing the death didn't rule it out. But in the end, the case was ruled an accidental death.

Parsons's Babalon working had culminated in a series of rituals in the Mojave Desert in early 1946. After the ritual on January 18, Parsons told Hubbard, his scribe and magical partner, that he'd succeeded: "It is done," he said.

Parsons returned home to the Parsonage to find his Scarlet Woman, his Babalon, in the form of Marjorie Cameron, a young artist and poet who'd arrived during his absence. The two at once became lovers and married later that year. Like Laura, Cameron had red hair and green eyes.

In the seventeen months since the discovery of Laura's remains, I've been able at last to let go of her. Despite the mystery of her disappearance and the bizarre questions raised by the finding of her remains, I've made my peace with Laura. Whatever drew her to the foothills and the Mount Lowe ruins was important to her, and I believe she finally found her place. Or time.

In July of last year, I met Sara, and we were married in December. Strong-willed and feisty, she was instrumental in helping me find my health and strength again.

Phil and Anne flew out for the wedding. When they heard Sara'd never been to California, they invited us to visit and stay with them in their Altadena home, and we accepted. We leave for a week on May 3rd, and among the things we plan to do is hike up to the White City ruins and the site of the Alpine Tavern, as well as visit the site of Parsons's Pasadena home, the Parsonage. Sara really wants to see them.

BIOGRAPHIES

Amy Sterling Casil

Amy Sterling Casil is a 2002 Nebula Award nominee and recipient of other awards and recognition for her short science fiction and fantasy, which has appeared in publications ranging from *The Magazine of Fantasy & Science Fiction* to *Zoetrope*. She is the author of twenty-six nonfiction books, over a hundred short stories, two fiction and poetry collections, and three novels. Amy is the founder of Pacific Human Capital, a founding member and treasurer of Book View Café and former treasurer of the Science Fiction & Fantasy Writers of America, and teaches writing and composition at Saddleback College. She is the founder of a new publishing company for the 21st century, Chameleon Publishing.

Dario Ciriello

Dario Ciriello is a professional author and editor, and the founder (2009) of Panverse Publishing.

Dario's fiction includes the novels *Sutherland's Rules,* a caper/thriller with a shimmer of the fantastic, and *Black Easter,* a tale of love, black magic, and demonic possession set on a remote Greek island. *Free Verse and Other Stories* is a collection of his short Science Fiction work. Dario's nonfiction includes *Aegean Dream,* the bittersweet memoir of a year spent on the small Greek island of Skópelos (the real *Mamma Mia!* island), and *Drown the Cat: the Rebel Author's Guide to Writing Beyond the Rules*. Visit him at www.dariospeaks.wordpress.com.

Jude-Marie Green

Jude-Marie Green is a writer of genre (science fiction & fantasy, plus the occasional horror) fiction. She lives in Southern California amid palm trees, orange trees, avocado trees, roses, and birds. Lots of birds.

She is a fan of long standing. Her first convention was in 1977 at the Los Angeles Airport Marriott. She attends many conventions, including NorWesCon in Seattle where she is frequently a panelist and professional author as part of the Fairwood Writers Workshop. Find her online at: judemarie.wordpress.com.

Andre Hardy

Andre Hardy is an MFA candidate at Antioch University Los Angeles. He is a graduate of St. Mary's College of California and was the fourth pick of the Philadelphia Eagles in the 1984 NFL draft. He writes hard-boiled, gumshoe stories with an urban twist.

Gabi Lorino

Gabi Lorino writes comedies starring socially awkward women who occasionally interact with men. Her tales are based on her 20⁺ years in the dating world and hilarious stories told by friends and sisters. Gabi is a proud member of Generation X, and she's heard more than once that her characters "act a bit younger than they are" and maybe "need an attitude adjustment," which makes her love them even more!

A Magical Time Called Later is Book One of the Socially Awkward Series. Gabi's stories within this anthology explore characters who are featured in *A Magical Time Called Later.*

Bonnie Randall

Bonnie Randall lives in a forest at the foot of the Rocky Mountains in Alberta, Canada.

Scribbling stories in coil-bound notebooks from the age of nine, Bonnie's first attempts at prose featured wicked dolls, evil grandmothers... and a romantic hero who just happened to be a professional ice hockey player (go figure). Clearly much has changed yet nothing has changed; Bonnie is still a sucker for true love, soul mates, smudgy shadows, and things that go bump in the night. *Divinity & The Python,* Bonnie's debut novel and the first in her Secrets & Shadows series, is available on Amazon. Look for the second Secrets & Shadows title, *Within The Summit's Shadow,* to be released in summer 2018, and visit Bonnie at https://randallbonnie.wixsite.com/mysite.

Allison Rose

Allison Rose is a novelist and screenwriter from Los Angeles. *Tick*, the first in her young adult science fiction series, tackles themes of mental illness, artistry, and violence. It has been followed by *Vice*, part two of the Tick Series. While Allison's stories vary in genre, her focus centers on the struggles of complex female characters.

Cody Sisco

Cody Sisco is the author of speculative fiction that straddles the divide between plausible and extraordinary. His Resonant Earth Series includes two novels thus far, *Broken Mirror* and *Tortured Echoes*, and a short story prequel, *Believe and Live*. The third novel in the series, *Altered Bodies*, will be published in 2019.

Cody is a 2017 Los Angeles Review of Books / USC Publishing Workshop Fellow. He is also a co-organizer of the Los Angeles Writers Critique Group. His startup, BookSwell, makes the book scene in L.A. easier to navigate, introduces readers to new writing, and weaves together digital and real-life literary experiences. Find out more at: www.bookswell.club.

MADE IN L.A. WRITERS

Made in L.A. Writers is a collaborative of Los Angeles-based authors dedicated to nurturing and promoting indie fiction. This 2018 volume is the first of the annual Made in L.A. anthology series. While our styles, themes, and story locales differ, our work is both influenced and illuminated by our hometown and underpinned by the extraordinary, multifaceted, and often surreal culture and life in the City of Angels.

As indie authors we face formidable challenges: fragmented audiences, intense competition in a crowded market, and traditional publishers' deep pockets.

If you enjoyed this book, please leave a review. Rave about us to your friends. Find us online and tell us how our stories made you feel. We're looking for connection; we hope to hear from you.

www.madeinlawriters.com